"LADY CARBERRY, THERE IS SOMETHING I MUST SAY TO YOU.

"Circumstanced as we are, madam, I feel obliged to ask you to do me the honor of becoming my wife."

"How can you be so ridiculous, my lord, as to offer marriage to one you hold in such complete dislike?"

"You may reject my proposal with scorn, but have you really given any thought at all to our situation here and the gossip that will inevitably arise as a result? Think again before you condemn us both to yet another infamous scandal!"

Nicola Cornick is passionate about many things: her country cottage and its garden, her two small cats, her husband and her writing, though not necessarily in that order! She has always been fascinated by history, both as her chosen subject at university and subsequently as an engrossing hobby. She works as a university administrator and finds writing the perfect antidote to the demands of life in a busy office.

TRUE COLOURS
NICOLA CORNICK

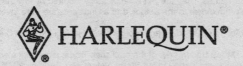

HARLEQUIN®

TORONTO • NEW YORK • LONDON
AMSTERDAM • PARIS • SYDNEY • HAMBURG
STOCKHOLM • ATHENS • TOKYO • MILAN • MADRID
PRAGUE • WARSAW • BUDAPEST • AUCKLAND

ISBN 0-373-51134-5

TRUE COLOURS

Copyright © 1998 by Nicola Cornick.

Prologue

Had matters fallen out differently they might never have met again. If his ship had not reached Plymouth early with a westerly wind behind it, or if she had not chosen that particular day for the journey into Somerset, or even if the hunt for Miss Frensham's lost reticule had taken just five minutes longer, the accident would have been averted and they would have passed on the road none the wiser. And later during the London Season, in some hot, airless drawing-room, an inquisitive matron would have fixed her with a sharp, avid gaze and said eagerly, 'I saw Lord Mullineaux driving in the Park today. Did you know that he was back in Town, Lady Carberry? You used to have some...small...acquaintance with him, I believe?'

And Alicia, Lady Carberry, would have put down her glass with a steady hand and responded in a colourless voice, 'Lord Mullineaux? No, I was not aware that he was back in England. But then, our acquaintance was not such that I would be likely to have heard of his return.'

And Mullineaux, hearing in his club the name of Alicia Carberry toasted on all sides as an Incomparable, would have said nothing, but reflected that money could buy much, even respectability, in a society that delighted in scandal.

But that was not the way that it was to be, as fate, which had first brought them together only to tear them apart again, took another decisive hand.

Chapter One

The accident happened on a stretch of road the locals called Verney Drove, on a bend where the track—for it was little more—abandoned its straight course across the Somerset Levels and skirted a small hill. Both carriages had been going too fast and neither could see the other before it was almost too late. The curricle grazed past the travelling chaise with less than an inch to spare and such was the shock and noise of its sudden appearance that the carriage horses took fright, rearing and plunging violently, and the chaise almost overturned. It lurched off the road into the water-filled ditch and there was a loud crack as the front axle broke.

For a few moments, all was panic and confusion whilst the groom leapt down to try to reach and calm the terrified horses, and the coachman found both himself and the team dangerously entangled in the reins. The groom had reached the horses' heads but was finding the frightened animals difficult to hold single-handed, and was shouting for assistance. The coachman cut the reins and tumbled down from his perch into the ditch.

Meanwhile, the driver of the curricle had pulled up his own team with an expertise that might have been admirable under other circumstances, and had passed the reins to his groom with instructions to drive on to the nearest village and warn them of the accident. He turned back and reached the scene at a run, just as the coachman, shaking the water off him like a dog and swearing horribly, joined the groom and grasped the reins.

The gentleman materialised beside the two of them as the horses were beginning to quieten and the groom cast a first dubious glance towards the carriage, uncertain whether to stay or go to the rescue of its passengers. The February afternoon was unseasonably mild after a long, cold spell and already the first heavy drops of rain were starting to fall from a leaden sky, threatening to turn the track into a rutted quagmire. The gentleman summed up the scene in one swift glance and turned to the coachman.

'Stay with the horses,' he instructed tersely. 'Keep them steady whilst I go to find your passengers. How many do you carry?' The rain was already running in rivulets down his caped driving coat and he pushed the soaking dark hair back from his forehead. In the sudden darkness of the storm the groom and coachman could discern no more of his appearance than a dark countenance with lowering black brows, and neither of them had the courage to ask him who he was; they simply responded to the voice of authority.

'There are two of them, sir,' the coachman volunteered. 'Two ladies.'

The gentleman swore briefly under his breath and turned his attention to the carriage. It was of the newest and most elegantly comfortable design, though it carried no crest. Leaning at a drunken angle, two wheels in the ditch and two on the road, it was immediately evident that it could not be moved without help. The horses were also of a high quality, though not so highly bred as his own team, and they were calm now and looking rather dejected in the rain. One, the left-wheeler, whickered softly and put its head down to pull at the sparse grass at the side of the track.

The gentleman had reached the carriage door when he was forestalled by it being scrambled open from within. The figure of a little old lady appeared in the aperture, raising her voice above the wind in querulous protest. Her actual words were lost but their meaning was plain—she was unable to get down, for the carriage was tilted at such an acute angle that the steps could not reach the ground, and she was diminutive of stature and far too elderly and proper to even think of jumping down.

'Oh, I am shaken all to pieces!' As he drew closer he could hear the quaver in her voice that denoted the beginnings of hysteria. 'This is quite intolerable! Jack Coachman, where are you? Help me down at once before I swoon!' Her gaze fell suddenly and suspiciously on the stranger—little more than a tall shadow in the darkness as he stood beside the carriage—and he could tell she did not know whether to faint with fright or appeal for help. In the event, common sense won.

'You, sir, whoever you are, help me down at once!' Her words came out imperiously but with an edge of fear, and she looked about her a little wildly. 'Oh, this is not to be endured! The steps will not reach to the ground!'

Sensing the real panic behind the lady's words, the gentleman stepped forward to the rescue. Without further ado she was picked up in a pair of strong arms and swung down onto the road in a flurry of petticoats and outrage.

'Sir, you are importunate!'

She made a desperate grab for her bonnet as the wind caught the brim, dropped her gloves in a puddle, and looked round forlornly for her reticule. She was shaking with both fear and reaction, and the stranger felt an immediate pang of compunction at having caused the accident in the first place and given anxiety to one so frail.

'I ask your pardon, ma'am.' He sketched an elegant bow which was incongruous in such inclement conditions. 'Pray accept my apologies both for the accident and for any further distress I may have caused you. You must allow me to make amends by helping you.'

His voice was low and attractive, and Miss Frensham's ruffled sensibilities began to feel a little soothed. Though at heart a timid woman, the necessity of earning her own living had trained her to be practical. She was still very shocked at the accident but decided that little would be achieved by succumbing to a fit of the vapours. She even allowed the gentleman to take her arm gently and draw her against the side of the carriage, which afforded a little shelter from the wind and rain. His attentions were all that was proper, she assured herself; he was clearly both reliable and, more importantly, well-bred.

'Allow me to present myself and my apologies to you at the same time, madam,' the gentleman continued. 'I am James Mullineaux, entirely at your service. We must see you conveyed to shelter, but first— am I mistaken in thinking that there was another lady with you in the carriage?'

There was no trace of urgency or alarm in his voice, but Miss Frensham froze and clapped her hand to her mouth with a squeak of horror.

'Alicia! Oh, how could I be so thoughtless?' She grasped James Mullineaux's arm in urgent entreaty. 'Oh, please, sir, could you see what has become of her? We were both knocked to the floor when the coach overturned and I could not rouse her! How could I forget so? I am the veriest monster!'

Her words dissolved into a wail of misery and once more she looked round hopelessly for a handkerchief.

'Do not distress yourself, madam.' Mullineaux pressed his own large handkerchief comfortingly into her hand. 'You have sustained a great shock, you know, and could not be expected to think of everything. Wait here—I will find your friend.'

'She is my charge,' Miss Frensham sniffed, inconsolable, 'and I should have taken greater care of her! Oh, whatever will Lady Stansfield say? I shall never be able to face her again—never!'

Her words had an extraordinary effect on the gentleman, although Miss Frensham was too distraught to notice it. There was a moment of absolute stillness, then he asked expressionlessly, 'Lady Stansfield, ma'am? Would that be the Dowager Countess of Stansfield?'

Miss Frensham sniffed assent, dabbing her eyes with the handkerchief, which was already soaked with rain. She was still too upset and preoccupied to realise that a digression onto rank and title was rather odd in the circumstances.

'Her ladyship is Alicia's grandmother, and much attached to her,' she confirmed. 'I promised to take care of her!'

'Lady Carberry is hardly an infant in arms,' James Mullineaux commented dryly, with more truth than tact. 'Surely she can be expected to take care of herself? She has always managed to do so extremely well in the past!'

This time there was no mistaking the sarcastic edge to his voice. Miss Frensham looked up, startled out of her preoccupation, but it was too dark to see his face.

'Are you acquainted with Lady Carberry, sir?'

Mullineaux returned no reply, and for a moment Miss Frensham had the oddest feeling that he was about to turn on his heel and walk away. The impression lasted only a moment, then he spoke brusquely. 'I knew Lady Carberry before her marriage.'

Miss Frensham stared in puzzled incomprehension, but Mullineaux said nothing more, merely turning back to the carriage and leaving her standing a little despondently in the road. A moment later, she saw him swing himself up easily into the darkened interior and disappear from her view.

Inside the coach the floor sloped sharply forwards and into the ditch. It was slippery with rain and there was almost no light at all. Nor was there any sound. Mullineaux steadied himself with one hand on the door jamb and paused for his eyes to adjust to the darkness.

Alicia Carberry was lying tumbled in the far corner. A faint glimmer of light touched the pallor of her face and he edged his way cautiously down the sloping floor towards her, bracing himself against one of the thick velvet seats. The creaking of the coach as it settled more deeply in the ditch was hardly reassuring. The rain drummed constantly on the roof.

After making cautious progress for a few moments, Mullineaux was able to kneel down beside Alicia Carberry's recumbent figure and reflect on what he should do next. She was unconscious but still breathing normally and he doubted that she was seriously hurt. However, it would be impossible to check her injuries until he had managed to get her out of the carriage. It seemed a little undignified to drag her across the floor, but he could not safely pick her up inside the carriage in case it toppled over completely. Anyway, in her current state she would scarcely be in a position to notice and he was disinclined to treat her with any particular care or consideration.

Mullineaux managed to get a grip on the material of Lady Carberry's travelling dress and manoeuvre her body back up the sloping floor to the doorway. Once there, it was a simple matter to jump down onto the road and scoop her up into his arms. She did not stir at all, which was probably just as well since it made his job easier and spared her the distress and confusion that would have inevitably followed had she regained consciousness.

She was surprisingly light, and Mullineaux found himself thinking with a certain grim humour that her years as a wealthy widow had evidently not taken their toll in rich living. He could not see her face clearly in the darkness. No matter—he knew exactly what she looked like. More disconcertingly he also recognised the feel of her in his arms, even after the passing of seven years.

'I knew Lady Carberry before her marriage...'

It was a ridiculous understatement from the man to whom she had once been engaged and from whom she had parted in such extraordinary and scandalous circumstances, when she had jilted him for a rich man old enough to be her father. Mullineaux, who had been out of the country since that time, reflected dispassionately on the ironic quirk of fate which had decreed that almost the first person he should meet on his return to England was the woman he wanted at all costs to avoid.

He had known that he would probably have to meet Alicia Carberry again some day. He had every intention of taking up once again his place in society, and he was well aware that Lady Carberry was one of its greatest ornaments and had been so for many years. However, he had anticipated that it would be easy to avoid her and to treat her with cold civility if their paths did cross. The past, after all, was dead, and with it any warmer feelings that he might have held for her.

Now, holding her reluctantly in his arms, he was conscious of an immense irritation at the situation in which he had been placed. But that was not all. Treacherously, dangerously, he became slowly aware of the scent of her skin, the brush of her hair against his cheek, the way her head rested so confidingly in the curve of his shoulder. It was intolerable to still feel an attraction towards her, particularly when his rational mind was telling him how much he disliked her. With a very forcible effort he blanked out the past and shut the door very firmly on his emotions.

As he stepped away from the wreck of the carriage Miss Frensham emerged from the shadows and hurried forward. She had retrieved her reticule, which had gone a long way towards restoring her composure, but she had started to shiver with cold and reaction and looked woefully frail.

'You have found her! God be praised! But—' she peered closer through the rain, pushing Alicia's wet hair off her face '—is she badly hurt, sir?'

'I have no doubt that she will survive,' Mullineaux stated coldly. 'Lady Carberry appears to have sustained a blow to the head, but I think it will not prove too serious, and I doubt that she has broken any bones. You may rest assured that she is strong enough to cope with worse than this.' He gave Miss Frensham a comprehensive look and his tone softened.

'But you are soaked to the skin, ma'am, and no doubt badly chilled, too. This benighted village must surely have an inn of sorts. Let us repair there and see what can be done. If you are able to walk a little way, ma'am, I shall carry Lady Carberry—' was there the slightest of hesitations on the word 'Lady'? '—and we may call a doctor once we are there.'

Miss Frensham did not dissent from this plan. The village of Ottery was a mere five hundred yards distant, and, though it was little more than a hamlet, there should surely be shelter there. James Mullineaux carried his fair burden along the muddy road with a cautiousness born of distaste, not care, while Miss Frensham trotted along by his side. She shivered as the wind hurled flurries of rain in her face and every so often cast anxious glances at Alicia's unconscious form.

The coachman had managed to extricate the carriage horses from their harness and had led them on ahead whilst the groom was now retrieving as much as he could of the luggage. Little could be done for the carriage itself, however, and the coachman and groom, after a muttered discussion, had decided to abandon it until daylight might bring the chance of salvage or at least the opportunity to consult with their employer.

The ill-assorted group had gone about half the way towards the village in silence when Alicia Carberry stirred. The chill of the rain against her face was the first sensation she recognised. She had no notion of where she was, or what had happened to her, but she felt the arms about her tighten in response to her involuntary movement and was obscurely comforted.

'Lie still,' Mullineaux instructed in a low voice. 'You are quite safe.' The last thing he wanted at this point was for her to regain consciousness for it would make matters too complicated. The sooner he could deposit her at the inn and leave her, the better.

Alicia immediately relaxed and did as she had been told. She did not know who had spoken and did not really care. There had been something reassuringly familiar about the voice although she could not place it. Her head ached abominably and it was pleasant to rest it against the broad shoulder so invitingly close. For the first time in a long while she relaxed into an unfamiliar feeling of safety and security.

Mullineaux glanced down at her nestling so confidently in his arms. Old passions and memories stirred instinctively within him again and he could not avoid a rush of protectiveness, followed swiftly by a greater rush of anger. Damn it, after all she had done to him, how could he still feel this way? He had not even seen her properly yet, but already he could feel that insidious pull of attraction there had always been between them reasserting itself and threatening to make a fool of him again.

He had been a man of twenty-five when they had first met, no mere stripling, and for some reason the fact that she had so thoroughly duped him then rankled more than if he had been a youth in his salad days. James, Marquis of Mullineaux, with his looks, title and reputation for wildness, was hardly a flat to be taken in by the pretty face of an adventuress. For that was what Alicia Carberry had been.

An adventuress. He faced it squarely. She was the granddaughter of an Earl and under the patronage of her redoubtable grandmother, she was the heiress to a fortune, she had beauty and to spare, but it had not been enough for her. He could still recall with bitterness the last words she had written to him to terminate their betrothal:

'...and so, dear James, I fear I must end our betrothal for I am sure we should not suit. Carberry will make me a much more comfortable husband, and though one should not refine too much on the value of a good financial match it is better than being poor as a church mouse. Your title is worth a great deal, my dear, but sadly not enough...'

As evidence of a grasping nature it could scarcely be surpassed, and after the first blinding flash of disillusionment James Mullineaux had had time to be shocked by both Alicia's sentiments and the fact that she had damned herself so eloquently in writing. That she had only loved his title, not his person he could just about accept, although if he had not seen the letter with his own eyes he would not have believed it of her. She had seemed so innocent, so devoid of conceit or greed. He had thought that he had found a kindred spirit in her, recognising instinctively a bond between them, and yet he had been totally mistaken.

The Mullineaux title was an old one and although in recent years the family's fortunes had dwindled considerably James had still been hunted exhaustively by the matchmaking mamas and their resourceful offspring. He had thought Alicia Carberry different and had been sadly disenchanted. He had been in love for the first time since his youth and not only had his feelings been engaged but his pride had been seriously dented by her defection. His judgement had always been good and he'd found his confidence severely impaired by the way in which she had so cleverly duped him. She had snared him, then ruthlessly dismissed him when a richer prize had come her way.

Such bitter reflections on the past served only to reinforce his antipathy towards Alicia, and by the time they reached Ottery he had his feelings well in hand and viewed her with nothing but strong dislike. The village itself hardly lifted his spirits, for it was the merest huddle of cottages down each side of the road, and though there was indeed an inn its peeling doors were very firmly closed. This did not dissuade Mullineaux, however, who was resolved to rid himself of his burden, and strode firmly up to the main entrance and pulled the bell with determination.

A harsh peal sounded somewhere in the depths of the building and it seemed an unconscionably long time to Miss Frensham, shivering on the doorstep, before there was the sound of footsteps on stone and the bolts were drawn back reluctantly. The door opened a crack to reveal a villainous-looking individual.

'Horses! Carriages! And now this!' the man began indignantly. 'I tell you, we're not open——' But James Mullineaux cut him off ruthlessly.

'There has been an accident on the road,' he began, in tones which brooked no refusal, 'and we are in sore need of shelter. Be so good as to show us to your best parlour and call your wife to attend to these ladies. I take it that my groom and curricle are already in the yard?'

Then, as the landlord still stood gawping on the threshold, he lost his patience.

'Come along, man; we are like to die of cold if you keep us standing here any longer!'

Whatever alarm had previously been raised by the arrival of the curricle, it had not stirred any concern within the landlord, who now sniffed loudly and opened the door only a crack wider. He stumped off down the dimly lit corridor, grumbling at the whims of the gentry and leaving them to follow if they chose. With ill grace he opened one of the doors off the hallway to reveal a dark, mean little room with peeling walls and the unmistakable sound of mice in the wainscot. The stale smell of beer seemed to have seeped into the very fabric of the building. The light was faint, and there was no fire in the grate. Mullineaux looked about him with incredulity, distaste, and a sinking heart.

'It's the best I 'ave to offer,' the landlord said, with no trace of apology. 'Curricle an' horses are out back, but they ain't in no state to travel. Soaked through, the lot of them!'

He gave the bedraggled trio a look which clearly told them that beggars could not be choosers, turned on his heel, and disappeared down the corridor.

Mullineaux, meanwhile, won a brief but violent battle with his temper. It could be some miles to the nearest alternative hostelry and they currently had no means of transport. Lady Carberry might well require the services of a doctor, and Miss Frensham was beginning to look decidedly unwell. He could go out in the rainstorm to search for shelter in a vicarage or sympathetic manor, but he did not know the area well and to approach strangers in that way would involve him in precisely the complicated explanations he wished to avoid. Anything which associated him with Lady Carberry or kept the two of them together for any length of time was anathema to him. He would have had no compunction about abandoning her there and then had it not been for the miserable spectacle of Miss Frensham, dripping onto the taproom floor as she waited in vain for the arrival of the landlady.

No, all he could do for the present, Mullineaux thought with resignation, was to make sure that the ladies were attended to and see what better alternatives presented themselves. He had still not given up hope that he might be able to leave them and travel on further, thereby avoiding all embarrassing confrontations with Lady Carberry, but for now he could not in fairness abandon Miss Frensham alone to the mercies of the landlord.

He deposited Alicia Carberry somewhat unceremoniously in the parlour's only armchair and straightened up. It seemed that she had either lost consciousness once more or fallen asleep, for when Miss Frensham hurried over to her she did not stir. After hovering ineffectually for a moment, Miss Frensham had the happy idea of extracting her smelling salts from her bag and waving these vigorously under Alicia's nose. A few moments later their pungent smell began to have the desired effect.

'She's awake!' Miss Frensham exclaimed excitedly and somewhat superfluously as Alicia moved slightly and opened her eyes, only to close them again immediately. 'Oh, sir—' she turned to Mullineaux, who had been watching her efforts with sardonic amusement and no offer of help '—do you think we should send for the doctor? My poor Alicia, she will be very shaken you know, and perhaps the best thing would be for her to lie down at once!'

'I am perfectly well, Emmy.' Lady Carberry spoke for the first time, making her companion jump. Her voice, normally low and unhurried, sounded a little strained. 'Pray do not trouble to send out for a doctor. You know how I hate fuss! A little rest and perhaps a cup of sweet tea will suffice. I shall feel completely better directly.'

She rested her head on one hand and kept her eyes closed. Miss Frensham, used to her ladyship's decisiveness through long experience, did not trouble to contradict her but pursed her lips with disapproval. She caught the tail-end of an ironic smile from James Mullineaux, which prompted her to look at him more closely. It had begun to dawn on her that the gentleman appeared in no hurry to offer Lady Carberry any further assistance, but still she felt a sudden shock as she assimilated the expression in his eyes as they rested on her charge. She was used to gentlemen surveying Alicia with every shade of expression from shy admiration to blatant lust. She could remember no one, however, who had looked at her with such a very cold, hard dislike. Miss Frensham unconsciously drew herself up straighter.

It was the first opportunity that the companion and the gentleman had had to consider each other properly, and there was some curiosity in the look which they now exchanged. The dim light revealed Miss

Frensham to be a little wisp of a lady. Of indeterminate age, she was sensibly dressed in a practical grey cloak over a black bombazine gown, which spoke her calling more clearly than any words. Fussy rows of beads, her only concession to adornment, clashed with each other about her neck. Her hair, which had no doubt started the day neatly curled, was now hanging in damp white strands under her bonnet. She was shivering occasionally and appeared soaked to the skin. Her eyes, large, anxious and grey, moved from Alicia Carberry to James Mullineaux with a puzzled appeal.

Mullineaux turned abruptly to the doorway and gave vent to his feelings by shouting peremptorily for the landlord to come to light the candles and make the fire up immediately. That might at least be achieved, though the cup of sweet tea was looking an increasingly unlikely prospect.

Miss Frensham, for her part, desiccated spinster though she was, was not completely indifferent to the appearance of the gentleman before her. She was familiar both with the gentlemen of *ton* society and with the heroes of the marble-backed books from the circulating library, and James Mullineaux appeared to combine the attributes of both. He had a tall, broad-shouldered physique which any man of fashion would envy, setting off to perfection his immaculate tailoring. Both his eyes and hair were black, which combined with his tanned face to give him an almost piratical air, Miss Frensham thought, a little faintly. She had never seen any pirates, but she knew they would look like this. He might almost be said to possess classical good looks, were it not for the fact that some air of arrogance suggested that he would scorn such an accolade.

His bearing had both the easy assurance of authority and a latent elegance in its economy of movement, but the hint of amusement showing in his eyes at her scrutiny was belied by the hard line of that firm mouth, which betrayed no humour at all. Indeed, there were lines around his mouth which suggested bitterness and unhappiness, rather than a willingness to laugh. Yet a moment later Miss Frensham was obliged to revise that opinion when he smiled at her with quite devastating charm.

She dropped a prim, disapproving curtsey. She was a stickler for convention, and felt instinctively that this man would not conform to any recognised conventions at all. The knowledge was disturbing, but good manners had still to be observed.

'I do not believe that I have thanked you, sir, for your prompt rescue of myself and Lady Carberry,' she said, a little uncertainly. 'Nor have I introduced myself properly. I am Miss Emmeline Frensham, one-time governess and now companion to Alicia, Lady Carberry.'

The gentleman took her hand and raised it to his lips in a gesture so gallant that Miss Frensham felt a most unexpected shiver along her nerves. His smile, she reflected dizzily, was wickedly attractive.

'Although I deplore the circumstances of our meeting, I am most happy to make your acquaintance, Miss Frensham,' he murmured. 'As I mentioned earlier, I am James, Marquis of Mullineaux, very much at your service.'

Miss Frensham's memory had always been tiresomely unreliable, and now at last it suddenly presented her with the reason why James Mullineaux's name had seemed vaguely familiar to her. Her recollection of who he was and his precise connection with Alicia Carberry followed swiftly. Her hand fell from his grasp, her eyes widened to their furthest extent, and her mouth formed a perfectly round, horrified 'O'.

It was at that exact moment that Alicia opened her eyes.

Alicia Carberry was generally held to be a diamond of the first water, although her looks hardly conformed to the accepted standard of beauty of the day. Even James Mullineaux, who held her in such strong dislike, could not deny her physical beauty and now found to his annoyance that he could not tear his gaze away from her.

The hood of Alicia's bronze-coloured cloak had fallen back and her mass of dark auburn hair had escaped its pins and tumbled in glorious profusion about her shoulders. She had inherited the distinctive heart-shaped face that was a feature of her grandmother's family and with it the high cheekbones and determined chin which gave fair warning of her temperament. But it was her eyes that compelled attention, for they were a vivid emerald-green, brilliant and direct, framed by thick black lashes. Not even the unfashionable sprinkling of freckles across the bridge of her small nose could mar Alicia Carberry's looks, for they merely made her seem more endearing, less remotely beautiful.

The faint colour was returning to her face now, and to James Mullineaux she looked at once the same and poignantly different from the nineteen-year-old debutante he had known. Her looks had, if anything, improved with age. There was a sophistication and air of aloofness about her which had replaced the innocence of the country girl fresh to London. Temperamentally too, he sensed that she was far more complicated and interesting.

Alicia raised her head and their eyes met and held for a long moment. 'I thought that it was you,' Alicia said slowly, 'but then I thought I must have imagined it.'

Mullineaux's expression was as blank and unwelcoming as a stone wall and as he seemed disinclined to say anything appropriately gallant or charming in reply to this Miss Frensham rushed into the breach.

'The Marquis was good enough to stop and help us after the carriage accident, my love, and has conveyed us to this inn, where we hope to find refuge!' She looked a little forlorn on this point, since the landlord had not yet reappeared to light the fire and the room was as bleak and unwelcoming as when they had entered it.

Alicia sat up a little straighter, unwrapping her sodden cloak with distaste. She tried to rise, but winced and fell back, closing her eyes for a moment and resting her head against the back of the chair. Miss Frensham made a sound of distress at Alicia's evident discomfort and hurried back to her side, but Mullineaux did not move at all. A minute later, Alicia opened her eyes again and her gaze swept comprehensively from the anxious face of her companion to the Marquis's blank one.

'His lordship stopped to help us, indeed!' she marvelled sweetly. 'How very chivalrous of him! I remember little about it, of course, but was not he the cause of the accident in the first place? I am sure that I recall something of the sort—assuming that he was the driver of that curricle which flashed past us with such wicked speed!'

This outrageous statement threw down the gauntlet with a vengeance, and the direct challenge in Alicia's eyes only served to underline it.

She had been aware of Mullineaux's antipathy from the moment that she regained consciousness; the air positively crackled with it. The suddenness of the encounter had left her with no time to examine her own feelings but she responded instinctively to his animosity. So he held her in contempt, did he? She had no very high opinion of him, if it came to that! Here was a man whose protestations of love had meant so little that when her father had forced her into marriage with another he had stood by and said not one word against the match. Worse, he had damaged her reputation irrevocably with his denouncement of her as a fortune-hunter.

Pride had always been the besetting sin of the Mullineaux family, Alicia thought resentfully. James Mullineaux had been unable to bear the whispers and gossip of the *ton*; he had moved to disassociate himself from her immediately it appeared he would be tainted with scandal. Her disillusion had been intense; helplessly in love, hopelessly inexperi-

enced, she had waited stubbornly like the heroine of a romance for
James to arrive and rescue her. Even after her father had forced her to
send the letter breaking the engagement, she had confidently believed
that she and James Mullineaux were so close, so attuned, that he would
instantly know it for the fraud it was.

It had not been so. As the days had stretched to a week, Alicia had
begun to realise that something was wrong. Finally her father had triumphantly shown her a copy of a scandal sheet in which her own
identity was very thinly veiled indeed in a cruel story relating how the
lovely, duplicitous Miss B had been scorned as an adventuress by the
handsome Marquis who had previously been at her feet.

Alicia determinedly pushed her memories back into the past where
they belonged, and met Mullineaux's contemptuous look with an
equally acerbic one of her own.

'Your own carriage, madam, was travelling at a pace hardly considerate to other road users,' Mullineaux said coolly. 'I had no time to
react to your sudden appearance other than in the way I did. I am,
however, relieved to discover that a knock on the head has in no way
impaired your faculties. You appear to be remarkably resilient, but then
I already knew that to be so!'

'You, on the other hand, are no more gallant, sir!'

Such an inimical look immediately flashed between the pair of them
that Miss Frensham once more attempted to be conciliatory.

'It's true, you know, my dear, we were travelling very fast! We were
late leaving Glastonbury, if you recall, and you did tell Jack to spring
the horses!'

'So I did.' There was a glint of amusement in Alicia's look which
did nothing to calm her companion's fears. For a moment Miss Frensham indulged in the uncharitable wish that Alicia had been completely
incapacitated by her injury. This miraculous recovery of hers was proving to be most uncomfortable. Miss Frensham knew Alicia very well
and had already divined that her ladyship intended to be very difficult
indeed. As for Mullineaux, he was looking so forbidding that Miss
Frensham doubted she would get any help there.

She pursed her lips. She had been Alicia's governess until her charge
had been sent to Miss Hannah More's school in Bath, and had later
assumed the role of companion upon Alicia's widowhood. In the intervening years had occurred Alicia's London Season, under the aegis of
her grandmother, Lady Stansfield—and the ill-fated betrothal to the
Marquis of Mullineaux. Alicia had never spoken to Miss Frensham of

her broken engagement and subsequent hasty marriage, and Miss Frensham had been far too well-bred to pry, but she could tell that some very painful memories still troubled Lady Carberry. As for the Marquis of Mullineaux, he had gone abroad immediately after Alicia had jilted him and tales of his exploits on the Continent and in Ireland had filtered back to Society over the years. As far as Miss Frensham knew, this was the first time he had returned to England since then.

'What a very great surprise to meet with you here, Lord Mullineaux,' Alicia was saying with a syrupy sweetness which somehow managed to convey that meeting him was the least pleasant aspect of their current situation. 'I am sure everyone had thought you settled abroad this past age... Italy, was it, or perhaps France? What can have brought you back to England? Your grandfather, perhaps... He is quite well?'

Her words were courteous but Mullineaux chose to read into them an implication which was in all probability there. Despite his lengthy sojourn abroad he was still heir to his grandfather, the Duke of Cardace, whose health had taken a decided turn for the worse recently. The Duke was one of the premier landowners in Britain. Mullineaux flushed at the suspected insinuation, but managed a tolerably polite reply.

'His Grace is well, I thank you, ma'am.' His tone showed how plain was his dislike of having to converse with her. 'I am, in fact, on my way from Cardace Hall now. I landed at Plymouth but two weeks ago, and made my grandfather my first call.'

'Such devotion,' marvelled Alicia in dulcet tones. 'I do not wonder at it. Your grandfather is very rich, is he not?'

Now the implication could not be missed, and Miss Frensham drew her breath in sharply at such pointed bad manners. She hurried in with a question of her own. 'And do you intend to settle back in England now, my lord?'

Mullineaux's face immediately lightened as he turned to her. 'I hope to do so, ma'am. Now, by your leave, I will go and rout out the landlord. You need some light, a fire and a warm drink, not to mention rooms for the night. Then I shall go to the stables and see how matters progress there.'

Miss Frensham opened her mouth to thank him but was forestalled.

'So eager to escape us, Lord Mullineaux?' Alicia asked, mockingly, from her armchair. 'No time for pleasantries, and such indecent haste!'

This time she had the satisfaction of seeing James Mullineaux provoked into anger. His dark eyes narrowed in a way Miss Frensham could only describe as murderous. 'I would not choose to stay here a moment longer than I must,' he ground out and, turning on his heel, stalked from the room.

'There now,' Miss Frensham said exasperatedly into the sudden silence, 'look what you've done! Was there any need for that, Miss Alicia? I didn't know you had it in you to be so ill-bred!'

Alicia had the grace to look a little ashamed. Such strictures were very uncommon from her normally timid companion, but she knew she had behaved extremely badly. She leant against the chair-back for a moment and closed her eyes. Her head was aching and she felt very close to tears. She had dreamed plenty of times about meeting James Mullineaux again. Why did it have to be like this? She turned her head to look at Miss Frensham, who was fussing with the ribbons of her cloak and laying it out to dry over a chest in the corner of the room.

'I know it was very bad of me, Emmy, but he evidently despises me and I cannot abide being treated in such a way!' Alicia's face took on a mutinous look. 'I will *not* allow Mullineaux to judge me, not when he was as much at fault as I! If he had ever cared a jot for me he would have known that the breaking of our engagement was none of my doing!'

She warmed to her theme, her eyes flashing. 'But he chose to believe the worst of me—and did not scruple to tell everyone else so! Oh!' It came out with a vehemence she could not hide. 'Of all the pieces of bad luck—to be obliged to spend some time in enforced contact with Mullineaux!'

This somewhat jumbled speech led Miss Frensham to conclude that Alicia was genuinely upset and she relented a little. Lady Carberry was normally the most serene of characters, at least superficially. But then, Miss Frensham thought a little sadly, she had never seen anyone move Alicia beyond the superficial. No man had had the power to affect her in all the years Miss Frensham had acted as her companion—until now. The Marquis of Mullineaux had achieved in five minutes an impact no one else had even approached in five years.

'Well, to be sure it was very bad of him to behave so, but that is all in the past now!' Miss Frensham observed, in an attempt to console. 'Can you not at least *try* to be civil to him? After all, he has done us a considerable service in rescuing us both! I had not the least idea he was back in this country,' she added reflectively, 'but if the two of you are to meet at all in future, my love, you will need to preserve at least a semblance of politeness!'

'I see no reason to speak with him at all,' Alicia returned, sulkily, but there was the glint of tears in her eyes and Miss Frensham sensibly chose to let the matter drop. It was very unusual to see Alicia put so out of countenance. Although she was renowned for possessing the fabled temper of the Stansfields, this loss of control was quite another matter. No doubt she had been more shaken by the accident than she would care to admit.

'Let me have that sodden cloak, my dear,' she urged, changing the subject and coming across to help Alicia to her feet. 'Indeed, I am sure I do not know how long it will be before we get a fire in here! This really is too bad! No fire, no bedchambers, and no doubt no one to go for a doctor!'

'I do not need a doctor,' Alicia repeated fretfully. 'Truly, Emmy, I shall be very well with a little rest.' She let Miss Frensham take the cloak from her and place it across the back of the chair, shivering slightly in the damp air. The matching bronze travelling dress beneath was not damp, for Alicia had not been out in the rain for as long as Miss Frensham, but her right wrist was starting to ache badly. She was determined not to mention it and add to her companion's anxieties.

Shaking out her skirts, Alicia cast her first critical glance around the room and gave a silent sigh. Not only mental turmoil to contend with, but physical discomfort as well! Her gaze moved thoughtfully on to Miss Frensham and she was concerned by what she saw. There was a hectic flush in that lady's cheek and a glitter in her eyes which Alicia did not like the look of at all.

'It looks as though you are the one in need of a doctor's attentions, Emmy,' she observed judiciously. 'You must have taken a chill. Since Lord Mullineax has evidently failed to raise the landlord, I shall do so myself. We must see you to a bed immediately!'

Miss Frensham gave a muffled groan. She had suddenly started to feel very unwell with the combined effects of the soaking and the worry of it all, but it made her feel even worse to contemplate Alicia wandering the corridors of an alehouse alone. Not that Lady Carberry, being a widow, required chaperonage in the sense an unmarried girl would, but Miss Frensham was a dragon for preserving the proprieties—it was one of the reasons that Alicia had employed her. She sat down rather suddenly in the chair Alicia had recently vacated.

'Oh, no, my love, you cannot go looking for the landlord! I feel sure that he will be here directly, and only imagine if you should meet anyone; we should be quite undone!'

'Nonsense, Emmy,' Alicia said robustly. She was already halfway to the door. 'This is no time to be worrying about the conventions! I am well able to take care of myself, and besides, there is nobody else here!'

Whatever reply Miss Frensham might have given was drowned out by a sudden noise outside the inn. Alicia moved across to the grimy window to try to see what was happening but the rain was lashing down so violently now that it was too dark to see anything at all. A moment later the doorbell pealed sharply. Alicia and Miss Frensham exchanged a look and Miss Frensham stifled another moan. This was the worst thing that could befall them, alone and unprotected in a seedy alehouse—she had temporarily forgotten the dubious protection available from the Marquis—with goodness only knew what kind of disreputable travellers about to burst in on them.

'Who could possibly be out on such a night? Oh, Lady Carberry, I fear we shall be ravished in our beds—or worse!'

Alicia forbore to point out that they did not even have any beds in which to be ravished, for she did not think this would help. In silence they waited. Once more it was an extraordinarily long time before they heard the sound of the landlord's reluctant footsteps and the drawing back of the squeaky bolt. There was a swift, decisive but indistinguishable altercation in the corridor, and suddenly the parlour door was thrown open and the room appeared to be full of people, all talking at once.

The landlord was in full flow, involved in a heated exchange with a large and forceful lady. A portly, middle-aged gentleman was also present, talking and gesticulating wildly. Just as matters appeared to be getting out of hand, the lady made a dismissive gesture and accosted Alicia across the room.

'So it *was* your carriage, Lady Carberry! I thought I recognised it, and obliged John to stop here to see if there was aught we could do to help!' She was a plump, comfortable-looking woman of middling years and she shook the nerveless Miss Frensham by the hand with the warmth of an old friend, before turning back to Alicia with a quick look of concern.

'My dears, are either of you hurt in any way? Lady Carberry, you are looking a trifle pale, if you will forgive me! Can we be of service to you?' She cast an unfavourable look around the room. 'Indeed, you cannot possibly stay here! John, tell them they must not stay!'

'Indeed, my dear ma'am, you cannot stay here!' her husband echoed obligingly.

The landlord, who had at last lit the candles and started to make up the fire, glared at them, but Mrs Henley ignored him with superb indifference. As the wife of the local squire she considered all village matters to be her business and made no secret of the fact that she thought the Crown and Anchor inn a disgrace in terms of hospitality. She repeated her offer of help energetically and it was a moment before Alicia could get a word in.

'We are well enough, thank you, ma'am,' Alicia replied, with a smile, when at last the flow of words had ceased. 'Neither Miss Frensham nor I too much the worse for our accident, but I am afraid that she may have taken a chill.'

Mrs Henley had just turned back to Miss Frensham with an exclamation of alarm and sympathy that had that lady shrinking back in her chair, when the parlour door opened again and James Mullineaux strode in. He seemed unperturbed to find the room so full of visitors and strolled forward with easy charm to make their acquaintance.

After a swift glance at Alicia, who was standing stubbornly silent, Miss Frensham struggled to her feet and made the introductions in a failing voice.

'Mrs Henley, this is the Marquis of Mullineaux, who was so good as to assist us after the accident.' She ignored Alicia's snort of disgust and ploughed on. 'My lord, may I make you known to the Squire and Mrs Henley, who have stopped to offer us their help?'

Mrs Henley's shrewd brown eyes opened a little wider as she registered Mullineaux's name, but she was too well-bred to show curiosity. She also noted that Alicia's mouth was set in lines of obstinate dislike, and that, for his part, Mullineaux viewed her with no less antagonism. She became even more interested as Mullineaux launched into an easy explanation of the presence of so ill-assorted a group in such a small village on such a bad night. No inquisitive questions were required on her part whatsoever, for Mullineaux seemed determined to make the details of their unfortunate encounter crystal-clear in order to avoid the suspicion that he and Alicia had intended to meet.

Alicia stood listening to his admirably factual explanation of their accident with growing irritation. He showed nothing but the most impersonal concern for Miss Frensham's welfare and none whatsoever for her own. Mrs Henley missed none of the nuances, and, watching Alicia covertly, concluded that there was a very interesting by-play going on between the two of them.

'And so, ma'am, sir, if you would be so good as to recommend a more reputable hostelry, I should have no further worries about the safety of these ladies,' Mullineaux finished smoothly. 'I, alas, am fixed here for the night as my cattle are chilled to the bone and it is now too late for me to continue my journey. However, I am sure that the landlord could muster a gig to convey the ladies a short distance.'

'Lord Mullineaux is anxious to be rid of us, ma'am,' Alicia said with so much honey in her tone that Mrs Henley was barely able to suppress a smile. 'We are a sad burden on him.' She looked down at Miss Frensham drooping in her chair and added silkily, 'There is one aspect of Lord Mullineaux's commendable speech with which I would disagree, however. It does not seem to me desirable to subject Miss Frensham to the rigours of another uncomfortable journey. I am sure we shall do very well here.'

There was a flash of irritation in Mullineaux's eyes and as he drew breath for a scathing remark Mrs Henley hastened into the breach, much as Miss Frensham had done earlier.

'I will not hear of you putting up at this or any other inn tonight, Lady Carberry,' she said decisively. 'Ottery Manor is but a short distance from here and I am happy to convey you both there immediately as our guests. Nonsense.' She cut across Alicia's protests decisively. 'It will be a pleasure!' She turned courteously to Mullineaux. 'You are also most welcome to join us at the Manor, Lord Mullineaux!'

Alicia watched with malicious pleasure as Mullineaux tried to think of a way to decline without giving offence. She knew full well that only his dislike for her was prompting him to stay at the inn and refuse Mrs Henley's invitation.

'Alas, ma'am,' Mullineaux was saying with every evidence of sincere regret, 'I would be honoured to accept were it not for the fact that I must continue my journey at first light. I would not wish to inconvenience you in any way, and I am sure I shall do very well here.'

He could not be persuaded otherwise and eventually Mrs Henley accepted his refusal with resignation, not in the least fooled as to the reason for it. Bowing to them all but Alicia, who got the curtest of nods, Mullineaux went out to bespeak his lonely supper.

A smile twitched Mrs Henley's lips. She had never met the Marquis of Mullineaux before, but rumour certainly had not lied about him. He was without doubt a very attractive man and a formidably determined one. It was also beyond doubt that Lord Mullineaux wanted nothing more to do with Lady Carberry and viewed this whole incident as a profound nuisance. Meanwhile Lady Carberry herself, unaccustomed to being disliked, resented such cavalier treatment and could be very provocative when she chose. Lady Carberry was not spoilt, Mrs Henley reflected fairly, but it was unusual for men not to fall at her feet. Even the squire, who had never given Mrs Henley a moment's worry in twenty-five years of marriage, was gawping like a foolish schoolboy, ready to leap to Alicia's aid if required.

Alicia was looking particularly lovely in the candlelight, with her hair drying in tangled curls and the fire bringing a glow of colour to her almost translucent complexion. But clearly James Mullineaux was immune and, remembering the past history of Alicia and the Marquis, Mrs Henley could not really be surprised at it.

She had heard all the slanderous talk—the hastily arranged marriage to the grossly libidinous George Carberry, the sudden death of the bridegroom on the wedding night—from over-excitement, so the wags said—the bitter denunciation by James Mullineaux of his former betrothed, the wild tales that had circulated in the clubs... Alicia Carberry's name had been dragged through the mud so thoroughly that it had been thought she would never recover.

Mrs Henley had always had her own theory about the hastily arranged marriage to George Carberry. She gave no credence to any of the wilder tales about Alicia, but suspected that the Carberry match had been forced on her by her father. In the county of Somerset, Bertram Broseley's ruthless dealings were known at first hand, from the money he had made from the slave trade to the hard-driven land deals which had enabled him to expand his own estate immeasurably. Broseley was quite the most unpleasant man of Mrs Henley's acquaintance, and she was sure he would not scruple to use his own children as a business asset.

Time could bring about great changes, Mrs Henley reflected. The enormous social power of the Dowager Countess of Stansfield had been brought into play to help rebuild her granddaughter's place in Society, and after a while those who had been disposed to censure Alicia had seen only a rich and beautiful widow who had made an improvident marriage. Seven years had passed in which the lovely Lady Carberry had been courted by Society's most eligible bachelors, but had shown no sign of remarrying.

Mrs Henley frowned slightly, drawing on her gloves. Mullineaux's return from Ireland would whet the appetites of even the most jaded of society's gossips, she thought, with a certain degree of speculative interest. He was a vastly handsome man with a certain reputation as far as women were concerned, and there would be any number willing to put it to the test. And then there was the delicate matter of his future relationship with Lady Carberry. This unexpected meeting must have been embarrassing for both of them, and no doubt the fur would fly in the future. It was going to be a very interesting Season.

The door closed behind Mullineaux and Mrs Henley turned her warm smile upon Alicia, who was still looking a little dubious at foisting both herself and Miss Frensham unexpectedly on the Henleys' hospitality.

'I have guests already, Lady Carberry, and shall be happy to augment the party,' Mrs Henley reassured her comfortably. 'However, therein lies the only problem—my visitors are in the carriage outside, neglected shamefully, I know, but I hope they will forgive me! However, it means that I have room to take up only one more person at present. So perhaps—' she turned to Miss Frensham '—if you do not mind waiting, dear ma'am, I will take Lady Carberry to the Manor now, and send the coach back for you directly.'

Miss Frensham, who had been in a feverish doze in her chair, started to agree, but Alicia interrupted quickly. 'By your leave, ma'am, Miss Frensham has been exposed to the rain for longer than I, and is of frailer disposition. I should be happier if you could take her up first and return for me.'

Mrs Henley and Miss Frensham exchanged a look. Miss Frensham stood up shakily.

'It would be most singular, my love, to leave you here alone,' she observed carefully, worry reflected in her grey eyes. 'I am grateful for your consideration, but I will do very well here for a little longer. Perhaps—' her face brightened '—we could both wait, ma'am, if you will be so good as to send the carriage back for us when you have delivered your guests.'

It would have been the best plan, but Alicia was so used to taking decisions that she hardly hesitated.

'Stuff and nonsense, Emmy—you are shivering with ague,' she said strongly. 'You must get into the warmth as soon as possible. As for the proprieties—for I take it that is what concerns you—I doubt Lord Mullineaux will even return before the carriage comes back to collect me, and even if he does the landlady may stand my chaperon for five minutes! I beg you, ma'am—' she turned to Mrs Henley '—do not let us delay you any longer!'

Mrs Henley nodded. 'Very well, it shall be as you wish, Lady Carberry! Come, ma'am—' she took Miss Frensham's arm '—we will have you right in no time! I have a herbal mixture which is sovereign against the ague!'

So it was settled, and, whatever her private qualms, a secretly grateful Miss Frensham went out to the carriage.

Chapter Two

Ten minutes later, James Mullineaux re-entered the parlour from the direction of the stables, whistling under his breath.

Whistling! How very pleased he must be to be rid of us! Alicia thought crossly. Nevertheless, there was a hollow feeling in the pit of her stomach as she contemplated having to deal with him without Miss Frensham's soothing presence, and she smoothed the material of her dress down in an unconsciously nervous gesture.

Mullineaux stopped dead on seeing Alicia sitting alone before the fire and a swift frown descended on his brow. His dark hair was ruffled from the wind and he brought with him from outside the scents of fresh air and leather. The casual shooting jacket fitted his broad shoulders to advantage and despite the events of the previous hour his buckskins were clean and fitted to perfection. Only his topboots indicated that he had spent some time wading through the mud outside. Realising suddenly that she was staring, Alicia removed her gaze to his face and surprised there a look which could only be described as antagonistic. Her nerves tightened.

'What's this? I understood you to have gone to the Manor with Mrs Henley!' There was a dangerous control in the Marquis's quiet voice.

'Miss Frensham has gone with Mrs Henley,' Alicia said, with more composure than she was feeling. 'There was only room for one in the carriage and Miss Frensham has, I think, already started to develop a chill. The carriage will return for me shortly, my lord.'

Mullineaux appeared to be having difficulty in grasping what she was saying. He ran a hand through his dishevelled black hair, which only served to make him look even more attractive. Alicia noticed, and chided herself for being so susceptible. Unfortunately it seemed all too possible to find someone physically attractive whilst simultaneously disliking them intensely.

'You have sent Miss Frensham on ahead and stayed here alone?' Mullineaux repeated, carefully expressionless, looking at Alicia with something approaching incredulity. He crossed the room and turned to face her, his back to the fire.

Alicia, feeling intimidated and determined not to show it, rose to her feet. She met his eyes squarely. 'That is correct, my lord. Miss Frensham is not feeling at all well and it seemed only right that she should be taken to shelter immediately!'

The astonishment in Mullineaux's dark eyes was turning swiftly to anger. 'It may have been the right thing to do, but it was hardly wise!'

Feeling her own temper rising, Alicia decided to be deliberately obtuse. He really knew how to bring out the worst in her. 'Why, whatever can you mean, my lord?' she enquired coolly.

Mullineaux looked exasperated. 'I cannot believe you so naive as to fail to understand me! It would be unexceptionable for a lady of advanced years to be alone here with me. It is rather more singular for you to choose to stay here unchaperoned!'

He was, of course, quite correct. As a widow Alicia had a certain latitude of behaviour allowed to her that was denied unmarried girls, but even so she could not expect to retain her reputation for virtue by spending time alone with a man in an isolated inn. Given the circumstances of their previous relationship it was particularly unfortunate. Alicia mentally acknowledged this, but she was scarcely going to give Mullineaux the satisfaction of agreeing with him. She shrugged with every appearance of nonchalance.

'Oh, I do not have such a slavish regard for the conventions! You refine too much upon this, my lord!'

'I see.' His expression was contemptuous. 'I can only assume that your reputation was lost so long ago that it is of little consequence to you. Or perhaps—' he looked at her thoughtfully '—you deliberately contrived to stay here with me?'

Alicia had inherited her grandmother's temper along with the red hair. Normally it lay fairly well-buried, but now she could feel her control slipping away rapidly. Damn his presumptuousness! 'What a very good opinion you must have of your own attractions, Lord Mullineaux!' she said scathingly. 'Alas, I must disillusion you. There is no basis for your arrogance—I scarce chose to stay here in order to be with you! And you may acquit me of any attempt to compromise you! I assure you, you are quite safe with me!'

'Thank you for your reassurances, madam,' Mullineaux snapped, 'It is gratifying to know that you are more concerned for my reputation than for your own! I suppose I should not be surprised by your comments. Seven years ago you made it abundantly clear that you did not wish for my company. At least you are consistent!'

Even as he spoke, half of Mullineaux's mind was marvelling at the speed with which they had jettisoned polite convention and slipped into conflict. He was well aware that Alicia had been deliberately trying to provoke him all afternoon and that she had succeeded in getting under his guard very easily. Her unwanted company was a complication he could well have done without. His anger was intensified by the discovery that he was hardly indifferent to her. He might reasonably have expected the passage of seven years to have weakened, if not destroyed, any appeal she had once held for him. It was infuriating that this was not so.

Alicia herself was both angry and confused by their mutual antipathy. Whilst it would have been impossible to imagine that they could ever be on friendly terms, this instinctive antagonism was difficult to deal with. An icy reserve would have been more her usual style, but, shaken out of her habitual cool composure, she was unable to get back onto the sort of footing with Mullineaux that might at least have enabled them to preserve the minimum of cold civility. Whilst she struggled to regain lost ground, Mullineaux pushed them further into conflict.

'You say that I am safe from your attentions, ma'am.' He gave her a dispassionate look that was so indicative of scorn it brought the colour up into Alicia's face. 'Have you considered that you may not be safe from mine? Behaviour such as your own is an open invitation!'

'It might be construed as such by a man of your stamp!' Alicia pushed the heavy waves of burnished hair away from her face with a hand that was shaking. 'You never could believe yourself resistible, could you, Mullineaux?'

The tone of this extraordinary conversation could only degenerate further.

'I had heard that you were enjoying to the full the licence your widowed state allows you!' Mullineaux took a step towards her. 'It is what I would have expected. And it ill becomes you to play the innocent now, Lady Carbery. Had I realised that all candidates for your hand in marriage had to be old, rich and degenerate I should never have troubled you with my attentions! Not,' he added coolly, 'that it is marriage that is on my mind at the moment—far from it! But now that I understand you better, perhaps we could find a more interesting way of passing our time here?'

Alicia whitened. Her own comments had been provocative, but she was shocked by the ruthless cruelty of his response. He evidently considered her to have lost every shred of reputation and to be fair game for his advances. She had been in society long enough to recognise that she had tested his precarious self-control to the limit by the attitude she had assumed. He could not know that her apparent lack of regard for the conventions was mere bravado. In fact, she had reinforced his own prejudices by her wanton disregard for propriety. She struggled to regain some lost ground before it was too late.

'Your comments are both inaccurate and discourteous, sir! Pray do not make arrogant assumptions when your knowledge is so incomplete! Added to which, I find that strictures on behaviour come somewhat strangely from you! A man who abandons his responsibilities for seven years for the pursuit of pleasure is not in a strong position to criticise the behaviour of others!'

'Pray do not make arrogant assumptions, madam!' Mullineaux said, through his teeth. His look of scorn swept over her comprehensively, from copper curls to kid slippers. He did not even hesitate. 'At least I have never sold myself for a fortune!'

Even as he was speaking, he knew that he had gone too far, but her false protestations of innocence had infuriated him, and her comments on his own behaviour had touched a raw nerve. The tension that had been building between them from the very first moment had reached such an intensity that it had to defuse itself somehow.

As for Alicia, she was conscious only of her anger and resentment building with searing intensity. She wanted only to hurt him for the pain he had so carelessly inflicted. She raised her hand to strike him, but Mullineaux read her intentions quickly enough to prevent it finding its mark. He caught her wrist in an unbreakable grip. Their eyes locked in furious confrontation.

And then it happened. Mullineaux's hand slid from wrist to elbow in a caress that made Alicia shiver, but no longer with nerves. It had always been like this—like recognised like and reacted instinctively, and the conflict between them gave the attraction an edge that had not previously existed. Rational thought was suspended as he drew her closer. She could not tear her gaze away from his, realising that whatever it was that drove her also had him in its compulsive grip.

A corner of Alicia's mind acknowledged that in another second he would kiss her and she would not be able to resist, would not want to resist, and then God alone knew what might happen....

The door of the parlour opened and the landlord entered. Mullineaux dropped Alicia's wrist and stepped back unhurriedly, and the landlord smirked meaningfully in their direction.

'Road's flooded over by Ottery Down,' he said with gloomy relish. 'Ain't no ways they'll get a carriage through there from the Manor.' He peered out of the parlour window at the dark sky. 'Still rainin' too,' he remarked with obvious satisfaction. His gaze darted from James Mullineaux to Alicia and back again. 'Reckon you'll be needin' that room, sir!'

'Make that two rooms, please, landlord,' Alicia said hastily, and turned away from both the landlord's knowing leer and James Mullineaux's too penetrating gaze. She felt sick and shaken with reaction after what had just passed between them. Her injured wrist had started to ache badly and she put the other hand up to it, wincing as she touched it. It was nothing to the pain she felt inside. How could they have quarrelled so horribly when they had only just met again? And then for her to almost fall straight into his arms as though she were as promiscuous as he suspected her! And the final and all too predictable disaster of them being stranded together... Everything in the world felt so irrevocably wrong that Alicia was sure it could never be right again.

James Mullineaux did not appear similarly disturbed. The driven quality of a moment before had left him and he seemed once more the cold, remote stranger. He put up a hand to halt the landlord as he was leaving the room.

'Bring me some bandages, if you please,' he instructed quietly, then, at the landlord's look of dumbstruck amazement, he added with an edge of sarcasm, 'You do have such a thing in the house, I presume?'

'A horse bandage is the best I've got,' the landlord said churlishly. 'Will that do for your Honour?'

Alicia could have sworn that Mullineaux nearly smiled. 'That will have to do,' he said. He caught her look of mingled surprise and hostility, and added expressionlessly, 'Your wrist clearly pains you. You will do better with it bandaged up until you can see a doctor.'

His consideration had the effect of making Alicia feel even worse. It would have been more in character, she thought numbly, for him to tear her off a strip for her folly in causing this whole disaster. She hoped fervently that she would soon awake from this nightmare but it seemed unlikely.

James Mullineaux was standing before the fire watching her with an incalculable expression she found most disconcerting. He did not say a word about their recent argument or about the coil they now found themselves in, no doubt believing that the facts spoke for themselves. Perversely, Alicia wished he would say something, anything, to break that intolerable silence. She did not wish to feel beholden to him.

'Thank you for your thoughtfulness,' she said, trying not to sound ungracious, 'but surely the landlady could tend to my wrist?'

Mullineaux raised a sardonic eyebrow. 'I have not even seen evidence that there is a landlady, let alone assessed her ability to minister to the sick! If my help is so repugnant to you, you will just have to suffer the pain! Make your choice!'

Alicia's face flamed. For once she floundered for words.

'I did not mean...I did not say...I am grateful to you for your offer of help, but—'

'The landlord is returning with the bandage,' Mullineaux interrupted her laconically. 'You had better make up your mind! What's it to be? Common-sense or pride?'

Alicia acquiesced with ill grace. Somehow he had made her feel like a gauche schoolgirl, and an unappreciative one at that. She sat down and watched him untie the bandage, extending her arm unwillingly, as though his touch would burn her. Her wrist showed faint marks of bruising and was already beginning to swell. Mullineaux probed it gently, looking up as Alicia could not avoid a small gasp of pain.

'Not broken, I think,' he said thoughtfully, 'but a nasty sprain. If you will bear with me a little longer whilst I bind it up, that should ease the discomfort.'

His long, tanned fingers were deft and gentle as he bandaged the wrist with impersonal skill. To her horror, Alicia found her throat had closed with tears—tears which she was determined not to shed. She looked down at his bent head as he knelt next to her chair. The candlelight turned his dark hair the blue of a raven's wing and cast the exaggerated shadow of his eyelashes along the line of his cheek. Alicia was swept by a physical longing so intense it hurt her. All the feelings she had buried deep had been exposed in the most sudden and cruel way possible. She wanted to throw herself into his arms and cry away all the pain and misery of the last seven years.

She bit her lip viciously to hold back the tears and pulled her sleeve further back out of his way. As she did so, the slender bracelet she always wore slid down her arm and caught the light, the glow from the fire sliding over its intricate gold and silver tracery. Mullineaux's gaze fastened on it, drawn by the sudden glitter. For a moment he stared at it, completely still, then he looked up into her eyes with the dawning of puzzlement and disbelief in his own. It had been his betrothal gift to her and she always wore it.

It was too much. The accumulated shock of the accident, the strain caused by seeing Mullineaux again and his evident dislike for her, the impossibility of ever having the opportunity to explain the past to him— all these combined to drown Alicia in a huge wave of grief. With a sob she tore her arm half-bandaged from his grip and ran out of the room to seek sanctuary, any sanctuary, away from his astonished gaze and disturbing presence.

Alicia got very little sleep that night. The best bedchamber the inn had to offer was a bleak garret facing north and battered by the storm which raged outside. The walls were cold and damp to the touch, and the sheets were no better.

At first Alicia curled up on the bed and cried as if her heart would break, too unhappy to think of anything at all except the huge weight of her own misery. Such a flood of tears could not last for ever, though, and when she was at last drained and exhausted she looked up and shivered at the grim, grey room with its icy chill. The solid warmth and comfort of Ottery Manor, a mere half-mile distant, could only be imagined but even though she was desperate Alicia rejected the idea of trying to walk there and no doubt developing pneumonia in the process.

She got up, lit a candle and washed her face in the stale water from the pitcher, peering at her unprepossessing appearance in the speckled mirror. Alicia was not vain, for Miss Frensham had successfully managed to instill in her a respect of person, not appearance. However, the red-rimmed eyes which looked back at her from a deathly pale face did make her shudder. She felt suddenly hungry, but was too tired to bother with the effort of requesting a meal which would as likely as not be inedible. She wrapped herself in her cloak, blew out her candle and lay down on the bed. She found that she could not think at all; her mind appeared to be completely frozen. Soon she fell into a light doze.

Some unmeasurable time later Alicia was disturbed by a tapping sound and before she awoke sufficiently to enquire who was there the door opened and a thin, pale woman entered carrying a tray. She marched into the bedchamber and deposited her load on the chest of drawers with something of a crash, then turned to Alicia rather defiantly.

'The gentleman below insisted that I bring this to you, miss. He thought you might wish to partake of some food but prefer not to come downstairs. I'll leave it here for you.'

Her sniff and the toss of her head were indicative both of her un-willingness in performing the errand and her opinion of members of the so-called gentry who managed to get themselves into such compro-mising situations. She gave Alicia a look full of contemptuous curiosity and did not wait for any response but marched out in the same manner in which she had entered.

Alicia moved the tray onto the small bedside table and looked at its contents dubiously. The game pie was cold, but it turned out to be tasty enough to tempt her into eating a little and she found the wine pleas-antly reviving in its effect. After she had finished she sat quite still, trying to decide what to do. The process took a long time, for her head was still aching with the aftermath of sleep and her mind was under-standably reluctant to face the facts of her situation. She could get up and go downstairs, but the prospect of confronting James Mullineaux again so soon filled her with horrified embarrassment.

Although she acknowledged his kindness in thinking of sending her some food, she scarcely felt able to sit down with him to a game of cards to while away the evening! She had no books or needlework with her and there could be little else the inn would offer in the way of entertainment. Besides, she felt suddenly tired and light-headed from the wine, and her wrist, which she had finished bandaging inexpertly herself, was aching badly. In the end she merely wrapped the cloak about her again and lay down on the threadbare bedspread.

It seemed that the thoughts and memories which she had kept at bay whilst she was awake could not be denied, for as soon as she was asleep she began to dream almost immediately.

The scene was familiar: the ballroom at Stansfield House, lavishly decorated as it had been seven years previously on the night of Alicia's come-out ball with a richly coloured fresco of harvest fruits and an extravagant display of real, exotic fruit and flowers. The room was full of music and chatter, rainbow colours and ostentatious jewellery, as the cream of the *ton* mingled and gossiped, all so eager to see the new sensation that they had begged, borrowed or stolen an invitation. Alicia herself, slender in a white dress overlaid with silver net, moved through the crowded rooms and could feel the thrill and excitement of the evening almost tangible on the air.

The dream continued in a blur of laughter and music. Alicia had no concept of time passing as she danced every dance. Then suddenly everything slowed down and became sharper than crystal as she relived moment by moment all that had happened next...

It was the supper interval and Alicia was swept up into the group of people surrounding her friend, Caroline Oxley. She felt immediately welcome in the circle of friends, included in their light-hearted banter and with several of the young men making their admiration for her very plain. The food was delicious, the company great fun, and Alicia was thoroughly enjoying her introduction into society.

There was a lull in the conversation, and Alicia looked up to see a girl seated further down the table who was simply sitting staring, her spoonful of strawberries suspended inelegantly halfway to her mouth. Following her rapt gaze, Alicia realised that her eyes were riveted on a man who was threading his way between the tables and was being hailed on all sides. His tall, broad-shouldered figure seemed to draw all eyes and Alicia's neighbour was not the only lady who was frankly staring.

The stranger had reached Lady Stansfield now and was bowing elegantly over her hand before straightening up to give her a wicked smile. Alicia was amazed to see her grandmother positively preening herself—she who reduced most fashionable young men to stammering incoherence! Still, Lady Stansfield was not completely immune to good looks and this was a very personable young man indeed.

At that moment, Caroline Oxley looked up, gave a shriek and dug her brother Charles painfully in the ribs with her fan.

'Charles, only look! It's James Mullineaux, of all people! He never usually attends these affairs!'

'Too afraid of being pounced upon!' her brother agreed caustically. He turned to Alicia. 'You must know, Miss Broseley, that James Mullineaux is considered one of the biggest catches on the marriage mart and is always fighting off eager women! He came into the Marquisate last year, and has been under siege ever since! But I suppose one can't blame him for that and he's a capital fellow, really!'

Caroline tutted. 'Really, Charles! Must you give Alicia the wrong impression from the very start? James Mullineaux is all very well as long as one does not take him too seriously!' Her perceptive blue gaze swung back to Alicia, and there was the tiniest shadow of concern in her eyes. 'James is a reckless but charming flirt. He has an air of careless arrogance which many women seem to find fascinating, but, Alicia—' again, there was that hint of concern '—do not believe a word he says, I beg you!'

The Marquis had reached their table by now and was greeting Caroline's cousin, Charlotte Anstey. Watching Charlotte blush becomingly, Alicia felt a hitherto unexperienced emotion sweep over her which she had no trouble at all in placing as pure jealousy. Judging by the expression on the faces of other ladies nearby, she was not alone.

Fool! she chided herself, but it was without heat. The impact of this man hardly lessened at close quarters, and she could scarcely expect herself to be immune when all about her were devastated by his charm.

Then he was beside her and was demanding an introduction. There was an odd moment of tense silence before Peter Weston complied— as Alicia's self-constituted beau for the evening, Weston was not best pleased at the sight of such a rival. James Mullineaux noted his friend's reluctance and the possessive way his arm lay along the back of Alicia's chair, and his smile deepened.

'Miss Broseley, this is James, Marquis of Mullineaux.' Weston sounded even more sulky than he looked. Charles Oxley caught his sister's eye and they exchanged a meaningful glance.

The Marquis took Alicia's hand. His dark eyes trapped and held Alicia's startled green gaze for what seemed like forever. Then he smiled and spoke as though they were quite alone.

'My grandfather told me once that he had been one of Lady Stansfield's greatest admirers in their youth. He said that she was the most beautiful woman he had ever met and he fell hopelessly in love with her. They say that your resemblance to her at that age is very strong, Miss Broseley, and as soon as I saw you I realised how my grandfather must have felt.'

There was a long silence. Seeing Alicia's complete inability to reply in kind, Caroline Oxley came to her rescue.

'A pretty compliment indeed for my friend, sir!' she observed pertly. Her smile encompassed the whole group. 'Pity me that the Marquis of Mullineaux has always viewed *me* as a sister!'

Mullineaux relinquished Alicia's hand reluctantly and joined in the general laughter at this.

'Allow me to tell you that you look very fine tonight, Caro,' he offered, with a smile.

'Pah, a paltry piece of flattery!' she replied, with laughing disgust.

'Then you must rely on Marcus for the necessary compliments, I think,' Mullineaux commented with a sideways glance at his friend, Marcus Kilgaren. He drew up a chair beside Charles Oxley and the conversation became general again, but Alicia was all too aware of that dark, intense gaze resting thoughtfully on her face from time to time. Her heart was still beating erratically and she felt a frightening breathlessness. Well, she had been warned. She was not to believe a word he said.

Later, Mullineaux cut Peter Weston out for a dance with her and continued to pay her the most outrageous compliments whilst doing so. Alicia had regained sufficient composure to parry his comments quite effectively, but it was proving quite impossible to remain indifferent to him. She was young and fresh from the country and whatever her sensible intentions had been she was hardly proof against the sheer overwhelming magnetism of the man.

What was perhaps more surprising was that James Mullineaux, cynical and notorious breaker of hearts, should have found himself so genuinely drawn to her. Yet he had felt exactly the same as she had. Alicia had known that from the first moment he had looked into her eyes. The feelings wrapped themselves around her again as she slept. It had been recognition and danger, excitement and warmth, security and elation, all mixed up together. It had been perfect...

Alicia woke with a start. The damp and heavy bedspread had somehow managed to tangle itself around her in her sleep and was pressing down on her like a shroud. She struggled out of it and discovered that her face was wet with tears. The warmth of the dream fled, leaving her feeling cold and bereft. Shivering a little, Alicia crossed to the chest of drawers and washed her face again. There was a bitter taste in her mouth and she felt a little sick. The inn was quiet and the storm had died down, no longer battering the corners of the building. The candle had burned down and the room was dark and lonely.

The dream was still in her mind and all thought of sleep had fled as she contemplated the past. What a naive innocent she had been in those days, convinced that because she and James loved each other all would be well! Her father had had different ideas. To him, Alicia's undeniable beauty and social lustre had just added to her value as a marriageable asset. He had never had any intention of allowing her to choose her own bridegroom. Summoned hotfoot to London by the news of his daughter's imminent betrothal to one he considered entirely unsuitable, he had wasted no time in acquainting her with his alternative plan for her future.

Alicia stood by the window, staring out into the windy dark. She swallowed painfully. She had resisted his plans with all her strength, but the things that he had done to coerce her into finally agreeing to marry George Carberry were best left unremembered. Strangely, it was not her father's brutal treatment which had distressed her the most, but the slow, lonely disillusionment about James Mullineaux...

At first, the pain of loss had been excruciating and she had not known how she would survive it. She had lain awake for night after night, going over in endless detail the time she had spent with James, his every word, her every feeling. Every emotion had flared into vivid and unbearable life and when the searing pain had finally died down she had been an empty shell, a shadow of her former self.

A tear trickled down Alicia's face, mirroring the raindrops on the pane outside. Widowhood had not been unpleasant for her. She was rich, beautiful and much courted, and though she knew there were those who would always consider her bad *ton* because of the scandal of her marriage they would never say so to her face. She had her friends, her charitable works, and her grandmother. She had enough money to do whatever she wanted and if there was a monotony and emptiness about her life it was at least materially comfortable and undemanding.

She would never marry again. Alicia had known that already, before the unexpected encounter with Mullineaux had opened up wounds which had never truly healed, but could perhaps have been tacitly ignored. Unconsciously she had always compared every man she met with him and found them all wanting. And now he had come back... She shuddered at the prospect of meeting him socially in some dowager's drawing-room and being obliged to treat him as the merest acquaintance. A moment later, her mind presented her with the even less palatable picture of Mullineaux choosing one of the approaching Season's debutantes as his wife and she could not prevent a shudder of misery. Jealousy, long dormant, stirred in her again.

Shivering in the draught from the ill-fitting window, Alicia groped her way back to the armchair and drew her cloak about her for comfort. She was stiff and tired, but her mind stubbornly refused to rest. Huddled in the chair, she thought about their quarrel.

It was all too obvious now that Mullineaux considered her to be without a shred of honour. Briefly she tried to imagine explaining it all to him and gave up almost immediately. They were as strangers after seven years—she could never tell him the terrible events which had overtaken her.

Emotionally exhausted at last, Alicia settled herself to sit out the rest of the night. The inn had a long-case clock at the foot of the stairs and she heard it chime every hour through the night.

Alicia did not look her best the following morning, although she had done what she could with no clean clothes, no hot water and no maid to help her. Jack had managed to retrieve her valise the night before, but it was both crushed and soaked from resting in the ditch and its contents were largely unusable. Alicia knew she looked wan and pale in her crumpled dress, and about as young as a schoolroom miss with her hair in one long plait down her back. Looking and feeling scruffy gave her none of the confidence she needed to face James Mullineaux over breakfast.

She pushed open the door of the breakfast parlour somewhat apprehensively and found Mullineaux moodily eating buttered eggs and toast. He rose to his feet, unsmiling, as she entered.

His immaculate appearance made Alicia feel both dirty and resentful. There was not a mark on the close-fitting buckskins and his boots had a high gloss again. The coat which fitted his shoulders without a wrinkle was not of Weston or Stultz's making, but had an indefinable continental elegance for all that. He had not shaved and the stubble already darkening his tan only served to emphasise the piratical air Miss Frensham had observed the previous day. It did not detract from his spectacular good looks. Alicia, feeling as tongue-tied as a new debutante, looked away and hoped her colour had not risen.

'Good morning.' Mullineaux's observant gaze did not miss the violet shadows beneath Alicia's eyes, nor the fine lines of fatigue on her face. 'I trust that you slept well and are feeling better this morning?'

'I feel very well thank you,' Alicia responded with obvious untruth, but in tones that dared him to argue. It won her an assessing glance, but he did not comment and she almost immediately regretted the impulse which set her on the defensive and made her snap at him when she was barely in the door. Fortunately the landlady came into the parlour at that moment and with her customary good grace slapped a plate of eggs and toast down in front of Alicia. There was also a pot of coffee which both smelled and tasted surprisingly good.

Mullineaux showed no inclination for conversation, simply staring out of the window in an abstracted sort of way, and it was Alicia who finally broke the silence between them when it threatened to become prolonged.

'Do you plan to continue your journey today, Lord Mullineaux?'

'I do.' The dark gaze focused back on her in a most disconcerting manner. 'I have sent to enquire after both Ned and Jack this morning, and they are both well despite their soaking. Ned tells me that my horses are none the worse and have taken no chill.' He smiled suddenly in a way that Alicia found immediately familiar and her heart gave a little jolt. 'Indeed,' Mullineaux added, 'I believe Ned takes better care of them than he does of himself and would count it a personal insult were they to come to harm!'

'Do you have far to travel?' Alicia asked, determined to show she was perfectly able to pursue a civil conversation.

Mullineaux reached for the coffee pot and poured himself another cup. The strangeness of sharing breakfast with him suddenly struck Alicia forcibly; its intimacy made her abruptly aware of the sorts of rumours which would no doubt surface as a result of their enforced stay. She put her hand up to a head which was suddenly aching. She really was not feeling capable of thinking about that at the moment.

'I am going to Monks Dacorum for a few days,' Mullineaux was saying, effortlessly casual. 'I own a small property there which has been let for the last few years. I wish to make sure all matters such as tenancies are in order before I leave, as I do not intend to spend much time in these parts in future.'

That, Alicia thought as she bent her head over the buttered eggs, could be interpreted in several ways, none of them favourable. Mullineaux was as aware as she that his estate of Monks Dacorum bordered on her own at Chartley, since it was the Marquis's father who had sold that part of his estate to George Carberry some twenty years before. The Mullineaux family had never seemed fond of the house, however, preferring their homes in London and Oxfordshire. It could certainly not be wondered at that James Mullineaux would not wish to make his home so close to her! Alicia chewed the bitter crusts of misery and wished that the effort to make polite conversation, which so obviously came easily to him, were not such a trial to her. But then, he simply did not care, whereas she cared too much. Every moment in his company was a torment which Alicia hurried through in order to escape him as soon as possible.

Mullineaux put down his empty coffee cup and rose to his feet, crossing to the window where a sliver of watery blue sky was visible above the bare trees.

'Lady Carberry, there is something that I must say to you.'

He was standing half turned away from her and had his back to the light, but she could still see that he was frowning. Alicia's first thought was that she disliked intensely the sound of her married name on his lips. Her second was that she did not in the least wish to hear what he wanted to say. Whether he was about to resurrect ancient history and demand an explanation for her behaviour seven years ago, or merely to ring a peal over her for her behaviour as recently as yesterday, she simply could not cope. She had no wish to dissolve into tears yet again. However, she had no opportunity to make a graceful excuse and retreat, for Mullineaux had already started to speak.

'Circumstanced as we are, madam, I feel obliged to ask you to do me the honour of becoming my wife.'

For one dazed moment Alicia wondered whether she had misheard, or misunderstood his pompous words. It seemed unlikely, however, that one would mistake a proposal of marriage for anything else, and as Mullineaux merely waited silently for her reply Alicia found her indignation growing. He could at least have waited until she had finished her meal before he put her off her food so completely! Her appetite fading rapidly, she pushed her plate away and gave him her full attention.

'How can you be so ridiculous, my lord, as to offer marriage to one you hold in such complete dislike?' she demanded, with characteristic candour. 'I declare I cannot believe that you would do anything so ill-judged! But perhaps I misheard you? Indeed, your enthusiasm was so half-hearted that I fear I may not have understood you properly!'

She watched with no little satisfaction as the angry colour came into his face. He already looked as though he would like to strangle her.

'You did not mishear, Lady Carberry, nor misunderstand, as well you know!' Mullineaux spoke through gritted teeth. His hands were clenched tightly by his sides and his whole body was taut with anger. 'Nothing but the situation in which we find ourselves would induce me—' He broke off and resumed as politely as he was able, 'In short, I am making an offer in an attempt to limit the damage of this discreditable escapade, and would hope that your own sense of propriety would prompt you to accept!'

Alicia would not have believed that she could feel so furious so quickly. Normally she had her temper under tight control. She reluctantly rejected the idea of responding as her grandmother might have done—Lady Stansfield would no doubt have said, 'A pox on your propriety, sir!' or some such well-chosen phrase. That would not really help matters, tempting as it was. She bit her lip, trying to regain control of her temper.

'I believe that it is customary for a lady to express herself honoured by a proposal of marriage,' she said carefully. 'However, I cannot find myself grateful for a proposal which clearly caused you as much pain in the offering as it did myself in the receiving. So I thank you for your chivalry, my lord, but I fear I must decline.'

Too late she wished she had been a little more conciliatory, for Mullineaux looked no less furious as he came across the room to lean on the table in front of her in a way Alicia found completely intimidating. His mouth was a tight, angry line and Alicia could sense his rage, elemental in the tense lines of his body. She shivered, unable to help herself.

'You have no choice.' Despite his anger he spoke softly, which was somehow even more chilling. 'You must see that you have compromised yourself!'

'I have a choice.' Alicia met his gaze very steadily. 'I accept that my reputation is compromised, but I cannot regard that as good enough reason to marry you. To accept your reluctant proposal would surely cause more speculation than to continue as though nothing important had happened.'

There was a moment of silence as Mullineaux held her gaze, his own thunderous with disapproval. Then he straightened up and turned away.

'Very well, madam! Let me put this another way! You may reject my proposal with scorn, but have you really given any thought at all to our situation here and the gossip which will inevitably arise as a result? You think that you can ignore it? Think again, before you condemn us both to yet another infamous scandal!'

His arrogance took her breath away. Once again Alicia felt her temper rising and made a grab for her self-control. How dared he insult her by his insistence on doing the honourable thing when his dislike of her was so obvious? Only the previous night he had suggested that she no longer had a good reputation to protect, and whilst that might have been said in the heat of the moment his opinion of her was scarcely high. In her book it would always be better to face the scandal and ride it out than tie herself to so reluctant a suitor.

'You are overstating the case, sir,' she said, as calmly and coldly as she could. 'Certainly it is unfortunate—'

'Unfortunate! The most damnable mess imaginable!' Mullineaux strode back to the window. 'You may feel that you have the—"licence" was the word I believe you used last night—to do as you wish, but even your credit will suffer from a story that you spent a night alone in an inn with a man whom you once knew exceptionally well!'

He swung round to glare at her again. 'And the story which goes round will not be that we were marooned here as a result of a carriage accident and inclement weather—a far better tale would be that I returned from a long stay abroad and arranged a secret rendezvous with you.'

His tone took on a wealth of anger and bitterness. 'Then they will say that you deliberately sent your chaperon away and chose to spend the night with me—how romantic; how deliciously scandalous! And how does that suit your ladyship?'

It suited Alicia very ill and she could hardly deny it. Knowing society as she did it was impossible to believe that there would not be a great deal of speculation about the two of them and that the story which circulated would not be highly coloured; it was so much more interesting than the truth. Even so, she thought stubbornly, that was no reason to consent to a marriage where her feelings were still hopelessly engaged, and his were based on nothing but contempt. But how ironic! Alicia grimaced. She had just rejected the only man she had ever considered marrying!

She dared to raise her eyes to meet that furious dark gaze, and tried to speak composedly.

'I take your point, my lord. I might even apologise for unintentionally causing this situation. However, I would have thought that to become betrothed to you so suddenly would only give rise to a great deal of speculation on its own account! It is no solution! No, I still would not marry you were the gossip twice as loud!'

Mullineaux ran his hand through his disordered black hair in a gesture she knew well.

'You seem to take a perverse enjoyment in making life as difficult for yourself as possible!' he exclaimed. 'Of course there would be conjecture over our betrothal, but it would not be nearly as harmful to you as the gossip which will inevitably suggest that we are lovers!'

Alicia lost her patience. His scorn seemed to make a mockery of the feelings which she had tried so hard and so unsuccessfully to suppress.

His persistence when it was obvious that he detested her was the veriest insult.

'Lovers! I would imagine that anyone with half an eye would quickly realise that there was no truth in that and that we could not bear each other!' she retorted unwisely. 'And for my part I cannot see that it would make my life any easier to be betrothed to you! Are you suggesting that we should break off this false betrothal after a respectable time has elapsed, or do you feel we should go through with the charade and actually get married? I am sorry, my lord, but I find the whole idea nonsensical in the extreme!'

'I thank you, madam; you have said quite enough!' Mullineaux interposed with exasperation as she paused to draw breath. Their gazes clashed and held, both bright with anger. After a moment Mullineaux shook his head slowly in disbelief. He was not at all clear how they had managed to get into such a situation of conflict yet again. Why did she always bring out the worst in him?

He knew that the terms of his proposal had scarcely been flattering and was not even sure what quixotic impulse had led him to make it. He'd had no intention of doing so until he had seen her that morning; indeed he blamed her recklessness for compromising them both. Yet she had seemed so small and tired when she had come down for breakfast and so in need of protection. How misleading, when she had proved as little in need of protection as a tigress!

Her spirited rejection of his suit had perhaps been deserved, and, of course, she was right in that to become betrothed would be madness. He had no wish for their names to be linked, and his reputation would suffer far less than hers by the gossip that would inevitably follow this escapade. Nevertheless, her refusal rankled with him. And, confusingly, some element of him felt an obscure disappointment, but he knew he could not afford to examine why. Already his emotions were becoming dangerously involved.

'I thought that you would be glad to add a better title to your fortune,' he said, to give vent to his feelings, and almost immediately felt ashamed that he had allowed his distaste for her past behaviour to force him into rudeness. He watched the hot colour flood her face at the insult. How amazingly good she was at playing the hurt innocent! But what was the point in pretending to him?

Not for anything would Alicia show him how much his accusations hurt her. They cut through all the protective layers she had painfully built up over the years and exposed the unhealed scars beneath. This man had once held her in his arms and murmured words of love in a tone so far removed from his current one that it seemed like another world, another time... That man and this The change was too great. She rallied all her forces to defend herself.

'You may consider me an adventuress, Lord Mullineaux,' Alicia said, getting up to leave the room, 'but had you thought that *you* might be seen as a fortune-hunter in proposing to me? After all, you would be regaining a piece of your lost patrimony. And I am so very rich, you see,' she added sweetly, 'that no doubt people would quickly recognise the temptation my fortune, if not my person, presents to an impoverished Marquis!'

Well, Mullineaux thought, smothering a sudden grin, he had asked for that. She was quite capable of countering his ill-bred accusations with her own. At nineteen, Alicia Broseley had had plenty of spirit, but a sweet nature to accompany it. Now she seemed both decidedly outspoken and unfashionably quick to offer an opinion.

'Well, then, no doubt I should simply be grateful to have escaped marriage with a shrew!' he stated unforgivably, and once more they were left glaring at each other with bitter hostility.

The sky was a pale washed blue later that morning as Alicia trudged along the road to Ottery Manor. The road was still damp underfoot, but most of the flood waters had receded beyond the ditches, and lay across the low flat fields like a silver mirror. The faint, plaintive call of the curlew floated across the drowned landscape, and a single buzzard wheeled high overhead. The fresh breeze had brought a little colour back into Alicia's cheeks, but she was less inclined than usual to pause to enjoy the scenery.

Only the coldest words of farewell had passed between herself and the Marquis of Mullineaux. He had gone to the stables to oversee the preparation of his curricle, eager to be away, and Alicia had consulted Jack about the salvage of her carriage before setting off to the Manor. Jack had been hopeful that the repairs might be effected that day, which left Alicia with the dilemma of how to pass the time before she could resume her journey. The thought of whiling away time at Ottery Manor under the curious eyes of Mrs Henley's guests was almost intolerable, but the prospect of spending more time at the inn was equally unacceptable.

Alicia's thoughts turned back to Mullineaux and she felt sick at heart at what had passed between them. He was worse than a stranger, someone to whom instinct persistently drew her, whilst fate placed apparently insurmountable barriers between them. It was horrible that she still found him so undeniably attractive when he held her in the deepest contempt. For the sake of her sanity she would just have to keep out of his way in future. This melancholy reflection brought her to the stone gateway of Ottery Manor, and the low, rambling building came into view.

If Mrs Henley was taken aback to receive a visitor when her guests were still at breakfast, she hid it well. Shutting the breakfast parlour door in the frankly curious faces of Mrs Eddington-Buck and her daughter, she drew Alicia into a charming, sunlit drawing-room and settled her in a chair by the fire. Her shrewd brown eyes appraised Alicia's face with concern.

'You look a trifle out of curl this morning, Lady Carberry, if I dare say so,' she ventured at last. 'I am so very sorry we were not able to return for you in the carriage; indeed, John did try, but the Lilley had burst its banks, and the road was under several feet of water. We were at a loss as to what to do, and Miss Frensham was nearly beside herself with distraction!' She did not add that Miss Frensham's usual discretion had deserted her and that her wailed lamentations had added immeasurably to a scandal which her guests had been quick to seize upon.

Alicia looked up, her tired green eyes meeting Mrs Henley's observant brown ones and seeing nothing but kindness there. The urge to confide in someone was overpowering. Alicia swallowed a lump in her throat.

'Oh, my dear ma'am, do not apologise! The fault was all mine for thinking it best to send Miss Frensham on ahead, although—' she shuddered '—I would hardly have wished to condemn her to a night in that appalling inn! But now Miss Frensham has probably taken a chill anyway, and I have lost my reputation—which is, I suspect, a longer-lasting handicap!'

It seemed that her granddaughter resembled old Lady Stansfield in plain speaking, Mrs Henley reflected. Certainly Lady Carberry was very likeable, and one could not but sympathise with her predicament. Even so, Mrs Henley hesitated to offer advice and chose to address the easier part of Alicia's comments first.

'Well, I fear Miss Frensham is rather poorly this morning, my dear. She did not feel able to take any breakfast and has stayed in bed to rest. I expect the news of your arrival will cheer her, though. As for your own dilemma...' she took a look at Alicia's expression and decided to risk it '...well, it is rather difficult, is it not?'

Alicia managed a smile at this masterly piece of understatement whilst still looking despondent. Watching her unconscious grace even whilst she was drooping with tiredness, Mrs Henley felt grateful that her impressionable younger son was not at home. At nineteen he was ripe to fall in love, and Alicia was the perfect romantic heroine.

'You are very welcome to stay here as we had originally planned,' Mrs Henley ventured, with complete truth, 'but I fear that it might be rather uncomfortable for you. Mrs Eddington-Buck is an unkind creature, and as for Mrs Evelyn—well...' She did not need to complete the sentence, for that lady's lack of discretion was legendary. 'I imagine,' Anne Henley said carefully, 'that they may be capable of inventing all kinds of fascinating tales for public discussion. Not that I do not believe you able to cope with such tabbies, Lady Carbery, but—'

'But it would be poor repayment for your kindness, ma'am, to cause you such trouble,' Alicia finished. 'No, I will not stay. If I may trespass on your hospitality further and beg to borrow a carriage, I will continue the journey which was interrupted yesterday. My own vehicle may be ready on the morrow, but I have no wish to delay my business. Miss Frensham may have told you, ma'am, that we were on our way to my father's house.'

'Indeed, my dear,' Mrs Henley murmured. Now she was very surprised. To her knowledge, Alicia and her father had not met for seven years.

'Nothing could be simpler than you borrowing a carriage,' she added, 'if that is what you wish. And perhaps you are right in thinking that the scandal will die down in your absence. Certainly I will do all I can to squash it. Does the Marquis of Mullineaux have plans to travel on today?'

Alicia smiled faintly. 'I believe he does, ma'am, although I know little of it. Believe me, the Marquis was too displeased by my folly to think of indulging in much conversation!' She stared miserably at a bright square of sunlight on the carpet. 'Not,' she added suddenly, 'that any blame for this situation can lie with him. He was generous enough to offer me the protection of his name, but I declined.'

Mrs Henley's eyes opened very wide at her words. What sudden impulse could have prompted Mullineaux to offer for Alicia Carbery when he so clearly despised her? And why did Alicia feel that she had to refuse him but still make it clear that he had behaved as a gentleman ought?

'I had no choice but to refuse his offer,' Alicia was saying softly, more to herself than to Mrs Henley. 'How could I accept, knowing that he detests me so?'

Their eyes met and what Anne Henley saw reflected there made her think that perhaps she understood. Lady Carberry's predicament was worse than she had originally imagined, for, whatever Mullineaux's motives had been in proposing, Anne Henley knew Alicia had refused him because she had the misfortune still to be in love with him.

Chapter Three

Alicia slept for most of the journey from Ottery to her father's home north of Taunton and woke only as the carriage turned in at the black iron gates of Greyrigg. Despite the wonders worked on her appearance by Mrs Henley's maid, who had both dressed her hair and miraculously removed all dirt from her clothing, Alicia felt both worn and tired. Her eyes were gritty from lack of sleep and she already had a slight head-ache which she wryly ascribed to tension. Her first meeting with her father after seven years was bound to be difficult and she did not feel best prepared to face it, but having got this far she was determined to go through with it.

A line of bare chestnut trees bordered the gravel drive which led up to the house. Greyrigg had once been the home of an impecunious Viscount but had been purchased some twenty-eight years previously by Alicia's father, Bertram Broseley, who was a fabulously wealthy nabob. Broseley had made his fortune in trade with both the Indies and the African continent, and the Viscount, who had considered him to be an upstart of the most encroaching sort, had nevertheless seized the opportunity to turn the least favoured part of his estate into hard cash.

It was easy to see why the Viscount had felt no attachment to the house. On this wintry day the grey bulk of the building was uncom-promisingly ugly as it stood amidst its park. Not even the carpeting of wild snowdrops beneath the trees could lend it any charm. It was as though the house had absorbed some of its owner's characteristics over the past decades, and now it had an air of gloom and neglect.

As the carriage drew up outside the imposing portico, the door of the house opened and a liveried butler emerged. The groom jumped down and opened the carriage door for the occupants to descend. Alicia tilted her head to gaze up at the massive edifice and could barely repress a shiver. Taking a deep breath to sustain her, she turned to greet the butler, who was advancing across the gravel with an unctuous smile on his face.

'May I welcome you to Greyrigg, my lady.' Obsequiousness did not become Castle, who had the physique of a prizefighter and, indeed, was more at home in dealing with the unsavoury side of Bertram Broseley's business affairs than in greeting his guests. His black boot-button eyes flicked over Alicia with an unpleasant expression which reminded her of their last meeting. Things were different now. She raised her chin.

'Thank you, Castle.' She sounded as coldly regal as the Dowager Countess of Stansfield herself. Nothing would induce her to say that she was pleased to be home.

Alicia preceded the butler up the steps and into the gloomy entrance hall with her borrowed maid trotting along behind, seemingly awed into silence by the oppressive atmosphere.

Although Alicia had been nineteen when she had left Greyrigg for her London Season, the house now looked smaller, as though she had previously seen it through a child's eyes. There was a smell of mustiness and decay in the hall which she did not remember. Huge cobwebs festooned the grimy central chandelier and there was a spartan emptiness which suggested the recent removal of various pieces of furniture. Alicia wondered briefly if her father's business affairs were ailing and the neglect of his house was a direct result. Certainly the marble floor had not been cleaned for an age and the air had a stale smell which made her wrinkle up her nose in disgust.

The front door closed and Alicia had the oddest idea that a trap had closed with it. She shrugged the fanciful idea away impatiently. It was natural that she should feel uncomfortable, for she associated her father with the unhappiness of her marriage and her recent meeting with James Mullineaux could only put such matters back at the forefront of her mind.

Even before the meeting at Ottery, she had never had any intention of staying long at Greyrigg, having come reluctantly at Broseley's behest only to take her sister to London for the forthcoming Season. It would be pleasant, Bertram Broseley had written, for Annabella to have the opportunity for a come-out, just as Alicia herself had done. This had seemed perfectly reasonable, but Alicia had felt both hurt and manipulated. Three years before, when Annabella had been fifteen, Alicia had tried to mend the breach with her father so that she could see her sister again. Her approach had been brutally rebuffed by Broseley, who had never contacted her again until the day three weeks before when his letter had arrived out of the blue.

Despite their past differences and the fact that all Alicia's letters to Annabella had been returned unopened, she had unwillingly bowed to her father's pressure, anxious to prevent a fate similar to her own from befalling her sister. Broseley's letter had pointed out urbanely that Alicia's home at Chartley was close enough for her to come to Taunton to collect Annabella, and Alicia had not been able to find a gracious way to refuse. Now she wished she had tried harder.

Suddenly the door of her father's study was flung open and Bertram Broseley himself came striding across the floor to greet her, hands outstretched as though she were the prodigal daughter.

'Alicia! My dear! It is a happy day for us now that you are once more beneath the roof of your home!'

He met his daughter's sardonic eye but did not falter. Castle smirked. Alicia, overwhelmed by a feeling of revulsion, found that she was utterly unable to respond in kind. In fact, she was unable to respond at all and simply stood, struck dumb. She had underestimated how unpleasant it would feel to be confronted with her father again. Old fears and memories were stirred up, confusing her. As she struggled to frame a suitable response, Broseley spoke again.

'We expected you yesterday and were somewhat concerned when you failed to arrive. I hope you did not experience trouble on the journey?'

'Merely some damage to my carriage on the Ottery road,' Alicia replied, dismissing all the events of the previous twenty-four hours in one fell swoop. She was already feeling profoundly uncomfortable. She had hoped that Annabella would be ready to leave immediately, yet there were no trunks in the hallway, no signs of imminent departure. Suspicion stirred, faint but disturbing.

'It's a bad road,' Broseley commented, his shrewd grey gaze making an inventory of his daughter's appearance as though totting up exactly how much her clothes and jewellery had cost. An indefinable hint of satisfaction entered his manner. He had already calculated how expensive her outfit was.

'Never mind, you are here now. And you are looking very...' He paused, and for an insane moment Alicia thought he was going to say 'rich'. 'Very well indeed. I hope that you will feel able to stay for a little time.'

Nothing would have pleased Alicia less. She tried to think of a polite rebuff, but once again the effort of framing the appropriate words defeated her. Fortunately the silence, which was already threatening to become strained, was broken by the sound of running steps on the stair and by Annabella's voice.

'Lud, sister, can it really be you?'

Alicia could have said much the same thing. The voluptuous beauty who had reached the bottom step and was now pausing for effect bore little resemblance to the skinny little sister of eleven whom Alicia had not seen in seven years. Annabella Broseley justified the term statuesque and her clinging scarlet riding habit made her charms abundantly clear. Unlike Alicia, who had, of course, inherited the glorious but unfashionable copper hair of their maternal grandmother, Annabella was blonde. Her eyes were of a paler green than her sister's and hers was a bold, flaunting beauty which she used to advantage on all the men she met.

Annabella's gooseberry-green eyes were now appraising her sister with a patronising regard. She was deeply jealous of Alicia, though she would never have admitted it. Not only was her sister very wealthy in her own right, but she was also an acknowledged beauty who had earned the sobriquet of the most desirable widow in Society. Society's opinion mattered a great deal to Annabella and it seemed unfair to her that a widow of twenty-six, who should have been at her last prayers, should have such an enviable existence.

Both sisters had the same heart-shaped faces, but the dramatic lines of the cheekbones and the determined chin which gave Alicia both beauty and resolution were already blurring into fat on Annabella's face. Her mouth was accustomed to droop with bitter discontent and her low voice was cultivated to be deliberately sultry.

Alicia's taste in clothes was far too subtle to appeal to Annabella, who, unlike her father, dismissed the superbly cut bronze travelling dress as plain in a single glance. Mrs Henley's maid had taken Alicia's hair up beneath the elegant bronze wide-brimmed hat and this, with its contrasting ribbon, was again too simple to win her sister's favour. Patting her own be-ribboned and flower-decked hair with complacency, Annabella walked around Alicia, inspecting her as one might the points of a horse.

'La, Alicia, you are so thin!' This was not a virtue in Annabella's eyes, for she saw her sister's slenderness as ugly. 'And so pale!' She eyed Alicia's porcelain skin suspiciously. 'I see you do not favour cosmetics to improve your looks. Oh!' She gave an affected little shriek. 'Never say those are freckles on your nose! Are freckles become the fashion in London, then?'

The words were naive but the look which accompanied them was anything but simple. Belatedly she offered her own enamelled cheek for her sister's kiss and stood back to watch the effect of her words.

Alicia merely smiled at her sister's malice. Annabella had always been like a kitten sharpening its claws, although now the kitten showed signs of having developed into a fully grown cat. For a brief moment she wondered how the two of them could possibly coexist peacefully during the next London Season, at the end of which she hoped Annabella would be safely married and off her hands. It looked as though it was going to be a difficult prospect.

'You are looking very well, Annabella,' she observed peaceably. 'Are you intending to go riding? I had hoped to be away as soon as possible, for it is a few hours' journey back to Chartley, and—'

'Oh, but you must stay for refreshments at least!' Annabella had flashed a look at their father who had stood silent throughout this exchange. She slipped her arm through Alicia's, steering her in the direction of the drawing-room.

'Unfortunately I have a prior engagement to go riding, but there is plenty of time, and I know Papa hopes for the chance of a chat! Perhaps we might stay until after dinner? Or indeed until tomorrow, since I do not suppose you to wish to travel after dark?' She made it all sound comfortably domestic and cosy, and her gaze was bright and innocent. There was no reason for Alicia to feel the same vague uneasiness stir within her, but she did and she could not place the reason. Perhaps it was Annabella's deliberate insouciance, or perhaps she was simply imagining things.

'I would prefer to leave today,' she said, a little stiffly. Above all, she wished to be home at Chartley to achieve a little peace. 'I had made no arrangements for an overnight stay.'

'Oh, very well.' Annabella seemed to dismiss it as of little importance. 'But tell me about London! We hear much about you, even buried here in the country! We are so dull.' She pulled a face. 'I saw Severn's heir when he was staying with the Milburns at Stoakely Manor. You must have had windmills in your head to refuse his proposal, sister dear—a Viscount, and so handsome! Thirty thousand a year! Why, I declare, if I had half your chances I should not waste them as you do! Lud, to think—'

'Annabella—' There was something in Bertram Broseley's voice which brought the colour rushing to Annabella's face. She paused in the drawing-room doorway.

'La, here I am running on so, and you must be fagged to death after your journey! I will ask Mrs Rivers to send in refreshments, and—' she turned to the maid with a dazzling smile '—Castle will escort your maid to the housekeeper's room whilst you wait. Until later, then, sister dear!'

She swung out of the main door, shouting for her groom, and Bertram Broseley took Alicia's arm in a firm grip and guided her into the drawing-room. She found that she had to make a conscious effort not to brush him off, so strong was her feeling of distaste. The atmosphere of constraint in the house seemed very strong; this visit was proving even more difficult than she had imagined. She had seldom felt so uncomfortable, although her father seemed quite unaware of her feelings.

'Do you ever see your cousin Josiah?' he enquired sociably as they crossed the threshold and the door was shut on Annabella's demanding voice.

Alicia sighed. It was scarcely a happy choice of question with which to start the conversation rolling after seven years. Josiah Broseley, the son of Bertram's younger brother, was foolish and feckless, and aspired to live the life of a gentleman in London. Alicia seldom saw him unless he came begging for funds, but despite her exasperation with him she found she could not dislike him, for he had a surface charm that was engaging. What worried her more was the knowledge that, in his more impecunious moments, Josiah had undertaken some work for Bertram Broseley. He was not discriminating when it came to funding his more questionable habits, nor was Broseley selective if he felt he could use someone to his advantage.

Alicia returned some slight, negative reply to his enquiry and looked about the room with interest. It was dark and oppressively hot. There were heavy curtains which all but hid the windows. It was an ugly room, and Alicia realised that it had not been altered since the last time she had been in it. Now the furnishings looked old and outmoded, the wall-hangings a threadbare shadow of their former rich show. An huge fire was burning in the grate and added to the overpowering warmth. The heat and tension between them were combining to make Alicia's headache much worse, but Bertram Broseley seemed totally unaffected.

He had spent much of his life in tropical climates, and no doubt felt the cold, particularly during an English winter.

Alicia took a seat on one of the puffy sofas which had looked so elegant twenty years previously, but now were merely lumpy and uncomfortable. Since she had been manoeuvred into spending at least a little time at Greyrigg she would try to make it tolerable, though how she would manage this defeated her. She would have wished to avoid a tête-à-tête with her father above all things. She watched his easy confidence as he moved to pour her a glass of Madeira, then helped himself to brandy from another decanter. He seemed completely at ease. Alicia could even hear him humming under his breath. She accepted her glass with a stiff word of thanks but could make no attempt to initiate conversation.

'May I repeat what pleasure it gives me to see you once again at Greyrigg?' Broseley began pompously, seating himself at a right angle to her and crossing his legs. 'You have been too long away, Alicia.'

His shrewd grey eyes met hers with an expression of guileless innocence. Any daughter should have been moved by the paternal sentiments, but Alicia had learned in a hard school just how far he had her interests at heart.

'My absence is hardly surprising,' she said coldly.

'A difference of opinion, perhaps...' Broseley sounded vague, waving his hand in an indeterminate gesture of dismissal. He took a sip of his brandy, eyeing her over the rim of the glass. 'I am sure that time must have gone a long way to healing the rift between us, and today we have a chance to further that process.'

Alicia almost gasped in disbelief. How could he assume that a reconciliation would be so simple? She set her glass down with a snap that made the delicate crystal shiver. This was intolerable. Her nerves were already on edge from the other events of the day and she felt utterly incapable of sustaining a travesty of politeness.

'Let us be quite plain from the start, Father, and avoid any insincere sentimentality. It was my intention never to set foot in this house again and I am only here today because you suggested that it would be good for Annabella to spend the Season in London with me. As you know, I have always been anxious to re-establish my relationship with my sister.'

Broseley winced at such plain speaking but his daughter did not relent. She eyed him thoughtfully. 'I am beginning to think that there was more to your invitation, however. I do not see much urgency on Annabella's part to be on her way!'

Broseley's expression was one of hurt innocence. 'My only other motive in inviting you here was an earnest wish to see you again, my dear Alicia!'

His daughter raised a cynical eyebrow. 'Come now, Father, do you expect me to believe that? Annabella may well wish for a Season in London, and you may well be pleased for her to go, but there is more to this than that! Do you take me for a complete fool?' She bent over to pick up her reticule. 'I have no wish to effect a reconciliation between us. If it is indeed your intention that Annabella have a Season, I suggest that you send a groom to find her and bring her back so that we may leave immediately. I asked for my carriage to be ready within the hour. If you do not want her to go with me, I will take my leave now.'

'You are too hasty, my dear.' Broseley looked pained at her lack of finesse, but managed to summon up a wintry smile. The light fell across his face as he leant towards her. He looked much thinner than Alicia remembered, for his face had lost a lot of its fullness and the portly figure—the result of years of good living—had become almost gaunt. Only the slate-grey eyes were as sharp as ever beneath their lowering brows and the mouth was a thin, cruel line. He steepled his fingers and spoke weightily.

'I'll allow that a Season in London for Annabella was the reason I gave to ask you here, and, of course, I wished to heal the breach between us. But as you are so perceptive, my dear Alicia, I'll admit that there are other options which I wished to discuss with you.'

He paused, but Alicia remained silent, looking at him with nothing more than polite enquiry. It was as she had suspected. Bertram Broseley wanted something but he could never approach his objective directly. She was deeply distrustful, but it would be far safer to know his intentions now rather than to get an unpleasant surprise later on.

'It was always my intention that Annabella should have the benefit of a Season in Town—as you did, my dear,' Broseley was continuing, 'but the little minx is hot to marry Francis St Auby, and pesters me night and day for my consent.'

Alicia raised her eyebrows, but managed to keep her tone neutral, revealing none of the agitation she was starting to feel. The suggestion of a Season for Annabella was looking more and more like an excuse—hence the lack of luggage and Annabella's reluctance to make plans for departing. So where was all this leading?

'Is it St Auby that Annabella is riding with today?' she asked.

Broseley nodded. 'It is. He is a reckless youth, but I can see that they would be well-matched. Annabella would like to join the accepted ranks of the local gentry and she and St Auby have much in common.'

'And does this marriage have your blessing, Father?'

'Not yet.' Broseley looked secretive. 'But it would be quite a good match for Annabella—she would like to be Lady St Auby—and besides, she wants Francis.'

'I am sure that she wants both the man and the title,' Alicia observed dryly. She knew Francis St Auby to be a handsome young man with an unsavoury reputation. She also remembered the St Auby family, and privately reflected that they must be desperate indeed to consider an alliance with Broseley when they had always considered him to be a jumped-up nobody. But poverty made for strange bedfellows and the St Aubys possessed endless debts as well as an old title and an over-weening pride. Perhaps they had been consoled that Annabella's grandfather had been an Earl and that her pedigree, on her mother's side at least, was immaculate.

'You know the St Aubys a little,' Broseley was saying, in a concil-iatory way so far removed from his usual manner as to be suspicious in itself. 'What is your opinion of them?'

Alicia paused. 'I should say that Francis St Auby is a dissolute youth and his father thinks of naught but his hounds and his women, no doubt in that order,' she observed after a moment. 'They have no money and are snobbish and small-minded. It amazes me that you are considering an association with the gentry, father. I thought that as a class you despised them.'

Broseley flushed angrily, but managed to shrug with an approach to nonchalance. His hatred of the aristocracy to which he had once aspired was notorious and his dislike of the landed gentry, amongst whom he had never been accepted, was almost as strong.

'To tell the truth it was not my intention originally,' he admitted grudgingly. 'But, as I said, Annabella is keen to have him.' His gaze flicked over Alicia, and it was not kind. 'She wishes to have a title to outrank yours, amongst other things.'

His taunt missed its mark, for Alicia only laughed. 'That would not be difficult, poor Carberry being a mere knight! But a baronetage is scarcely more and Sir Frederick St Auby may live for years if he does not break his neck on the hunting field.' She paused. 'If you are willing to buy a title for Annabella, could you not make more sure of one? Or buy a better one? Annabella would improve her chances immeasurably by coming to London with me. If I make it known she comes with a fat dowry she might even catch herself an Earl!'

It was a comment very close to the mark and Broseley held onto his temper with an effort. He had always considered his elder daughter to be a headstrong chit with a regrettable tendency to speak her mind. Annabella he understood, for she was very like him, but Alicia had always been a mystery to him. He knew that she was the image of her grandmother and that did her no service in his eyes. Of course, she was considerably older than when they had last met and no doubt possession of an independent fortune had only strengthened this deplorable attitude of self-assurance in her. He schooled his features to a semblance of pleasantness, and struggled to regain lost ground.

'Come, come, we must not quarrel, you and I. After all, this is supposed to be a reconciliation! The truth is that Annabella and St Auby...' He paused delicately. 'Well, they are very close. They have already—'

'Anticipated the pleasures of the marriage bed?' Alicia finished for him sardonically. She was not particularly shocked, for she knew Francis St Auby's reputation. Nor did Annabella seem concerned over her apparent fall from grace. 'Is she expecting a child?'

'No!' Broseley snapped, abandoning subtlety in the face of his elder daughter's outspokenness. 'At least, she assures me that she is not! The little madam—she came and told me as bold as brass—' He got a grip on himself and finished grudgingly, 'You must see that it changes matters...I am obliged to agree to her demand that they wed!'

Alicia thought that she saw rather well. No doubt Broseley had mooted some arranged match for Annabella and her sister, preferring Francis's undeniable attractions to some middle-aged libertine, had acted on her own plans rather than her father's.

'I am touched to see that you are more solicitous for Annabella's happiness than you were for mine, sir,' Alicia said smoothly. 'But in what way does this paternal dilemma affect me?'

Broseley seemed not to notice her sarcasm.

'I simply wanted to discuss my predicament with someone I could trust,' he said with a plaintiveness that was so ludicrously uncharacteristic that Alicia almost laughed aloud.

'And so you chose me?' she said incredulously. 'Pay me the compliment of believing me less gullible than that, sir! It seems that my sister has made her own decision! Francis St Auby's attributes were clearly more attractive than a Season which could not guarantee a richer prize! You knew that, but still you chose not to disabuse me! You used Annabella's future as your excuse to bring me here—now, what was your true purpose—those other options to which you referred earlier?'

It never occurred to Bertram Broseley that some part at least of Alicia's tenacity could only have been inherited from himself. He abandoned his attempt at pathos but still tried to pin on a friendly smile.

'How very direct you have become, my dear!' It was not a compliment. 'Since we are being so matter-of-fact, I will not waste any more of your time! It occurred to me recently that we might be able to do business together, you and I. I know that you have considerable capital which could be invested wisely, were I to advise you. Or, alternatively, you might wish to consider marrying again. I have a business associate who is much taken with the idea of an alliance. It could be an advantageous financial match!'

Alicia's overriding reaction to this crassly insensitive suggestion was blind fury. He evidently thought that, having benefited so handsomely from the forced marriage to Carberry, she would be willing to enter a second arrangement of her own free will!

'I am surprised that you did not offer him Annabella!' she said wrathfully. 'That would be more in keeping with your usual style, would it not, Father?' Her eyes narrowed as she considered his flushed, furtive face. 'Or perhaps you did, only to be circumvented by her conduct with St Auby! I cannot believe that you truly thought that *I* would consider either of your suggestions seriously! I have no interest in going into business with you, and I certainly have no intention of marrying to oblige you again! What conceivable benefit could there be to me from such a match?'

'The prospect of enlarging your fortune?' Broseley suggested, still hopeful.

Alicia was not impressed by this evidence that he thought her as venal as he.

'My fortune is already too great, sir, and achieved by means that I detested!'

Too great a fortune was not a concept Broseley could understand. By now he was rigid with the effort of holding onto his temper in the face of his daughter's defiance.

'I do not believe that one can ever have too much wealth, my dear Alicia,' he said, condescension just winning over annoyance in his tone.

'Then that is the difference between us!' Alicia snapped furiously. Her headache was worsening and she took a sip of the unwanted Madeira in an effort to help clear her thoughts. It had never been a favourite drink of hers and the taste of the wine was strong and cloyingly sweet. Already her head was starting to spin and the edges of the room were beginning to blur in the dark and the heat from the fire. Sweet wine, but with a slight, bitter aftertaste which was almost undetectable... She put her glass down again with such a jolt that some of the liquid splashed onto the table.

She might be mistaken, of course, but her father appeared to favour such drinks as this. He had given her a sweet, drugged wine to soften her resistance once before: when she had refused to marry George Carberry. Alicia looked at the glass pensively. There was no way of telling if this drink had been doctored, but drugged wine and an overpoweringly hot room would combine to make her feel very ill...so unwell that she would probably be unable to leave Greyrigg and would be vulnerable once again to Broseley's machinations for her future.

Alicia shivered convulsively. The shock had helped to clear her head. She could see the gardens outside in the pale sunlight and hear the birds twittering in the gutters, but here in this dark room it was possible to believe that Bertram Broseley was capable of anything. To him it would only be a means to achieving an end. He was watching her intently.

'I do not care much for your taste in wine, Father,' she observed as coldly as she could. 'And I care as little for your plans. Now let me be quite plain. I do not wish to invest in your business and I do not wish to remarry. You may tell this mysterious suitor that I have no desire to be treated as yet another commodity!'

'Indeed, my dear, you wrong my colleague,' Broseley murmured, with a smile Alicia neither liked nor understood. 'You are fair and far out in thinking that he would have taken Annabella—it was always you he meant to marry!'

'My money, you mean!' Alicia snapped, refusing to fall for this appeal to her feminine vanity. 'How fortunate that you broached the subject with me first, Father—I have a dislike of being rude to complete strangers!'

'But no compunction over showing your father a most unfilial ingratitude!' Bertram Broseley was now letting his anger get the better of him. 'Your duty as my daughter should at least prompt you—' He broke off as Alicia made a noise indicative of her contempt.

'Come now, sir, that is taking it too far, even for you! You lost the right to ask for such filial respect seven years ago!'

Broseley's nature had always been choleric, especially when crossed.

He had been keeping a hold on his temper for a long time, but now his face suffused with blood and he brought his fist down on the arm of his chair with a force which made the dust rise in a choking cloud.

'I see that you are still the same ungrateful chit you were those seven years ago, miss! To whom do you owe your pretty little title and your fine fortune? Had I not exerted myself for your benefit you would have thrown yourself away on that wastrel who was wild to a fault and spent all his money at his tailor's or in the gambling clubs! Who was it who arranged the wedding settlements so that you would inherit all George Carberry's wealth and property? And how did you repay me?' He did not wait for an answer. 'By running to your grandmother when my back was turned and destroying all that I had worked for! And now that you have the opportunity to redeem yourself you throw my generosity back in my face!'

Alicia stood up. The heat, the sticky sweetness of the wine and her own anger had combined to give her a blinding pain behind the eyes. She could barely tolerate being in the same room with him, but there was something she had to do before she left. She locked her hands together to prevent them from shaking.

'How you delude yourself, Father! No—' as he made a move towards the bell-pull '—you will hear me out! That may be your interpretation of events seven years ago. Let me tell you mine!'

She gripped the back of her chair to steady herself, her fingers digging into the faded brocade, and cut across his bluster incisively.

'You refused to allow my betrothal to the man of my choice and told a farrago of lies as to how I preferred George Carberry. You made my name a byword for scandal in the clubs and finally you forced me into marriage with that…that disgusting old man! Throughout it all you were motivated by nothing but commercial gain! Oh, no,' she corrected herself angrily, 'I mistake! You had another purpose—to make my grandmother look a fool because you had never forgiven her for refusing to accept you as her son-in-law!'

'You always were a sentimental fool!' Broseley was on his feet, vicious in his anger, his rage matching her own. 'All that happened was that I arranged a good match for you and you were headstrong enough to think of opposing me! If Carberry had not died, he would have knocked this ingratitude out of you—'

Alicia rounded on him, her eyes blazing. 'You tried that when I refused to marry him—do you remember? How could you forget? Beating your own daughter into submission and starving her, and worse—'

Her voice broke. 'But Carberry *did* die and you were too drunk at the time to stop me from going, and I thank God that I will never be drawn into your wicked designs again!'

The hot tears filled her eyes and overflowed down her cheeks. She dashed them away with an impatient hand. Broseley's expression had changed suddenly and miraculously from a convulsion of fury to a rather calculated and sickening look of concern. He came to her side, taking her arm in a proprietorial grip.

'My dear, you are distraught.' His sympathy was far more objectionable than his anger. 'I will send for Mrs Rivers at once to take you to a room. You cannot possibly travel in this condition—'

'You mistake, Father.' Alicia shook him off abruptly. 'I intend to leave directly.'

True to her word, she marched to the door and wrenched it open and Castle practically fell into the room, demonstrating all too clearly that he had been listening at the keyhole.

Alicia glared at him. 'Castle, summon my maid and my carriage. I am leaving.'

There was a moment of silence and indecision as Castle looked to his master for guidance. Broseley himself was looking at Alicia's barely touched glass of wine and frowning heavily. Alicia could read his mind all too easily.

'I may be a foolishly sentimental chit, Father, but I am not so green a girl as to be caught by the same trick twice. So you see I did learn something from the experience of my first marriage! Now, will you let me go, or are you intending to restrain me by force?'

She knew quite well that he was capable of doing so, but would he dare? Even now, she could hear the spattering of the wheels on the gravel outside as Jack, following her earlier instructions, brought the coach round. Broseley heard it too and made his decision.

'Really, my dear, I would have expected more courtesy of you! Such a breach of manners!'

'It's the company I keep,' Alicia snapped. She turned to find Mrs Henley's maid hurrying to her side, drawn like half the other servants by all the noise in the hall. 'Come, Joan, we are leaving!'

The carriage drove off moments later at a spanking pace and the door of Greyrigg slammed shut behind them. Broseley and Castle were left standing silently in the hall as the sound of its wheels died away down the drive.

'Your daughter has turned into a formidable lady, sir,' observed the butler to his master after a moment, with his habitual smirk.

Broseley glared at him. 'I'll bring her down,' he ground out, his West Country accent thickening as it always did under stress. 'Aye, and her grandmother with her, that old troublemaker!'

He retired to the privacy of the drawing-room where he smashed the offending glass of Madeira in the fireplace. He had had no interest in mending the breach with his daughter for the sake of it, but he had devised an opportunity to regain control of both her and her fortune and to use both to further his own ends. He stared furiously into the pier glass. So he had misread her. He had hoped—believed—that inheriting such a huge fortune would have made her more materialistic. How many people in such a situation would not see the benefit of increasing their wealth? Not many that he knew! Unfortunately, Alicia had proved to be one such and the prospect of augmenting her fortune held no interest for her. The nineteen-year-old girl whom he had forced into marriage had been replaced by a woman of considerable character who could not be either persuaded or threatened.

For the umpteenth time Broseley reflected bitterly on the malign fate which had caused George Carberry to die on his wedding night. He could hardly have anticipated such bad luck. To have worked so hard, only to lose it all! He allowed himself a moment to dream of the ventures he and Carberry had planned together. What he could have done with such money! Carberry had been as rich as Croesus.

Broseley turned to stare unseeingly out of the window. It gave him a bitter satisfaction that he had managed to sabotage Alicia's relationship with the Marquis of Mullineaux so thoroughly. Alicia had never known that Mullineaux had come round to Bruton Street day after day, demanding to see her. Impetuous hothead! Broseley's mouth twisted with cynical disdain. Mullineaux had represented everything he had grown to hate about the privileged classes.

Broseley's train of thought turned back to his commercial dealings. His business associate would not be pleased with the day's outcome. Mr Wood, as Broseley liked to think of him, had never been interested in Annabella and had only ever wanted to marry Alicia. She had divined the reason correctly—her money—but she had never thought to ask his name. This had saved Bertram Broseley the trouble of inventing another lie, for his associate was actually known to Alicia and was very anxious that his connection with her father remain a secret, at least until the marriage contract was signed.

Broseley sighed. He hated to be proved wrong. His associate had warned him that his approach was misguided. He had correctly predicted that Alicia would reject both an invitation to a business partnership and a marriage of convenience. Further, he had pressed Broseley to allow him to try his fortune under his own colours. Broseley had been dismissive. Now it seemed that he would have to allow it. He moved over to the fireplace and rang the bell vigorously for Castle. There were matters to attend to.

Alicia, exhausted by the scene with her father, had quickly resolved that she could not bear to return to Ottery Manor and the malicious whisperings of Mrs Henley's guests. Instead, she decided to throw herself on the mercy of one of her grandmother's oldest friends, the Reverend Theophilus March, who held a country living which included the parish of Ottery as well as several others. An elderly bachelor with a fearsomely respectable housekeeper, he inhabited a spacious and well-appointed vicarage in the village of Ashlyn, some five miles from Ottery.

The vicarage was warm and quiet, a haven after Greyrigg. The Reverend Theo was delighted to see her. Stooping slightly, he came forward to greet her warmly and kiss her on both cheeks.

'Alicia, my dear child! What a splendid surprise! No, do not apologise for intruding; I could not be more delighted! Mrs Morland will see your luggage taken up. I must apologise, but the green room is already taken—I have another guest, you see...' He was ushering her into the library as he spoke. 'The grandson of an old friend...called this afternoon, after a considerable time abroad...I persuaded him to stay for dinner...'

Alicia had a presentiment of disaster a second before the library door swung wide to reveal the Marquis of Mullineaux, a tattered copy of *The Meditations of Marcus Aurelius* in his hand. He was smiling as he looked up from the book, and for a heartbreaking moment he looked exactly like the boyish young man she had known all those years before. Then he saw her and an expression of complete astonishment was followed swiftly by incredulous disbelief, before he assumed a carefully cultivated indifference.

Alicia, horrified to find herself confronted with such an unexpected problem, was already backing out of the door and bumping into Theo, who was trying to follow her into the room.

'Oh, no! Dear Theo, I did not realise...' She took a grip on herself as she saw the faintest hint of amusement touch Mullineaux's mouth at her discomfort. 'I would not dream of intruding on your reunion! It is of no consequence...I can easily stay elsewhere...'

The Reverend Theo, a scholarly and spiritual man, was rather unworldly and seemed completely unaware of her very real reluctance, and of Mullineaux's sudden withdrawal.

'My dear Alicia, do not think of it! I could not be more delighted by your unexpected arrival, and I am sure James shares my sentiments! James, dear boy, may I introduce Alicia, Lady Carberry? Alicia, this is the Marquis of Mullineaux, whose grandfather was up at Oxford at the same time as I. I used to coach James on his Sophocles during his school holidays!' He smiled reminiscently.

Mullineaux took Alicia's reluctantly proffered hand with an equal lack of enthusiasm. This was, she knew, the moment to reveal to the Reverend Theo that they knew each other already, but she felt a curious reluctance to do so, aware that the attendant explanations could be difficult. Mullineaux seemed equally reticent. He dropped her hand with a murmured word of greeting, and went to return the copy of *The Meditations* to the bookshelf. Alicia remembered, at least ten minutes too late, that Lady Stansfield had once mentioned that Theo was a mutual friend of herself and the Duke of Cardace, James's grandfather. Alicia mentally conjured up as many unladylike epithets as she could muster.

'We are dining early,' the Reverend Theo was continuing, in blissful ignorance of the turmoil affecting Alicia, 'for James could do with a good square meal and a proper night's sleep! Do you know, my dear, he had the misfortune to be involved in a tiresome carriage accident yesterday with some careless fellow traveller?' He tutted loudly. 'Too many people drive with a total lack of consideration these days!'

Alicia's eyes met James's for a long, silent moment. He was looking studiously blank.

'I always say exactly the same thing myself,' Alicia said sweetly. 'Do you know, Lord Mullineaux, by an extraordinary coincidence, I too was involved in an accident on the road yesterday and I believe the other party was very much to blame?'

A muscle twitched in Mullineaux's cheek. 'Indeed, ma'am,' he said colourlessly. The Reverend Theo beamed to see his guests in such harmony.

As she dressed for dinner in the blue bedroom, Alicia took stock of her situation. It was the most confounded nuisance to meet Mullineaux again so soon and unexpectedly, but she had to manage as best she could. Her preferred strategy of avoiding him was obviously impractical, so she had a choice between languishing over her feelings like the heroine of a bad melodrama, or taking her courage in both hands and the battle to his camp. She knew which she preferred. She raised her chin defiantly at her reflection in the mirror and went down to dinner.

Mrs Morland, privy to the servants' gossip, might have been able to enlighten her employer as to the relationship between his two guests, but she never offered an unsolicited comment. Wrapped up in his world of parish matters, the Reverend Theo had never paid much attention to events in the outside world, and since neither Lady Stansfield nor the Duke of Cardace had mentioned the broken engagement between their grandchildren at the time he remained in happy ignorance.

'And so I told him to send the creature to the horse-coper!' he finished triumphantly, coming to the end of a long anecdote which had taken up the best part of the first course. He roared with laughter and both his guests smiled politely.

Alicia had been studying James Mullineaux covertly since the beginning of the meal. Immaculate in a coat of black superfine over a dove-grey waistcoat, there was something austere in both his dress and manner. She had already divined that he intended to ignore her for the most part, for he never looked at her directly and addressed not one word to her. Invited by Theo to take Alicia in to dinner, he had graciously seceded the privilege to his host in a manner so charming that Theo had suspected nothing, whilst Alicia had been left fuming with indignation. He had taken a seat opposite Theo, which kept her out of his line of vision, and for the most part they had all talked on generalities such as the weather before Theo had begun his anecdote about the horse.

Alicia swallowed the last of her turbot and watched entranced as the dressed capon was brought in, accompanied by asparagus and new potatoes. For a country parson, Theophilus March certainly did not stint himself. She remembered that he had a private income and also assumed he would be killing the fatted calf for the return of this particular prodigal. Her attention was caught as she realised Theo had started off on another of his unpredictable trains of thought.

'Excellent shooting at Monks Dacorum in your father's time, my dear James,' he was saying, through a mouthful of rich sauce. 'The woods between Monks and Chartley were always flush with pheasant. Why, I remember—' He broke off as an idea appeared to strike him for the first time. 'I say, Alicia, do you realise that this chap is your near neighbour? Well, I declare, what a happy coincidence! You will be able to show him around the neighbourhood!'

Alicia thought she saw James shudder slightly. 'I should be delighted,' she said warmly. 'Lord Mullineaux has been so long away, has he not, that I dare say he can scarce remember where his own tenants live!'

That earned her a look at last, dark and direct. Theo did not notice, for he was nodding enthusiastically. He leant towards James confidingly. 'You should know, my dear boy, that Lady Carberry is a considerable benefactress to this neighbourhood!' He waved his fork about in vague description. 'The schools she has started, the businesses saved from closure... Her work has given employment to plenty of young men who might otherwise have gone to the bad, driven by a want of education and honest toil! I always preach her example from my pulpit!'

James Mullineaux's lip curled slightly. 'Very commendable, I am sure, my dear sir! Lady Carberry must be an example to us all!'

Theo missed the sarcasm completely, but Alicia did not and flushed with mortification. She began to perceive that Theo's ignorance of their situation might be awkward. She had no wish for him to sing her praises to James Mullineaux of all people.

'Dear Theo, you exaggerate,' she said gently, hoping to stem his flow. Unfortunately it had the opposite effect. He looked injured, peering at her short-sightedly from under his thatch of grey hair.

'Alicia, dear, do not hide your light under a bushel! His lordship should know of your good works!'

'You need not praise Lady Carberry to me, sir,' the Marquis of Mullineaux said smoothly. 'I already know all I need to form my opinion!'

Only Alicia saw the dismissive look of contempt in his eyes. She felt her temper rising with the unfortunate effect his scorn always had on her. Arrogant, overbearing man! She took several reckless mouthfuls of Theo's excellent wine.

'Your reputation precedes you also, Lord Mullineaux,' she observed with saccharine sweetness. 'I imagine the county has not had so much excitement in an age! Your...pursuits are legendary!'

Mullineaux's gaze touched hers for a brief moment, then he looked away with an apparent lack of interest.

'Plenty of country pursuits here!' Theo was chuckling, oblivious to the undercurrent running between them. 'Hunting, shooting, fishing... Take your pick, my boy!'

'And what pursuits do you indulge in, Lady Carberry?' Mullineaux asked suddenly. Only his tanned fingers, drumming a ceaseless rhythm on the table, betrayed his irritation at her subtle provocation. 'Other than the exercise of your benevolence, that is! Balls and parties, perhaps? Or would a masquerade be more to your taste?' He put the very slightest emphasis on the word and Alicia's over-sensitivity did the rest. So he thought her charitable activities were all a pretence, did he? She had never boasted of her philanthropy but it infuriated her to think that Mullineaux was judging her a fraud.

'My favourite activity,' she said, determinedly squashing her anger with a demure smile, 'is my gardening, sir.'

It was such an innocuous reply. Theo beamed again and Mullineaux almost choked on his wine. He cast her a cynical look. She met it with a defiant sparkle in those green eyes.

'Alicia's garden is a joy to the whole neighbourhood,' Theo commented as a redcurrant syllabub and the dessert wine were brought in.

'Are the village children permitted to play there?' Mullineaux enquired innocently. 'It would seem a charitable act to allow them to do so!'

Now it was Alicia's turn to choke on her food. She took another draught of wine, regarding him thoughtfully over the rim of her glass. Mullineaux had turned to Theo, courteously praising the quality of his wine cellar.

'And that is a genuine compliment from Lord Mullineaux, who is a connoisseur of such matters!' Alicia observed smartly. 'Of all the areas of Lord Mullineaux's expertise, that is surely the only one suitable for *your* ears, dear Theo!'

Even the Reverend Theo was not so obtuse as to misunderstand that comment. He swallowed convulsively, his baffled gaze travelling from Alicia's flushed face to Mullineaux's politely expressionless one. Mullineaux might, in fact, have been forgiven for administering the setdown which Alicia so richly deserved for this, but he said not one word. Theo wriggled uncomfortably, greeting the butler's arrival with the port as though he were a long-lost cousin.

'Alicia, my dear, the port...would you mind? Mrs Morland has tea served in the drawing-room... Perhaps you would be so good... We will join you later...'

The relief on his face as he saw her rise to her feet was almost comical.

Alicia was suddenly feeling very light-headed. Her poor night's sleep the previous evening and the strain of her day had led to an immense, unexpected lassitude. She found that she had to enunciate her words very clearly.

'Please excuse me. I am very fatigued and would retire. Thank you for your hospitality, Theo.' She nodded distantly in Mullineaux's direction. 'Goodnight, sir.'

Mullineaux put down his napkin and rose to his feet. 'I will escort you to the stairs, Lady Carberry.'

Hysteria rose in Alicia. She realised that she was feeling very odd indeed. Why should she need his escort? Did he think she would get lost? The vicarage was a sizeable house, but not that large! She almost laughed, and just managed to swallow a hiccup.

Mullineaux was holding the door for her and somehow she found herself standing with him in the relative darkness of the hallway. He was lighting a candle for her with grave concentration, the flame catching and illuminating his face from beneath with its soft light. Alicia's mouth dried. She could not look away. His dark eyes were hooded and the candlelight shadowed the hard, determined line of his jaw, his mouth...

He looked up and shattered her mood.

'Do you always drink too much at dinner?' he asked casually.

Alicia stared at him in outrage. 'How dare you insinuate—? I am not drunk!'

'No?' Mullineaux looked at her with cool disinterest. 'Then you have even less excuse for that ill-bred display in there! Be careful, Lady Carberry! Drinking too much and failing to realise it is the first sign of danger for a lonely, middle-aged widow—'

'How dare you?' Alicia's voice was rising. 'I am *not* middle-aged!'

She saw his sardonic smile and could have slapped him. 'Maybe not,' he agreed readily, 'but you are becoming repetitious! And as to how I dare, well, it seems to me that no one else does dare tell you any home truths, my lady!'

Outrage and misery struggled for ascendancy within Alicia. She had had enough of his officious, interfering ways! Here he was again, judging her with such insufferable arrogance! She glared at him speechlessly.

Mullineaux seemed completely unaffected. He handed Alicia the candlestick, but when she would have taken it and marched off upstairs he did not let go. She looked up into his face, confused. What new indignities was he about to heap on her head?

'Lady Carberry, tell me one thing.' There was an odd note of urgency in Mullineaux's voice. 'The schools…and the businesses…is it all true?'

Alicia felt as though she was looking into his eyes for ever. A welter of thoughts tumbled over themselves inside her head. Tell him the truth, one voice urged. Damn his presumption, said another. Well, damn him, and damn her as well. Some imp of perversity prompted her to confirm his poor opinion of her.

She gave a little, catlike smile. 'Oh, it is true as far as it goes, my lord. But you should know that sound businesses make more money than ones that are poorly run! I never invest where there is no profit to be made!'

She took the candle and swept off upstairs, but not before she had seen the disillusion and scorn return to his face. It was his habitual expression when regarding her, she thought.

She slept heavily and woke with a headache, heartache, and a severe case of guilt towards Theo, who did not deserve his hospitality to be abused in the way she had done the previous night. She need not have worried about meeting Mullineaux again. He had left before she even came down to breakfast.

Chapter Four

For a week after her return home, Alicia had been pondering whether she dared venture near Monks Dacorum now that she knew that the Marquis of Mullineaux was in residence. She felt so bruised by their recent encounters that she had no wish to see him again for a very long time. Unfortunately, a short while before Christmas, she had accepted an invitation from Mrs Patch of Monks Farm to take tea that very Thursday and she was loath to cancel the engagement and give offence.

In the event the hour she spent at Monks Farm was very enjoyable. She admired the small Patch children and received Mrs Patch's assurances that the yield from the estate had increased since she had been so kind as to lend them the money for drainage of the five-acre field. The tea was strong and the home-made cake delicious. It was only as Alicia was leaving the farmhouse with her arms full of fresh vegetables and two small children clinging to her skirts that disaster arrived in the shape of the Marquis of Mullineaux on what was evidently a tour of the estate.

It was perhaps to be expected. It was the first fine day of the week, with a fresh, crisp feel that made it perfect for riding out. The hedgerows still glistened with frost and the puddles in the farmyard were slippery with ice. Mullineaux, on a raking grey hunter, looked formidable and every inch the lord of the manor as he rode slowly into the farm court-yard, glancing round with evident approval at its trim tidiness. Then his gaze fell on Alicia, defiantly clutching a large marrow, some sprouts and a bag of potatoes, and a less easily definable expression crossed his face.

Mrs Patch was curtseying clumsily, drawing the children to her side like a protective mother hen. She was horrified at the unexpected intrusion.

'My lord, if only we'd a' known you were coming to visit! Farmer Patch is down the five-acre field—I'll send to fetch him at once!' Belatedly she realised that she did not sound very welcoming, dropped another hasty curtsey and added, 'We're most honoured by your visit, my lord, to be sure!'

Mullineaux had dismounted and was quick to put her at her ease. 'I was just passing, Mrs Patch, and thought to stop and renew old acquaintances. Don't trouble to disturb Patch now—Tadcaster and I will drop by in a few days for a proper chat with him about the farm. And these must be your children.' He smiled at them, and they smiled back, completely dazzled. 'What a delightful pair! I believe your daughter favours you, Mrs Patch.'

Mrs Patch looked overwhelmed by such magnanimity. Tom Patch, a sturdy six-year-old, stood braced, gazing up at the Marquis as though he had seen a god. Four-year-old Matilda looked more dubious, but was coaxed into a smile again as the Marquis squatted down beside her and asked her gently if she enjoyed living on a farm. Alicia, feeling distinctly *de trop*, tried to edge away only to be thwarted as her bag of potatoes burst and scattered its contents all over the cobbles.

Tom whooped with glee, chasing them round the yard. Mullineaux straightened.

'Your servant, Lady Carberry. It is something of a surprise to see you here.'

Alicia was immediately on the defensive, as was Mrs Patch who was quick to detect the hint of disapproval in his tone. In her haste to smooth matters over she stumbled into disastrous speech.

'Lady Carberry has always taken an interest in the farm, my lord, ever since we had that terrible flooding last year and she advanced Patch the loan to drain the five-acre field! It's made such a difference to us, my lord, you would not believe! Why, if it hadn't been for her ladyship...' Her words trailed away, conscious of Mullineaux's sudden silence.

'Monks Farm is now the best purveyor of fresh fruit and vegetables in the locality,' Alicia added, knowing she sounded completely inane but anxious only to prevent Mrs Patch from making any further damaging disclosures. Judging by the black frown on Mullineaux's brow, it was already too late.

'Thank you, Tom,' she added as the young Patch solemnly presented her with her potatoes. She turned to Mrs Patch with a warm smile. 'And thank you for your hospitality, Mrs Patch. I hope to see you again soon. Good day, Lord Mullineaux.'

It was not to be supposed that she could escape so easily. As she turned to walk away, her arm was caught in an iron grip.

'Let me escort you to your carriage, Lady Carberry,' the Marquis of Mullineaux said, in tones which brooked no refusal. 'This ice is most treacherous and I would not care for you to slip and hurt yourself.'

Alicia looked up suspiciously, but the dark face above her was completely bland. She was acutely conscious of his gloved hand beneath her elbow, holding her lightly now but in a grip that nevertheless made her nerve-ends tingle. They crossed the courtyard in silence and reached the gate, where Alicia's coach was drawn up to one side of the archway.

'Now,' Mullineaux said, very pleasantly, as they paused beside the hawthorn hedge, 'we can either talk here or in the relative privacy of your carriage. Which do you prefer, Lady Carberry?'

Alicia looked mutinous. 'Neither suggestion would seem appropriate, my lord,' she said coolly. 'I have nothing to say to you.'

'You are mistaken, however.' Mullineaux still sounded pleasant but there was an expression in his eyes that belied his tone. 'You will tell me, if you please, exactly how much the Monks Dacorum estate owes you for the drainage of Patch's land. I do not care to be indebted to you.'

Alicia almost gasped at his words. He had wasted no time on polite conversation. The gloves were off with a vengeance.

'I shall do no such thing,' she said hotly. 'The arrangement between Farmer Patch and myself was a private transaction and nothing to do with the estate!'

Mullineaux was tapping the end of his riding crop impatiently in the palm of his other hand, and Alicia wondered suddenly if he was about to use it on her. He looked angry enough to be thinking of it.

'I do not care for you to be making private transactions with my tenants,' he said, with silky politeness. 'Tell me the figure and I shall see it repaid at once.'

'I doubt it!' Alicia flashed, stung into fury by his desire to be rid of all obligation to her. 'Having been away so long, you may not realise, my lord, that drainage is prohibitively expensive. The reason Farmer Patch approached me in the first place was because your agent had told him the estate could not afford to pay!'

Mullineaux's eyes narrowed. 'You are telling me that Tadcaster knew of this transaction and permitted it? Good God, how could he allow Patch to be bled dry by a private loan?'

Alicia felt a spark of triumph prompt her to provoke him further. 'He permitted it because a man's livelihood was at stake, my lord! And,' she added sweetly, 'you quite mistake the case! The loan is interest-free and based only on Farmer Patch's ability to pay! But now that you are aware of this obligation on your estate perhaps you would wish to take over the repayments to me?'

Murder flared in Mullineaux's eyes. 'You little—!' He got a grip on himself. 'You sound like a cursed money-lender, madam!' He flung away from her, to turn swiftly back and view her with a narrow, contemptuous gaze. 'Devil take it, that's what you really are, isn't it? Tell me.' He came to stand menacingly over her. 'What other insidious little arrangements have you made to undermine my estate? A loan here, a business started there... Buying the loyalty of my tenants because that's the only currency you really understand, isn't it? Well, hear this! I will not tolerate your damned interference any more!'

A great wave of desolation hit Alicia. No matter what she did now she would never be able to alter his opinion of her. Whenever she tried to avoid him, a malign fate seemed to cast her in his way just so that they could argue again and part on bad terms. Remembering their previous encounter, she blushed with embarrassment. Not only did he view her as mercenary but as a sad, lonely woman whose fondness for drink led her to make ill-bred observations! She knew that there was little she could say now to counteract his bad opinion, but at least she could try.

'Whatever I have done for your tenants has been done with the best of motives, my lord,' she said, so quietly that he could only just hear her words, 'and perhaps I was wrong to interfere. Are you sure that your anger springs from genuine concern and not mere resentment? I bid you good day.'

In the silence that followed, she turned on her heel and would have got into the carriage without another word had not Mullineaux caught her wrist again to stop her. This time Alicia gave a gasp of real pain, and too late he saw the new white bandage below the sleeve of her dress, and remembered the accident at Ottery. He dropped her wrist as though scalded and stood back.

Alicia was shaking now. The pain had pierced the artificial calm which she had managed to preserve under his last, furious attack and now she felt horribly close to tears. Not again, she thought despairingly. She was turning into a complete watering pot.

'Lady Carberry...' There was a note in Mullineaux's voice she did not recognise, did not understand, but she knew she could not cope with it now. She ignored his half-outstretched hand and brushed past him to the carriage where Jack, his ears pink-tipped with the embarrassment of overhearing their argument, was waiting to help her inside.

James Mullineaux stood in the road watching the carriage disappear. He had just remembered Alicia telling him that she never struck a bargain unless it was to her financial advantage. And yet she had apparently offered Patch a loan whose terms were generous in the extreme—terms he could substantiate simply by asking his agent. Mullineaux frowned. Perhaps it *was* time he asked a few questions. There was something going on here that he needed to understand. He stood in the empty road until Tom Patch emerged from the yard to tug on his hand and offer to show him the sheepdog's new puppies.

It was evening, and in the library of James's house at Monks Dacorum sat the Earl and Countess of Kilgaren, playing at chess. They had arrived earlier in the day and had been highly diverted to discover that their host was absent, having been held up by estate business for longer than expected. Caroline Kilgaren had wasted no time and taken charge in her usual capable fashion. Soon the servants were eating out of her hand, the beds were aired, the fires lit and a delicious cold supper was resting on a side table, for Caroline was certain that James would be sharp set after a day out in the fresh air.

Monks Dacorum was a small house, tranquil in atmosphere, and retaining many of its original fifteenth-century features. Over the centuries it had become an appealing but rather inconvenient muddle of medieval and modern, with a great deal of charm and individuality. The library was a cosy room panelled in dark wood with shabby, leather-bound volumes filling its oaken bookshelves and similarly shabby leather armchairs set before the huge stone fireplace. Caroline and Marcus sat in front of the fire, the chessboard spread out on the table between them.

The rainstorms of the previous week had returned with the dusk, but in the room there was a companionable silence as they concentrated on the game. The candlelight burnished the fair heads of both players and cast flickering shadows across the chessboard. The only noise was the tap of the pieces on its wooden surface and the ticking of the ormolu clock on the stone mantelpiece.

The clock had just chimed seven when there was at last the sound of an arrival.

Caroline finished her move with a flourish which suggested that she had checkmated her husband very neatly, then both of them rose to their feet as the door of the room opened and James Mullineaux strolled in. Caroline, always demonstrative, gave a shriek and flung herself into his arms, careless of the fact that he was still wearing his caped driving coat and that rivulets of water were making their way down from it onto the carpet.

'James! It's wonderful to see you!'

Caroline was tiny, and it was easy for James to pick her up off her feet and spin her round, before planting a kiss on her cheek and holding her at arm's length to take a closer look at her. It was several years since they had met and they had known each other well, even before Caroline had married James's closest friend—and he had almost married hers.

The sparkle in Caroline's bright blue eyes owed as much to tears as pleasure, but it did not prevent her frank appraisal of him. She had always been very fond of James Mullineaux for they had grown up together, and it was probably that very familiarity which had preserved her from the danger of ever falling in love with him. Others had done so with an inevitability which she had felt was tiresome and predictable, but her feelings had never been remotely threatened. This had not prevented her from admitting, however, that he was quite devastatingly attractive, and whilst it had always been difficult to quantify this attraction it owed something to his height and presence, as well as his expressive dark eyes, carefully disordered black hair and immaculate tailoring.

Not that he made any pretensions towards high fashion these days, Caroline thought, but time had transmuted the arrogance of a young nobleman into an unconscious self-assurance, and age—he and Marcus were both almost thirty-three!—had done little to diminish his spectacular good looks. Perhaps he appeared to have a harder, more incisive edge to him, but he was indubitably the same James Mullineaux.

James let go of her and gave her an approximation of the wicked smile which had set so many hearts fluttering in the past.

'Well, you haven't changed at all!'

It was Caroline who spoke, but James could have said much the same about her. Caroline Kilgaren might now be a society matron, the proud mother of two delightful offspring, but her diminutive figure had not altered and the only difference he could see in her piquant face was a becoming gravity. He was willing to lay bets, however, that this solemnity would soon be banished by the same irrepressible high spirits that had led her, as Caroline Oxley, to be one of the toasts of her generation.

Marcus Kilgaren was waiting quietly to greet him, his casual calmness as much of a foil for his wife as ever. It had always been Marcus who had counselled against the wilder escapades of their group of friends and who had soothed the ruffled feelings of disapproving dowagers with his charm and apparent good sense. The same spark of humour still burned in those shrewd blue eyes as he shook James's hand.

'My apologies for not being here to greet you,' James said as he handed his sodden coat to a hovering footman with a word of thanks. 'I spent far longer out on the estate than I had intended. It was all very interesting—' He broke off as a small, wet bundle of black and white fluff streaked into the room with a triumphant barking, and sat down at his feet to gaze up as adoringly as Tom Patch had done.

The hapless butler arrived a moment later, out of breath. 'I'm sorry, sir! I had him down in the kitchen and he suddenly took off when my back was turned! Shall I take him away?'

James was laughing as he bent to scoop the puppy up in his arms. 'Don't worry, Russell! He may stay here with us for the time being.'

'I don't think he is house-trained, sir...' Russell continued with a worried frown, but James waved him away airily.

'House-trained or not, I'll swear he is as hungry as I am!' His eye fell appreciatively on the table, groaning under the weight of the supper dishes. 'I detect your influence here, Caro! Let's eat, shall we?'

There was much news to catch up on during the meal. They ate informally on their laps and James entertained his visitors with some of the more light-hearted anecdotes from his time abroad. They had stayed in touch during the past years and picked up the threads of their old friendship without any trouble. The conversation ranged widely from the French political situation to the latest fashionable plays, and the time passed agreeably for them all. The puppy, which Tom Patch had solemnly assured James was called Nod, sat beneath James's chair and ate the bits of food surreptitiously passed to him by all three.

The last of the cold chicken and ham pie was finished and James rose to put more logs on the fire whilst Marcus poured the port and rang for a pot of tea. Caroline had stated with characteristic frankness that she had no intention of withdrawing whilst the men drank and chatted together. Thus they settled themselves in a circle before the fire and a contented hush fell upon them which no one felt inclined to break. After a few moments, however, Caroline stirred herself. She could never sit quietly for long.

'I do like this house, James. It has a very restful atmosphere.'

'Yes.' James looked around him with surprised approval. 'I have scarce been here since I was a boy and could hardly remember it, but it is rather charming. I had intended to let the place shortly,' he added thoughtfully, 'but it's usefully placed between London and Cardace Hall. If I am to visit my grandfather much, it might prove a convenient staging post.'

'How is your grandfather?' Marcus enquired. 'Did you find him improved?'

'Fortunately I did, although he was out of charity with me!' James smiled, albeit ruefully. 'Not surprisingly, he was ill-disposed to forgive me my neglect of him over the past few years! I shall have to work hard to regain his approval. I wish now that I had not stayed away so long.' He remembered suddenly Alicia's searing indictment of him as a man who had cared nothing for his responsibilities, and shrugged irritably. She had an uncanny aptitude for finding out his weaknesses.

Caroline and Marcus exchanged a look. 'Why did you not come back sooner, James?' Caroline asked, tentatively for her. 'We have all missed you, you know!'

James's face softened and he smiled at her. 'Thank you, Caro! To tell the truth, I never planned to be away so long; it just turned out like that.' He looked sombrely into the flames. His confrontation with Alicia was still at the forefront of his mind, the urge to talk about her was strong.

'I suppose,' he said slowly, 'that I left in the first place for all the wrong reasons. I was young and I had too much pride.'

'You mean because you could not tolerate what Alicia had done?' Caroline asked directly. 'Don't glare at me, Marcus! We both know that's what James meant!'

James smiled, a little reluctantly. 'Near enough, Caro! And, once away, I found that I had no inclination to come home. Until now.'

'So you went to Paris and plunged into two years of dissipation and dangerous living,' Marcus observed, deliberately cheerful, and after a moment the tense lines on James's face eased and he laughed.

'Well, Paris is the best of places for that!'

'So I'm told!' Marcus looked at him with speculative amusement.

'The whole of London Society heard of your exploits with Ghislaine de Fleuriot, *and* Marguerite Santony, *and* that delightful actress...'

'Not forgotting that Italian opera singer,' Caroline added mischievously. 'The one who apparently entertained her guests one evening wearing your pearls and very little else, James!'

'I see you know more of it all than I do,' James commented, undisturbed by their teasing. 'It was an...educational two years, one might say, but there were pressing matters relating to my father's estate which still needed to be dealt with, so I went to Ireland to sort them out.'

'And exchanged a life of dissipation for one of seclusion?' Marcus prompted, with a grin.

'Hardly that,' Caroline objected. 'They say Dublin Society is very fast—is that not so? And remember the tales of Jane Clancy and that heiress—Elizabeth Daubenay? Rumours reached us that you were to marry her, James!'

James managed to look amused and cynical at the same time, and for a moment there was an expression in his eyes which led Caroline to reflect whimsically that she could perfectly understand why the besotted Elizabeth had tried so hard to fix his interest. He seemed so dangerously attractive, she thought soulfully; the temptation would always be to try to reform him. Then she smiled at her own fanciful ideas.

'There was never the least possibility of my marrying Elizabeth Daubenay!' James was quite definite. 'Such stories were much exaggerated, Caro! I was too—'

'Exhausted?' Marcus suggested wickedly.

'I was going to say busy, actually!' His friends' teasing was having the desired effect and James appeared to be relaxing. Both the Kilgarens had noticed the latent tension within him earlier and were curious to learn its cause, but they also knew well enough that he would tell them in his own time if he wanted them to know.

'Turning the stud farm around so that it became profitable again took both more time and more work than I had anticipated,' James finished, by way of explanation.

'Well, you've been remarkably successful,' Marcus commented. 'The pair of greys you sent to Tattersall's last autumn were sweet goers and I know Saltburn paid a fine price, so keen was he to secure them. But what do you plan to do now that you are back in England, James?'

The arrival of the tea tray provided a short distraction at this point and Caroline poured for herself whilst the port decanter made another round. Once the footman had withdrawn, James tossed another log on the fire and turned back to the question.

'I've made arrangements to sell the stud, and I intend to settle back in England permanently.' He looked thoughtful. 'It's plain to me that I need to consolidate my estates and there's a lot of work to be done putting them in order. First I had planned to see Tadcaster, my agent, and arrange for a new tenant here with a view to selling eventually. However, I am not so sure now that I wish to let the house, since I may need to keep it for my own use.' He sighed unconsciously. 'There is another complication in that, however.'

When he did not elaborate, Caroline glanced at her husband, then seized the bull by the horns in her usual blunt manner. 'You mean because of your proximity here to Alicia Carberry? But surely you would not be intending to spend a great deal of time here, James—it should be possible to avoid her if you try hard enough!'

James looked up, aware of an undercurrent in Caroline's voice that made her own feelings on the subject quite plain. He knew full well that Caroline and Alicia were still close friends, and until the previous week he had not seen why this should affect him at all. Now he realised that this had been naive—if he intended to avoid Alicia and the complicated effect she appeared to have on him, he needed to make a complete break with everyone and everything connected with her. He sighed. He had no desire to lose Caroline's friendship.

'It's not as simple as that, Caro. Bear with me and I shall explain in a moment. As for the rest of my future plans—in a few weeks I am travelling up to Worcestershire to see Louisa and her family, and finally—' he grimaced '—I plan to open Cardace House for the Season. My grandfather feels himself so improved that he wishes to come up to London for the first time in an age.'

'That'll cause a stir,' Marcus commented. He was happy to follow James's lead and not press him on the subject of Alicia Carberry, but he knew that James's hint had already led to Caroline being consumed with curiosity. 'You don't seem very enthusiastic at the prospect of the Season,' he added. 'Has middle age caught up with you already, James? You used to be so sociable!'

James shrugged. 'I don't know.' Once more a touch of constraint entered his manner. 'Perhaps I'm simply not looking forward to having all the old history raked up. In my heart I knew that I could not escape it, but now the prospect of having my past picked over by a bunch of quizzes is hard to bear!'

Caroline poured herself another cup of tea. 'You must confound them all by being a pattern-card of virtue!' she said, with a hint of malice. 'Perhaps you should take a wife! That should silence the gossips!'

Unbidden, infuriatingly, the image of Alicia Carberry rose in James's mind once more. Alicia, who had refused his proposal only last week. Alicia, whose memory was provoking, infuriating, tantalising... With a painful jolt of the heart he wondered if he would ever be free. He shook his head abruptly to dispel the image. Caroline was watching him over the rim of her cup with her steady, perceptive gaze and he was afraid that she might see too much, but she said nothing and a moment later an impish light had entered her eyes.

'We could help you in your search for a wife,' she suggested lightly. 'We know all the eligible debutantes who will be making their come-out this year.' She wriggled down comfortably in her seat. 'Let's see,' she mused.' Amanda Edgecot is pretty and biddable, but perhaps a little young for you at seventeen? Do you remember her? A skinny brat with pigtails? What would you prefer, James—a demure young thing, or perhaps someone slightly older, with a little more conversation?'

James winced. He had acknowledged to his grandfather that he needed to find himself a wife, but now the whole process sounded horribly commercial and—worse still—a dead bore. His thoughts turned once more with a predictable inevitability. Alicia... She was never boring or insipid...difficult, perhaps...challenging, even... Now he was starting to get really angry with himself for his preoccupation with her. He completely missed the conspiratorial glance which flashed between Marcus and Caroline Kilgaren, so profound was his combined distaste at an arranged match and his annoyance with himself.

'Well,' Marcus continued casually, when James had failed to answer, 'I don't doubt that you will be viewed as quite a matrimonial prize!' He met Caroline's eyes with a smile and they both studiously ignored James's look of disgust.

'If you do prefer someone older,' Marcus pursued, 'there are several sensible girls who have been out for a few seasons. They are up to snuff and would not expect too much from you!'

It said a lot for James's preoccupation that he completely failed to realise that they were teasing him. Caroline picked up the cue neatly.

'Yes,' she said thoughtfully, 'there is Maria Marston, although I hear she is a little...' she paused delicately '...well, stupid really, but ideal if you require an amenable wife! Or Georgiana Stapleford,' she added hopefully. 'Now, she is *very* beautiful!'

'But equally spoilt and selfish!' Marcus said roundly. 'No, my dear, I doubt we can foist Georgiana off on James even if he were not too particular in his requirements! Now, how about——?'

'When you two have quite finished!' James put his glass down with a snap indicative of irritation as much as amusement. 'I fail to see why my matrimonial plans cause such fascination! Not,' he added ironically, 'that I could not do with some assistance! Only last week I had a proposal of marriage rejected out of hand!'

The reaction to this deliberately provocative statement was all that James could have desired. Caroline gave a smothered squeak and clapped her hand to her mouth, the teacup in her other hand tilting at a dangerous angle. Even Marcus's habitual nonchalance suffered a severe blow. He ran his hand through his fair hair, adjusted his cravat and cleared his throat.

'Well, if that don't beat the Dutch! Dash it all, James, you can't just leave it at that!' A twinkle entered his blue eyes. 'Who is the lady who is discerning enough to reject your suit?'

James smiled sardonically. 'We have already mentioned her name. Five days ago, I offered my hand in marriage to Alicia Carberry!'

Caroline's eyes were the size of saucers. She stared, but could utter no sound. Marcus, showing no further visible sign of disturbance, carefully removed the cup from his wife's hand and put it down gently on the table. She did not even notice.

'Well, James,' Marcus said ruefully as the silence stretched out, 'you have achieved your object of silencing us both! Now you owe us an explanation! It is stretching credulity too far to expect us to believe that you have been nurturing a secret passion for seven years and have now come back to fulfil it—not after the terms of your parting from Alicia!'

James gave a reluctant laugh, lying back in his armchair and stretching his long legs towards the fire. 'True enough! But you are vastly behindhand in your knowledge of my reacquaintance with Lady Carberry!' A wicked twinkle came into his eyes. 'In the space of one week I have been involved in a carriage accident with her, spent a night in a lonely inn in her company, indulged in several heated arguments with her and had my proposal of marriage put to scorn!'

'James! Enough of this provocation!' Caroline held up a hand in mock surrender. 'If you do not instantly indulge my curiosity I will burst!'

James laughed aloud at that. 'Acquit me, Caro! I will try to make amends!' He paused to sort out his thoughts. 'Where shall I start?'

'The beginning would seem appropriate,' Caroline said, with asperity.

'Very well,' James agreed obligingly. He picked up the soft, sleepy puppy and settled him on his lap.

'On my way up from Cardace, my curricle was in collision with Lady Carberry's coach. No one was seriously hurt,' he added hastily, seeing Caroline's look of sudden alarm. 'I helped the ladies to the shelter of the inn at Ottery. It was a godforsaken place, but I had given up hope of being able to convey them to a better establishment as we had no useable vehicle. Then, fortuitously, Squire and Mrs Henley stopped, having seen Lady Carberry's carriage in the ditch. They offered hospitality at the Manor.' The hint of amusement left him and his tone took on a heavy irony. 'The Henleys had guests and could not take up both ladies at once, so Lady Carberry, for reasons best known to herself, sent Miss Frensham on ahead.'

'Oh, dear,' Caroline said faintly, sensing disaster.

James gave her a rueful grimace. 'The road was flooded,' he said, with weary patience, 'the carriage could not return for her ladyship and thus we were marooned together overnight at the inn!'

'How uncomfortable for you both!' Marcus commented, with a twitch of the lips. 'Dare I ask how you felt about this meeting? And how you passed the time?'

James shot him a darkling look. 'My feelings could best be described as mixed! As for the rest, we spent most of our time together in argument! I accused Lady Carberry of a reckless disregard for the conventions and the conversation degenerated from there! She retired to her room and I did not see her for the rest of the evening. The following morning I mistakenly conceived it to be my duty as a gentleman to offer her the protection of my name. I was rejected.'

Marcus looked perplexed by this foreshortened tale. He frowned.

'Hold on a minute, James, you're not making sense here! By your own admission you have no very good opinion of Alicia Carberry, yet you could have come out of this encounter an affianced man! Doing it a bit too brown, old chap!'

James smiled reluctantly. 'I know! Misplaced chivalry...' He shrugged with an attempt at lightness. 'No doubt I should be grateful that Lady Carberry had the sense to refuse me!'

There was an inflection in James's voice that caused Marcus to look at him curiously. After all this time one might have expected there to be nothing but indifference between James Mullineaux and Alicia Carberry, but this was evidently not so. James had spoken lightly, but

Marcus knew his old friend and sensed that James's feelings were neither detached nor clear-cut. His interest sharpened.

'So how did you find Alicia after all these years?' Marcus enquired, the casual nature of the question belied by the acute interest in his eyes.

A black frown descended on James's brow. 'I found her wilful, proud, selfish, spoiled and arrogant,' he said shortly. 'Perhaps she was always all of those things and I was simply too infatuated to notice!'

He saw the expression on Caroline's face change and felt instantly contrite. 'I am sorry, Caro. I realise that you have remained Alicia Carberry's friend.'

There was an awkward pause. Mullineaux picked up the poker and moodily stirred the fire up into a blaze again. Caroline was watching him with a thoughtful look in her blue eyes. She felt no need to justify her friendship with Alicia, but she did feel an obligation to her friend. For once she thought very carefully before rushing into speech. She met her husband's steady gaze in a look of complete understanding. He did not say a word.

'No doubt you find it odd that I should still be a friend to Alicia after all that happened,' Caroline began carefully, 'and if it is your wish, James, we shall not mention the matter again. However, I should like to explain.' She saw his discouraging look, hesitated, then ploughed doggedly on when he did not speak.

'I am still close to Alicia because I do not believe that she was ever a...' she searched for the right words '...a scheming adventuress who was out to marry for money or a title. Alicia did not change—she is still the same person we all knew, and we knew that she was not like that! She has never told me the circumstances of her marriage, but I *know* Bertram Broseley forced the match and I am willing to believe that he exerted a lot of pressure to do so. I cannot blame Alicia for a situation of which I feel she was as much a victim as you were!'

There was silence. James looked totally unconvinced by this undeniably heartfelt plea. After he had clearly thought about and discarded several potential replies, he merely said, 'I'm sorry, Caro. I know you are sincere and I admire your loyalty even whilst I think it misplaced, but I cannot feel the same way as you do.'

Something closed in Caroline's face. 'No, of course not.' She put her teacup down gently and rose to her feet. 'Well, if you gentlemen will excuse me, I think I shall have an early night.'

Her gaze met Marcus's and a powerful message passed between them. Both men rose politely to their feet as she went out, closing the door softly behind her. James hesitated, put the pup down then walked over to the desk, reaching for the brandy decanter this time. Nod raised his head from his paws and gave a sleepy snore.

There was the companionable quiet that often existed between old friends and Marcus yawned, stretching in the warmth of the fire. He had not been remotely disturbed by the conversation between Caroline and James Mullineaux. He had great respect for Caroline's judgement and for his own part he had always liked Alicia Carberry. Like Caroline and a great many of their immediate friends, Marcus was certain that Bertram Broseley had compelled Alicia to marry George Carberry by some very questionable means. The fact that Alicia had never spoken of this even to her closest friends suggested to Marcus that it must still be very painful for her to recall.

However, he felt it would be naive to expect James to hold the same opinion. Whatever the truth had been, the relationship between James and Alicia was smashed beyond repair.

'So what happened after Lady Carberry dented your self-esteem with her rejection?' Marcus enquired lazily, looking up as James passed him one of the balloon glasses of brandy. 'You mentioned arguments in the plural—have you met since Ottery, then?'

James looked rueful. 'You don't miss much, do you, Marcus? I have met Lady Carberry on two subsequent occasions and our antagonism has not waned! The rest of the time I have been obliged to hear all and sundry sing her praises! It's enough to try the patience of a saint!'

Marcus grinned. 'So you don't list yourself with her admirers, then, old chap!' He stole a quick look at James's face and added guilelessly, 'It seems you still hold her in complete dislike!'

Surprisingly, James did not immediately agree with this. He turned his empty port glass over absent-mindedly between his fingers a few times, then he looked up and smiled.

'Cut line, Marcus—you know you don't really believe that! I never could fool you, could I, not even when we were in short coats? Damn it, my feelings really don't bear examination at the moment, but, despite that, I think you had better tell me whatever it is both you and Caroline feel I should know about Alicia.'

Their eyes met in a split second of tension, then Marcus gave a nod of acknowledgement.

'Well, you don't miss much either, do you, James? I suppose it's only fair...I cannot speak for Caro, but for myself it's simply that I dislike injustice and I think Alicia has been misjudged. Like Caro, I believe that she was forced into marriage with Carberry. I can't prove it, of course,' he added quickly. 'Alicia is the only one who could tell you the truth, but it grates on me that she should be condemned without a hearing.'

James's gaze rested on him with acute intelligence. 'There's more to this than that, though. You both remain convinced of her innocence when all the evidence points to the contrary. You must have some basis for your belief in her integrity.'

Marcus shifted a little uncomfortably in his chair. 'Yes, there is something... But it's hardly my secret to tell. Can you not take my word for it?'

There was a silence, then James shook his head slightly. 'On anything else I would say yes without reservation, Marcus. But you are asking me to agree to something without letting me judge the evidence myself—something which has profoundly affected my own life! I can't do it.'

Marcus sighed resignedly. 'I take your point. Well, this is Caroline's tale rather than mine, but I do not suppose that she would grudge my telling you.' He paused, aware of the sudden tension in the room.

'Caroline was one of the few people who saw Alicia immediately after George Carberry had died. She had heard that Alicia was back at Stansfield House and went to see how she was. That was typical of Caro,' Marcus said, his pride showing in his voice. 'Everyone else was talking scandal, but all she was concerned about was Alicia's welfare.'

He looked up to see James's gaze fixed on him with grave intent.

'Anyway, at first Lady Stansfield refused point-blank to let Caro in, but you know how persistent she is! In the end Lady S. agreed that it might help Alicia to see a friend, but she warned Caroline that Alicia was very unwell.' Marcus looked sombre. 'I called to see Caroline later in the day and she was still very upset by the experience. She poured it all out to me—how Alicia was covered in disfiguring bruises and cuts and was so disorientated that she barely had any idea where she was—even who she was!' Marcus shrugged uncomfortably. 'It was profoundly distressing.'

James's eyes had narrowed in disbelief at the story he was hearing. 'What are you saying, Marcus? That Carberry—or Broseley—did this to her?'

Marcus met his eyes directly. 'Precisely, James.'

There was a silence whilst James struggled with what he had been told. Then, suddenly, the enormity of it struck him. He looked aghast. 'Marcus, I cannot believe... Why would Broseley do such a thing?'

Marcus looked grim. 'Who can say for sure? It was in his interests to achieve a marriage between two mercantile empires and this was a good way to seal such an arrangement. If Alicia cut up rough at his plans, he would have to change her mind for her, somehow. After all, persuading unwilling offspring into marriage is hardly a new concept!'

'Last century, perhaps, but in this day and age...?' James ran his hand through his hair. 'I'm sorry, Marcus, but I really can't believe this...'

Marcus shrugged. 'That is your privilege, of course, and I would not seek to change your mind. All I know is that Caro would not lie.'

'No, of course not...' James was struggling to equate his own view of events with this new evidence. 'But perhaps she misunderstood? Damn it, Broseley told me Alicia had chosen Carberry of her own free will!' He slammed his fist down on the arm of the chair as his feelings caught alight. 'Marcus, Alicia's letter damned her more eloquently than I ever could! It was the most blatant piece of self-seeking greed that I have ever come across!'

Marcus drained his glass. 'She never *told* you to your face, did she, James?'

'No.' James was looking impatient. 'But—' He broke off. 'What exactly are you suggesting? That Broseley contrived it all? That he made her write something against her will?'

'Precisely,' Marcus said again. He waited for this to sink in and watched the conflict of thought that was clearly displayed on James's face.

'But—' James was really struggling now '—there were all those stories circulating in the clubs that Alicia had always been up to the highest bidder, that she had married Carberry for his money...'

Marcus looked at him a little pityingly. 'Come on, James! Anyone can put a tale about—you should know that! Who do you think started those rumours?'

James looked incapable of commenting. He was scowling into the heart of the fire, but it was not the flames that he was seeing. His imagination was quite capable of summoning up all kinds of demons prompted by Marcus Kilgaren's words. It all sounded so horribly plausible and yet he had never even imagined it. Wrapped up in his own pride and disillusion, he had never questioned his interpretation of events. He had swung from the extreme of love to hatred and disenchantment, and had joined the chorus of those who had condemned Alicia to social damnation.

James shook his head in disbelief. 'Why did she never say anything if it were true? Why didn't *you* ever say anything before?'

Marcus laughed at that. 'When would you have liked me to tell you? If I'd written to you immediately after you'd left the country, how much credence would you have given the story? We're talking about it seven years later, in cold blood, and you're still having difficulty believing it. Besides, as I said before, it is Caro's story about Alicia, not mine—I had no right to tell you things Alicia might not wish you to know. Even now I only spoke because I felt you were maligning her.'

'If what you say is true, everybody has maligned her,' James observed sombrely. 'Why has she never told anyone the truth?'

'Would you?' Marcus asked bluntly. 'It's hardly an edifying tale, is it? For a start, I imagine that it was too personal and painful for Alicia to want to discuss it and, God knows, the scandal was great enough as it was! Would anything Alicia said have had any effect other than to fan the flames? Also, she was very ill after this happened. Lady Stansfield took her away for a long time and it was generally said that that was to allow the scandal to die down, but I think it was because she was very ill indeed.' Marcus paused reflectively. 'No, I think Lady Stansfield handled it in the only way possible—by subtly hinting that Alicia had been the victim of a forced marriage, and by reintroducing her into Society in as slow and circumspect a way as possible.'

Marcus did not add that James's own defection had done immeasurable damage to Alicia's reputation. His public denouncement of his betrothed could only add weight to the story that she was an adventuress who should be drummed out of Society. James was, however, quite capable of working that out for himself. He reached almost blindly for the brandy decanter.

'Indulge me,' he said after a moment, 'and answer some more questions.'

'If I can.'

'Why do you suppose that Alicia has not remarried? Surely she could have added a better title to her fortune by now?'

Marcus laughed 'She has hardly been short of offers! They say that Peter Weston proposed to her six times before he settled for Maria Loseley, and Severn's heir was the latest to try his luck and end up nursing a bruised ego at her rejection! She does not covet a title,' Marcus added with certainty.

'Then what else is there? Money, property, status—she has them all,' James pursued.

'I suppose,' Marcus agreed, 'that there's very little anyone could offer her which she does not have already. Respectability she has won by hard work, which leaves only love, and I expect Alicia feels she has burned herself badly enough on that in the past! Now I can only imagine her choosing to marry for companionship.'

'Is there no one she might wish to marry?' James asked quizzically.

Marcus laughed. 'No one! Alicia lives like a nun, James! She has become such a figure of virtue that she is almost a caricature! She has a reputation for coldness to the point of frigidity.'

James slanted a look at him. 'Is that a rumour spread by those whose suit has not prospered?' he suggested with a smile. 'It's usually the way!'

Marcus smiled reminiscently. 'Well, those who have offered a carte blanche do not make the same mistake twice! Alicia has a temper to rival her grandmother's when she wishes to use it!'

'I know!' James said with feeling. He picked up one of the chess pawns, idly admiring the intricate carving. 'And Christopher Westwood?' he asked, with apparent casualness.

Marcus looked surprised. 'Oh, so you've heard about him, have you? Well, he is Lady Stansfield's great-nephew, and as such I suppose he has a legitimate reason for hanging on the family's coat-tails. I don't like him,' he admitted, 'but Alicia seems to enjoy his company. There's no more to it than that, though, even though he moons about her like a lovesick puppy! She won't marry him,' Marcus concluded, with certainty. 'Alicia's reputation for coldness is well-founded. Whether to avoid fortune-hunters or the intimacies of marriage it would be difficult to ascertain, but, for whatever reason, it is true.'

Now it was James's turn to laugh. 'Coldness?' Involuntarily he remembered the intense physical awareness that had flared between himself and Alicia. 'Maybe on the surface she appears cold, but it is only skin-deep. The fire is banked down, not burned out.'

Marcus gave him a look of genuine curiosity. 'Is that so? Well, if you saw that much, old fellow, you must have had more of an effect on her than anyone else in the last seven years! But then, you did catch her at a disadvantage. Next time you meet her, I expect she will have resumed her habitual chilliness!'

James slanted a smile at him. 'So you think that there will be a next time, do you, Marcus?'

His friend gave him a very straight look. 'I would lay odds on it, James!' He yawned suddenly. 'Well...I must retire, or Caroline will come looking for me! We always keep early hours in the country. Goodnight, James!'

James stayed by the fire for a little while, finishing his brandy and stroking the somnolent puppy he had lifted back into his lap rather absent-mindedly.

There was something about the name Westwood that was nagging at the edge of his memory, although he could have sworn that he had never met the man. He moved the chess pieces thoughtfully back to the side of the board, deliberately avoiding any thought of Alicia. And then he remembered. He *had* met Westwood before, and the circumstances of it gave him pause.

It had been seven years previously, and play at White's had been high and drinking deep. It was only a couple of nights after Alicia's scandalous defection and James had been trying to drown his sorrows. He had been on a phenomenal winning streak, but even he knew that there had been an explosive element in his own behaviour, just waiting for release. Westwood had given him the opportunity, by being amongst the first to sling mud at Alicia's name.

James frowned, remembering with unpleasant clarity the real hatred on Westwood's white face as he had made those claims about Alicia, claims which had found their mark with James because he was vulnerable and in two minds about her innocence himself. The whole of White's cardroom had heard Westwood denounce her as a duplicitous adventuress who had the benefit of an innocent face hiding an amoral soul. James had raised his fist to hit him across the room, but Marcus had caught his arm in a grip of iron and persuaded him rather forcibly to let the matter drop. James, half inclined to agree with Westwood's assertions, had gone and got seriously drunk instead, after which he remembered nothing. Unfortunately there were plenty of kind souls who later reminded him that in his cups he had damned Alicia with more colourful invective than Westwood had ever used.

Remembering all this, James found it odd in the extreme that Westwood was now so close to both Alicia and her grandmother. In those days Westwood had not been a visitor at Stansfield House, but had pursued a far more rackety existence on the fringes of Society, always wagering more than he could afford and indulging in some very expensive habits. There were many such, living beyond their means and gaining membership to the exclusive clubs such as Whites' by extracting a favour from some luckless sprig of the nobility over whom they had some hold.

James wrinkled his nose with disgust. Something had evidently occurred to help Westwood overcome his loathing of his fair cousin to the extent that he now wished to marry her. Or perhaps, James pondered, he simply saw ingratiating himself with his Stansfield relatives as the best hope for the future. Either way, it left a rather unpleasant taste in the mouth. James wondered whether Lady Stansfield, normally sharp as a razor, had ever known that Westwood had been one of the first to denounce her beloved granddaughter. Still, it was none of his business, after all.

What had become his business was the truth about Alicia. For the first time in years he allowed himself to wonder if he had made a mistake, and to think of the Alicia Broseley he had once known, with her bright, indomitable spirit. To think of that life and brightness crushed and defaced by the likes of Bertram Broseley and George Carberry was almost intolerable.

He put down the pup and raked out the embers of the fire. He was determined to see Alicia again. He had to make her tell him the truth. Only then could he be free of the past. He paused, remembering the lovely, heart-shaped face, the flashing green eyes, the perfect, curved mouth…and felt a rush of desire that took him by surprise. He was hardly a callow youth to be enslaved by a pretty face and neat figure! If he was not careful, he could find himself in as deep as he had been seven years before.

James Mullineaux had always been a gambler, but he seldom took an uncalculated risk. It meant that he did not often make mistakes. But now he knew the course he had chosen was going to be dangerous. It made no difference. He had made his decision.

Chapter Five

Chartley Chase had changed since the days when a young James Mullineaux had been taken there as a protesting child to visit some indigent maiden aunt. In the pale sunlight of the late February morning its creamy stone gleamed warm. In his memory was the smell of camphor and sal volatile—now he noticed the mingled scent of beeswax and lavender in the air, and paused to appreciate the sparkling stained glass of the landing window as the sun scattered its colours over the graceful, curving stair. The whole house exuded an understated good taste and subtle, welcoming warmth that was a reflection of Alicia's hospitality.

Alicia was standing by the drawing-room window looking out over the garden to the moors beyond. She turned as the Marquis's name was announced and came forward unhurriedly as he started to cross the room towards her. She was wearing green, a colour which established a satisfyingly subtle contrast with that glorious auburn hair, today piled on the top of her head in an artfully contrived knot of curls. She looked every inch the Society hostess; no genuine emotion could be discerned in her manner or countenance. Her smile had exactly the right degree of warmth in it for one dealing with a surprise visit from a mere acquaintance, which put him in his place, James reflected ruefully. Marcus had been quite correct. There was a chilly composure about Alicia which suggested that her defences were firmly in place. Well, they would see.

Alicia, contrary to her outward calm, was shaking inside. When Cheffings had announced that the Marquis of Mullineaux had called to see her she had been astounded, for she hardly considered that they were on calling terms. Her second reaction, following swiftly on the first, had been a cowardly instinct to avoid James by pretending to be out, but in the end the urge to see him again had proved too strong. She had put aside her book, pressed her palms together in a brief, nervous gesture, taken up her stance by the window, and sent Cheffings to show James in.

She watched him cross the room towards her, casually elegant and assured.

'Lord Mullineaux.' Alicia summoned up a faint, distant smile. She felt a little colour come into her cheeks as he took her hand in his, and took a deep breath to steady herself. 'How good of you to call, sir. Will you take a seat? May I offer you some refreshment?'

'Thank you, but no.' James inclined his head, as formal as she. 'I am to join Caroline and Marcus Kilgaren at Pilton Abbey shortly, so this is only a brief visit.' He took the chair that she indicated and returned his attention to his hostess, allowing his gaze to travel over her in a thoroughly disconcerting manner.

'Caroline and Marcus both send their best wishes. They are looking forward to seeing you later in the week. I called to enquire whether you had recovered from your accident,' James added, in an impersonal tone. 'The last time we met, I had no opportunity to enquire after your health.'

And whose fault was that? Alicia thought rebelliously. He had been too busy hurling accusations to indulge in polite conversation! She crushed down the prickles of resentment. Today he would *not* get under her guard. Today, her equilibrium restored, she could view him as a mere acquaintance. She knew she was lying to herself, but did not want to stop and think about it.

'How kind of you to ask,' she said coldly, drawing on the strength which had seen her through so many trials in the past. 'As you see, I am much recovered.'

She thought she saw James's lips twitch slightly at her formality.

'You are still a trifle pale, perhaps, but I see that you have had your wrist attended to properly,' he observed solemnly.

'Yes, indeed.' Alicia glanced down a little self-consciously at the bandage, its pristine whiteness reminding her of their last meeting. 'The doctor tells me that it is a slight sprain, nothing worse, but that I must rest it for a week or so more.'

'You were fortunate that your injuries were not more severe,' James commented.

The conversation lapsed. Alicia wished he had agreed to a glass of Madeira—at least it would have given them something to do to pass the time. She was aware of a feeling of resentment growing within her as she watched him marking time to the end of what must constitute for him a tedious, duty visit. He could not have made clearer that he had called only out of a sense of social obligation. She wished that he had not bothered. The nature of her feelings for him had inevitably led her to hope for more than the grudging consideration he was according her.

'And Miss Frensham?' James enquired, after a strained pause. 'Do you have any news from Ottery?'

Alicia fought down the sense of irritation that this superficial conversation was provoking in her. It seemed they could never be comfortable together, for they must always be either coming to blows or talking in trivialities. She pinned on a bright, insincere smile.

'I hear that Miss Frensham is recovering well from her ordeal,' she replied. 'She hopes to return here in a couple of weeks. Mrs Henley also mentioned in her letter that you had called to enquire after Miss Frensham's health before you left Ottery.' A shade of genuine warmth came into her tone. 'That was most kind of you, sir. I know that Miss Frensham deeply appreciated the help that you gave her that evening.'

James was also suffering from the artificiality of the conversation. Matters were not progressing as he had intended, but he seemed powerless to bridge the gap between them. Alicia's chilly welcome had set him at a distance and she had seemed disinclined to allow him any closer. He, in turn, had responded by taking his cue from her and talking at only the most shallow of levels. He was beginning to find their stilted words deeply frustrating.

Alicia was fidgeting with her dress, pleating and re-pleating the material between her fingers. James looked at her bent head and felt a sudden acute pang for what they had lost.

Alicia looked up abruptly and met his eyes. Just for a moment she surprised there an expression which she thought she recognised, before his face was wiped clean of all emotion. She must have imagined it. Once again, she summoned up a brilliant, superficial smile.

'I hope that you have found the house at Monks Dacorum to your liking, my lord.'

James shifted restlessly. 'Monks Dacorum is a fine house. I like it a great deal.'

'And the estate?' Alicia continued politely. 'You must have found much to interest you in the past week.'

'Yes, indeed.' James leant forward, a sudden flicker in his eyes. 'I have heard much spoken of your good works, Lady Carberry. Tell me, how do you equate your apparent determination to make a profit with the almshouses you have had built? And how much revenue does the village school generate for you?'

Alicia opened her mouth to deny all knowledge and met his quizzical gaze. She swallowed hard. Suddenly finding she could not prevaricate, she tried to make light of it. 'It is no great matter, my lord.'

'No?' James refused to smile and let it drop. 'I believe I owe you an apology, Lady Carberry. You misled me with your insistence that you always sought financial gain, but I believe I should not have been so quick to condemn. The facts do not bear out your words.'

Neither did the facts seven years ago, Alicia thought with sudden anguish, but you waited for no explanation then. She had to turn away from him, so acute was the sudden pain in her breast. It took a moment for her to regain her composure, but then she was able to turn back with a gracious, social smile.

'I repeat, my lord, it is of no great moment.'

'I think it is.' James was looking sombre. 'It is easy to make false assumptions.' He held her gaze very deliberately with his own. She could read there the one question he did not put into words: *Why did you lie to me*?

Alicia could not even begin to consider the implications of that question. She broke the contact between them with an effort.

James now found that he was the one in danger of losing his temper. He scrutinised the flawlessly perfect face before him, but Alicia was looking completely unmoved. James was suddenly determined to break through the polite triviality of the conversation. If she would not respond to his veiled comments on the past, he would try a different provocation.

'Lady Carberry, will you explain something to me?' He was looking at his most satirical, Alicia thought, with misgiving. Where was this line of questioning going?

'When I was at Ottery Manor it became apparent to me that Mrs Henley's guests were all aware of my ill-considered proposal to you, and your still more reckless refusal. Whatever possessed you to make them free of such information?'

Alicia felt the humiliating colour flame into her face. Her green eyes widened with a mixture of mortification and anger. She could feel her façade of bland courtesy wavering and it suffered another blow when she looked at James and saw that he had recognised her discomfiture. With all her strength she struggled to regain her composure, wipe all expression from her face and achieve an appropriate level of civility.

'I am very sorry that you should have been exposed to such speculation,' she commented, with constraint. 'I spoke to Mrs Henley in private and cannot believe that she would break a confidence. I can only assume that our conversation was overheard. I must offer you my apologies,' she finished stiffly.

James was appalled at the violence of the frustration that shot through him. When they had met at Ottery, Alicia had been at a severe disadvantage, hurt and distressed, unable to deploy her defences as she was doing now. But how much more attractive had been that more brittle, accessible Alicia—even at the height of their conflict he had preferred the real flesh-and-blood woman to this infuriating cipher.

'Pray do not apologise, Lady Carberry,' James said, a little grimly. 'All that I believe you owe me is an explanation for your wilful courting of Society's disapproval! To have become stranded with me was folly enough, but to let it be known that I had offered the protection of my name only to be rejected was madness!' His voice took on a reflective quality. 'I find a strange contradiction here. Over the past couple of days, more than one person has commented to me that you behave as a pattern-card of conformity. How is it, then, that in your dealings with me you appear to feel a compulsion to challenge the rules all the time?'

This was coming uncomfortably close to the mark, and he was pushing her very hard, far harder than good manners allowed. Alicia knew it, but could not imagine what was prompting his behaviour. She was not to know that it was James's sole intention to provoke her into losing her temper, for paradoxically he knew that he could get far closer to her if she dropped her guard. Their explosive encounter at Ottery had proved as much.

But not this time. Alicia stood up, a faint, wintry smile on her lips, indicating that their meeting was at an end.

'I do not believe that I have anything further to explain to you, sir,' she said sweetly. 'Do not let me keep you from your other engagements! I thank you for your consideration in calling on me. Please convey my best wishes to Caroline and Marcus. Good day to you!'

James gave her a long, level look, which she met with nothing but an impervious blankness in return. He got to his feet slowly. After a moment's hesitation he took her hand and bowed over it.

Alicia felt the tension uncoil within her a little. At last he was going to go away and leave her alone! She should have been more careful, knowing his complete unpredictability; it was only a momentary lack of vigilance on her part, but it was enough. With great deliberation, James turned her hand over and kissed the palm, watching with amusement as she snatched her hand away and took several hasty steps back. She knew that for a long moment her expressive face gave her confusion away, then, as movement returned to muscles which appeared temporarily frozen, she turned hastily aside to pull the bell for the butler, addressing him in arctic tones as the door opened. 'Cheffings, be so good as to escort the Marquis of Mullineaux out. He is leaving now.'

Despite the coldness of his dismissal, James was smiling as he sauntered down the steps and out into the crisp morning air.

'Well, miss, you must have windmills in your head if you think that I'm going to accept this latest piece of nonsense!'

The Dowager Countess of Stansfield descended from her ancient carriage onto the gravel in front of Chartley Chase and addressed her granddaughter in her usual pugnacious terms. Alicia repressed a smile.

'How lovely to see you again, Grandmama! But what can you mean?'

'Humph!' Lady Stansfield made a noise reminiscent of a camel snorting and looked Alicia over critically. The bright green eyes, exactly like her granddaughter's, were still as shrewd and sharp as ever. She was attired in vivid red, her favourite colour, and a hat adorned with many and varied feathers sat atop her white curls. She fixed Alicia with her ferocious gaze.

'This tale going the rounds concerning a secret rendezvous between yourself and the Marquis of Mullineaux! Barely is the man back in this country and you are running off to meet him alone in some country inn! What do you have to say for yourself, miss?'

Alicia remained calm beneath the interested gaze of the coachman, several footmen, her own butler, her grandmother and Christopher Westwood, who had assisted Lady Stansfield from the carriage and now stood on one side still waiting to greet her. This, it seemed, was only the start of the onslaught. Still, there was no point in retaliating with Lady Stansfield, who could give as good as she got anyway. Alicia gave her grandmother an unconcerned smile.

'How gossip does travel!' she marvelled innocently. 'Why, the only thing I have to say, ma'am, is that were I to arrange a secret meeting I would do so more efficiently and no one would know of it!' She turned to greet Westwood, signalling that the topic was at an end. 'Good day, Christopher, I hope that you had a comfortable journey!'

Lady Stansfield took this set-down in good part. Alicia had learned a long time ago that the only way to deal with her outspoken grandmother was to refuse to submit to her bullying. This had endeared her to the old lady rather than the reverse and Lady Stansfield's eyes now took on a distinct twinkle as she came forward to kiss her granddaughter.

'Well, well, that's as maybe, miss! Christopher is quite out of charity with you! It doesn't do to make him jealous!'

Lady Stansfield had always had a squirm-inducing habit of talking about people as though they weren't there, and Westwood was far too deferential to object. He merely stood looking sheepish and shifting uncomfortably from one foot to the other.

Alicia gritted her teeth. There was no point in telling her grandmother that Christopher Westwood had no right to question her behaviour— that would only give the old lady another opportunity to remark on the sense in the two of them marrying. It was no secret that Lady Stansfield wished to promote such a match and Westwood was more than willing. Only Alicia's stubbornness was opposing it.

'I am fagged to death after the journey,' Lady Stansfield continued, her gold-topped cane tapping across the gravel and up the steps. 'I wish to rest. We shall talk later, my dear. You—' Her beady gaze turned on Cheffings, who looked somewhat unnerved. 'You are not Fordyce! Where is he?'

'Fordyce is in London, opening up the house for the Season,' Alicia replied patiently. 'This is Cheffings, Grandmama, and I do beg you not to terrify him!'

'In London! So early in the year! And two butlers! How extravagant!' Lady Stansfield looked scandalised, as though Alicia had admitted to some perversion. Her accusing gaze swept over the hapless Cheffings as though it were all his fault. 'Well, Cheffings, I suppose you will have to do! Show me to my room!'

She swept regally up the staircase, trailed by the startled butler. Alicia was left with Christopher Westwood, who was looking positively miserable.

'She means no harm, you know,' he offered pacifically, his fair, good-humoured face troubled. 'We heard all the gossip and were only at pains to think how best to help you.'

Alicia reflected that that was exactly the sort of appeasing comment that put her out of humour with him. It might be unfair to blame him for being so eager to please, but she could not deny that it annoyed her. Ushering him into the library, she turned to order refreshments then closed the door thankfully on her grandmother's retreating back. She felt exhausted already, and the rest of her house party had not even arrived yet.

They talked on trivialities such as the weather and the state of the roads whilst the refreshments were being served, but it was clear that Westwood was somewhat preoccupied for his answers to Alicia's questions always seemed to be a little late on cue. He was a fair young man who was related to Lady Stansfield through her sister. Cultivated and refined, he affected dandyism in his style of dress, and his shirt points were high, his cravat a miracle of intricacy and his boots as highly polished as the library mirrors. Yet despite, or perhaps because of, his regard for fashion, he did not seem able to achieve the careless elegance of James Mullineaux. Nor did he have any of James's instinctive authority. Alicia found herself making the comparison and disliked herself for it, but she could find Westwood amiable, nothing more.

On this occasion he had a more than usually anxious look on his face and Alicia wondered what was distracting him. He knocked his glass over, set it to rights and cleared his throat, then sat forward and fixed her with an earnest look.

'Alicia, this business with Mullineaux—' He broke off immediately, clearly unsure how to proceed.

'Yes?' Alicia asked unencouragingly, determined to make him suffer. She was still out of charity with him and did not see why he had to pry into her personal affairs. And anyway, the last thing she wanted to do was talk about James Mullineaux.

'Well...I mean...surely it was an accident?'

'Certainly.' Alicia deliberately misunderstood him. 'A carriage accident.'

Westwood had the grace to look slightly ashamed of himself. The hot colour flooded his face. 'I hope,' he said constrainedly, 'that you came to no harm?'

'Fortunately not, thank you,' Alicia said, with composure. 'I injured my wrist in the accident, but it is only a slight sprain and already on the mend. However, Miss Frensham caught a chill from standing about in the rain and she is still at Ottery Manor with the Henleys.'

'I am sorry to hear it,' Westwood murmured, still abashed. He seemed to steel himself. 'No doubt it is unpleasant for her to have taken a chill, but surely it is worse for you, Alicia! To have spent a night alone in an inn with Mullineaux... Well, you can see how people will be talking!'

Alicia wondered briefly whether a scream of aggravation would put an end to this topic of conversation. It seemed likely, but rather an extreme measure to take. She smiled politely.

'I can understand perfectly. However, I rely on you to squash the rumours, of course.'

Westwood looked taken aback. Clearly whatever outpouring of regret or apology he had expected would simply not be forthcoming.

'Of course,' he agreed doubtfully. 'But, Alicia—'

Alicia cut across him decisively. 'Indeed, it's very unfortunate that Miss Frensham is still indisposed! We should not be so careless of the conventions as to meet like this without chaperonage, Christopher! Not everyone views our family connection in the same light as we do!'

Westwood swallowed hard. It seemed a little ironic to him that Alicia should choose to play propriety now, having spent a night alone in an inn, however innocently, with another man. He stole a glance at her charming profile, but learned nothing. Her expression was as calm and serene as usual, although he fancied he could detect a hint of determination in the set of her jaw. Westwood sighed unconsciously. He knew Alicia could tie him in knots should she choose, but it made little difference to his main aim, which was to marry both her and her fabulous fortune.

He had been finding it more and more difficult to get Alicia on her own in recent weeks, and suspected that this was because she deliberately avoided this. Now he had his opportunity and he intended to make the most of it. Although he had not planned to speak so soon after his arrival, he was in such a state of pent-up nervousness and anticipation that he could not help himself.

'I am glad Miss Frensham is not with us,' Westwood said desperately, 'for there is something I particularly wished to say to you, Alicia.'

Alicia was aware of a sinking feeling in the region of her heart. She could hardly be unaware of what was coming. Westwood's attentions had been becoming so marked over the past few months that she had known it could only be a matter of time before he made her a declaration. With vague amazement she realised that a week ago she might have even considered his suit. Now, as her thoughts slid imperceptibly but inevitably towards James, she knew that she could never marry Christopher Westwood.

It was evident that Westwood, having announced his intentions, was unsure of exactly how to begin. He cleared his throat a couple of times, leapt restlessly to his feet and finally burst into speech.

'Confound it, Alicia, I have been trying to show you for months— no, years!—how I feel about you!' he went down on one knee before her, and seized her hand. 'Marry me! Give me the right to protect you! I know it is presumptuous of me even to think of proposing to you, but we would deal well together, I know it! We enjoy each other's company, and—' he seized on another advantage to strengthen his suit '—your grandmother would be delighted!'

His intense grey eyes were fixed unwaveringly on her face and he raised her hand to press a feverish kiss on the back of it.

At this passionate and highly inconvenient moment, the door opened to admit a footman with a message from Lady Stansfield. Alicia had never been so glad to see anyone. Westwood dropped her hand as though he had been burned and scrambled to his feet, his countenance flushed with mortification. The footman, equally scarlet, hovered hopelessly in the doorway, his tray tilted at such an alarming angle that the missive slid off it onto the floor.

'Please come in, Liddell,' Alicia instructed coolly, quite as though nothing untoward had occurred. She retrieved the note, read it and waved him away without a reply. The door shut behind him with indecent haste as he shot downstairs to regale the servants' hall with the news that Mr Westwood was proposing.

Westwood himself was clearly furious at the interruption but could not see any way of resuming his declaration without appearing even more foolish.

Alicia seized her chance. 'Dear Christopher,' she said gently, 'I am very flattered that you wish me to become your wife, but I really must decline. You know that I esteem you as a friend, but I do not believe that we should suit.'

The hot colour rushed back into Westwood's face. Already humiliated by the tactless entrance of the footman, he was in danger of losing his self-control.

'Why not?' he demanded, with more indignation than manners.

Alicia bit her lip. This was difficult, as she was well aware that she had given him every indication that she enjoyed his company, whilst not having the least desire to marry him. Worse, she realised with a guilty pang that she had used him to keep other admirers at a distance, even whilst she had been aware of his growing regard for her.

'I am too used to having my own independence now to comfortably adapt to another arrangement,' she temporised. 'I am used to running my own estates and ordering my life, and all that would have to change were I to marry.'

'If you wanted to remarry, none of that would be of the least consequence,' Westwood retorted, unanswerably.

Alicia sighed. She could hardly tell him that she found him dull, and that life with him would be lacklustre. When he had touched her she had felt none of the explosive chemistry which was between herself and James Mullineaux. What a trying week it had been! Three marriage proposals, albeit one was by proxy, and none of them acceptable!

Westwood was still gazing down at her with a dogged determination. How could she finish this? Briefly she toyed with the idea of bursting into tears, thus putting him firmly in the wrong. After all, no gentleman should persist in an unwanted suit. A moment later, however, she rejected such a shabby idea. She had treated him badly enough as it was.

'Please come and sit down, Christopher,' she urged, patting the seat beside her. 'We have been good friends—must it all be at an end?'

Some of the sulky, mulish expression left Westwood's face, and he sat down beside her with an ill grace. He gave a despondent sigh.

'Suppose I never really thought you'd accept,' he admitted ruefully. 'After all, you turn fellows away by the barrowload, and why should I be different?' He was already looking more cheerful, as he had a disposition which could not sulk for long. 'Still, can't blame me for trying!'

He looked at Alicia thoughtfully, then added, 'I don't suppose it's anything to do with Mullineaux, is it?'

Alicia jumped involuntarily. 'What do you mean?'

Westwood looked a little confused. 'Well, you're forever turning away proposals from eligible men. I wondered if you were comparing them with some ideal? And as you have just met him again...'

This was surprisingly perceptive of Westwood, who was not known for his sensitivity to others' feelings. Alicia, who had no inclination to examine her own feelings on this point, ignored the difficult part of his question to concentrate on the bit she could deny.

'Well, disabuse yourself of the notion that Mullineaux was—or is—

some kind of ideal!' It came out more fiercely than she had intended. Remembering their disastrous encounters and the even more dangerous feelings which James could arouse in her, Alicia felt tormented beyond bearing.

'When he was younger,' she said coldly, 'James Mullineaux was arrogant and conceited, and time has improved him into a man over-bearing beyond toleration and downright rude! We met by complete chance and it was undoubtedly the worst piece of luck I could have had!'

'You don't like him, then,' Westwood said, without irony and with complete satisfaction.

Annabella Broseley's wedding took place on a bright afternoon in early March with the first blossom bursting out on the trees and the breeze setting the daffodils dancing on the green before Taunton Castle. That the wedding was being held in Taunton had been the first bone of contention between the St Auby family and Bertram Broseley—he had wanted to hold the ceremony in St Mary Redcliffe in Bristol, at the heart of his mercantile empire. The St Aubys had thrown up their hands in horror. No smell of the shop was going to infect the wedding of their only son, no matter how much he was going to benefit from the profits of trade after the event. So the wedding was held in Taunton and the St Aubys invited half the county in the hope that some of them would actually attend.

Alicia had agonised over her invitation for what felt like an age. It had arrived shortly after her return from Greyrigg and she had hidden it behind the clock on her mantelpiece, unwilling to see her father ever again. She felt very little kinship with Annabella either, and acknowledged to herself that this was a great shame. It seemed that she had made her choice and that her grandmother could be her only family now. Nevertheless, a niggling sense of guilt had caught her every so often and in the end she had found herself at her escritoire, penning a stilted little note to her father to the effect that Lady Carberry would be very happy to attend the marriage.

So here she was. The church was as flower-bedecked as Annabella herself, whose huge organza frills resembled nothing so much as a large meringue dessert, to Alicia's mind. She was clearly very pleased with herself, casting languishing looks at her young husband throughout the service and tossing her golden curls as she trilled with excited laughter. Alicia found it all vaguely sickening, particularly as before the service had started she had also spotted Francis St Auby exchanging looks of an intimate nature with a fast-looking matron in stripes. Worse, from Alicia's point of view, Bertram Broseley had made sure she was installed very ostentatiously beside him on the front pew and had joined her, beaming, after he had given away the bride.

Relations between them had been superficially pleasant so far. Shortly after her arrival at the St Aubys' house, Alicia had rather tartly enquired whether her father had invited his mysterious business associate to be amongst his guests, sure that he would not miss this opportunity to try to promote the match he had mooted to her before. Rather to her surprise, Broseley had appeared to find this highly amusing, relating that Mr Wood, as he referred to him, had a previous engagement in the county and could not attend. A little later, Alicia had caught her father's eye resting upon her roguishly, as though he was enjoying a good joke, and she had even thought she saw his shoulders shake slightly. Vaguely irritated, she had dismissed it as of no importance.

Also absent from the nuptials was Josiah, whom Alicia had expected to see at an occasion where he could have played the gentleman. Again, her father had seemed amused by her enquiry after her cousin, telling her Josiah was indisposed and could not attend. Alicia, concerned, had asked if his illness was serious, at which Broseley had looked as though he was about to burst out laughing. It was all rather odd and, Alicia thought, rather childish of him.

Alicia sighed. The St Auby family were Catholic and had insisted on a wedding mass, and the service was lasting some considerable time. Annabella appeared not to mind, no doubt caring little about the religious denomination of her husband as long as she could hang upon his arm in front of the assembled throng. Francis was a slender youth whose delicate fair looks might well appeal to some women, but whose nature could be described as neither delicate nor fair. Alicia did not like him at all. From her vantage point she could see him shifting from one foot to the other and trying to catch the eye of the stripy lady whilst Annabella's attention was distracted. Beside her, Broseley exuded all the confidence and complacency of the self-made man.

Alicia could feel her own attention wandering as the priest's voice droned on. She turned her head, idly scanning the rows of guests in the side aisles, mostly the local gentry who had decided for whatever reason to grace the occasion with their presence. Lady St Auby had managed quite a creditable turnout, Alicia thought with surprise. She had expected most of the gentry to spurn the invitation on the grounds that

Broseley was a jumped-up nobody, but evidently curiosity had done the trick... Her train of thought came to an abrupt end as she recognised a familiar dark head across the other side of the church, at the front of the congregation. Surely it could not be! Whatever could he be doing here? Alicia stared harder to make quite sure. And at that moment the Marquis of Mullineaux turned his head and met her startled gaze with the very faintest sardonic glint in his own eyes. He inclined his head in acknowledgement.

Alicia removed her gaze hastily, blushing furiously and flustered at having been caught staring. What on earth was Mullineaux doing there and how could she possibly have missed his arrival? He must have already been in the church when she went in, for Alicia had arrived deliberately late and some of Bertram Broseley's acquaintances had kept her talking until just before Annabella had arrived.

Alicia was utterly dumbfounded by Mullineaux's presence. She realised that she was breathless, gripping her dainty reticule between clenched fingers, brought close to panic by the sudden and unexpected nature of his appearance. She took a deep breath in an attempt to calm down. The congregation was standing up, indicating that the service was almost over. Annabella and her new husband were walking slowly down the aisle and Bertram Broseley was offering his arm to her as the St Aubys swept out in front of them. Alicia took the proffered arm numbly, all her thoughts suddenly centred on Mullineaux and the necessity of trying to avoid him during the rest of the celebrations.

This proved relatively easy to begin with. The wedding breakfast was being held at the St Aubys' town house in Fore Street and Alicia was relieved to find that her place at table sandwiched her between Sir Frederick St Auby and his elder daughter, Lady Grey. James Mullineaux was out of Alicia's sight, as Lady St Auby had claimed the hostess's privilege and put him on her right hand as an honoured guest. Although Alicia could not see James, her senses seemed intensely aware of him. She knew, for instance, what a commotion his presence at the wedding was still creating, as guests clamoured to greet him and speculate over his motives in accepting Lady St Auby's invitation. In her mind's eye, Alicia could see the friendly greetings of the men and the fawning of the women, and could imagine the tilt of Mullineaux's head, that slow, devastating smile, the sleepy look in those dark eyes which masked the shrewd appraisal as he summed up his fellow guests.

Alicia was no less perplexed than they about his presence, though perhaps for different reasons. It was natural for Lady St Auby to have invited him, she supposed. Together with the Piltons and Cavanaghs, the Mullineauxs must be considered one of the premier families in the county whose appearance at the wedding could not but add cachet. To leave Mullineaux off the guest list could have been interpreted as a monstrous snub. On the other hand, Alicia, not normally prone to gambling, was willing to bet that Lady St Auby had never expected Mullineaux to accept and had probably had a fit of the vapours when he had done so.

And why had he done so? Alicia could not puzzle it out. Surely any event involving her family would naturally lead him to cry off? He was certainly making no attempt to seek her out, and whilst this relieved her she also found to her annoyance that it piqued her as well.

The banquet over, the guests began to mingle and chat. Alicia was immediately pounced upon by Richard, Viscount Pilton, the youthful heir to a local earldom, who made a beeline for her side and stuck fast.

'Splendid wedding, Lady Carberry, quite splendid!' His fair, cheerful face beamed with good humour and good claret. 'Such a shame Lady Stansfield could not be here!'

Alicia did not enlighten him. Her grandmother had not been invited.

'Splendid to see James Mullineaux back amongst us,' Pilton continued, oblivious of the tactlessness of his observation. 'Always said he had been away too long!' He looked across the room to where Mullineaux lounged at ease, one shoulder resting against a pillar, a faint smile on his lips as Francis St Auby's inamorata plied him with wine and conversation. 'Taken up where he left off,' Pilton said enviously. 'God, I wish I had his style! Francis won't be pleased—' He broke off, flushing as he encountered Alicia's quelling gaze, and realised that such a comment was hardly appropriate to the sister of the bride. But a moment later Alicia smiled charmingly at him and he instantly forgot his tactlessness and smiled back, completely enraptured.

A hand fell on his shoulder.

'Richard,' the Marquis of Mullineaux said in his distinctive drawl, 'your aunt Marion is looking neglected. Go and fetch her a glass of lemonade, there's a good fellow!'

Pilton was already halfway across the room before he stopped to wonder how Mullineaux, who a moment before had appeared engrossed in flirtation, could possibly know of his aunt's need for refreshments. He scowled, but it was too late.

Mullineaux watched him go with a slightly pitying smile on his face.

'So easy to mislead,' he mused, with mock sadness. 'Modern youth has much to learn!'

'Doubtless he has not your wealth of experience,' Alicia said sarcastically, and saw him smile with appreciation.

'True enough, I suppose! And by the same token he is out of his depth with you, Lady Carberry!' Mullineaux's frankly admiring gaze approved her dress of aquamarine velvet, lingering on its fichu of almost transparently fine lace. 'I was merely saving our young friend the inevitable humiliation of falling prey to unrequited love!'

'Not a misfortune ever likely to afflict you, sir,' Alicia snapped, before she had time to bite her tongue. His comment had caught her on the raw for she already seemed to have fallen prey to that undesirable condition herself. Her hypnotised gaze travelled over him. His coat of darkest blue, worn with pale buff pantaloons and a cravat immaculately tied in the Mathematical, gave him the same indefinable elegance that she had noted at Ottery. His black hair was carefully disordered and as her eyes met his she saw that he was watching her with interest and not a little amusement. Alicia felt her colour rising and cursed the perfect, pale complexion which betrayed her so easily.

'Oh, I do not know about that,' Mullineaux said thoughtfully, his disturbing dark gaze never leaving her face. 'And you, Lady Carberry—do you have any experience of that melancholy state yourself?'

Drat the man! He was too perceptive! Alicia was certain that some degree of her discomfort must be showing in her face. She said the first thing that came into her head in order to distract his attention.

'Whatever are you doing here, anyway, Lord Mullineaux? I would scarce have expected to meet you at my sister's wedding!'

'Nor I you perhaps, Lady Carberry,' James Mullineaux said, somewhat obscurely. His wicked grin lightened his expression suddenly in a way that always made her heart turn over. 'We really must make an attempt to greet each other with more originality! This must be the second or third occasion on which one or other of us has uttered those words! But I suppose I should be grateful, for at least they have helped me place your mood.' He gave her a sideways look. 'And now I perceive that you intend to be eccentric. How am I to answer such a blunt question? I could be courteous and claim a close friendship with the St Auby family, or flattering and claim I wished to see your beautiful sister wed...'

They both looked over to where Annabella stood in a group of admiring young bucks, tossing her fair curls and giggling girlishly. Mullineaux grimaced.

'But then, alas, I would be lying!' His dark eyes moved over Alicia's face feature by feature, with a grave consideration. 'In some ways you look very alike,' he said thoughtfully, then added softly, 'But you are very different in character, are you not? And she cannot hold a candle to you, Alicia.'

Alicia's breath caught in her throat. The expression in his eyes was making her feel both hot and dizzy at the same time. There was a dangerous intimacy in that dark gaze, a disturbing power which held sway over her senses. For a moment she saw the white heat of a remembered passion flare in his eyes, then it was replaced by his customary cool detachment.

'Or,' Mullineaux finished lightly, as though the intervening moment had never occurred, 'I could just admit that I was bored and succumbed to the impulse to discompose your father by appearing at a public function where I knew he could not cut me dead!'

Alicia, still trying to recover her poise, barely took in his words at first. Had she been concentrating she might well have chosen not to take him up on a comment which might well lead to trouble. But now she regarded him with some puzzlement.

'Why should you wish to do that, my lord? I was not aware that you had ever met my father!'

Mullineaux viewed her with weary cynicism. 'Oh, come, come, Lady Carberry, you can do better than that! It may be old history, but let us not pretend that it never happened!'

Alicia raised her chin stubbornly at this reference to what she could only assume was their previous, unhappily concluded relationship. 'I have no wish to pretend anything, my lord,' she observed frigidly. 'However, I do not understand you. I did not know that you had ever met my father.'

Mullineaux looked exasperated, both with himself for raising the subject in the first place and with her for pursuing it.

'It seems, then, that we must be very frank, you and I,' he said dryly. 'You must know—none better!—that your father and I are old adversaries! We met on the fateful occasion when I called in at Bruton Street to question your sudden betrothal to George Carberry and he had me thrown out into the street on your—'

He broke off as all the pretty colour fled from Alicia's face, leaving her chalk-white and her eyes huge and stricken pools of green. She opened her mouth, but no sound came. Mullineaux instinctively took her arm, fearing she would faint. Then her attention was claimed by Broseley himself, insinuating his large bulk between the two of them with the superficial social smile reserved for such occasions.

'Alicia, my dear! May I make you known to some friends of mine?' His glacial gaze touched Mullineaux briefly and slid away. 'Excuse us, Lord Mullineaux.' He shepherded his daughter away with a possessive arm around her waist.

Alicia looked back at Mullineaux over her shoulder as she walked away. She looked completely shattered, the lovely, heart-breaking innocence he remembered showing clearly in her eyes, overlaid with disbelief and puzzlement. The truth burst over him with the power of a tidal wave. She had never known. Broseley had never told her.

Mullineaux put down his drink gently and turned to answer some casual question put to him by an old acquaintance. But his mind was elsewhere. He had had enough of rumour, half-truth and equivocation. There and then, he resolved that he would make Alicia tell him what had really happened, if it was the last thing that he did.

Monks Dacorum Hall was very quiet. Caroline and Marcus Kilgaren had left the previous day to join Alicia's guests at Chartley. James was alone in his study, attempting to formulate a reply to his sister Louisa, who had written to ask him to postpone his visit to Worcestershire. Two of the children had developed chickenpox, she wrote, and the house was all at sixes and sevens. If he could delay for a week or two, they could give him a better welcome.

With surprise, James realised that it would be no hardship to stay at Monks Dacorum for another week. He put the letter down on his desk and stared out of the window into the dark. Before he had gone abroad he had considered the country to be good only for hunting and a dead bore otherwise. He had had no desire to live on any of his country estates, finding amusement and company only in London. The West Country was particularly alien to him with its mixture of wild, heather-clad uplands and its flat, waterlogged levels. Yet now...

He picked up his pen again, and it was then that he heard the music. High, sweet and piercing, it was the sound of a single violin. Intrigued, James leant on the desk in order to peer out of the mullioned window. The ivy grew close, but he could just distinguish the dark outlines of the garden and the retaining wall which bordered the road.

The moon was a silver disc, high and bright, in a cold black sky studded with stars. By its light, he could just discern a procession of shadowy figures moving along the road. At first he wondered if it was the fabled free-traders who were particularly active in the Bristol Channel, but they would hardly herald their approach with music. James turned back to the lamplit room and rang the bell.

'Russell, what is going on outside?'

The butler was a local man and for a moment it seemed that he had caught some of the excitement in the atmosphere outside. He struggled to regain a suitable gravity.

'It's the annual cider wassail, my lord.'

'Cider wassail?' James raised his eyebrows. 'What sort of festival is that?'

The butler scratched his head. 'Every spring, folk from all the surrounding villages come to the orchards to celebrate the previous year's crop and drink a toast to the next harvest, my lord,' he explained. 'There have been cider wassails for generations in these parts. Why not go along and see for yourself, sir?'

James almost dismissed the idea out of hand. It sounded to him like an excuse for excessive drinking and precious little else, but something gave him pause. He had nothing else to do that evening—why not experience a little local colour?

'Where is it being held, Russell?' he enquired casually.

'On Chartley land, sir,' the butler replied. 'Lady Carberry provides the food and drink, and a barn for the dancing. There's no side to her ladyship! Why, sometimes she even attends herself!'

'Does she, indeed?' James murmured, and as he made for the door the butler could have sworn that his master was smiling.

It proved very easy to find the revels. The sound of the fiddle was still faintly audible above the soughing of the wind in the trees as James set off on foot down the track to Chartley. He felt a sudden lifting of spirits to be out in the fresh air after a day spent poring over the estate books. And there seemed to be something in the air that night—something of magic, excitement and anticipation. James shrugged the feeling off as fanciful, but it persisted.

There were many orchards thereabouts which stretched from the fertile east of Chartley village towards Monks Dacorum, but only one barn large enough to house the celebrations. As he drew near, James observed that the wassail was already well advanced. Figures were milling around the wizened trunks of the apple trees, torches flared, and the cider flowed freely from a multitude of casks. Someone at the front of the crowd was making a speech—there was much laughter and shouts of encouragement—and as James drew close the crowd burst into spontaneous applause before breaking up and streaming towards the open doors of the huge tithe barn.

Torchlight and firelight spilled out from its doors. There was a delicious smell of roasting meat and James, anonymous on the edge of the crowd, could just see inside, where wicker baskets spilled their contents of fruit over the cobbled floor and the village children picked them up with cries of excitement. Oranges and lemons were expensive commodities—no doubt these had also been provided by the philanthropic Lady Carberry. James smiled to himself. There really was no stopping her.

The press of people about the barn was so great that not everyone could get inside. Trenchers of food and huge, overflowing tankards of cider were passed good-humouredly out to those in the cold. James glimpsed bottles of liquid other than cider being passed surreptitiously from hand to hand, and wondered fleetingly how many of the locals augmented their wages with free-trading. It was an accepted fact that smuggling was rife in the Bristol Channel—perhaps the charitable lady of the manor also bought her brandy without paying duty?

James stayed at the back of the crowd, preferring to remain unrecognised. He felt almost like an interloper in this merry throng. All around him the conversation buzzed and the laughter grew raucous as the cider made the rounds again. People were beginning to disperse a little now. Some amorous couples, oblivious of the cold night air, drifted off between the trees, absorbed in each other. An area was cleared at the front of the barn and the fiddles struck up again, several of them in haunting melody. It was time for the dancing. James was about to slip away when he received a surprise.

A small party of people were coming forward from inside the barn where they had been out of his line of vision. With a slight shock he recognised Caroline Kilgaren, her piquant face upturned to Marcus's, her eyes bright with excitement. A fur-lined cloak framed her fair curls. Marcus's head was bent towards her and in a moment he grinned, took both her hands, and whirled her into the dance. A small ripple of applause went through the throng of watchers and some of them came forward to join in.

There was another girl there whom James did not recognise, but whose identity he could guess. Caroline had mentioned that the Stapleford family would be joining them at Chartley—this, then, must be the celestially fair but unfortunately rather spiteful Georgiana, whom they had maliciously put forward as a potential bride for him. She was indeed very beautiful, James thought dispassionately, but her beauty was marred by her expression, which at the moment mirrored her shock and disgust that members of her party should condescend to join in the festivities with the local peasants. Clearly she felt that it was all very well to be seen to patronise the event, but a suitable distance should be maintained.

The reel finished and one violin immediately took up an air for a jig. Caroline and Marcus showed no inclination to stop dancing. Georgiana Stapleford turned to look for the rest of her party. Evidently her parents and Lady Stansfield had considered themselves too staid and ancient for such revelry, particularly on a cold spring night. Which only left...

Then he saw them. The torchlight burnished Alicia's hair with a dark copper glow and shadowed the brilliant green eyes with a deep mystery. She had her hand on Christopher Westwood's arm and was speaking urgently to him. Westwood's expression was unencouraging; in fact, it was a close match with Georgiana's. Apparently he would not be obliging her by dancing, no matter how much Alicia wanted him to.

James was not aware of having moved until he had almost reached them. The crowd parted silently to allow him through and then he was bowing before Alicia and looking down into her wide, startled eyes.

'Would my lady care to dance?'

He felt, rather than saw, Westwood stiffen beside him, as though he was about to object. But it was Alicia he was looking at and only her. She absorbed his whole attention and the look she gave him was one of pure, uncomplicated pleasure.

'Gladly, my lord.'

He took her hand and drew her into the dance. A murmur ran through the crowd, but James barely noticed. His awareness of Alicia was intense. The firelight gave her skin a golden glow and lit her eyes with luminous brightness. She burned with an excitement he could feel emanating from her whole body. Around them the other dancers dipped and whirled, but it was as though the two of them were alone, absorbed in the same magic that had touched James earlier. The wind whipped back the hood of Alicia's cloak and she laughed aloud in pure enjoyment. Despite their large and very interested audience, James could simply have picked her up and carried her off there and then. He wanted her more than any woman he had known.

But all dreams must end. The musicians had already played one extra chorus and now the dance drew to a close. Alicia was rosy and breathless but the magic was draining away. The violins finished with a flourish and a moment later Marcus and Caroline Kilgaren were at James's shoulder.

'You never told us you intended to be here tonight, James! We could have made up a party!' Caroline's speculative gaze slid from him to Alicia with puzzlement.

Some element of restraint had entered Alicia's manner, as though she could not believe what she had just done. James knew that during the dance she had felt exactly the same as he had done but now her glance was suddenly shy as it met his. 'We should be glad if you would come back to Chartley with us for refreshments, Lord Mullineaux,' she said, with constraint.

Christopher Westwood was lurking behind her with a face like thunder, whilst Georgiana Stapleford's avid blue gaze moved from one face to another ceaselessly. For James, too, the descent to reality had happened too quickly and he bowed abruptly.

'Thank you, Lady Carberry, but I must decline. Your servant, ma'am, Lady Kilgaren...'

He turned on his heel and walked away without a backward glance. The murmur of the crowd rose to a crescendo behind him and over it could be heard Georgiana Stapleford, in a voice as sharp as daggers. 'So *that* is the dangerous Marquis of Mullineaux! *What* an attractive man!'

'All I am saying, Alicia, is that such behaviour cannot help but fuel the rumours that there is some kind of illicit relationship between yourself and Mullineaux!'

The entire household could hear Christopher Westwood's complaints on the subject, for he was standing stubbornly in the entrance hall at Chartley Chase and would not move. He was white with anger and determined to have his say.

Alicia strove to keep her own temper and to keep her voice level. She knew that Westwood was right and that her actions had been ill-considered. But how could she explain to anyone, least of all Christopher Westwood, the spell which had held her captive from the moment she had seen James Mullineaux stepping forward to take her hand? At that moment nothing on earth would have prevented her from dancing with him. Now, it seemed, she must bear the consequences.

'Since you know such rumours to be false, Christopher, I can only suggest that you disregard them!'

'But you are encouraging them! Why dance with the man if you wish to quash the speculation?'

'What would you have me do?' Alicia snapped. 'Must I refuse to even speak to him just to satisfy you? I am not so poor-spirited as to regard this gossip, and neither should you be!'

'But you should have seen yourself! The look on your face alone—'

Alicia turned on him, eyes flashing. All enjoyment she had derived from the evening, and in particular her dance with James, had long fled.

'I was simply enjoying myself! Really, Christopher, you are becoming the most complete puritan!'

'Dash it, Alicia, will you not take this seriously? Your reputation is hardly such that it can afford another scandal!'

Westwood regretted the words as soon as they were said, for Alicia was looking at him with a glacial expression very reminiscent of her grandmother. The fact that he had spoken nothing but the truth did not really help.

'Thank you for your consideration, Christopher. I do not believe that I have given you the right to judge such matters, however.'

Westwood winced. For someone who looked so sweet, Alicia had a damned unpleasant way with her sometimes! He stood his ground.

'Nevertheless, as your friend I feel I must say something!'

'But not in front of the servants, Christopher! Very bad *ton*!'

Lady Stansfield's voice carried with the clarity of a bell from the first landing, where she was standing dressed in a silk kimono of dashing but unorthodox design. It was clear that she had been roused from her slumbers by the altercation and was in a very bad mood. She had no difficulty with criticising others for faults which she had herself, and addressed herself to both of them, oblivious of the embarrassed footman standing by the front door.

'You, Christopher, will hold your tongue and show a little more self-control! Alicia, you will come up and talk to me! At once!'

Westwood flushed to the roots of his fair hair and slammed off into the library in search of a drink. Alicia sighed and started up the staircase. It was useless to argue with Lady Stansfield in such a mood. She followed her grandmother into her bedroom, which smelt strongly of snuff, and took a seat in one of the armchairs disposed beside the fire. The room was dimly lit, the embers of the fire glowing hot in the grate. An abandoned piece of embroidery lay on the table, and Alicia's heart sank further. Lady Stansfield only ever resorted to what she termed 'frippery, female pursuits' when she was very bored and it inevitably put her in an even worse mood. Her evening with the Staplefords must have been a tedious one.

Lady Stansfield eased herself into the other chair and turned her sharp gaze immediately on Alicia.

'Well, miss! Here's a fine to-do!' Her expression was at its most autocratic. 'I've been wanting to talk to you! I think it's best for you to tell me the whole—what is the relationship between yourself and James Mullineaux?'

'Our relationship is mainly categorised by ill-temper and conflict,' Alicia said, with a touch of bitterness.

She hesitated, but knew better than to try to argue with her grandmother in her current mood. She related the carriage accident and her subsequent rescue by James, how it had come about that she had compromised them both by sending Miss Frensham away, their quarrel, their subsequent meetings, and finally her dance with him that night. She left nothing out of her factual account, but made no reference to her feelings. Let Lady Stansfield make of that what she would.

When she had finished, Lady Stansfield stirred a little in her chair. Throughout Alicia's account her attention had not wavered.

'So Mullineaux is not in fact your lover,' she observed thoughtfully.

'I fear I cannot claim that privilege,' Alicia said, very dryly. 'The terms of our relationship could scarcely be described in such a cordial way!'

'Humph! A pity!' Lady Stansfield looked her over comprehensively. 'Still, I am hardly surprised. I would have expected you to look much more cheerful if he were!'

'Grandmama!' Alicia had never grown out of being scandalised by her grandmother's plain speaking. 'Do I understand you to be encouraging me to indulge in a love affair?'

'I should think so!' Lady Stansfield said energetically. 'You are too strait-laced, Alicia, and I have given up all hope of you ever losing your puritan streak! Lord, a man wants a cosy armful in bed, not a block of ice! I know that your marriage gave you a disgust of a physical relationship, but that is all in the past now. You should allow yourself a little amusement!'

Despite herself, Alicia's wayward mind presented her with a series of images which all too graphically suggested what it might be like to take James Mullineaux as a lover. Carberry had been gross and grotesque, but James's lithe body would be quite a different matter. With an effort she tore her mind away and found her grandmother watching her with amused comprehension.

'Exactly! In my day we were not so shy to follow our inclinations! Why, I remember—'

'Grandmama!'

Lady Stansfield subsided with a sniff. 'Oh, very well, very well, I can see that you mean to be odiously strict! But it's no good you denying that you still care for Mullineaux, for I can see it as plain as a pikestaff!'

Her assertion made Alicia face squarely up to the facts that she had been trying to ignore since meeting James again; not only did she find him intensely attractive but she also still cared deeply for him. It did not seem to matter that he held her in contempt and that they always seemed to end up quarrelling. She had loved him for over seven years and his return had only served to stir up all the old emotions which had never really left her. He is arrogant and high-handed, she told herself severely, but it made no difference to her feelings.

Alicia was aware that her grandmother was still watching her like an inquisitive sparrow with its head on one side. She shrugged uncomfortably.

'I cannot deny it, Grandmama! Oh, I have tried to tell myself that what is in the past is over, but my feelings are not so easily dismissed. And at least you should now see why I am not able to marry Christopher!'

Her look dared her grandmother to contradict her, but the old lady was silent. She knew that a man like Christopher Westwood was no substitute for James Mullineaux.

'I thought Mullineaux had never met my father,' Alicia said suddenly, 'but at Annabella's wedding he told me he had been to Bruton Street all those years ago to demand to be told what was happening. I always thought...I never believed...' Her anguished gaze met that of Lady Stansfield. 'He had no reason to lie to me, did he?' she appealed.

Lady Stansfield smoothed the silk of her kimono. 'None at all,' she said, a little gruffly. 'It don't surprise me—the last time I ever saw James Mullineaux he swore he would visit your father to demand the truth. I always liked Mullineaux,' she added, with a smile. 'Oh, he was impetuous, but he was generous with it and he could charm the birds off the trees. And he loved you, Alicia. Really loved you.'

She looked at her granddaughter's downbent head. 'You always believed he had deserted you, didn't you, Alicia? And now you know it is not true you have very little left to reproach him for—'

'Except pride,' Alicia snapped. 'I don't forgive him for being so quick to condemn! The arrogant conceit of the man! That is one thing about him that has not changed!'

Lady Stansfield hid her smile. 'Whereas he,' she continued, 'has rather more to forgive—or so he thinks.'

'For Mullineaux it is not a matter of forgiveness,' Alicia said bleakly. 'He has made his judgement. Why should he wish to change it?'

Lady Stansfield shifted slightly in her chair. 'Those encounters you describe hardly suggest a disinterested man... If he holds you in such dislike, surely he would never have offered you his help at Ottery!'

Alicia smiled. 'I can only assume that, being a gentleman, he came to the rescue of Miss Frensham only to discover that he was faced with the unpleasant task of rescuing me as well!'

'True.' Lady Stansfield had her head on one side once more. 'But he need not have made you a declaration the following morning, particularly as it was all a bumblebath of your own making!'

'Thank you! I am well aware that I was to blame! But I can offer no explanation, I fear, Grandmama, other than the prosaic one which is that Mullineaux conceived it to be his duty!'

Lady Stansfield looked unconvinced. 'Stuff!' she said, with finality. 'There is more to this than you think, Alicia. And, leaving that aside, why did he seek you out here, let alone go to the wassail and draw such attention to the pair of you by asking you to dance?'

Alicia did not reply. She hardly understood herself the impulse which had prompted James to ask her to dance and her to accept. It had been unreal, a moment out of time. But she was not foolish enough to build any hopes upon it. To do so would only leave her more distressed and disappointed in the end. She made a slight, dispirited gesture.

'Do not refine upon it too much, Grandmama. I do not! As we are alone, I will admit that it was foolish of me to encourage the gossip by dancing with Mullineaux tonight, but there is no real cause for speculation. The meeting at Ottery was the merest chance, what followed was bad luck, and how I feel is really irrelevant given that Mullineaux will never think of me as anything but a fortune-hunting adventuress who jilted him to marry a richer man!'

Lady Stansfield snorted with disgust. 'The facts don't fit the case, my love, but by all means believe them if you must! How did you find your father after all these years?' she added, changing the subject as she saw Alicia's instinctive rejection of her words.

Alicia looked up and met her eyes squarely. 'Oh, he was just the same! He scares me, Grandmama. I feel as though I can never be free of him.' A darker shadow touched the shadowed room. Alicia shivered convulsively. 'All the time his presence is there, even when he is not!'

She did not add that she had already received a letter from Bertram Broseley inviting her to stay at Greyrigg. Annabella was still on her wedding journey in the Lake District and Broseley was claiming to be lonely without the company of either daughter to comfort him. Alicia had crumpled the letter up in disgust, but it had brought back all her feelings of disquiet.

'Bertram Broseley, faugh!' Lady Stansfield wrinkled her nose as though there was a vile smell beneath it. 'The man was always an out-and-out bounder, for all he is your father!' A faraway look came into her eyes. 'He was a cit trying to buy his way into good company when he met your mother. We knew Julia was taken with him—looked like a god, did Broseley in those days, with his fair hair and finicky gold waistcoats!' Lady Stansfield snorted in disgust.

'I never spoke to him,' she continued, with the unconscious aristo-cratic arrogance which had led her son-in-law to detest her, 'but I could see how he turned heads and Julia always was a silly piece.'

Alicia sighed. She did not remember her mother very well, for Julia Broseley had died at Annabella's birth, but she did recall a gentle, soft-voiced creature with an anxious face framed by soft brown ringlets. Julia had inherited none of her mother's acerbic wit or hot temper. Such strength might have protected her from Broseley's casual cruelty. As it was, the runaway match had been an unmitigated disaster. The Earl of Stansfield had refused to accept Broseley as his son-in-law and since Bertram had only married Julia to increase his social stature he had viewed the alliance as worthless. It was only after the Earl's death that Lady Stansfield had been able to make contact with her granddaughter, and by then Broseley himself had been deeply embittered and the breach could not be healed.

Lady Stansfield patted Alicia's hand comfortingly with her own be-ringed one. 'But your father cannot touch you now, Alicia. You are quite safe.'

Alicia shook her head. She did not believe Bertram Broseley could be dismissed so easily. She got to her feet.

'If you will excuse me, Grandmama, I am very tired. I must seek my bed now.'

She kissed her grandmother's cheek and straightened up.

'Alicia.' Her grandmother's voice halted her as she had her hand on the doorknob. 'Just one small piece of advice. Think twice before you play off any tricks on Mullineaux again. He is hardly the man to tolerate them for long! I predict that you will find it more difficult to avoid him than you think.'

Alicia smiled a little sadly but did not reply and the door closed softly behind her. After a moment Lady Stansfield sighed. The fire had gone out and she was cold. With an old lady's stiffness she rose and went to bed.

Chapter Six

Alicia reined in her horse on the top of the moor, her cheeks becomingly flushed with the sting of the cold afternoon air. The ride up from Chartley Chase had been exhilarating for she had given Savannah her head, the mare's inclination for a gallop coinciding with Alicia's own inclination to escape.

The spirits of the Chartley house-party had not managed to reassert themselves in the days following the cider wassail. Christopher Westwood was still nursing a fine sense of grievance and was displaying his disapproval of Alicia by sulking. Georgiana Stapleford was making life a misery with her sharp looks and sharper comments, Lady Stansfield was suffering from rheumatism and was inclined to snap, and Alicia herself was unable to throw off the depression which had possessed her after that evening. Despite the visits, card parties and impromptu theatricals, it had somehow proved impossible to please people and it had been very tiring for Alicia in trying.

One look at the sullen faces around the breakfast table that morning had prompted Marcus Kilgaren to suggest a trip out, in the hope that the fine day might dispel the bad humours. After some discussion it was agreed that the whole party should drive over to Pilton Abbey for the day, both to admire the fine house and to take Countess Pilton up on the hospitable invitation she had issued the week before. There had been general agreement to the plan, but Lady Stansfield had declined to go, saying that Hermione Pilton bored her to death, and Alicia had pleaded a headache in order to be excused. She was desperate for a little solitude.

A false air of calm had settled on Chartley Chase as the carriage and the riders had clattered away through the village in the early afternoon. In the blue saloon Lady Stansfield had snored over her post-prandial cup of chocolate and, peeping around the door, Alicia had seen that she was dead to the world. She'd needed no further encouragement, for she had never had any real intention of resting that afternoon. In her room she'd hastily donned a riding habit of apple-green, severely styled and most becoming, and braided her hair into one fat plait beneath her round-brimmed hat.

There had been a little more activity in the stableyard where Alicia's groom, Jem, had willingly led out Savannah for her. The mare's coat was gleaming with good health and it seemed that she was as keen for exercise as Alicia herself. Jem had smiled as he'd looked up at them. They seemed very well matched.

'Reckon you shouldn't be riding out without a groom, ma'am,' he'd offered thoughtfully, knowing full well his advice would be rejected.

Alicia had laughed, already impatient to be off. 'In the country! I assure you I am quite safe, Jem!'

She had wheeled the horse round and made for the moor before Jem could reply and he had only smiled and scratched his head as he made his way back into the tackroom. Her ladyship was a law unto herself like the old Countess, and no one could gainsay her, least of all Mr Westwood. In company with the other servants, Jem had heard of the failure of Christopher Westwood's suit and he'd smiled to himself again. It would take more than that tailor's dummy to appeal to Alicia Carberry.

From the top of the hill there was a spectacular view across the patchwork countryside to the Bristol Channel, gleaming like a silver ribbon in the sun. Chartley Chase was a tiny dolls' house below her, with the village scattered beyond it. A light breeze fanned Alicia's face and stirred the tendrils of hair beneath her hat. Savannah snorted softly and turned away from Chartley, picking her way over the hillside in the direction of Monks Dacorum. Alicia made no effort to change direction.

The mare had picked up one of the old drover's tracks across the moor and was now trotting briskly along, her chestnut ears pricked. The heather and bracken were springing back after the winter and the peat track was firm beneath the horse's hooves for there had been no rain for several weeks. The air had a keen, pure feel and there was not a single person in sight. Alicia, feeling her tensions slipping away with a rush of relief that was almost too euphoric, urged Savannah to a gallop.

They slowed to a reluctant trot when the heathland gave way to cultivated fields again, and took a road that wended between drystone walls and high hedges. Alicia had lost her sense of direction completely but had no worries for she knew that she would eventually find a village where she could take directions back to Chartley. For now, just the sense of escape was enough. She had not realised how oppressed she had become by both the talk of scandal and the pressure of constantly having to put on a public face. But for now she need think of nothing but the sting of the cold wind, the scent of leather and her pleasure in being out of doors.

The road ran on between the fields, then into a small, coppiced woodland through which the distant, rhythmic thud of the forester's axe could be heard. Savannah splashed through a ford and the narrow track began to climb again. Pallid blue sky stretched overhead and the breeze had a cutting edge to it. Alicia's spirits lifted with every step away from Chartley Chase.

They had gone perhaps a couple of miles along the track when the trees fell back suddenly to reveal a sinister huddle of cottages. They were all empty, walls crumbling and once neat gardens overrun with weeds. An old estate wall on both sides culminated in a pair of iron gates swinging on rusty hinges. Alicia allowed the mare to walk forward slowly, almost afraid to disturb the stillness. The track was grassed over now and the horse's hoofbeats were muffled. She picked her way with dainty care between the half-open gates.

So this must be one of the neglected entrances to Monks Dacorum. Alicia had never seen the house, for old Mr Rowley, the previous tenant, had been a recluse who never entertained. Those of her neighbours who could remember the days of the previous Marquis had told her that the house was vastly pretty and charmingly modernised. Caroline, too, had declared it to be a delightful house, if somewhat neglected in recent years.

The obvious course of action now was to turn back. The house would be empty, of course, for James Mullineaux would have left a week ago to visit his sister and the servants would have been laid off until a new tenant could be found. However, that hardly gave Alicia the excuse to indulge her curiosity and go further. But still she hesitated and Savannah, who clearly had different ideas, set off down the drive at a lively pace.

They passed a lodge where a family of blackbirds flew off with shrill cries of alarm at their approach. The house was empty, its windows dark and unfriendly. The track was descending quite steeply now under a thick canopy of trees whose bare branches knitted together overhead. The pale winter sun could not penetrate here. Rhododendrons grew close to the track and weeds smothered it. There was one more sharp bend to the left and the trees ended suddenly, revealing to Alicia's fascinated gaze the scene which lay before her.

In the distance she could see a village nestling amongst the fields. Curls of smoke plumed into the winter air and a church spire cut the pale sky. In the foreground, cradled in the hollow of the hill, was the most perfect house Alicia had ever seen. It was small, half-timbered, and built around a central courtyard. There was a medley of decorative chimneys and a show of gables, orioles and leaded casement windows.

The whole house and garden were surrounded by a moat of glassily green water on which she could see an assortment of swans and ducks preening and swimming. The moat was fed by a narrow river which wended its way towards the village in a series of lazy curves, and in one of these lay the ruins of the abbey church that had originally given the house its name. The pattern of gardens was fascinating—Alicia recognised an overgrown maze and the outlines of a knot garden, both almost choked with weeds. The blank, mullioned windows of the house stared back at her solemnly.

Alicia dug her heels into Savannah's sides and the mare trotted obediently down the drive, passing the unkempt lawns carpeted with wild daffodil and narcissus, and over the moat bridge into the stableyard. At close quarters the house was eerily quiet, its windows shuttered with ivy. Alicia, held as she was in the grip of some powerful enchantment, dismounted and tied the mare to the block by the stables. Her footsteps sounded loud on the gravel as she made a circuit of the courtyard and peered beyond the stable doors into the musty and disused interiors. The house and the stables themselves appeared in good condition, unlike the neglected gardens, but there was an air of emptiness about the place.

The house was built in an L-shape around two sides of the courtyard, with the stables in front of Alicia and on her left a high wall dividing the courtyard from the gardens. There was a door in the wall and it was open a few inches. The temptation was too strong. She pushed the door tentatively and it yielded with only a squeak of hinges.

Alicia found herself standing in a walled garden—a mellow, secret garden set between the moat and the high courtyard wall. She stared about her, entranced, all sorts of ideas coming into her head. In the summer the sun-warmed stone would be covered with sweet-scented honeysuckle and ancient, fragrant roses. The flowerbeds would hold columbine, speedwell and flax, mingling profusely with cornflowers and valerian. She could imagine tall Canterbury bells nodding at the back of the borders and bees lurching intoxicated from flower to flower.

There was an old rustic bench under the gnarled branches of an apple tree and Alicia sat down and let her thoughts drift over the warm, hazy days of summer. If only she were able to buy Monks Dacorum she could re-create the gardens just as they would have been in Elizabethan times. But James Mullineaux would never sell to her...

Alicia sat there until the March chill began to seep into her bones and made her shiver. The colour fading from the sky warned her that evening was already closing in and it was time for her to return home. She got to her feet and shook out the skirts of her riding habit. The feeling of enchantment had begun to fade as she grew colder, and almost immediately the extreme impropriety of her actions became apparent. Though the house was empty, that was no excuse to indulge her curiosity and trespass in this shameless way! The light was fading and there was suddenly something sinister about the neglected gardens and shuttered windows. A feeling akin to panic rose in Alicia and she almost ran down the path to the old door in the wall.

Grasping stems of wild roses caught at the skirts of her riding habit, detaining her. She wrenched the material free of their thorns and fled precipitately to the doorway.

A mere five steps brought her to the door, which still stood open, and to confront the man who stood with his shoulders propped negligently against the frame, blocking her path. And this time there was no moonlight, and no enchantment, and she was looking up into eyes which were as dark and cold as the chill of a winter's night.

Alicia felt herself to be at a distinct disadvantage. To have been caught trespassing could only be proof of a most vulgar curiosity. Worse, she had now provoked a confrontation with the one man she would have chosen at all costs to avoid. They had not met since the night of the cider wassail, an occasion which brought her to the blush when she remembered the abandonment of her behaviour. She felt paralysed with embarrassment.

No such problem appeared to afflict the Marquis of Mullineaux, however. His dark, direct gaze was unflinching, quizzical and slightly mocking.

'Good afternoon, Lady Carberry. What a pleasure to see you again!'

'Whatever are you doing here?' Alicia could have bitten off her tongue as soon as she had asked such a naive question. Caroline and Marcus had said that he would be away, but they had obviously made a mistake—a mistake which was proving costly to her. Flustered, she could feel herself blushing and was even more annoyed.

James Mullineaux raised an eyebrow and straightened up, driving his hands into his jacket pockets.

'It *is* my house! Surely it is more appropriate for me to make that enquiry of you? If only I had known that you planned to visit Monks Dacorum, Lady Carberry, I would have been at pains to show you round myself!'

The words were smooth, but Alicia did not miss their sarcastic undertone and it brought more blood up into her face. She gritted her teeth.

Odious, odious man! Still, she was forced to admit that she was firmly in the wrong. What could have possessed her to come here in the first place? She was utterly mortified. Worse, James was still blocking the doorway and seemed completely at ease and in no hurry to move. Alicia was seized with panic. She simply had to get away. With a great effort of will she overcame her embarrassment sufficiently to look at him. She could not quite meet his eyes—almost, but not quite.

'Lord Mullineaux.' Alicia's voice still sounded annoyingly squeaky with emotion. 'I must apologise for my presence here. You are quite right to view it as an unwarrantable intrusion and I have no wish to prolong a meeting which must be so mutually disagreeable.' She tried to gather up her skirts into her hand. 'I shall take my leave.'

It was a creditable speech, only marred by the fact that Alicia could feel her hat slipping backwards and could see that her skirt was already tangled again with the treacherous roses. She was quite prepared to push James Mullineaux aside, so single-minded was her desire to escape the turmoil of her emotions and that unremittingly quizzical gaze.

James allowed her to wrench her skirts free of the thorns again without comment, but when it appeared that Alicia was about to flee past him he laid a restraining hand on her arm.

'Just a moment, Lady Carberry. Surely you do not expect me to let you go as easily as that? We need to talk, you and I. You cannot just walk away as though you had not met me!'

There was a silence which felt to Alicia as though it lasted several hours. Her mind seemed incapable of understanding the implication of his words. She had focused so completely on getting herself away from him and the embarrassment of the situation that she had not contemplated an alternative. And why should James wish to talk to her anyway? He had never given any indication that they should be anything other than mere acquaintances.

All this went through her mind as she stepped through the doorway into the courtyard, and James tightened his grip on her arm and drew her towards the main door of the house.

One of the stable doors was open and a groom was leading a docile Savannah towards it. The mare was still within reach, but Alicia had barely half formulated the idea of grabbing her reins and riding off when James disconcertingly read her thoughts.

'I wouldn't even think about it if I were you,' he said, pleasantly but definitely. 'It's only in stories that a lady encumbered by a side saddle and long skirt is still able to make some dashing escape. You would merely look foolish, and I would be put to the trouble of bringing you back!'

Alicia fumed, resolving that he was quite the most unpleasant man she had ever met. On the principle that attack was her best form of defence, she stopped dead on the cobblestones and rounded on him.

'So you intend to keep me here by duress? Might I enquire to what purpose?'

James did not appear disconcerted. 'But you came here of your own free will, my lady! I could ask what you are doing here at all!'

'I wish to buy Monks Dacorum,' Alicia snapped, half-truthfully. 'I thought that you had left for Worcestershire, and I came over from Chartley to inspect the property.'

'How very unorthodox,' James observed mildly, with a smile that made Alicia's blood boil. 'Most prospective purchasers would surely contact my agent first! But you, Lady Carberry—' it was said with exaggerated politeness '—you are always different!'

Alicia's understandable humiliation at being caught on the property was fading fast before this mockery.

'You still have not answered my question, my lord,' she pointed out frigidly. 'Do you intend to hold me here by force?'

The corners of James's firm mouth twitched in a smile. 'How very melodramatic! If you insist on expressing it in those terms, then yes, I intend to keep you here for a while!'

An Important Message from the Editors

Dear Reader,

Because you've chosen to read one of our fine romance novels, we'd like to say "thank you!" And, as a <u>special</u> way to thank you, we've selected <u>two more</u> of the books you love so well, <u>plus</u> an exciting mystery gift, to send you absolutely **FREE!**

Please enjoy them with our compliments...

Rebecca Pearson

Editor

P.S. And because we <u>value</u> our customers, we've attached something extra inside...

EDITOR'S
FREE GIFT
SEAL
THANK YOU

Peel off seal and Place inside...

How to validate your
Editor's FREE GIFT "Thank You"

1. Peel off gift seal from front cover. Place it in space provided at right. This automatically entitles you to receive 2 FREE BOOKS and a fabulous mystery gift.

2. Send back this card and you'll get 2 brand-new Harlequin Historicals® novels. These books have a cover price of $4.99 each in the U.S. and $5.99 each in Canada, but they are yours to keep absolutely free.

3. There's no catch. You're under no obligation to buy anything. We charge nothing—ZERO—for your first shipment. And you don't have to make any minimum number of purchases—not even one!

4. The fact is, thousands of readers enjoy receiving their books by mail from the Harlequin Reader Service®. They enjoy the convenience of home delivery...they like getting the best new novels at discount prices BEFORE they're available in stores...and they love their *Heart to Heart* subscriber newsletter featuring author news, horoscopes, recipes, book reviews and much more!

5. We hope that after receiving your free books you'll want to remain a subscriber. But the choice is yours— to continue or cancel, any time at all! So why not take us up on our invitation, with no risk of any kind. You'll be glad you did!

6. Don't forget to detach your FREE BOOKMARK. And remember...just for validating your Editor's Free Gift Offer, we'll send you THREE gifts, *ABSOLUTELY FREE!*

GET A **FREE** MYSTERY GIFT...

YOURS FREE!

SURPRISE MYSTERY GIFT COULD BE YOURS _FREE_ AS A SPECIAL "THANK YOU" FROM THE EDITORS OF HARLEQUIN

Visit us online at
www.eHarlequin.com

A breeze rippled along the surface of the moat and shivered down Alicia's spine. Savannah had now gone into her stall and Alicia could hear the groom talking softly to her as he rubbed her down. The shadows were lengthening in the courtyard and the air was cold. In the slowly gathering dusk the ancient house looked less approachable.

So there it was. James wished to speak with her and was prepared to follow the unconventional route of holding her against her will in order to achieve his aim. This was presumably the cue for any gently bred lady to faint or have hysterics, Alicia reflected. Being held hostage might seem appalling to some and romantic to others, but Alicia was not a reader of Mrs Radcliffe's gothic novels and doubted prosaically that she was in any serious danger. Clearly, all James wanted was information, not to force his attentions upon her.

Alicia abandoned the idea of creating an awkward scene. On a practical note, she was fairly certain that James would only throw cold water over her if she had a fit of the vapours.

She stole a glance at his profile and sighed inwardly. Beneath the tan his face was set in hard, uncompromising lines which did little to reassure her that the coming interview would be a pleasant one. She took a deep breath. She might as well make one last attempt to persuade him of the impropriety of his actions. They were crossing the gravel towards the oaken front door now, and Alicia stopped again. James slanted a look down at her, but did not release her arm.

'Whenever we have met, my lord, you have made me well aware that you disapprove of my flouting of convention,' Alicia observed quietly, tilting her head to look up at him properly. 'It therefore seems strange that you should be breaking with propriety yourself in behaving like this.'

'That's true.' James appeared to give the statement serious consideration and now sounded infuriatingly reasonable. 'I accept that word of any meeting between the two of us here would damn for-ever your hopes of overriding the previous scandal. However, I want to talk to you, so you will stay and hear me out.' He gave her a thoroughly unnerving smile. 'You think me high-handed, no doubt. Well, so I am, but there is not a great deal that you can do about it. A novel situation for the self-sufficient Lady Carberry, I suspect.'

Alicia gave up. She was not going to give him the satisfaction of retaliating in any way. She made the tacit admission to herself that she was as much his prisoner as his guest, and steadfastly refused to think about what her grandmother might say if news of this latest escapade reached her ears. She would worry about that later; just now she needed her wits about her to deal with whatever it was James intended to say to her.

James was waiting with scrupulous courtesy to allow Alicia to precede him into the house, and after a moment she stepped over the threshold and found herself in a dark, stone-flagged hallway. The ceilings were low above walls of beautifully moulded plaster, with heraldic devices entwined with flower designs and mythical beasts. There were fresh flowers on the highly polished table and the scent of beeswax in the air. It was both charming and welcoming. Alicia forgot both her hostility and her embarrassment, and gazed about her, captivated. James gestured to a door at the end of the passage.

'Will you step into the Hall?'

The Great Hall, with its huge, dominating stone fireplace and minstrel's gallery, appeared little altered from its original style. It was a coldly impressive, baronial room, the only concession to modernity being the long windows which looked out across a terrace to the moat and the woodland beyond. A suitably large fire was burning in the grate, but made little impression on the chill air. Alicia shivered. Even the pools of light cast by the multitude of candles appeared cold, and the shadows beyond the light were deep. There was something awesome about such splendour, but it was chilling too.

In such a setting James Mullineaux seemed peculiarly at home. On the walls were the pictures of his ancestors—Sir James Mullineaux, who had been an Elizabethan privateer and had bought Monks Dacorum and a peerage from the Crown with the ill-gotten gains of piracy; the fourth Baron Mullineaux, who had been a rake and a gambler, and a close friend of Charles II; the sixth Baron, an astute politician who had been granted the Marquisate for services to the Crown, followed later by the Dukedom of Cardace to crown his glittering career. The dark, patrician countenances all showed the same elements of danger and excitement; the watchful eyes held a gleam both wild and calculating. James, in the casual hunting jacket that so became his lithe physique, was the epitome of the reckless attraction that had been the hallmark of the Mullineaux family down the centuries.

Alicia allowed her gaze to travel to the opposite wall, where the ladies who had married into the Mullineaux dynasty looked down with a painted disdain that matched that of their menfolk. There was more variety here in terms of appearance and expression, but all had one characteristic in common, and that was a determined look which suggested that they had no intention of letting this parade of charismatic manhood overawe them. Alicia smiled despite herself. The Lady Henrietta, who had almost single-handedly defended the Oxfordshire estates against Cromwell's men, looked to have been a fearsome battleaxe, and even Lady Rose, James's famously sweet and beautiful mother, had a set to her chin which suggested that she would take no nonsense no matter how amiable her reputation.

Alicia turned impulsively to James, whose unreadable gaze had never left her face as she'd assimilated her surroundings.

'In truth, it is very imposing, my lord, but rather cold! Surely you must find such grandeur a little lonely on a day-to-day basis?'

James smiled, and the change was remarkable. For a moment the bitter lines were smoothed away and it was like coming face to face with the young James Mullineaux, beloved of the matchmaking mamas. Alicia's heart did not simply skip a beat, it did a somersault. The illusion lasted only a moment, however, before the shutters came down again.

'Indeed I do,' James was saying, 'but it seems peculiarly appropriate for this evening. You will, I hope, honour me by staying to dine?'

His tone was wholly courteous, but it was hardly a question, more a statement. Alicia hesitated. She could scarcely send a messenger to Chartley with the news that she was dining alone with the Marquis of Mullineaux; that would fan the flames of gossip to a positive bonfire. On the other hand, if she did not send word, her grandmother for one might be unnecessarily worried. She bit her lip.

'Thank you, Lord Mullineaux, but I must return to Chartley soon. I have guests, and they will become concerned if I am missing for any length of time...'

Her voice trailed away as she saw his ironic smile.

'No doubt you thought of that before you chose to go riding alone? Tell me, Lady Carberry, do you always do exactly as you please?'

Alicia's eyes widened. Here he was again, watching her with the critical amusement one might show to a spoiled child! She felt her simmering resentment rising, but before she had framed a suitably crushing reply he had turned away.

'Never fear, I will arrange for Lady Stansfield to be sent an appropriately reassuring message! And I will see you safely escorted back to Chartley—after dinner. Now, will you not take a seat?'

Rude, arrogant, high-handed... Alicia ran out of mental epithets, and, rather to her surprise, found herself already installed in a high-backed chair before the huge fireplace. James poured two glasses of wine and passed one to her gravely. Their fingers touched and Alicia felt her pulse rate increase. Tearing her gaze away from him, she chided herself for being a fool. It was intolerable to want to be free of the spell he had cast on her, but to find herself welcoming his touch with a shiver that owed nothing at all to revulsion. She had no control at all over her wayward response to him.

'So you did not know that I was still here?' James asked. Sitting opposite her with his long legs crossed negligently at the ankle, he looked both relaxed and watchful at the same time.

'No, I did not!' Alicia blushed at the possibility of him thinking she had intended to meet him. 'It was not my intention to seek you out, my lord!' Her tone implied that nothing on earth would have induced her to go to Monks Dacorum knowing he was at home, and she saw him smile as the point went home. 'I set out for a ride with no fixed intent, and when I reached the gates here I thought to take a look at the house. I know it was an unpardonable intrusion, but I scarcely expected—'

'That the price of curiosity would be so high?' James finished for her, very dryly.

Alicia kept a tight grip on her temper. Her well-known cool serenity was under severe attack and was all but lost. 'You are severe, sir. I have already apologised *several times!*'

James smiled slightly. 'Yes, I suppose it was unhandsome of me. And in fact your coming here is very convenient—I had been hoping for the opportunity to speak with you privately and could not have contrived a better one than this.'

Alicia's nerves tightened. She did not speak, not wanting to pre-empt anything he might say. She waited for him to explain, but James did not continue immediately; he got to his feet and placed another couple of oak logs on the fire, settling the remaining wood with his booted foot. The logs split apart, the fire jetting up to illuminate his intent features, the dark eyes which held no warmth for her any more. His expression was sombre.

'When we met last month at Ottery, I thought myself the unluckiest man alive to have been obliged to meet with you so soon after returning to this country. I had wanted to put the past behind me and think on it no more. I certainly thought that we two had no more to say to each other.' He drove his hands deep into his pockets. 'Yet now I find that I cannot simply forget it. In order to be free of the past I must know the truth of what happened and I think that at the very least you owe me an explanation.'

He finished and simply stood looking at her.

Alicia found herself to be struggling with a cocktail of emotions. Part of her was not surprised by the sudden demand, since she had suspected that that might be what he wished to discuss with her. However, she was shocked and resentful at the abrupt way in which he had spoken, and beneath her anger ran the undercurrent of pain which was always there when she remembered the events leading up to their separation. He had implied that she owed him an apology, and, whereas before she would have given anything for the chance to explain it all to him, now she felt that she could not bear to expose so harrowing a tale to his critical analysis. Instinct and reality were at war again; intuition was telling her that this was the same man she had loved so much before, but reality was showing him to be a stranger to her. She found that she was shaking her head, retreating for defence behind a determination to say nothing.

'I regret, Lord Mullineaux, that I cannot offer you the explanation you seek.'

James's voice was expressionless. 'Caroline and Marcus both spoke for you. They implied that I had misjudged you in thinking you a common jilt or, if you prefer, a fortune-hunter. I was prepared to be persuaded, but only you could tell me the truth. As you are declining to do so, I can only assume that my original assumption was correct.'

'You have no right to ask for an explanation now, Lord Mullineaux.' It was only when Alicia tried to speak that she realised how upset she was, for it was almost impossible to frame the words without crying. 'The time for explanations was seven years ago, but you had so little faith that you did not wait for one. You have made some unforgivable, arrogant assumptions and I will not correct them just for your gratification!'

James's gaze had narrowed on her in disbelief. Alicia's green eyes were very bright with both defiance and tears, but he was in no mood to compromise or defer to her feelings. He had become obsessed with knowing the truth. Each time he saw Alicia his obsession worsened because he could not equate his opinion of her with what was before his eyes. The doubts which Marcus had planted in his mind nagged him and gave him no peace. Everywhere he went people spoke of Alicia in terms of the highest regard. She was the only person who could tell him the truth about the past and she was refusing to do so.

He crossed to her side in two strides and stood towering over her. Once again, as at Ottery, fury and frustration consumed him. She was so stubborn he could have shaken her. His fingers closed hard around her wrist and jerked her to her feet. The small table at Alicia's side toppled over with a clatter, cascading the glass of wine onto the flagstone floor in a ruby waterfall. The glass miraculously did not break, but rolled away to hit the hearth with a gentle click. Neither of them paid the slightest attention.

'So you think that I misjudged you seven years ago,' James ground out, 'and as a result you will behave like the spoilt child you are! Well, I thank you for your good opinion, madam! It's fortunate we were spared the chance of ever marrying—no doubt time would have proved it to be a disastrous mistake!'

Alicia itched to slap his face, but he was holding her too tightly and too close to him. It was impossible to speak with any dignity, but at least she was now wholly angry where before she had been upset. She glared up into the furious dark eyes only inches from her own.

'Oh, no, my lord, it is you who are spoilt and selfish! Just because you wish to know a thing, you care not how much pain you occasion others! This is hardly the first time I have had to endure your strictures on my character—from allegations of wilfulness to the indictment that I married for a fortune! You have insulted me in every way conceivable and now I can only suggest you let me go!'

She barely had time to draw breath before he wrenched her into his arms. It bore no resemblance to any embrace Alicia had experienced before; not even the most ardent of her admirers had treated her so, and James himself had always exercised considerable restraint in his dealings with her as an inexperienced girl of nineteen. But now he held her ruthlessly whilst his mouth moved over hers, the pressure forcing her lips to part. The intensity of the kiss did not ease even for a moment and Alicia was lost almost from the start. Even had she wished to escape, she could not have done so. The arms which held her seemed made of steel. Though she knew he had only kissed her out of anger and frustration, she found herself adrift on a sea of sensation, careless of thought, responding to him with a lack of restraint which she was powerless to prevent. Her senses had been starved of emotion for so long that her nerve-endings felt as though they were on fire. His mouth became more insistent, deepening the kiss still further, and she was achingly aware of every taut line of his body against hers. Then, as she was about to abandon thought completely, a small corner of her mind whispered that he did not care about her, did not trust her, and certainly did not love her as she still loved him.

It was like being doused by a bucket of cold water. Alicia tore herself from his grip and would have fallen had James not caught her elbow to steady her. She did not stop to think, but turned on her heel and made straight for the door with no clear idea of where she was going. James caught up with her as she reached for the latch and put his hand over hers to stop her.

'Please, Alicia...' His breathing was still uneven, but there was an urgent note in his voice. 'Please don't run away. I'm sorry. I know I've treated you unforgivably, but please give me a chance to explain.'

The heavy iron latch was cool under Alicia's fingers, but somehow it seemed too much of an effort to lift it. She felt dizzy and confused, hearing her own voice as though from a great distance.

'But I don't think I want to talk to you any more, Lord Mullineaux...I think it's a little too late for that...'

Alicia could feel the tears slipping down her cheeks and made no effort to stop them. She tried to dash them away with her hand, but they just fell all the faster. The room was blurring at the edges, and suddenly she was grateful for the dark because she was so tired. So tired, but there was no need to think any more—no need to do anything at all. She closed her eyes.

James caught her before she fainted, and carried her over to the chaise longue in an alcove by the side of the fire. Alicia had already started to stir by the time he put her down and for a moment she lay quite still, obscurely at peace. The only sound was the crackle of the fire, and the distant clatter of pans in the kitchen. Her eyes were closed, but her other senses seemed heightened. She could feel the thick velvet of the chair beneath her fingers, the softness of the cushion beneath her head, and she could smell the most wonderful aroma of food cooking.

Alicia turned her head slowly and opened her eyes with extreme reluctance. It was dark outside now, and the Hall looked even more austere with its stone-flagged floor and high ceiling wreathed in shadow. There was a step beside her, and James appeared, a glass of water in his hand. He helped her to sit upright and passed her the glass without comment, but when he saw that she was still shaking his hand closed around hers to steady it and raise the glass to her lips.

'Dinner is ready,' he observed quietly. 'You will feel much better once you have had something to eat.'

At that moment a maid appeared and started to set the long trencher table with silver and sparkling glass. James helped Alicia to her feet and escorted her over to the table with grave courtesy. She felt as though she was floating, too tired to resist or even think. Nor did James himself appear inclined to break the silence between them. Alicia could feel his reflective gaze resting on her, but she did not look at him, or speak.

The food was simple, consisting of a delicious home-made soup of winter vegetables, followed by a side of beef and finally apple pie and cream. However, it tasted as good as anything Alicia had ever eaten and she was surprised to find that she was ravenously hungry. After a while, her composure returning, she became more and more sharply aware of the man opposite her.

James looked up and met her gaze, and her heart jolted once, uncomfortably, as she saw the unhappiness reflected in those dark eyes. At once, as though avoiding any subject which might prove too emotive, he began to speak of his growing interest in the estate and to ask Alicia's opinion on several local issues. She answered his questions on everything from cider production to the village school with a clear interest and knowledge that intrigued and amused him.

'You evidently spend a great deal of your time at Chartley,' James observed casually, refilling their wineglasses. 'Do you prefer it to London? And do you have time to visit your other properties at all?'

Alicia considered. 'I usually spend the Season in London, and that's quite enjoyable. But—' she met his eyes squarely '—I love Chartley and the peace I find here. I have a house by the sea at Scarborough which I'll visit sometimes in the summer, but most of the other properties are let on a long-term basis.'

'To orphanages and other charitable institutions, often at a peppercorn rent, so I have heard.' James raised one black eyebrow. 'You may undertake your transactions through paid agents, my lady, but it is not so difficult to trace them back to you if one tries.'

Alicia looked at him reflectively. It was odd, she thought, how all constraint between them seemed suddenly to have vanished. It was as though they had passed the restrictions usually imposed by convention and could say anything to each other. So she had felt at nineteen, discovering with James Mullineaux an affinity that had been both comforting and exciting. They had been kindred spirits and had immediately recognised each other as such. Now, suddenly, that bond had reasserted itself, regardless of what lay between them, drawing them as close as they had been seven years before. It felt both stimulating and dangerous.

The candlelit room had an odd intimacy about it for so large a space and despite all that had happened Alicia knew suddenly that she would never be able to escape this feeling. She could refuse to discuss the past, she could claim never to want to see him again, but she would be lying and the awareness between them, which had flared into such explosive life earlier in the evening, could never be denied.

'You seem very well acquainted with my business, sir,' Alicia commented mildly. 'What else do you know? And why should you have troubled to discover so much?'

James smiled straight into her eyes. 'Because I wanted to know the truth about you,' he said, with shattering directness. 'You wrote me a letter in which you condemned yourself as an adventuress and at the time I was prepared to believe in your duplicity. I was young and very proud, after all.' He tilted the liquid in his glass, watching the firelight warm the rich ruby wine. 'What I said earlier was also true. I had considered the matter closed until I came back and met you again. Then I realised that you were not the caricature fortune-hunter I had built up in my mind, but I refused to accept the evidence of my own intuition. I spoke to Caroline and Marcus, and to the people here at Monks Dacorum, and they all spoke of your warmth and your kindness and your generosity—and I could not make the picture fit with my opinion of you.'

Alicia's gaze dropped before that intense regard, and after a moment James resumed.

'So the only thing I could do was to ask you directly. But, of course, I did it all wrong, because the gulf between the two of us was still so great that I could not bridge it. Now I will not press you for an explanation if you do not wish to give one.

'But, to answer your first question, I know that you have vast quantities of money tied up in charitable trusts, making more money for your beneficiaries. I know that you have invested heavily in local commerce and have opened schools and hospitals. And I must thank you for your care of my tenants while I have been away.'

Alicia had regained a measure of composure by now, and raised a hand in laughing protest. 'Enough, sir! You make me sound like a philanthropist!'

'Why, so you are!' James looked solemn. 'Why deny it?'

'Because I have a horror of being given credit for what I have done,' Alicia answered seriously. 'Unfortunately,' she added, a little sadly, 'the more schemes I think up to get rid of the money usefully, the more money it seems to generate!'

James burst out laughing. 'Vast fortunes have a habit of doing that, so I have heard! But why do you not wish to be thanked for the uses to which you have put your money?'

There was a silence. 'George Carberry's fortune was made by various dubious means, few of them legal,' Alicia observed at length, staring beyond James into the shadows. 'I wanted nothing to do with it and it should never have been mine. The only thing I could think of was to turn it to good—which I have tried to do.'

Their eyes met for a moment of tension. James sat forward, his gaze suddenly intent.

'Alicia, I know I said I would not press you for an explanation, but will you tell me what happened?'

Alicia looked at him for what seemed for ever, then she gave him a shaky smile.

'Very well, my lord. You will have your story.'

Chapter Seven

The study where previously James had entertained Caroline and Marcus Kilgaren was a small oasis of warmth and quiet, more intimate than the Great Hall, a place designed for confidences. It was lined on three sides with the bookshelves where reposed dusty tomes collected by generations of the Mullineaux family, some pristine and uncut, others whose well-worn covers bore testimony to their popularity. Once again, Alicia looked around her with interest. The furnishings were old and tattered, but had a comfortable quality that more than compensated for their threadbare appearance. It was a friendly house, Alicia thought, still showing the touch of Lady Rose, who had had the decorating of it thirty-five years ago when she had been a bride. Yet it was not just the outward appearance that was so welcoming; deeper than that was an atmosphere of warmth, of reassurance. Alicia shivered. She would need all that and more to help her tell her story.

Another exquisite plaster ceiling displayed the arms and devices of the Mullineaux family and those with whom they had intermarried. The only light came from the fire, which the servants had built up during dinner, and from one lamp which cast a golden glow in a corner of the room. In front of the fire was sprawled a very small black and white puppy. Alicia, recognising one of the Monks Farm litter, smiled to herself. The room was very quiet. The servants had seen to it that James and his guest had everything they needed, then they had slipped discreetly away, leaving the two in silence.

James could sense Alicia's tension as she sat uncomfortably on the edge of the chair Caroline had occupied the previous week. The food and wine had revived her colour and animation, but there was a wary look in her eyes as though she had already regressed some way into the past and was thinking on the events of seven years previously. She watched silently as he poured himself a glass of port and took the seat opposite her. She had declined any more wine, requesting a dish of tea, which sat prosaically on the table in front of her.

After a moment Alicia made a little gesture, almost of defeat.

'Well, I promised you the story, my lord, so I shall keep my word. First, however, I should tell you that no one else knows this, except my grandmother. I can only beg you to repay me by relating it to no one.'

James inclined his head. 'You have my word. But may I also know why you chose never to tell anybody else?'

Alicia smiled, a little grimly. 'When you hear the tale, sir, I doubt you will need an answer to that. Firstly, it was too...' she paused, searching for the right word '...too personal for me to tell. I did not wish to make an avid Society free with the details. And the scandal at the time was dreadful enough without my fuelling it further. I suspect— no, I know—that it would have been even worse had I chosen to make people aware of the true facts.'

She took a sip of tea, welcoming the comforting warmth.

'From something you said earlier, my lord, I imagine that Caroline and Marcus must have guessed at a version of events which may be close to the truth, but few people ever realised... Most drew their own conclusions—the most shocking, the most scandalous ones they could think of.'

James did not comment. He had, after all, been one of those very people. Now he had the opportunity to judge for himself. He never doubted for a moment that Alicia would tell him the truth—there was a brittle tautness about her which demonstrated all too clearly the profound effect that the subject still had on her. No, she would be telling him the truth and it would be at great personal cost. He watched her try to settle herself more comfortably in the chair. Her stress and reluctance to speak were almost a tangible thing, and James felt his own tension growing as a result.

'I suppose I must start with the day my father came up to Town,' Alicia said reflectively. 'You may recall that I had not mentioned beforehand that he was visiting, for I was unaware he even planned to open up the house in Bruton Street. I was very surprised to receive a message from him, but I was not suspicious in any way.' She shrugged.

'Why should I have been, after all? He asked me to call there, so, of course, I went.'

She looked thoughtfully. 'We had never been close, he and I — you may remember that I once told you how distant he had been as a father, wrapped up in his business affairs. Even so, I was a dutiful daughter. God help me, I even imagined that his arrival might herald a reconciliation between himself and my grandmother, and that the family might be whole once again.'

A log fell in the grate with a soft hiss and Alicia looked up to meet James's absorbed gaze.

'It was not as I had presumed,' she said shortly. 'Naturally not. The butler showed me into my father's study and there I was acquainted with his plans for my future.'

Alicia shivered as she remembered the obsequious Castle with his black button eyes. Pausing, she took another drink of tea and put both hands around the cup for reassurance. James had still not said a word but his gaze did not once falter from her face.

'He told me that he had arranged a match for me with George Carberry,' Alicia resumed. 'Carberry himself was there, in fact, and the pair of them were in fine fig with all their plans. I was slow to understand what they were trying to tell me, for first I had to appreciate the enormity of my father's scheming. Once I had grasped that, though, I put up strong resistance. I told them that a marriage between myself and Carberry was out of the question for I was already promised to you, and you would be asking my father for permission to marry me as soon as you knew he was in Town.'

Her voice was colourless. 'They both seemed to find that most amusing. My father asked scornfully what possible benefit such a match could bring him. He was adamant. And when I refused again Castle, the butler, came in and hustled me upstairs in less time than it takes to relate. I was locked in a bedroom for two days without food before they tried to persuade me again.'

There was a distant, inward-looking expression on Alicia's face, for she had become completely wrapped up in the past. She did not even look at James—it was as if he were only there by coincidence rather than as the reason for her to be telling the tale. She stared past him into the shadows, and her face was as remote and beautiful as a porcelain sculpture, but equally cold.

'When they chose, I was taken back downstairs and once again both of them were there with their proposals. Carberry called me a foolish child for still obstinately holding out against them. He said that you had repudiated me and that stories were flying round the clubs that I was nothing more than a jilt and a fortune-hunter. He told me all the names they were calling me. My father said that Society had finished with me and that I had best just accept it.'

Alicia stopped. She had said nothing of her confusion and loneliness, the feeling of terrible isolation, the despair of being hopelessly trapped, but it was all there in the tone of her voice. James could hear it all, see her expression as she remembered how she had felt, and imagine the feelings of a girl whose sheltered and privileged upbringing had scarcely prepared her for coping with such a shock. Alicia had been strong, or she would have capitulated long before; perhaps it would have been better for her if she had done so.

Alicia looked up suddenly at James, and her gaze refocused on him abruptly. He was sitting, head bent, watching the liquid swirling in his glass, and the increasingly grim set to his mouth was the only outward sign that he had heard her words. His very stillness was frightening to her for she could not interpret it. She hurried on.

'I still refused to accept Carberry's proposal. My father tried very hard to persuade me, but to me it would have been betraying you to agree. He blustered and threatened me, and finally he had me beaten for my disobedience.'

James drained his glass in one mouthful and reached for the decanter. 'Go on,' he said curtly.

'That night...' Alicia paused. Her green eyes mirrored shocking disillusion and pain. 'Forgive me, my lord; some things are not easy to tell. That night my father hosted a party for his cronies. I will spare you the details, but there was much heavy drinking and "entertainment", and towards the end of the evening George Carberry decided that he would like to take a look at his latest business acquisition—myself. I was dragged from my bed and taken downstairs.'

James got to his feet, as though better to bear whatever she was about to say. Looking at Alicia, he saw that her expression was once again quite blank. She had laced her fingers together to prevent them from shaking and the knuckles showed white with the pressure.

'It was not so bad, I suppose,' she said deliberately, meeting his gaze directly. 'Now I realise how much worse it could have been, but for a girl brought up as I had been, in so sheltered an environment, the humiliation of being paraded half-naked before such a drunken company, the humiliating looks and comments... Well, the shock was terrible for me. I imagine that my father believed that the shame and horror of it all would convince me that I was ruined and had no choice but to marry. But still he took no risks.

'The following morning, a maid brought me the first proper food and drink I had had for a week. Like a fool, I ate it all. I remember nothing of the next day—I do not even know how the day—or days—passed. The food must have been laced with a sleeping-draught, but I never imagined... Anyway, when I awoke, my father produced his final ultimatum.'

Her voice was now so quiet that James had to strain to hear her words, but when she looked up her gaze was full of emotion.

'He told me that if I did not agree to marry Carberry he would ruin you, destroy you.' She shrugged dismissively. 'In retrospect I wonder if he could have carried out such a threat. Perhaps so; perhaps not. At the time I was hardly in a fit state to think at all, but I would not have taken that risk anyway. So I agreed. God help me, of course I agreed.'

It was all far worse than James had even imagined. Although close to Marcus's version of events, told by Alicia in such factual terms it somehow became even more chilling. She had not tried to invest the words with any particular feeling, but her sense of desperation and hopelessness had come over strongly. James found that his anger and pity were so great that he could not speak and had to clear his throat first.

'I did not know...I had no idea.' He tried to think about it rationally, but found that he could not even begin to do so. It was too sudden and involved too much reappraisal to be dealt with easily. His mind was spinning, but overriding all else was an intense, impotent anger at what they had done to her—and a disgust with himself for believing her false when she had suffered all this for him.

'How could anyone do such a thing?' he finally burst out, with all the suppressed violence he would have liked to wreak out on Broseley himself. 'God damn him to hell, I could kill him myself.'

Alicia almost laughed. 'Locking up recalcitrant daughters to encourage them to marry their parents' choice is hardly a new concept,' she pointed out, in another unconscious echo of Marcus Kilgaren's observations. 'Many a young lady has changed her mind about a prospective suitor when under duress! In my case the duress was particularly severe and the suitor particularly unpleasant, but that is the only real difference!'

James was shaking his head in disbelief. 'You can say that? After everything that they did...! And so you married him. Of course you did! What choice did you have?' He brought his fist down on the mantelpiece with a violence that made the whole structure shiver. 'I wish...I just wish that I had known the truth!'

Alicia said nothing. No platitudes would make it any better. James was experiencing one small part of the anger, misery and shock that had been hers so long ago. After a moment he turned back to her, a question in his eyes.

'Did he tell you—did your father ever tell you that I went to Bruton Street to find out what had happened to you?' he demanded.

Alicia did not look surprised. A smile that could have been ironic touched her mouth fleetingly and was gone. 'No, he did not. But at Annabella's wedding, when you said you had met him, I realised... What did he say to you?'

James drove his hands forcibly into his pockets as though to restrain them from violence. 'For several days he would not receive me, although that thug of a butler gave me a message to the effect that you had gone to your father of your own free will. He implied that you had no wish to marry me and felt forced into it by Lady Stansfield. I flatly refused to believe him and went back every day demanding to see your father. The stories to which you referred earlier started to circulate in the clubs, but I tried to ignore them and finally Broseley granted me an interview—' He broke off, staring into the fire with a black frown on his forehead.

'I was almost demented with worry by that time. But if I had known—' He broke off again, then resumed. 'Anyway, when I saw him, your father confirmed that the stories were true and that you were marrying George Carberry. He said some terrible things.' James's dark gaze rested on Alicia thoughtfully. 'He implied that you were marrying for money, a course of action of which he thoroughly approved. Finally, he gave me the letter you had signed. You did sign it, didn't you, Alicia?'

'Yes.' Once again Alicia's voice was devoid of all expression. 'It was when he threatened to ruin you that he gave me the letter to sign. I did not even read it, I'm afraid. I just...put my name to it, whatever it might have said. Was it very bad?'

'Just bad enough to convince me that you meant it,' James said grimly. 'I realise now that my judgement was seriously flawed, but I was in such a state of tension that it seems understandable, if not forgivable, that I misjudged you so. I am so very sorry that I ever believed it, Alicia...'

He could read nothing but sadness in her face. 'I am sorry too,' she said slowly. 'For all that happened. But it is done with now.'

'But what of the rest?' James ran a hand through his hair. He paced over to the French window as though he was unable to keep still. 'You must finish the story.'

'There is little more to tell.' Alicia sighed. 'I married Carberry and we returned to my father's house. There was much carousing on the part of my father's friends and creative suggestions for the wedding night... Carberry died that night,' Alicia said deliberately. 'He was puce with drink, excitement and excess, and he died before my eyes. Better for me, perhaps, that he had been drunk—too drunk at any rate to consummate his marriage!

'I roused a servant to go for a physician—a reputable doctor who had attended my grandmother. He almost refused to come to such a house, but in the end he agreed, though there was nothing that could be done for Carberry anyway. My father was drunk in the arms of a maidservant, and so I took my chance and ran away. I ran all the way back to my grandmother's house, desperately hoping that she would take me in.' She paused, remembering with what trepidation she had hammered on the door of the darkened house. 'And when I arrived she was there, and I was safe at last. I think I must have lost consciousness—I believe Caroline came to see me, but I remember nothing of it, and it was a long time before I recovered enough to ask about you, and then my grandmother told me that you had gone abroad. I remember little after that, but I think I was ill for a very long time...'

A stray breath of wind set the candle flames dancing. James watched as the tears gathered with dazzling brilliance in Alicia's eyes. She cried soundlessly, but all the more poignantly for that, finding to her horror that once she had started she seemed unable to stop. It was relief, not misery that prompted her tears, for after so long a silence she could hardly believe that she had been able to tell James the truth. The relief of knowing that he believed her was overwhelming, and he had not turned from her in disgust—not yet...

It was only when the storm of her tears had begun to subside that Alicia realised that James had crossed the room to her side and had gathered her into his arms without a word. Her head was resting most comfortably on his shoulder and he was stroking her hair gently as he murmured soothing endearments. She felt warm and secure, and it was entirely delightful. This discovery was such a surprise that she stopped crying in order to think about it, then immediately realised the impropriety of their situation. She drew back with a small hiccuping laugh, for was it not a little late to be considering propriety?

James let her go without haste and handed her his handkerchief.

'I do apologise,' Alicia said unsteadily. 'I have ruined your jacket, my lord.'

'It does not matter.' She could hear the warmth in his voice although she found she could not look at him. 'I am not such a slave to my tailor as I used to be!'

His face was in shadow. 'I am only so very sorry that I ever believed ill of you, Alicia,' he said sombrely. 'I have treated you with the most appalling discourtesy and can only beg your pardon. When I think what you had to endure... The whole experience must have been quite dreadful for you, and then I had the insufferable arrogance to consider myself the injured party!'

He turned away, still driven by the oppressive fury he wanted to unleash on Broseley and Carberry. Well, Carberry was beyond his reach now, but Broseley... He would make him pay for everything that Alicia had suffered, but even then it would not be enough to compensate—it could never put things right for her. He tried to imagine how a young and gently bred girl would feel when confronted with the unbridled lust of a gross libertine such as George Carberry, and groaned aloud with despair. Such things were beyond his imagination. A moment later he was overcome with the most hopeless guilt at his failure to save her and was so ashamed that he could hardly look at her.

Alicia was trying to regain a little composure. She felt completely incapable of talking any more, or even thinking beyond the superficial, but seeing James's agony she managed a watery smile. 'You were not to know, my lord! And even if you had done, how could you have helped me? No one could intervene—not you, not my grandmother, nobody! It is best forgotten now for, believe me, I have learned to live with it in the intervening years. I am just grateful that we have had the opportunity to put matters to rights between us, even if it is a little late in the day.'

She tried for a lighter note. 'At least I shall now have no fear that we shall spend the Season avoiding each other—or cutting each other dead! No, we may be comfortable, you and I, knowing that the past is laid to rest and we are free of it.'

It was only what James himself had said earlier, but now it rang a little hollow. Now that she had got over her immediate relief at telling him the truth, Alicia found the prospect of a future of mild friendship with James almost as intolerable as their previous antipathy had been. The relationship between them had always been characterised by intense emotion—first love then hatred—but it had never been one of bland insipidity and she could not bear to think of it degenerating into that now. However, she had no way of knowing how James would feel once he had had time to assimilate her story. It was hardly an edifying tale, and she could not blame him if he never wanted to think of it again.

Neither did James himself seem much taken by her words for he did not smile. Watching her in the glow from the firelight, he was suddenly aware of an extraordinary shift in perspective. It was as if for the previous seven years he had lived with all his beliefs and values displaced. Now, suddenly and shockingly, they had shifted back like the changing colours of a kaleidoscope, abruptly forming the most perfect and brilliant pattern. The thread of affinity stretched between them once more, both precious and amazingly strong. He could not tear his gaze away from her.

The intensity of his regard disturbed Alicia. She felt completely exhausted from the effort of reliving the experience and suddenly ill-equipped to deal with her thoughts on the future. She was glad when the clock on the mantelpiece chimed the hour and broke the moment.

'Eight o'clock! I really must go before my grandmother has roused the whole county to look for me!'

'I sent a message before dinner,' James replied, with a smile. 'Your mare has thrown a shoe and you have been staying at the blacksmith's whilst the damage is repaired. They have given you some supper and you will be on your way home shortly!'

'I see!' Alicia smiled mischievously. 'He will gain a reputation as a remarkably slow worker! It can only have been three o'clock when I set out!'

'Yes, indeed... Alicia, before you go, there is something I should like to show you...'

James had moved back to the French windows which, like those of the Great Hall, gave onto the terrace at the back of the house. The latch was stiff and squeaky from disuse, but it lifted with only slight resistance and the door opened silently. The fire guttered and roared as the cold night air flooded in, then James stood aside to let Alicia pass and they were outside with the door closed behind them.

Alicia shivered in the cold air, but after the emotional scene in the study it acted like a tonic and helped to clear her head. Here at the back of the house the ivy grew thickly over the mellow stonework and tumbled down over the lichened terrace towards the sweep of grass above the moat. The air was filled with the scent of cypress and the sky was clear. The lamplit room behind them seemed suddenly distant. Alicia turned questioningly to James.

'Wait...' His voice was barely above a murmur. 'The moon is rising behind the hill. In a moment—'

He broke off as the moon topped the hill, pouring its light pure and clear along the water of the moat and turning its path to rippling silver. The night was suddenly alive, the shapes of the trees cut as sharply as sentinels, the gardens mercilessly exposed in the bright white light. As though on cue, a barn owl slid like a shadow from the trees, hunting along the edge of the moat before disappearing into the dark.

It had been a mistake to go out into the darkness. As Alicia moved forward to the balustrade at the front of the terrace, James put his hand on the parapet, barring her way. It was too dark to see his face, but she was acutely aware of his tall figure beside her, his proximity infinitely disturbing to her senses.

'Alicia...' She read the warning note in his voice a second too late, for he was already drawing her gently into his arms. This time was very different from before: his mouth moved softly, persuasively, over hers, keeping a tight control as the kiss became more searching. It teased and provoked her until the slow-burning in Alicia's blood threatened to overwhelm her defences completely.

She arched her body against his, running her fingers into the thick black hair so that she could pull his mouth back down to hers when he would have drawn back. She wanted more, much more. James groaned. He could not resist.

He knew he ought to stop, that the onus had to be on him because Alicia was too inexperienced to understand what she was doing to him with her breathless endearments and soft gasps of pleasure. The trouble was that his inclination and his duty were diametrically opposed—and duty had never appealed to him very much as a concept anyway. He kissed her again lightly, first one corner of her mouth, then the opposite one, waiting until she caught her breath on a moan before he captured her lips fully once more and resumed the slow, exquisite exploration of a moment before.

Alicia did not care about anything at all, other than that James should carry on kissing her. She slid her hands beneath his jacket, luxuriating in the warmth she could feel emanating from the skin beneath his linen shirt. Her caress wrung a groan from him and he savagely forced her lips further apart, the skilful, sensuous demand of his tongue causing a flaming heat to wash through her in response. For a long, mindless interval they surrendered to their mutual need, locked in each other's arms.

When James's mouth finally, reluctantly, left Alicia's, it was only to renew its torment, tracing a burning line from the point of her jaw to the delicate curve above her collarbone. Alicia's head fell back in pleasure, the auburn hair spilling over his arm as James lowered his lips to the tantalising swell of her breasts which were barely revealed by the severely cut riding jacket.

Fortunately, from James's point of view, the drawback of the high neck was more than amply compensated for by the row of tiny buttons down the front of the jacket. These proved no hindrance to his experienced fingers, and in very little time he had undone enough to lay bare much more of the deliciously creamy skin beneath. He let his mouth drift teasingly over the curves he had exposed until Alicia dug her fingers into his back in an agony of wanting.

To play with fire... They were engulfed once again in the same searing tide of emotion that had threatened them earlier in the evening, only this time it was a thousand times more potent, releasing all tension between the two of them.

James found himself perilously close to losing all self-control. He made a desperate grasp for his sanity, turning his face against Alicia's hair and breathing hard. The faint, flowery perfume that clung to her skin was almost his undoing, and when she instinctively pressed closer to him he gave a groan and put her forcibly from him. He had miscalculated in thinking that he could dictate the situation. He wanted her so badly that the physical ache was almost intolerable and the inclination to abandon all rational thought was almost as strong. They could blot out all of the past seven years in an ecstasy that would bind them closer than ever...

And yet James knew that he could not do it. Alicia was in such a vulnerable state now that whatever happened between them at such a time might be bitterly regretted by her later. He suspected that he would be able to seduce her very easily now because the chemistry between the two of them was in danger of carrying them beyond the point of coherent thought. But it would be a mistake. Alicia had suffered enough as a result of the careless whims of men who had used her for advantage—he would not add himself to their number. Nor did he simply want to take her and dismiss her casually when the moment had passed. She affected him too profoundly for that.

Acting in such a responsible way was hardly his specialty, James reflected sardonically to himself as he leant both hands on the parapet and attempted to bring his wayward impulses firmly under control. Under normal circumstances there could only be one outcome to an encounter between himself and a young and beautiful widow—particularly when she was alone with him at one of his establishments. But Alicia had always been different. Cursing under his breath, he admitted to himself that, whilst his feelings for her were all too obvious on one level, they ran very deep on others.

He took her very firmly by the arm and steered her straight back into the house.

'One thing I cannot have on my conscience is the responsibility for you catching a chill!' There was an undertone of laughter in James's voice, though he still sounded shaken. 'And you were right, Alicia—you had better go now! I can't deny that I want you to stay with me, but it would not serve. God knows, I must be getting old! I never thought to find myself acting so much against my own inclinations!'

He scanned Alicia's face, upturned to his, and his gaze softened as he smiled. 'Damn it, Alicia, don't make it any more difficult for me! I'm hardly a candidate for sainthood as it is!'

It was a mild evening for March and Alicia had not felt the cold at all until James had let her go. Then, slowly, sanity had reasserted itself and with it a bereft chill that had made her shiver. More than anything in the world she wanted James to take her back in his arms and blot out the cold for ever. She stared up at him, watching as desire for her darkened his eyes again, and the moment hung in the balance. She knew she could make him change his mind, wanted to do it... Then she pulled herself together, picked up her cloak and turned towards the door.

She was still shaking with the effect James had on her as she walked out into the central courtyard. It would be easy now to forget everything, to persuade James to let her stay with him and damn the consequences. She knew instinctively that it would take very little coercion on her part to accomplish her own seduction, for she could feel the tension in him as tight as a coiled spring and knew he had only a perilously slender grip on his self-control. Alicia also knew that she should be shocked with herself for even contemplating such a course of action but there was no point in self-deception. If James had tried to seduce her she would not have resisted; she would have been glad. But then, what would have happened next?

Alicia gave up the unhappy tussle with her emotions and drew on all the cold practicality she could muster. Whatever happened between them in the future, for now she had to return to Chartley and dissemble her feelings for the benefit of her guests.

They reached the stables, where Ned was saddling up Savannah. James's own raking grey hunter was already saddled and chafing impatiently at the delay. Alicia turned to James with a smile.

'For the sake of my reputation, I think you must let Ned escort me back to Chartley and not do so yourself!'

She saw James frown and hesitate visibly before he nodded in reluctant agreement. He had to admit that any story that Alicia had spent her missing hours visiting innocuously in the village would be immediately discounted if he were seen in her company.

'Very well. It's not what I would choose, but you will be safe enough, and Ned will bring word when you are home.'

Savannah's hooves rang out on the cobbles and Ned swung himself up onto the other horse. James raised an eyebrow.

'Tempting fate, Ned? That horse is as recognisable as I am!'

Ned grinned. 'I won't let anyone see me, my lord! And he does need the exercise.'

James held Alicia's stirrup for her and straightened up, smiling at her.

'So it is farewell, then.' He touched her cheek, a fleeting contact which nevertheless felt as though it burned her. His gaze was serious though his eyes still had a smile in their depths.

'Take care, Alicia. I cannot begin to thank you...'

Alicia wheeled Savannah round and trotted briskly out of the courtyard, Ned at her side.

Back at Chartley Chase, her excuses and apologies were received with little curiosity. The expedition to Pilton had been a success and the visitors had returned only shortly before Alicia, having stayed to dine. Georgiana Stapleford in particular was in high spirits for a change, for she had enjoyed the undivided attentions of both Richard Pilton and Christopher Westwood. Only Caroline Kilgaren gave her friend a particularly piercing look as Alicia guilelessly related the tale of her fictitious, unscheduled stop at the blacksmith's.

It was old Amos, the head groom, who was the only one to know that the story was not true, and he would never say a word. In the first place, he had glimpsed briefly the prime piece of horseflesh which Ned had been riding as he had bidden goodbye to Alicia at the gates. Amos had worked at Monks Dacorum in the days of the old Marquis, knew James Mullineaux well, and also knew his excellent taste in horses.

In the second place, Savannah had been rubbed down and fed with a care that Amos respected. And she had not had a shoe replaced that day, or recently.

Amos grinned a little to himself as he put Savannah back in her stall. All the servants had heard of Lady Carberry's meeting with the Marquis of Mullineaux at Ottery and it had given rise to much speculation. Most of them had been present at the wassail and had wagered it would only be a matter of time before the Marquis and the lady met again. Then there was Christopher Westwood, whose suit had not prospered. Hardly surprising, Amos thought, when contrasted with such a man as James Mullineaux. For certainly Alicia Carberry had been at Monks Dacorum that evening, and the dreamy expression on her face when she had returned owed nothing to a visit to the blacksmith!

They met unexpectedly at church the following Sunday. Chartley Church still had a Mullineaux family pew from the time that the Chase had been part of the estate, but in recent years it had never been occupied. The sight of James Mullineaux in that pew for the morning service riveted the entire congregation to the extent that the finer points of the sermon were completely lost on them, and the vicar would have been furious had his unexpected parishioner been someone less august.

Alicia also found James's presence most distracting. She had not expected to see him again until the Season started and had tried to come to terms with the flat feeling which the thought had engendered. Despite the demands of her guests, she seemed to have spent a great deal of time thinking about the meeting at Monks Dacorum, and found that her feelings were in even more of a turmoil after the meeting than they had been before. Before, she had had nothing to hope for, and although this had been depressing it had at least been certain. Now she could not help the great number of unspecified thoughts and dreams which always centred in some way on James rediscovering the feelings he had previously held for her.

She stole a sideways look at him through her lashes and wondered what on earth he was doing there. There was something about his clear-cut silhouette which set her in mind of the alabaster profiles on the tombs of his ancestors, which decorated both this church and the one at Monks. Whilst many of the Mullineaux family had chosen to be buried at their main seat in Oxfordshire, there was plenty of evidence to suggest that earlier generations had liked Monks Dacorum sufficiently to live and die there.

Well, Alicia thought, she supposed that James could attend church wherever he wished and scolded herself for the presumption that he might have chosen to come to Chartley in order to see her. Certainly there was nothing in his bearing towards her that suggested it. They had exchanged the briefest of greetings when he had taken his seat, and he had not looked at her once since. She imagined that it was just his way of behaving as though nothing untoward had ever happened between them. Perhaps, she thought, he was already regretting what had happened.

The service over, James spent a considerable time chatting to the vicar at the church door whilst the more forward members of the congregation stood about with ill-concealed interest and waited to greet him. As soon as he was free, Caroline hailed him in her usual blunt manner.

'James! We thought you had already gone to Worcestershire!'

'I travel tomorrow.' James smiled impartially around the group, and Alicia stepped forward with slightly more alacrity than she had shown at Ottery to smooth over his greetings to the Staplefords and Lady Stansfield, whom he had not seen for a very long time.

'Ha! Mullineaux!' Lady Stansfield raised her lorgnette and viewed him critically. She smiled suddenly. 'Good to see you again, boy! Do you go up to London for the Season?'

'I do.' He returned her smile. 'No doubt we shall all meet up then. You must excuse me—I have a hundred and one matters to attend to before I leave tomorrow. It was a pleasure to see you all again. Your servant, ladies and gentlemen.' He bowed to them all, caught Georgiana Stapleford fluttering her eyelashes at him, and gave her an appreciative smile.

As an exercise in discretion, it had been admirable. All fences had been effortlessly mended and a basis for future meetings established. Alicia had been in no way singled out, but had been treated with exactly the same degree of impartial warmth as everyone else. There was nothing left to gossip about. Alicia understood this and could admire James Mullineaux for his strategy even whilst she resented it. It made the heated passion of that night at Monks Dacorum seem a mere figment of her imagination.

They watched as he walked off to the lych-gate, exchanging greetings with those members of the congregation who still lingered.

'Charming man,' Lady Stansfield opined. 'Come along, Honoria! Got to get out of this demmed cold wind!' She slipped her arm through Lady Stapleford's and the party from Chartley Chase turned for home. Caroline caught Alicia's arm.

'Alicia, while we're here I'd just like to take a closer look at the church. No, it's all right, Marcus.' She smiled at her husband. 'I know you don't rate church architecture high on your list of entertainments, so please go on ahead! If Alicia doesn't mind waiting, we can have a little chat on the way back. I won't be long—' So saying, she dived back inside the doors and left Alicia standing in the porch.

Despite the cold breeze it was a beautiful day, and Alicia sat for a little while admiring the view across to the sparkling sea. After a few minutes, however, she realised she was becoming chilled and resolved to take a quick turn around the churchyard whilst she waited. Caroline had always been interested in history, and her minutes could stretch to an hour without too much difficulty whilst she wandered around an ancient building in enraptured silence. It was perhaps an unusual pastime for a Society matron, but Alicia liked Caroline for it. She never felt the need to apologise for her lack of conformity.

The cypress-lined path wended its way around the ancient graveyard. It was very quiet now that all the churchgoers had left and the bells had ceased their ringing. Alicia made one circuit, relishing her solitude, then another, appreciating the view over the hills. When she had almost reached the church door again, she decided she would really have to go in soon and prise Caroline away from the glories of the past.

Her hand was on the church door when she felt a touch on her arm and turned, startled. She had heard no one approach up the stone-flagged path and in the shadows of the porch it was a moment before she recognised James Mullineaux. She never had a chance to greet him. He slid an arm around her waist and pulled her against him, stifling her instinctive exclamation with his mouth on hers. One hand was in the small of her back, holding her hard against him, whilst the other dispensed ruthlessly with her bonnet in order to entangle itself in her hair and draw her even closer.

Had Alicia been able to think at all, she might have reflected that all she had heard of James Mullineaux's reputation had unexpectedly proved itself to be true—this was not the man who had tried very hard not to seduce her two nights before, but the predatory rake of all the stories, a man accustomed to take the opportunities which presented themselves to him.

His devastating expertise swept her beyond coherent thought. His mouth plundered the sweetness of hers, shamelessly insistent, and the response it provoked in Alicia was equally abandoned. She felt as though every inch of her skin was on fire, burning for his touch. She wanted to dispense with the heavy layers of clothing which separated them, and feel his naked skin against hers.

He let her go at last, dropping one final kiss on her parted lips.

'And that, Alicia, my sweet,' he said very softly, 'was in case you were tempted to forget. Be assured I shall remind you again, when the time does serve.'

Alicia sank down onto the stone seat, one hand to her bruised lips, the other steadying herself as she took a very deep breath. She watched for a second time as James walked down the path to the gate and disappeared down the lane towards Monks Dacorum. Conceited, presumptuous... She gave up. Once again she was becoming repetitious and none of those words came anywhere near describing the boundless audacity that characterised James Mullineaux's behaviour. At that moment Alicia could not even begin to work out how she really felt.

She had completely forgotten Caroline Kilgaren. She turned her head slowly, to see her friend standing in the church door, the expression of comical consternation on her piquant face stating clearer than any words that she had seen exactly what had happened.

It was either very good or very bad luck that Christopher Westwood arrived at the church gate approximately two minutes later. Had he arrived sooner, and seen her with Mullineaux, Alicia realised it would have been disastrous. On the other hand, Caroline had only got as far as saying, 'Alicia, what—?' when she broke off, and set her lips in a very tight line as Westwood came up the path.

The friends had no chance for a tête-à-tête that day, for the demands of her guests kept Alicia fully occupied and she was never alone. On the following day, a number of visitors came to Chartley Chase. Mrs Henley delivered Miss Frensham home from Ottery on her way to Bath and a visit to her married daughter. The other occupants of the Henley coach were none other than Mrs Eddington-Buck and her daughter, who were also set to devastate that unsuspecting city. Good manners obliged

Alicia to offer them refreshment on their journey, but she was profoundly grateful when the Henleys' coach lumbered off out of Chartley, weighed down with the Eddington-Bucks' monstrous amount of baggage.

'That woman is an ill-bred toad,' Caroline Kilgaren observed roundly if inelegantly, when all the visitors had gone and she and Alicia were alone. 'Did you hear her telling Lady Stapleford that her elder daughter Jane had had her heart broken by Peter Weston, of all people, and had thrown herself away on a half-pay officer when Peter did not return her love? What utter nonsense! Why, everyone knows that Jane Townley is the only woman of sense in that family, and she and Townley determined to wed from the moment they first met! Oh, it puts me out of all patience!'

Alicia smiled slightly. 'Now we have seen for ourselves how gossip starts, Caro!' She had been playing Scarlatti very quietly, so that the bright breeziness of the music was muted, but now she broke off and lowered the piano lid. 'I did hear her telling my grandmother that she intended to catch Mullineaux for her younger daughter, now that he no longer had a penchant for auburn hair!'

'It is blondes, not brunettes, that are all the rage,' Caroline observed without inflection.

'Very true.' Alicia smiled mischievously. 'And it was a foolish thing to say to Lady Stansfield, who told her that if she wanted to risk her daughter's reputation with so dangerous a man she should not regret it were he to ruin her!' She looked up and met her friend's blue eyes with a challenge in her own. 'There now, Caro, I have made it as easy for you as I can... Now, ask me what you want to know!'

There was a pregnant pause, then Caroline took a deep breath.

'I collect you mean about James Mullineaux...' She gave Alicia a frank look. 'I would do so if I dared! You must know I am expiring with a most ill-mannered curiosity!' She looked so uncharacteristically confused that Alicia felt quite sorry for her. 'I mean, I never thought that you and James had really—' She broke off and started again. 'When you met at Ottery, I thought it was an accident... James never suggested... Well, I suppose he wouldn't—' She broke off again, caught Alicia's amused look and met her eyes accusingly.

'Damnation!' she said abruptly. 'What I am trying to say, Alicia, is that it makes no odds to me whether you and James are lovers! I just thought that you would both have been honest with us!'

Alicia realised that the intimate embrace she had shared with James at Chartley Church must have looked particularly incriminating. If she had been Caroline, how would she have interpreted finding Alicia locked in James's arms in what appeared to be a pre-arranged secret assignation?

'I suppose I should have slapped his face,' she said casually, shuffling the sheets of music together. 'Unfortunately, he took me completely by surprise! I realise how it must have appeared to you.'

There was a pause. Caroline was looking even more thunderstruck as she took Alicia's meaning. 'You mean that you did not arrange to meet? That you had not intended—? But Alicia—'

Alicia made an expressive grimace. 'You know James's reputation as well as I do, Caroline! It would be difficult to judge which of the two of us was more shocked—you at witnessing the scene, or myself at being the unsuspecting recipient of James's attentions!'

Caroline swelled with indignation. 'Well, upon my word! The presumption of the man!'

'Indeed!' Alicia said, very dryly.

Caroline eyed her closely. 'You do not appear much offended, Alicia! Are you sure that there is not more to this than meets the eye?'

Alicia burst out laughing at that. 'You're very shrewd, Caro! Come on, let's go for a walk in the gardens—and I will tell you everything!'

Donning warm pelisses and stout boots, the two friends slipped out of the garden door and began to wend their way by common consent through the maze of garden paths. The gardens at Chartley were small by the standards of the major local estates, but Alicia had not lied when she'd claimed gardening as her passion, and they demonstrated a range of styles and plants carefully and lovingly cultivated. Now that spring was upon them, the Chartley grounds were beginning to show all their promise.

'So what's to tell?' Caroline asked bluntly, seeing Alicia was preoccupied with her thoughts. 'How about your meeting with James at Ottery? I have heard a little from other sources—indeed, James himself mentioned the encounter to us. I imagine,' Caroline said with a slight smile, 'that it must have been quite eventful!'

'Yes,' Alicia agreed reminiscently, 'but perhaps not so eventful as the scene at the church might have led you to believe!' Her smile faded. 'It was an uncomfortable meeting, to tell the truth. I was ill-prepared to meet James again after all that time, and he...well, he made his low opinion of me very plain! I accept that I was much to blame for sending Miss Frensham away, but at the time she was cold and ill, and I thought

I was doing the right thing! Anyway, James was very angry—I expect he told you—and we quarrelled very badly. As I said, it was an uncomfortable meeting!'

They turned into the herb garden, where the air was lightly scented with thyme. Caroline drove her hands more deeply into her fur muff—though there was a sun, the air was still cold.

'It seems even more surprising, then, that James proposed to you the following morning,' Caroline ventured, and watched with interest as the colour flooded into Alicia's face.

'As a gentleman, I suppose—'

'Oh, stuff and nonsense, Alicia!' Caroline reverted to type and forgot her gentle line of questioning. 'James never behaves as a gentleman ought; you should know that!' Their eyes met, and they both burst out laughing.

'No, Caro, that is too harsh!' Alicia protested, through her laughter. 'I can think of at least one occasion—'

'Just how many times have the two of you met?' Caroline demanded. 'James mentioned several heated arguments, but failed to elaborate on where they took place!'

Alicia counted on her fingers. 'Two at Ottery, one at Theo's vicarage, one at Monks Farm...I think that's all, for we were very civil on the other occasions!'

'More than civil,' Caroline said dryly.

'Oh, and, of course, we quarrelled at Monks Dacorum,' Alicia said, with a wicked twinkle in her eye. 'But that was before we had the chance to talk properly and sort matters out between us!'

Caroline gave an infuriated squeak. 'Alicia Carberry, I shall shake you in a moment! So you *were* at Monks Dacorum last week! Marcus and I thought so! Now how did that come about?'

They were walking through the orchard now, between the laden branches of the fruit trees, towards the greenhouses where some of Alicia's most prized vegetables were growing.

Alicia was looking amused. 'I met James by chance when I was out riding,' she said, quite truthfully, but with a little, secret smile which Caroline did not miss. 'He...persuaded me to dine with him and after dinner I told him what he wanted to know, which was the truth of my marriage to Carberry.' Her green eyes met Caroline's blue ones quite frankly. 'The past is now all explained and can be put behind us.'

'And what of the present and future?' Caroline demanded. A flush rose in her cheeks. 'Alicia, you can be the most vexatious creature at times! You tell me the merest outline of what must have been a very interesting meeting indeed and then you glibly gloss over the rest! Tell me properly!'

A rueful smile lit Alicia's face. 'I'm sorry, Caro! What do you want to know? I suspect that you and Marcus had already been instrumental in encouraging James to seek a meeting with me, and for that I must thank you. As for the rest, it is as I said; it seems that James did not desert me as I had imagined, and he now no longer believes that I jilted him to marry Carberry for money, so now we may all be comfortable, and act as though it never happened!'

'Pshaw!' Caroline gave a snort of disgust. 'You can hardly have forgotten that you were in love with each other once and pretend that that never happened! And, good God, Alicia, if you had seen the pair of you yesterday, you would have drawn the same conclusions as I, and have thought that the two of you were lovers!'

They had reached the gate in the wall which led through into the quiet churchyard. Alicia put out her hand and pushed it open. All amusement had fled from her face, and her voice.

'Love?' she said, a little bitterly. 'No, I do not forget that, Caro. But that was seven years ago, and people change. And are you not confusing two quite different matters? What you saw yesterday was nothing more than James indulging a whim! He had the opportunity—'

'And the inclination,' Caroline said dryly. 'This is all becoming a little sophisticated for me! Are you sure you do not mistake James's feelings? And what of your own?'

Alicia's pain showed in her eyes. 'I have had plenty of time to think about this,' she said, very quietly. 'For my part, my feelings have not changed in all the time I have known James, but I cannot expect him to feel the same. Since we cannot go back to how matters were before, we can only go forward as friends. Things will be more comfortable now—only imagine how intolerable the Season would have been if we were constantly avoiding or ignoring each other!'

Caroline looked unconvinced. 'My dear Alicia, the feelings between yourself and James were never *comfortable*—' she stressed the word with heavy irony '—either before or after you quarrelled! You can hardly expect them to be so now!'

They were walking along the cypress-lined path around the church. The air was a dim green beneath the trees. There was a rustic bench placed to allow visitors to take the view, and they sat down, looking out across the moors in much the same way as Alicia had done the previous day. For a while there was silence between them, then Alicia sighed.

'You are right, of course,' she admitted quietly. 'I am still in love with James, and though I am glad that the past is now settled between us I cannot see that it will make matters easier for me in the future. I shall always be wanting more than he is prepared to give!'

A blackbird squawked off overhead.

'Look, Alicia.' Caroline spoke energetically. 'Marcus had a long talk with James when we were at Monks Dacorum and he thinks that James is still in love with you, too. He may not necessarily realise it, or even want it to be so, but in the end he will have to accept it. He was very angry with you. That was getting in the way, but now, as you say, it is resolved.' She looked at her friend appraisingly. 'James evidently still finds you exceedingly attractive,' she said, with a hint of a smile. 'Who knows? Perhaps in time—'

But Alicia was shaking her head, smiling a tight little smile which did little to conceal her hurt.

'No, Caro,' she said, with finality. 'I will not allow myself false hope. I admit that, at Monks Dacorum, I thought there might be a chance—' She broke off, and resumed. 'But it only took me a little time to see that what happened that night was in the heat of the moment. It is better this way.'

Caroline was looking almost as shocked as she had done earlier. 'Alicia, are you telling me that James seduced you that night?'

'No,' Alicia said again, this time with the same small, secret smile which Caroline had seen earlier. 'In point of fact he did not. He could have done, but he was very careful not to!' The smile faded. 'So you see—' she shrugged '—even then, he was thinking far more clearly than I!'

'He has had more experience,' Caroline observed coolly. 'I'll say this for James—he works very fast!' She looked at Alicia thoughtfully. 'And if he were to offer you carte blanche, what then?'

'No,' Alicia said, for a third time. 'I won't deny I've thought about it, Caro.' The colour came into her cheeks. 'Oh, I dare say it was immodest of me even to consider...but anyway it wouldn't do! In the end it would only make me more unhappy. For me, it has to be all or nothing!'

She shivered suddenly, and rose abruptly to her feet. 'Enough of this! I feel a fit of the megrims coming on! Shall we take a turn around the village? I wanted to tell you of my visit to Greyrigg and the interview with my father, not to mention other matters.'

They walked to the lych-gate and went out onto the village green, circled the duck pond, and made a detour down the lane which ran along the garden wall of Chartley Chase. Once again, Caroline turned her enquiring blue gaze upon her friend.

'So what of those other matters that are on your mind? Is one of them Christopher Westwood—he has made you an offer, hasn't he?'

Alicia nodded, glancing sideways at her friend. 'Yes, and I have refused him.'

'I should think so!' Caroline had no very high opinion of Westwood. 'If you had agreed I should have disowned you! You could do much better than that, leaving aside your feelings for James!'

Alicia looked amused. 'I did think about accepting,' she admitted, 'before I met James again. I knew Christopher was going to make me an offer and I wondered if I should accept for the sake of companionship.'

'What fustian you do talk sometimes!' Caroline looked totally disgusted. 'Next you will be telling me that you should marry him because your grandmother likes him!'

'Well, and so she does—' Alicia began, caught her friend's eye and they both burst out laughing.

They walked on for a few moments in silence. Alicia knew that Caroline was quite right—none of the reasons she had thought of for marrying Christopher were compelling enough and compared to her feelings for James Mullineaux they paled into insignificance.

'I did not tell you,' she added presently, 'that my father had also proposed that I enter the married state again. His was a proxy proposal, on behalf of a business acquaintance, but it was even less tempting than marrying Christopher!'

Caroline stopped dead and stared at her. 'We thought it odd that Annabella had married and settled in Somerset when you were supposed to be giving her a Season,' she commented. 'Was it all a ruse, then?'

Alicia nodded sombrely. 'Yes, I think it was just an excuse to get me to Greyrigg.' She shivered suddenly. 'I had not thought of it much, my visit there having been overshadowed by other events lately, but it was a most unpleasant interview, Caro. I always feel that no matter what distance I put between myself and my father he is always there. I can't explain it...' she finished lamely.

Caroline was frowning, her hands deep in the pockets of her pelisse. 'This match... Did your father say who his business associate was?'

Alicia looked surprised. 'No, I never thought to ask his name... Why do you ask?'

Caroline shrugged. 'I'm not sure, really... It just seems an odd co-incidence that you should be the recipient of so many proposals at once!' She gave her friend a look of amused raillery. 'I know you reject them by the dozen, Alicia, but three in one month!'

Now it was Alicia's turn to frown. 'It does seem a little excessive, I know... But surely there can be no connection between the three! The idea's absurd!'

Caroline agreed, but she continued to frown. 'You do know that Christopher is in debt, don't you, Alicia? I'm not wishing to suggest that his affection for you is insincere, but...' Her voice trailed away unhappily.

Alicia had not known, and felt vaguely surprised. There was nothing in Westwood's demeanour or dress which suggested straitened circumstances, but that in itself was hardly unexpected. Often those with the smallest means put on the greatest show in the society in which they lived. She wondered suddenly whether a man like Westwood would borrow from the same sources as her cousin Josiah, for example. It was an odd thought, for there was such a fastidious, finicky element to Westwood's nature that she could not imagine him seeking out a money-lender in the backstreets of London...

Yet when she considered it there *were* similarities between her cousin's case and that of Christopher Westwood: the lack of visible means of financial support, the enjoyment of expensive living and the love of deep play... At the back of her mind a thought stirred briefly, but Caroline was pulling her arm, drawing her attention to the light, grey drizzle and the mist that was descending again on the moorland behind the house. Alicia forgot her thoughts as the two girls slipped in at the back gate of Chartley Chase and made their way up the damp path. Marcus Kilgaren and Christopher Westwood could be seen through the games-room window playing at billiards, and Alicia sighed unconsciously at the thought of returning to the drawing-room and the barbed observations of Georgiana Stapleford. Caroline gave her arm a comforting squeeze.

'Only a few days until we all leave you in peace!' she whispered irrepressibly. 'Then all we need to worry about is the Season, and how on earth we engineer your first public meeting with James!'

Chapter Eight

It was the most perfect dress that Alicia had ever seen. Her maid, Gibley, brought it forward into the light almost reverently and the dress fell like a golden waterfall over her arm, rustling softly as she moved.

The first major social event of the new Season—a ball at the home of fashionable hostess Mrs Laetitia Bingley—was taking place that evening. It was also to be the first meeting of Alicia and James before the *ton*. Dealing with a handful of former acquaintances in a Somerset churchyard was one thing, Alicia reflected; could James achieve a similar success under the critical, fickle gaze of his peers? Alicia knew that the two of them would be a cynosure for all eyes and the thought was a daunting one, even to one as accustomed as she to the whims and ways of Society. In addition, she had had to cope with her own rising sense of anticipation at the thought of seeing James again. Hence the gold dress—she needed to give herself confidence. Such an outrageous gown, she thought comfortingly, could not fail.

Like all of Alicia's clothes it was very simple and elegant. Slashed low across her breasts, it revealed a dizzying amount of bare skin and hinted at other delights only just concealed beneath its sinuous, flowing silk. To match the style, Gibley painstakingly swept Alicia's hair back in a simple Grecian knot, restraining the copper curls with a small gold circlet that added a regal touch.

Alicia studied her reflection thoughtfully. She looked cool, untouchable, and almost impossibly tantalising, a far cry from the nervous turmoil that shook her inside. You're a fool to yourself, Alicia Carberry, she told her mirror image astringently. You have had any number of offers from the most eligible *partis* in Town, and yet you persist in pining for the love of the one man who is beyond your reach. The girl in the mirror looked back at her with the faintest hint of a compassionate smile on her lips. No matter. Tonight her feelings would not be on view for public consumption. She intended to dazzle and deflect the barbs of the curious. And as an additional aim she would show the Marquis of Mullineaux that she was not about to fall into his arms again. The memory of the scene at Chartley Church was with her still. She raised her chin. Damn his impertinence!

Gibley smiled slightly, standing back like her mistress to admire her handiwork.

'You'll set the Town by the ears tonight, my lady,' she opined. 'Do you wish to wear any jewellery?'

Alicia's eyes met hers in the mirror. 'Just the green star,' she said softly.

Gibley was surprised and showed it. In her opinion, Lady Carberry had many pieces of beautiful jewellery and the fact that she seldom chose to wear any of them was a great pity. The green star, an enormous emerald, had been brought back from India by George Carberry and set for him in a barbaric and vulgar gold necklace. Alicia had immediately had the emerald reset when she had inherited it, but she had never shown any inclination to wear it—until now.

Gibley unlocked the case and brought the necklace across gingerly, almost as though she expected it to bite her. There was no denying that the single jewel was very effective, set as it was now on a plain gold chain. Around Alicia's neck, it suddenly took fire from her eyes and reflected the intense green light back again. Under any circumstances it would have drawn all eyes, but Gibley could not even begin to imagine what effect it would have that night in combination with the dress and Lady Carberry's luminous beauty.

Alicia moved slightly and the light struck the carved surfaces of the emerald, scintillating deep within its depths. A faint, satisfied smile touched her lips, and Gibley watched her curiously. Lord Charles Oxley was her ladyship's escort to the ball that night, but Gibley doubted profoundly that all this finery was for Lord Charles's benefit. He and Alicia had been friends for many years without her betraying even the slightest *tendre* for him. Whereas the Marquis of Mullineaux would also be at the ball, and Gibley rather suspected that Lady Carberry's feelings for him were another matter. There was no doubt that her ladyship was playing a deep game—a game designed to fool the *ton*, but possibly to deceive the Marquis as well.

Alicia stood up and the pale gold skirts shimmered around her. Lost in admiration, Gibley passed her the matching gold reticule and fan, and the gossamer-light scarf for her shoulders.

It was as Alicia was about to go downstairs to join Lord Charles and Miss Frensham that Gibley suddenly realised what was missing.

'Your bracelet, madam! Are you not wearing it tonight?'

Alicia paused in the doorway and smiled. 'Not tonight, thank you, Gibley. It does not suit the occasion.'

There was a whisper of silk, and she was gone.

When Charles Oxley saw Alicia he experienced serious misgivings about the decision he had made only the previous day to propose marriage to the debutante daughter of Lord and Lady Mountjoy. Compared with the wanton beauty before him, the youthful charms of Sarah Mountjoy paled into insignificance. A moment later, he recalled that he had already asked Alicia to marry him twice in the past, and she had turned him down and always would. He suddenly realised that he had been gaping like a fish ever since she had entered the room and tried to pull himself together.

'I say, you do look splendid tonight, Alicia!' Lord Charles considered the gold dress in more detail and felt his collar become rather constricting. He was almost certain that he had turned bright red. 'Splendid!' he repeated, finding it almost impossible to drag his gaze away from the green star, where it shone so seductively in the hollow between Alicia's breasts.

Miss Frensham, conservative in her usual lavender muslin, was also struck by the dress, but in a rather different way.

'Lady Carberry! Why, you *never* wear that style!'

'No. Does it not make a delightful change?' Alicia seemed blissfully unaware of her disapproval. 'I like it so much that I think I will place an order for several more with Madame Celeste!'

Miss Frensham murmured something fortunately inaudible, although Charles Oxley thought that he had heard the word '*demi-monde*' mentioned. He hurried forward with Alicia's velvet cloak, clumsy in his efforts to get something more substantial around her body. Alicia gave him a melting smile over her shoulder which raised his blood pressure even higher. He had always agreed with those who had categorised the lovely Lady Carberry as sexually cold, but it seemed he had been in grave error. Either that, or something extraordinary had happened to her since the last time they had met.

Miss Frensham was tutting in a worried sort of a way. The guardian of Alicia's reputation ever since her unfortunate marriage, Miss Frensham had a lowering feeling that matters were slipping from her rather tenuous grasp. First there had been that distressing episode at Ottery, although Lady Carberry had been all that was proper in quashing *that* scandal! Now, however, it seemed she was set on creating a whole new set of rumours of her own accord! Never had Miss Frensham seen her ladyship in so—she boggled at the word, but it was applicable—wanton a mood. It did not augur well for the rest of the evening.

The road outside the Bingleys' town house was already crowded with carriages as they arrived. Flaring torches lit the steps to the door and a multitude of people appeared to be going in. It was very early in the evening for such a crush and Miss Frensham could not help but wonder whether Alicia's meeting with Lord Mullineaux was the sole reason for all this interest. To judge by the avid glances cast their way, this was very much the case. Miss Frensham's timid heart sank even further, particularly as she caught sight of the wicked sparkle in Alicia's green eyes, a look which her long-suffering companion could not help but mistrust. With a slight moan, Miss Frensham excused herself and dashed into a side room where she administered herself a large dose of sal volatile and waited for her nerves to calm a little.

Fortunately, Miss Frensham played no more than a peripheral part in the encounter which Caroline Kilgaren had orchestrated so carefully for her friends. According to plan, Alicia and Charles Oxley now progressed into the ballroom, which Mrs Bingley had decorated with an oriental theme. Oxley, a simple soul, was inclined to disparage the opulent draperies and colourful Chinese lanterns, and he shuddered visibly at the murals of rampaging elephants. Alicia, who was feeling ever more nervous beneath her confident façade, thought that Mrs Bingley had perhaps overdone the theme a little, and was assailed by a fit of the giggles. Ever since some ambitious hostess had held a ball complete with a troutstream running through the ballroom, the fashionable had outdone themselves and each other to come up with new and original ideas.

The ballroom was filling rapidly and Alicia was soon surrounded by her usual court of admirers who found to their annoyance that it was impossible to prise her away from Lord Charles. Since Caroline had specifically told her brother to stay with Alicia until after James Mullineaux had arrived this was not surprising, and Charles was sticking doggedly to his duty. Not even the twinkling smile of Sarah Mountjoy could draw him across the ballroom, although he would have felt more comfortable next to her than in the orbit of Alicia's bright, particular star. She was dazzling in a way which made him feel quite ill at ease that evening, and he did little other than watch her silently as she automatically parried the compliments of others more articulate than himself.

It was strange, Charles reflected, what a change could be wrought in a person, and it was not simply the dress which had effected the transformation. Alicia had always represented all that stood for restrained good taste, with the emphasis very much on the restraint. Her clothes were faultlessly elegant, but seldom so provocative, and she never wore jewellery. Not simply that, but there was something in her manner, some suppressed air of excitement, that was positively sensual. Watching her flashing smile, Charles once again tried to ease the tightness of his collar. How could he ever have imagined her to be cold? She was giving off so much heat that he was afraid of burning up. And he was not the only one who was looking at her with a mixture of fascination and puzzlement. Several of her oldest admirers, who flattered themselves that they knew Alicia extremely well, were looking completely confused.

The noise level in the room was growing, as was the excitement in the air. Alicia's own tension levels were well ahead of the rest, however. She was barely able to prevent herself shaking visibly and found it incredibly difficult to concentrate on what anyone said to her. Lady Stansfield came in, fixed her granddaughter with a shrewd eye, and crossed the room to bestow on her a very public kiss of approval. Her arrival had the fortunate effect of removing some of the less respectable of Alicia's admirers and making space for Caroline's cousin Charlotte and her husband Perry Renwick.

Everything was happening at once now. Lady Stansfield drifted off to join the Staplefords and Christopher Westwood, then there was a ripple of excitement, and Alicia, turning with everyone else, saw that Caroline and Marcus had come in, accompanied by James Mullineaux.

'The Earl and Countess of Kilgaren. The Marquis of Mullineaux.'

The stentorian tones of the Bingleys' butler floated across the room, putting a stop to all conversations. Caroline and Marcus greeted their hostess and came down the steps into the ballroom first, Marcus resplendent in evening dress and Caroline ethereal in silver gauze. Meanwhile, Mrs Bingley was greeting James Mullineaux very warmly. To her natural pleasure at seeing him again was added the fact that his presence had just about guaranteed the success of her ball. And he was, after all, a very attractive man. She let him go with obvious reluctance as another flurry of guests arrived and he joined Caroline and Marcus, who were chatting with Peter and Maria Weston. Peter seemed very pleased to see his old friend again and from Maria James got a shy smile, and a kiss on the cheek. All was going according to Caroline's plan. She took James's arm, and the whole group turned towards Alicia and Charles.

The years rolled back and Alicia could suddenly see the tall figure of James Mullineaux crossing the Stansfield House ballroom towards her, moving with that lithe grace which was peculiarly his own. Tonight he was dressed with elegant simplicity in black and white evening dress and in many ways he looked the same as he had done seven years before; the same tanned, classically handsome features, the same intensely dark and disturbing gaze, the same lazy assurance in his manner...

The murmur in the room died to almost total silence. Only the music of the string quartet still tinkled in the distance. Caroline, performing the introductions, did not bat an eyelid at finding herself the centre of attention. She had always had a flair for drama.

'You remember my cousin Charlotte, don't you, James? And this is her husband, Peregrine Renwick. Perry, may I make you known to James Mullineaux?'

The two men exchanged bows. Renwick was a spare, sandy-haired, humorous man, who had heard plenty about James Mullineaux even though he had never met him. He gave the Marquis a penetrating look, quite disposed to like what he saw. Charlotte was blushing in much the same way she had when James had greeted her at Stansfield House seven years ago. She had never quite grown out of her admiration for him, although she had equally never felt quite comfortable with him—there was something about such blatant masculinity that was too dangerously attractive. She murmured a few words of greeting, moving instinctively closer to Perry's side, and James smiled at her and turned to Alicia.

'Lady Carberry you know already, of course.' Caroline's voice held only the faintest hint of mischief as she looked from one to the other, although she could sense as well as everyone else the peculiar tension emanating from the two figures before her.

James was not smiling any more. There was a pause—the entire room appeared to be holding its breath. On the one side were those who waited hopefully for James to administer the cut direct, a cruel snub to the woman he had once loved. On the other were those equally avid watchers who wanted confirmation of the rumours they had heard about a clandestine love affair between these two. There were very few uninterested observers.

James had intended to follow the same strategy as at Chartley, and acknowledge Alicia coolly and civilly before moving on. That would have squashed speculation on both sides and left the gossips with nothing to talk about. He had no intention of showing her any particular regard, despite his feelings, which could have been described as more than warm. Yet when it came to the point he could not do it.

He had been aware of Alicia from the moment he had stepped into the room. Leaving aside the effects of the outrageously provocative dress and the sheer ostentation of the green star, all his senses were conscious of her presence. Had he not exerted the most supreme self-control, he would have been drawn irresistibly to her side from the first moment. He had not seen Alicia for several weeks and had been astonished, chagrined and finally resignedly amused to discover how she had haunted his thoughts.

Now she was here before him and, sensitive to her every feeling, James realised that she was very nervous. He took her hand and smiled straight into her eyes. It was a smile for her alone, conspiratorial and full of shared amusement. The room took a collective breath.

'You dim the candlelight, Lady Carberry.' His voice was low, but not too low for those about them to miss his words. 'It is a great pleasure to see you again. May I beg the honour of a dance with you later?'

In silence Alicia handed him her dance card. Their fingers touched, and a quiver of awareness shot right through her. Her heart was beating suffocatingly in her throat. James scribbled his monogram against one of the dances and handed the card back to her. Their audience watched. Alicia made an effort to speak. She knew she had to do it, but found it was one of the most difficult things ever to confront her.

'Lord Mullineaux.' It came out a little huskily, but better than she had hoped. 'Welcome back to London.'

He gave her another smile which increased her pulse rate several notches further, then Charles Oxley was stepping forward to shake his hand and second Alicia's welcome. The noise level rose again as several people who had been holding back now came forward to greet James.

Soon he was at the centre of a circle of well-wishers and Alicia was able to slip away unnoticed.

She found that she was shaking. The whole encounter had been so short, but had affected her so profoundly. Aware that there were still plenty of people watching her, she turned round and found Christopher Westwood at her elbow. He was looking absolutely furious. He took Alicia's arm in an iron grip and practically dragged her behind a nearby group of statuary.

'Well, I don't suppose many people can be in any doubt about your relationship with Mullineaux now, Alicia!'

Alicia shook him off, careless of the watchers. 'Oh, don't be absurd, Christopher! Would you have had him cut me dead? Mullineaux always was outrageous in his compliments. I am sure nobody but you thought it odd.'

Westwood was flushed with anger. 'Really? I can assure you that everyone thought it most particular! No one has any doubts now that you are Mullineaux's mistress! I suppose it was beyond either of you to try for a little discretion!'

There was a frozen silence, more effective than any words would have been. Westwood realised he had gone far too far. He started to splutter an apology, but Alicia cut him off.

'Would you escort me back to the Countess of Kilgaren, please, Christopher? I feel sure that I shall find more congenial company elsewhere. Leaving aside my own feelings on what you have said, you have now single-handedly given the gossip-mongers plenty more food for thought. I congratulate you!'

She set off across the ballroom without waiting for a reply so that Westwood was forced to hurry to catch up with her. Once out on the floor in full view of the assembled throng, he was prevented from saying anything further by the risk of drawing even more attention to them, and spent the journey to Caroline's side in red-faced, tight-lipped confusion.

Around the room the fans were waving and feathers nodding as the matrons exchanged opinions. The evening was far exceeding expectation, and it had only just started. There was the Marquis of Mullineaux, as arrogantly attractive as ever. There was Alicia Carberry, extravagantly beautiful, who seemed to have overcome the dreadful scandal of their parting and been reinstated in his affections. There was the conspicuous opulence of the huge emerald at Alicia's throat—vulgar, some said, but enough to draw the fortune-hunters in droves. Finally there was Christopher Westwood, deep in the throes of a jealous passion and unable to hide it. What an entertainment!

The music was striking up. The crowd around James had hardly diminished at all, although some were now drifting away as the dancing started. As well as old acquaintances, he was now surrounded by people he had never met before who were taking advantage of the informality of the occasion to introduce themselves. Chief amongst these was Lady Corinna Dawe, a dark beauty married to a complaisant husband, whose love affairs since her marriage had titillated the whole Town. She was standing very close to James, one little white hand on his arm to claim his attention, all melting doe eyes and lustrous black hair. Lady Dawe leant closer to give him the full benefit of her voluptuous figure, and Alicia, watching from across the floor, suddenly decided that she disliked her very much indeed.

Charles Oxley came up to claim Alicia for the first dance and Westwood, who had been dithering beside her in agonised silence, went off in a huff.

'I say, Alicia, I'd almost forgotten what a capital fellow James Mullineaux is!' Oxley was full of the enthusiasm of relief that all had gone so well. 'Corinna Dawe certainly finds him to her taste!'

He chuckled, watching as Lady Corinna artfully inveigled James into the set that was forming. 'I'll wager that it won't be long before those two come to some mutually agreeable arrangement! Lady Corinna is not one to let the grass grow under her feet when she sees something she wants, and James always did have an eye for the prettiest faces!'

Alicia felt sick. James certainly appeared to be enjoying Lady Corinna's company, his dark head bent attentively to hers, a smile of genuine amusement on his lips. Well, the scandal-mongers had plenty to muse on now! It would be most piquant to imagine that a current and potential mistress of the Marquis of Mullineaux were both at the same ball!

'I don't think I will take your bet, Charles,' Alicia said, trying hard to keep all evidence of her true feelings from her voice. 'Lady Corinna is said to be irresistible when she decides she wants something—or someone—and Lord Mullineaux, as you say, has hardly been known for his inclination to resist beautiful women in the past! They deserve each other!'

Oxley was not a sensitive soul, but the waspishness of this reply penetrated even his slow brain. Giving Alicia a thoughtful look, he realised that this was perhaps not the most tactful of topics to broach with her and turned the subject to less controversial matters.

Alicia was glad when the dance came to an end. The initial purpose of the evening achieved, she realised that she was not enjoying herself at all and would have given much to retire from the ball. Knowing the speculation this would inevitably engender, however, she also realised with resignation that she was forced to carry on as though she were having a good time. The prospect of the whole Season suddenly opened up before her. Having got over the difficulty of meeting her again, James could now ignore her and concentrate on pursuing Lady Corinna, or indeed a whole succession of willing partners. At the same time he could be weighing up the merits of some youthful bride, and then what price the confidences of Monks Dacorum? It was as though it had never been. And Christopher Westwood would be pestering her with unwanted attentions—the whole thing would be intolerably tiresome.

Marcus Kilgaren came up to claim the next dance and needed only one look at Alicia's face to realise which topics of conversation were out of bounds. At the end of the dance he steered her unobtrusively towards Caroline, who was conversing with Perry Renwick, and for a while at least Alicia had the balm of their companionship. Her dance card was full, however, and she could not hide away for long. Peter Weston was her partner for the following set of country dances and by the end of that her usual coterie of admirers was re-forming, its ranks swelled by several gazetted fortune-hunters drawn by the dazzling lure of the green star.

James, meanwhile, had temporarily shaken off the attentions of the predatory Lady Dawe and was confusing the gossips even more by blamelessly leading out a series of starry-eyed debutantes. Returning the latest of these, the youthfully pretty Miss Osborne, to her beaming mama, James handed her over with a charming word of thanks and turned to scan the ballroom. A moment later, Marcus Kilgaren, his hands full of refreshments, collided with his old friend as James stopped dead in front of him.

'How well does Alicia know that fellow?' James demanded without preamble, a heavy frown marring his brow. Marcus followed his gaze to where Alicia was waltzing in the arms of a man in striking scarlet regimentals—a man whose very attitude and manner towards her indicated intimacy.

'Patrick Wickford? He's been paying half-hearted court to Alicia for years and getting nowhere,' Marcus observed. 'No doubt the sight of the green star made him feel it was worth his while to try again,' he added, with customary cynicism.

James was looking grim. 'I came across him in Dublin. He's got a very unsavoury reputation. His pockets are to let and he's been hanging out for a rich wife, but he's quite prepared to pass the waiting time in the pursuit of other women.'

'Well, perhaps Wickford has cast Alicia in the role of rich wife,' Marcus commented thoughtfully, 'although Alicia's no fool and I should say that she can take care of herself! Anyway,' he added pointedly, 'what business is it of yours, James?' He looked down at the disintegrating ice cream in his hands. 'I must get this ice to Caro before it melts completely! I'll settle for lemonade next time, in case you delay me again!'

So saying, he left James still glaring in the direction of Alicia and the dashing Captain.

Alicia, much to her own surprise, was finding solace in Captain Wickford's attentions. He was very handsome in a rugged way and the piercing blue of those eyes rested on her in a manner so blatantly admiring that it was difficult to resist. Soon after she had been widowed he had paid her very marked attention, but she had never deluded herself that his feelings ran any deeper than the bottom of her purse. She had repelled him then with the cool charm that had thwarted so many potential suitors and he had taken his dismissal with good humour. He had been surprised to find her so receptive to his advances now, but had been quick to define the cause. No matter if it was James Mullineaux's presence which caused her to smile so sweetly on him—he might be able to benefit from it.

Since James was leading Lady Corinna into supper, Alicia graciously accepted Captain Wickford's invitation to join him and shortly found herself seated with him in an intimate corner tucked away from the crowds. Her attention was drawn repeatedly across the room, where Lady Corinna's tinkling laugh rang out often and she could be seen hanging on James's every word. Two impressionable young ladies, hidden from Alicia by an intervening pillar, were also discussing the Marquis and his fair companion, and Alicia found herself eavesdropping shamelessly.

'Is he not so handsome you could swoon?' sighed one, whose languishing looks in James's direction had so far been ignored. 'Louisa Osborne danced with him, and says that he is *devastating*, but disappointingly quite proper in his behaviour. Although,' she added, with a touch of anxiety, 'Mama did warn me that he has a shocking reputation!'

'Oh, he has!' murmured her friend, with a fair attempt at sophistication. 'He is rumoured to be very dangerous! But I doubt that that will deter Lady Dawe—she has quite a reputation herself!'

'Camilla! Don't let your mama hear you say so! You know how she dislikes us even referring to ladies of that type! Lady Dawe is very beautiful, though, isn't she?' the first young lady added, with a wistful note in her voice.

Camilla was evidently more discerning. 'I consider her to be rather overblown,' was her damning response. 'All very well if one cares for that sort of thing, I suppose, but I would have had more respect for Mullineaux's taste had he fixed his affection with Lady Carberry. She is truly beautiful.'

'Oh, yes, but so cold! They say she has broken many hearts and cares not for anyone! Though in that dress,' the first young lady said hesitantly, 'well, perhaps she has decided to change her style! At any rate, you know there can be no affection between the two of them after what she did! It was the most appalling scandal at the time, so my mama tells me! Why, did you know...?' Her voice sank confidingly low, and Alicia, losing the thread of her eavesdropping, realised that Patrick Wickford was watching her with some amusement.

Captain Wickford had also been looking in the direction of Lady Dawe and the Marquis. He had been Corinna Dawe's lover a couple of years before and admired her very much, but she could never give him what Alicia could. He leant forward until his breath stirred the copper tendrils of hair by Alicia's ear.

'Camilla Bennett is surely in the right of it, Lady Carberry! Corinna Dawe's a very attractive woman, but she cannot compare to you. For you are truly beautiful...all ice where she is fire, maybe—but underneath the ice I think there lurks the passion they all believe you lack.'

His hand moved to cover hers on the table. Alicia looked at him. He was very close, those brilliant blue eyes holding an expression which Alicia recognised quite easily as genuine desire. The Captain might covet her fortune, but he also had no objection to her personally. But he was taking a grave risk—Alicia had always behaved with such unimpeachable virtue that she might not be very receptive to such flagrant flattery. Yet tonight, in that incredible dress, she seemed quite different. Intrigued, Wickford waited for her reaction.

Alicia smiled at him. It was exciting to allow herself the luxury of a flirtation just for once. At first she had been obliged to behave with propriety to regain Society's good opinion; then it had become a habit, and no one had ruffled the surface of her calm. Now the Marquis of Mullineaux had thrown a stone into that serene pool and stirred up old emotions and feelings. Looking at her with renewed interest, Patrick Wickford realised that his words had been closer to the mark than he had imagined. Lady Carberry's serenely cool exterior concealed enough passion to burn a man down.

Neither of them noticed the presence of the Marquis of Mullineaux himself, who had come across to claim Alicia for the first dance after supper. His shadow fell across them, and both looked up from their preoccupation, the Captain's eyes bright with challenge and amusement. James gave him a nod that was barely civil and Wickford pressed a leisurely kiss on Alicia's hand before letting it go.

James was looking very forbidding. 'I believe that this is my waltz, madam.'

Alicia got to her feet with every appearance of surprise and reluctance. 'Good gracious, has the dancing started again already? I had not even noticed!'

James's gaze moved from her innocent face to Patrick Wickford and back again. 'No, indeed, I can well believe that you were too engrossed to realise!' He stood back to let her pass and Alicia, with a sudden frisson of anticipation, allowed him to escort her out of the supper-room.

It would have had to be the waltz, Alicia thought savagely, feeling her treacherous body respond immediately to James's proximity as he took her in his arms. Compared to the earthquake that shook her now, flirtation with Wickford was shallow and empty, exciting in a certain way, but superficial in its effects. This was real and therefore infinitely more disturbing to the senses. But he need not think that she was willing to join the ranks of his conquests, Alicia thought resentfully. Let him practise his charms on Lady Dawe—she was made of sterner stuff!

The struggle Alicia had to master her feelings against the unsettling attraction James held for her was quite enough to keep her silent for two circuits of the floor and it was eventually James who spoke first, slanting a glance down at her face.

'I see that you are determined to be displeased with me, Lady Carberry, for you have not said a word! May I enquire what I have done to incur your wrath?'

Alicia tried to give him a repressive look, which was difficult when

she was so distracted by her awareness of him. Knowing him well
enough to guess that he was perfectly capable of referring to their last,
incendiary encounter at Chartley Church, she made haste to deny him
the opportunity.

'You mistake me, Lord Mullineaux! I am simply at pains to quell
any gossip by conducting our dance with decorum!'

'Indeed!' James raised a mocking eyebrow. 'You were not so scrupulous a little while ago when you gave such blatant encouragement to
your military admirer!'

'I!' Alicia had risen to that before she had time to subdue her temper.
'It is you, my lord, who has been setting the tongues wagging with
your attentions to Lady Corinna! Not,' she added hastily, reading his
look of amused comprehension, 'that it is of the least consequence to
me if you choose such company!'

James absorbed this evidently untruthful set-down without the smile
leaving his eyes.

'I see. But are we not both just amusing ourselves—I with the delightful Lady Corinna and you with the gallant Captain?'

Alicia had herself back in hand now and refused to be provoked by
that. 'Certainly I find Captain Wickford to be charming company,' she
said coolly.

'He is most accomplished in his gallantry,' James agreed with a
smooth sarcasm. 'I see that he even manages to remove his gaze from
your necklace long enough to look meaningfully into your eyes!'

Alicia gritted her teeth, all too aware that surrounding couples were
straining to hear their conversation and that she could not afford to let
her mask slip. She smiled at him sweetly.

'You seem quite certain that you have discerned Captain Wickford's
motives, my lord! I should say that yours towards Lady Corinna are
equally transparent!'

James gave a genuine smile at that. '*Touché*, my lady! But do you
not mean Lady Corinna's intentions towards me rather than the reverse?
She seems to be a lady who knows her own mind!'

'Oh, I am sure I shall see you fighting her off!' Alicia snapped,
abandoning restraint. 'And at least you may be flattered by the knowledge that she is not seeking you out for your fortune!'

Their dancing feet moved on smoothly enough, but neither of them
was paying any attention to the music any more.

'Oh, I did not mean to imply that Wickford is attracted by your
fortune alone,' James said affably. 'This evening—and in that dress

particularly—you seem to have forsaken your severe image in favour of something entirely more exciting. I am disposed to test whether it is genuine or just for show!'

Alicia gasped and tried to pull away from him, but he was holding her far closer than convention dictated and she could not move. The heat of his touch seared through the clinging silk of the gold dress. She might have been naked for all the protection it afforded her. She could feel the hard length of his body against hers and shivered convulsively at the undeniable reaction between them. Once again, the memory of his kiss invaded her thoughts and she felt herself tremble in response.

'You are the most insufferable man—' Alicia began hotly, aware that her cheeks were suddenly suffused with colour and that many interested observers were watching avidly.

James only laughed. 'Admit that you were playing up to Wickford only to provoke me and I may consider letting you go,' he said softly in her ear.

Alicia shot him a furious glance. How dared James assume that she would pay attention to Wickford only in order to engage his interest? 'I shall do no such thing! Your arrogance, my lord, is beyond belief!'

'Then I shall have to prove it to you,' James observed, still very quietly. He glanced about them. 'Not here, perhaps, although it's tempting to do so! Are you prepared to accept that challenge, my lady?'

'No, I am not!' Alicia struggled to free herself as unobtrusively as possible and was completely unsuccessful. 'Your behaviour is intolerable, sir—'

'Ah, there speaks the virtuous and respectable widow, not the provocative seductress who chose that dress and whom I held in my arms not so very long ago! Do you remember, Alicia?' His voice had dropped several tones. 'You were not so cold to me then. In fact, I could have sworn that you wanted me as much as I wanted you!' He spoke in her ear, so softly she could scarcely hear, so sensuously that she felt she might melt on the spot. She could not believe that he was doing this in the Bingleys' ballroom, with a very interested audience only a few feet away.

'You were very soft and sweet in my arms that day at Chartley,' James's voice continued, barely above a whisper, 'and your mouth tasted like honey. I wanted to take so very much more, Alicia...'

She felt his lips graze her neck with the lightest of touches and she thought that she would gasp aloud. At some point she had closed her eyes, and only the fact that James held her had enabled her to carry on moving to the music whilst her mind was a million miles away. Alicia, whatever are you doing? her inner voice prompted her. She knew the answer. She was permitting James Mullineaux to make love to her in front of three hundred people. She had broken all her resolutions.

Alicia opened her eyes and interrupted firmly before it was too late. 'Have a care, sir! Do you forget that you are indeed addressing a virtuous and respectable widow? Such comments may well do for Lady Corinna, but not for me!'

She looked up into his face and saw the derisive glint in his eyes.

'Oh, I have heard tell that you are a model of virtue, madam, and I do not doubt the truth of it! What I do doubt is the universal belief that the lovely Lady Carberry is as cold as the driven snow, which I have just proved to you is false, have I not? Be honest and admit that there is enough intensity of feeling between us to outrage these good matrons if they only suspected one tenth of it!'

James had spoken more fiercely than he had intended. Tonight, when he had seen Alicia with Wickford, he could gladly have run the man through on the spot, fortune-hunter that he was. It had made matters infinitely worse that Alicia was not indifferent to him and clearly relished his admiration. For once James was on the defensive, suddenly aware that any intentions *he* might have towards Alicia could also be construed as seeking fortune on the part of one whose estates needed an injection of hard cash. The irony of it, when he had once accused her of jilting him for a fortune!

And that was not all. Alicia might well be almost overwhelmed by the onslaught on her senses, but she had just demonstrated that she did not intend to succumb if she could help it. She was not going to make matters easy for him. Clearly the situation called for tact and patience, and James smiled to himself. He would win the game in the long run and enjoy the challenge in the meantime. For now, though, his current strategy had succeeded only in infuriating her ladyship, who, now that she had regained her composure, looked as though she would like to drill the heel of her dainty slippers into his foot.

Alicia, fortunately unaware of his thoughts, gave him a cool smile. 'Your observations on my character and our relationship, whilst fascinating, my lord, are scarcely appropriate for such a public place!'

'Then grant me leave to address them to you in private!' James said promptly, and encountered such a glare that he almost burst out laughing. Yes, he would enjoy this battle of wills.

'If you do not wish to have the distinction of being left standing alone on the dance floor, I suggest that you pursue a different line of conversation!' Alicia somehow managed to get the words out through gritted teeth whilst preserving a spurious social smile for the benefit of Mrs Eddington-Buck who was deliberately circling near them.

There was a flash of amused admiration in James's eyes. 'Egad, and you would do it too, wouldn't you? I beg your pardon, Lady Carberry.' There was no trace of apology in his tone. 'I will leave this discussion to a more suitable occasion!'

There were plenty who had viewed this encounter with varying degrees of interest, cynicism and jealousy. Patrick Wickford, watching with a smile of amused regret, turned his attention away from the dancing couple as a voice he recognised purred in his ear.

'Patrick, darling! I need you to do me some small...service...'

Wickford's lips twitched as he looked down into the entirely enchanting face of Lady Corinna Dawe. These days he was all but immune to her charms, but could still appreciate that she was a lusciously attractive woman. He gave her a smile and allowed her to draw him away from the throng to a quiet alcove. He already knew what she was going to ask him.

Lady Corinna was watching the dancers, a petulant frown on her pretty face. 'I need you to keep that little milksop, Alicia Carberry, occupied for a few weeks,' she began, without preamble. 'I don't want her getting in my way! Judging by the manner in which you were panting over her tonight, you shouldn't find the task too difficult. Do it for me, Patrick, please!'

Captain Wickford's smile grew. How interesting! He had once believed Lady Corinna far too clever in her pursuit of the opposite sex ever to make a mistake. Now he realised she had met her nemesis.

Very deliberately he allowed himself to consider the figures of Alicia Carberry and James Mullineaux as they still circled the room in the waltz. They were not speaking now, but there was a dreamy smile on Alicia's face and James's dark head was bent very close to hers. Lady Corinna was almost scowling as she followed his gaze.

'And what would be my reward for helping you out, Corinna, my love?' he asked gently.

Lady Corinna made an effort to tear her gaze away from James Mullineaux and smiled up at him. 'I'm sure I'll think of something,' she promised huskily, the sultry look in her dark eyes hinting at all sorts of delights to come.

Wickford did not trouble to tell her that she was wasting her time.

He was willing to take her commission just for the amusement, but he felt she had gravely miscalculated. James Mullineaux was not the sort of man to fall at her feet just because she gave him the nod. She had become too spoiled, too used to conquest. Nor was Mullineaux's relationship with Lady Carberry so easy to dismiss. In the moment that Mullineaux had come to claim Alicia for the waltz, Wickford had sensed all kinds of complicated factors at work.

But Lady Corinna had taken his silence for assent. She pressed a soft, lingering kiss on his cheek and wafted away to position herself close to the edge of the dance floor in anticipation of the end of the waltz.

The music drew to a close and James and Alicia thanked each other with perfect solemnity. Alicia excused herself and slipped away to the ladies' anteroom, but not before she had had the irritation of seeing Lady Corinna Dawe drift back to James's side in a swirl of exotic draperies. The sight did nothing to calm her turbulent emotions, and she sat down rather heavily in an armchair to take several deep breaths.

A few moments of quiet reflection were sufficient to restore a degree of calmness, although Alicia still felt inclined to burst into tears and was quite exasperated with herself. She felt humiliated that, despite her best intentions, she had allowed James so much licence. She had let him take up exactly where he had left off at Chartley, and it was making a mockery of her feelings! Damn it, how could he remain so calm when he was wreaking havoc on her senses? And for him to behave in such a way, and then to go straight into the arms of Lady Dawe! Well, if James wished to avail himself of Corinna Dawe's blatantly offered charms that was no concern of hers, Alicia thought crossly, but if he intended to involve her in his little games as well he would find her less tractable in future! She checked her somewhat wan appearance in the mirror and emerged from the room as the quadrille began.

The ball was nearing its end and many guests had already left, mostly going on to other functions in the certainty that they had had full value of any scandal the evening could offer. The crowd in the ballroom was therefore thinning, but there were still plenty of couples dancing. Alicia's jealous gaze almost immediately picked out James's tall figure at the side of the room, still engaged closely in conversation with Lady Corinna. Neither of them seemed aware of anything except each other.

Alicia suddenly had no taste for the evening any more. She could see Patrick Wickford coming towards her, but the thought of resuming her flirtation with him irritated her, and none of her other suitors seemed remotely attractive. In a far corner behind some potted ferns Lady Stansfield still held court, but Alicia resisted the impulse to go across to her, for she could see Christopher Westwood hovering assiduously at her grandmother's side, plying her with refreshments. Alicia danced three more dances, had some desultory chat with the Renwicks and the Westons, and decided that enough was enough.

Marcus and Caroline Kilgaren were in the hallway, conversing with Charles Oxley and a few others, whilst James could be seen in the cluster of people around Corinna Dawe. He was helping her with her cloak and Alicia, as well as a score of other people, was able to see the way Lady Corinna put her hand over his with a brief, meaningful look and a soft word.

Alicia turned away hastily, unwilling to add to her own distress by dwelling on the imminent relationship between the two of them. Miss Frensham was tripping across the hall with her cloak and she grabbed it unceremoniously, determined to leave before James saw her. But it was too late. Leaving Corinna Dawe pouting, he crossed swiftly to Alicia's side, taking her hand.

'Am I forgiven for earlier, Lady Carberry, or are you still displeased with me?'

Alicia ignored the treacherous frisson of excitement that went through her at his touch and fixed him with her most quelling look. So he thought to play her off against Corinna Dawe, did he? This was the moment to end all play-acting and pretence!

'Displeased, Lord Mullineaux? Why, I do not even recall the incident...' She managed to hit exactly the right note of perplexity.

James laughed aloud. 'How bad you are for my self-confidence, Lady Carberry! To have my attentions so easily dismissed... Shall I remind you?' The wicked glint was back in his eyes again. 'Perhaps I should—'

'James!' Lady Corinna, sharp as glass, was at his elbow. 'We are leaving now! Do you come with us or not?'

James turned to her unhurriedly. 'I shall be escorting Lady Carberry home, I think,' he said pleasantly. 'I look forward to seeing you again soon, Lady Corinna.'

Such a polite brush-off amazed Alicia and it was certainly not at all what Lady Corinna had had in mind. Her black eyes flashed furious fire as they swept over Alicia with comprehensive dislike.

'There is no need, Lord Mullineaux,' Alicia interposed hastily, anxious to avert a confrontation. She gestured towards Miss Frensham who was hovering on the edge of the group. 'It is but a step to Upper Grosvenor Street, and I have Miss Frensham to keep me company.'

James looked amused, whether at Alicia's reluctance or Lady Corinna's ire it was difficult to tell.

'No doubt,' he said smoothly, 'but I wish to speak to you. Good evening, Lady Corinna!'

Her ladyship could take a hint and flounced petulantly away without another word. Alicia sighed.

'There was no need for that,' she said, with a minatory glance up at him. 'Believe me, sir, your best interests lie in that direction!'

That earned her a flashing look, full of amusement. 'Do you say so, Lady Carberry? Whatever could lead you to such a conclusion?'

All Alicia's disappointment and frustrations seemed to lodge in a tight lump in her throat. 'Because she understands your games,' she snapped furiously, 'and she is willing to play them! And now, I fear, you will have to work hard to reinstate yourself in Lady Corinna's favours—she may not even be prepared to forgive you!'

'You are doubtless correct.' There was an absent look on James's face, as though Lady Corinna's tantrums held no interest for him. He took Alicia's arm, turning her towards the entrance.

'But how would *you* have me behave, Lady Carberry?'

Alicia thought she would burst at his persistence. 'With circumspection!' she said, angry with him for pursuing the subject and also with herself because she knew deep down she was lying. 'And perhaps you could start by confining your attentions to Lady Corinna rather than pestering me with meaningless flirtation!'

James laughed. 'Are my attentions really so unwelcome?'

Alicia gave him a fulminating look. 'Your reputation alone suggests that no woman of sense should take you seriously! And you are certainly undiscriminating, sir!'

Miss Frensham, who had been trotting along behind them, totally riveted by the conversation, gave a despairing squeak at such plain speaking. James winced and held up a hand in mock surrender. 'You are too cruel, Lady Carberry! Very well, you have convinced me!' He sketched a mocking bow. 'Your wish is my command! I'll bid you goodnight!'

He strolled off down the street in the direction of White's, and the only consolation Alicia was left with was that she had seen Lady Corinna's party depart in the opposite direction. Well, she had not wanted his false attentions, she told herself fiercely. Better that he should leave her alone rather than seek to entertain himself at her expense. Idle flirtation with him held no charm for her. She would only end up with hurt feelings and an empty, aching heart when it was all over.

The carriage drew up and Alicia waited patiently whilst the Bingleys' footman helped Miss Frensham inside. She settled herself on the opposite seat and they set off towards Upper Grosvenor Street, her mind still preoccupied with thoughts of James. And what if he had wanted to take it further than mere flirtation? the devil's advocate inside her suddenly prompted. Do you really want him to take up with Lady Corinna, when that could be you? Admit that you want him. You know how much passion there could be between you. You could persuade him easily. If you really love him, you would want him on any terms...

With a shock, Alicia realised that they had arrived in Upper Grosvenor Street and that Miss Frensham was watching her with puzzlement, waiting for her to descend from the carriage. The cold night air made Alicia shiver as she hurried into the house. It was utterly alien to her nature to be thinking in such a way, but then James aroused in her emotions completely different from any she had ever experienced before. She had lived to the age of twenty-six without ever feeling true desire, and now that James had awakened those feelings in her they demanded fulfilment. For a moment Alicia recalled the delicious weakness which invaded her senses at his touch, the pressure of desire building within her, consuming her. She trembled again, this time with remembered pleasure.

'I hope you have not caught a chill, my dear,' Miss Frensham said, with a worried frown. 'You look quite pale and I noticed you shivering earlier. I will ask Cook to make up a posset for you.'

Alicia turned a blank green gaze on her, which only confirmed her companion's worries about her state of health. As Miss Frensham hurried off to fetch her a drink and hot-water bottle, Alicia reflected that there was something ailing her, but that the remedy was neither simple nor indeed suitable for discussion with her eminently respectable companion.

Chapter Nine

To Alicia's private dismay, James took her at her word and confined
his amorous attentions to Lady Corinna Dawe. It took him just one
week to reinstate himself in her favours. Usually so casually cruel to
her admirers, her ladyship was apparently besotted to the point of obsession, according to malicious gossip. James's own feelings were less
clear, but he seemed prepared to indulge the lady, ostentatiously escorting her to parties, routs, soirées and picnics. He squired her to a
Pantheon masquerade and to a fireworks display in Vauxhall Gardens,
where Lady Corinna lured him down the Dark Walks and was observed
behaving in an amatory fashion more suited to a cyprian than the wife
of a peer. It was all highly diverting for Society—as good as a play,
Lady Stansfield had commented, thereby earning herself a glare from
her granddaughter.

Over the weeks, Alicia had also found herself in James's company,
but in far more staid circumstances than Lady Corinna. He had been in
a couple of theatre parties of Caroline's contriving and he had stood up
with Alicia for a dance or two at the balls they had both attended. He
had even taken her for a drive in the park on two occasions, but then
Lady Corinna was seen driving with him at least three times a week.
The only sensation James had caused when he had taken Alicia up with
him had been occasioned by the presence of a small black and white
dog, which had accompanied them on James's phaeton. The next day,
everyone who was anyone had had a pet dog accompanying them on
their ride in the park.

All the gossip about James and Alicia had withered once he had
taken up with Lady Corinna, most people concluding that their rela-

tionship was indeed as tame an affair as they had always maintained. This was, in fact, close to Alicia's own opinion of the situation, for she had had no private conversation with James since the night of the Bingleys' ball, and the discussion they had had then seemed like a dream. What remained all too real to her, however, were her own private longings, which she found difficult to ignore. They made the blameless time spent in James's company even more difficult for her.

Though they could now talk about all kinds of subjects in public, from his impressions of London after his time away to the latest literary work of the shocking Lord Byron, the conversation never became more personal. James behaved with impeccable propriety, just as Alicia had demanded of him, and she was intensely irritated with herself for wanting matters to be different. In her heart of hearts she knew that James had simply been passing his time in flirtation with her and now Lady Corinna was offering him something much more exciting. She tried to ignore the welter of pain and jealousy this thought engendered, but this proved difficult. At the back of her mind were the thoughts that had not left her since the night of the ball—if only she had been brave enough, it could have been her...

To make matters even more complicated, she had found herself the unexpected object of Captain Wickford's persistent gallantry. This had amused her to start with, and it was consoling in a vague sort of way in the light of James's obvious lack of interest. However, Wickford was now starting to become most particular in his attentions, and Alicia knew she would soon have to dissuade him. She sighed. It was almost possible to believe that some malicious fate was deliberately designing torments for her!

Domestic matters provided little diversion from this absorption. Before her that morning were the household accounts, but the price of candles, however monstrously expensive, could hardly distract her thoughts. She looked out of the window at the bustle in the street beyond, and wondered idly whether a walk in the park would improve her spirits.

'Excuse me, madam.' Fordyce was hovering, a slightly mournful look on his face. Alicia welcomed the interruption with relief, although she recognised from experience that his long face denoted something distasteful to report. She put down her sheet of accounts in order to give him her full attention.

'Yes, Fordyce?'

The butler cleared his throat. 'I must apologise for failing to give you this information before, madam. It was most remiss of me.' He looked slightly embarrassed. 'Whilst you were out of Town, madam, your cousin, Mr Broseley, came to call on you.'

Alicia raised her eyebrows in surprise. She seldom saw Josiah above twice a year. She remembered that he had missed Annabella's wedding through ill health and frowned. 'A social call from Cousin Josiah? What did he want, Fordyce—money?'

'Well, yes and no, madam.' Fordyce's expression became even more lugubrious. 'He did mention a pressing need for cash, but I do not believe it was his primary motive in coming here. Mr Broseley arrived at three in the morning, madam, and was—' here he cleared his throat discreetly once more '—somewhat the worse for drink. He was most insistent that he see you, and when I explained that you were from home he begged to be allowed to stay here.'

Alicia waited without comment and after a moment Fordyce continued.

'As you were not at home, madam, I judged it unwise to allow Mr Broseley to stay. I hope that I did the right thing.'

'You did indeed, Fordyce,' Alicia agreed. It seemed unkind, but Josiah was a determined scrounger. One summer several years before he had taken advantage of Alicia's absence in Brighton to move himself and several cronies into the house and there had been a most unpleasant scene when she had had him forcibly ejected. So much damage had been done to the house and her possessions in the short time that he had been there that she had scarcely been able to believe it. After that, relations had been somewhat strained between them until Josiah had arrived with a huge bouquet and a most hangdog expression. Alicia had known it was mostly humbug, but she had not been able to prevent a smile.

'Pardon the liberty, my lady,' Fordyce was saying now, 'but Mr Broseley seemed badly frightened.' He hesitated, then added; 'I wondered whether he had had some disagreement over cards. He resisted most strenuously when Dawson and I ejected him—surprisingly so for a man so badly foxed!'

'Did he leave a message at all?' Alicia asked, frowning. She was very puzzled, for Josiah had not been in touch at all since her return to Town. She could only assume that whatever had been so important before must have ceased to matter.

'Not really, madam. He was too intoxicated to be coherent.' Fordyce's lips primmed with disapproval again. 'The only matter which appeared clear was that he had come to warn you.'

'To warn me?' Alicia echoed, even more at sea.

'Yes, madam. About what, Mr Broseley was not specific. As I said, he was in some considerable fear and ran off down the street as though all the devils in hell were at his heels!'

It was an unexpectedly picturesque turn of phrase from her usually staid butler, and it was possibly that which made Alicia's mind up for her. She could visualise the clear, moonlit night, her cousin's white, strained face, befuddled with drink and fear as he tried to resist the attempts to expel him from the house. He had wanted to see her urgently, yet he had not called in the four weeks since she had been back in London. She had no real reason to be concerned, and yet she was.

Alicia sighed.

'Fordyce, I think you had better send out to find Mr Broseley for me.'

Fordyce's face was schooled to calm though inside he was very surprised. Since when had Lady Carberry actually sought out her cousin?

'Yes, madam,' he said respectfully. 'Where might Mr Broseley be found?'

This was a good question. Depending on the state of his purse, Josiah could be in any one of a number of gambling hells or brothels. Alicia sighed with vexation, already regretting her impulse.

'Send Frederick to the Feathers in Southwark, for a start, then try the Guineas,' she suggested, reflecting that it was fortunate her grandmother was not there to hear her reveal her extensive knowledge of the London stews. 'Even if Josiah is not to be found there, I believe there is a maidservant who is—' She broke off at Fordyce's look of appalled horror, and finished carefully, 'Anyway, she may well know of Josiah's whereabouts.'

Fordyce bowed without another word and went out, stiff with outrage at the mission which had been entrusted to him. Alicia stifled a giggle. Really, he could be the most ridiculous stuffed shirt sometimes! Admittedly, Lady Stansfield had chosen him for Alicia particularly for his respectable qualities, but there was no point in trying to pretend that the seamier side of life did not exist—nor that it did not involve her cousin.

Fordyce had been unfortunate enough to have to deal with the aforementioned maidservant when she had arrived on Alicia's doorstep one day the previous year, demanding money for herself and an accompanying infant whom she had claimed was Josiah's progeny. Alicia had never forgotten his look of shock as she had led the girl and the baby into the drawing-room for a chat. The encounter had ended with the girl surprising both Alicia and herself by grudgingly admitting that Josiah was not the real father, asserting that he was no gentleman either. Alicia had been forced to agree with the latter comment, and had given the girl a sum of money for the baby anyway, which had had the girl kissing her hand in gratitude. Whether the relationship with Josiah had survived to this day she would find out soon enough.

She put the matter from her mind, glad to be distracted by a call from Charlotte Renwick, who easily persuaded Alicia to join herself and Caroline in a trip to Bond Street. They spent an entertaining couple of hours selecting gloves and hats before returning home to prepare for the evening's entertainment. Alicia had also engaged herself for a soirée at the Renwicks' house that night, but her secret hope that James might also attend was dashed when Marcus announced casually that his friend had gone to the theatre. Alicia did not need to ask who had accompanied him. She found the rest of the evening a dead bore and reproached herself for her lack of appreciation of Charlotte's hospitality.

It was in fact the following afternoon that she had the answer to her questions about Josiah's whereabouts, and they were not at all what she had anticipated. At the Guineas, Frederick had found the girl voluble in her accusations against Josiah, whom she had not seen for seven weeks and who had apparently left her without a feather to fly. She had suggested rather sullenly that Frederick should try Josiah's lodgings in Deptford, but the landlady had been away. Frederick had waited to see the landlady, and now he was standing in Alicia's library, a place which made him uncomfortable anyway, since he only felt at home in the stables. He twisted his flat cap around in his hands, his fair, weathered face flushed and unhappy.

'I'm sorry, my lady, to be the bearer of such bad news...I wanted Mr Fordyce to be the one to tell you, but he said you might have questions for me—' He broke off and stared fixedly at a patch of carpet.

Alicia waved him to a seat and he perched on the edge of it as though expecting it to explode under him.

'Please do not be worried, Frederick,' she said kindly. 'Just tell me what has happened. Am I to understand that some sort of accident has befallen Josiah?'

Frederick nodded unhappily. 'Oh, ma'am...' It came out in a rush.

'I'm sorry, ma'am—Mr Broseley's dead! They buried him in St Aldate's, in a pauper's grave!'

There was silence whilst Alicia sat quite still and Frederick waited miserably for her to speak. Alicia realised that she did not feel shocked or even particularly surprised. Josiah's excesses had always been going to lead him into trouble. But she did feel a sadness which took her by surprise. Josiah had been troublesome, ineffectual, exasperating, but he had still been her cousin and she had had an unwilling affection for him.

'How did it happen, Frederick?' she asked quietly. 'My father mentioned a couple of months ago that Josiah had been ill—was it some sort of disease that carried him off?'

The groom looked even more uncomfortable. 'No, ma'am. His landlady said he fell in the river when he was drunk. She was right sorry she did not let you know, my lady, but she said she knew nothing of how to contact Mr Broseley's relations. She was most sorry because he still owed her three months' rent when he died!'

Alicia smiled reluctantly. That sounded just like Josiah. 'I will send to pay her,' she said.

'Oh, no, ma'am,' Frederick said, eager to be able to impart some good news. 'That won't be necessary. The landlady said Mr Broseley's other cousin had arrived and settled his debts when he identified the body.' He lowered his gaze. 'Begging your pardon to have to speak of such matters, my lady.'

Alicia was frowning, but not at his reference to the corpse. 'Mr Broseley's other cousin? He does not have any other cousins, Frederick, apart from my sister. Are you sure she did not mean his uncle rather than his cousin?'

The groom looked confused. 'Oh, no, ma'am, for I remember it most particular! The landlady was surprised you did not know of the death on account of the fact that she thought your other cousin would tell you!'

Alicia digested this. 'What was the name of the other cousin, Frederick?' she asked, without much hope.

Frederick shook his head. 'Don't rightly know, my lady. I didn't think to ask. All I know is that this gentleman settled up and took all Mr Broseley's effects. All except the letter for you, that is.' He brightened. 'He must have missed that. The landlady found it in his room behind the washstand. She was about to send it on, but gave it to me instead.' He patted his pockets and brought out a dog-eared missive.

Alicia thanked him gravely and he went out with relief. She picked up the letter thoughtfully, turning it over in her hands. It bore her own name in Josiah's extravagant flourish, and was stained with something that could have been tears but Alicia suspected was really gin. She was about to slide the letter-opener beneath the seal, when she realised that she was not alone. The library door was half open and a figure was hovering in the aperture. A moment later Alicia realised it was Christopher Westwood and cursed the fact that he had chosen that very moment to pay a visit. She had never felt less like receiving guests.

Westwood, appearing oblivious to any tension in her manner, threw his gloves and cane in the general direction of Fordyce and sauntered past him into the room. The butler's figure was stiff with rage. He had already intercepted Westwood in the hall and intimated that Alicia was not receiving, only to be told that she would see family.

'How are you, Alicia?' Westwood enquired affably. 'Fordyce said you were not at home, but I knew you would see me!'

Fordyce's mouth turned down even more in disapproval. Alicia looked at him with resignation.

'Thank you, Fordyce,' she said austerely. 'And I am not at home to visitors.'

Westwood, in the process of divesting himself of his coat and hat, brightened to hear this. He had been very unsure of his welcome, for Alicia had been as cold as ice to him since he had made the scene in the Bingleys' ballroom. However, if she wished to be private with him it must augur well. He sat down close to her in a way Alicia found tiresomely proprietorial and she deliberately got up, choosing a seat as far away from him as possible.

Westwood did not appear discomfited. He picked up the letter from the desk, looking at its designation without even concealing his interest. Alicia stood up again, crossed to the desk, then with great deliberation took the letter from him and put it in a drawer. She resumed her seat to turn on him her most bland and superficial smile.

'Is aught amiss, Alicia?' Westwood's bright grey eyes dwelt on her with interest. 'You seem a little troubled this afternoon.'

'I am perfectly well, I thank you,' Alicia snapped. 'However, I have just heard that my cousin Josiah has died, which is why I am not receiving.'

Westwood raised his eyebrows. 'So Josiah Broseley is dead, is he? I am sorry to hear it,' he commented with so obvious a lack of concern that his words were robbed of any sympathy. 'You were hardly close, however,' he added, even more insensitively. 'Surely a formal period of mourning would be a little excessive?'

Alicia eyed him with dislike. 'I would not claim that Josiah and I were very fond of each other, but the news of his death was still a shock! Really, Christopher, I would have expected you to have a little more consideration!'

'I'm sorry, Alicia, but one might have foreseen that Josiah would end in such a way.' Westwood gave a negligent shrug. 'What did he die of?' he added carelessly.

'I believe he fell in the Thames,' Alicia said shortly, and saw a smile she did not understand briefly touch Westwood's lips. For some reason this irritated her even more.

'Careless of him,' Westwood murmured. 'He was drunk, I suppose.'

'I was not aware that you were familiar with Josiah's habits,' Alicia said frostily, and wondered what she had said when he gave her a very sharp look, totally unlike his usual languid pose.

'Did you hear from him at all before he died?' Westwood asked, allowing his gaze to wander along the library bookshelves, as though Alicia's answer was of no real interest to him. The question put Alicia in mind of her father's enquiry on the occasion of her visit to Greyrigg, which made her even more irritable. She had managed to forget Bertram Broseley for the few brief weeks she had spent in London. Must matters always be reminding her of him? She decided that it was time to get rid of Westwood's unwanted presence.

'No, I did not. Did you want something in particular, Christopher, or is this just a social call?'

Even Westwood was not so insensitive that he could view this as a particularly encouraging comment. He straightened in his chair.

'I am here on an errand from your grandmother,' he said, with a return to his normal equable manner. 'She suggests that you dine at Stansfield House before the masquerade next Friday—nothing formal, just family. Will you come?'

Alicia hesitated. She felt tempted to cry off and anyway she suspected this to be a plot of her grandmother's making. Lady Stansfield had made it plain that she wished to see better relations established between her granddaughter and great-nephew. She had apparently not given up hope that Alicia would accept Christopher's marriage proposal since recent events appeared to dash any hope of Alicia marrying James Mullineaux. Still, there was nothing to be gained by sitting at home fretting over Josiah's death. Despite the insensitivity of Westwood's comments, he had been right in suggesting it would be hypocritical of her to go into formal mourning for Josiah. Westwood was awaiting her reply, his gaze full of eager hope. Alicia stifled her irritation.

'Please thank my grandmother for her invitation to dine, Christopher,' she said carefully. 'I shall be pleased to do so.'

'Capital! Lady Stansfield will be delighted!' Westwood had brightened considerably at her acceptance, not least because it meant he could now escort her to the masquerade and had a legitimate excuse for staying at her side all evening. Taking her hand, he pressed a fervent kiss on it. Alicia sighed. The day was proving to be very trying.

After Christopher Westwood went out, Alicia sat still for a moment wondering what it was about him that had been different during their conversation. It was Josiah's name that had prompted the change, she thought. Christopher had barely bothered to utter the conventional platitudes of sympathy over his death, and for a man who prided himself on his proper behaviour under all circumstances that was rather remarkable. She frowned. He was certainly acting uncharacteristically.

Shaking off her puzzlement, Alicia moved back to sit behind the desk, and took out the letter from Josiah again. This time the knife cut through the seal and she unfolded it to read the message.

Alicia,
Be careful. You may know that your father has plans for you, but there are others closer to home you should watch.

Here there were some other words—a name?—heavily crossed out and illegible.

I can say no more, but I must see you. I am in fear of my life.
When you get the letter, send for me to the Guineas.
Your loving cousin,
Josiah.

Alicia pulled a face. Josiah's habitual penchant for melodrama had resulted in a letter which told her very little indeed. She could imagine him sitting in his shabby room, his bottle of gin by his side, plumped up with a sense of importance as he penned the theatrical words to warn her and summon her to his aid. She considered the letter again. Yes, she knew her father had wanted to marry her off again, but what did the reference to someone closer to home mean? There was no one closer than her father, unless one included the Countess of Stansfield, and it seemed ludicrous to imagine that she was plotting something sinister.

Alicia got up to put the letter in the fire, but as she was about to throw it into the flames she paused and looked at it again. Josiah stated quite plainly that he was in fear of his life. Fordyce had confirmed this when he had said that Josiah had resisted being thrown out of the house and had subsequently run off down the road in a frenzy. There could be any number of reasons for Josiah's terror—the money-lenders could have been foreclosing on him, or he could have fallen foul of some card sharp—but there was a definite implication in the letter that the matter involved Alicia in some way. She flung the letter down on the table in exasperation. Why did Josiah have to be so obscure? Now she would never be able to ask him what he had meant.

She remembered what Frederick had told her about the mysterious cousin, and frowned. She knew that Josiah had no cousins other than herself and Annabella. Perhaps this mystery man was some connection of her father's? Alicia was suddenly aware of a very strong desire to leave well alone. She did not want to become embroiled in Josiah's murky affairs, to discover things that were better left unknown. But Josiah had been in fear of his life. And Josiah had died. Alicia frowned. She thought about her cousin; he had been reckless, foolish and spend-thrift, but was she really going to leave him in his pauper's grave and think no more about it? Surely she owed it to him to try to find out what had happened?

She rang the bell for Fordyce, and soon his stately tread could be heard approaching across the marble hallway. Alicia grimaced a little as she thought about the instructions she was about to give him for Frederick. Delving into Josiah's domestic arrangements had been bad enough, but now she would be fortunate if he did not decide to leave her service!

Alicia refused all invitations the following week as a mark of respect to her cousin. She had discussed this with Lady Stansfield, who, as an arbiter of taste, felt that her granddaughter had a fine line to tread between appearing to have no concern over her cousin's death and appearing hypocritical by going into excessive mourning for someone she'd hardly ever seen. Most of the *ton* barely knew of Josiah's existence anyway, and took the news of his demise without much comment. As for Alicia, she found the time alone quite soothing for once, giving her the opportunity to read and to write letters—and studiously avoid thinking about James Mullineaux.

One thing which Alicia did not discuss with her grandmother was her concerns over Josiah's death and the warning he had issued to her. She had no wish to worry the old lady unnecessarily. But she found herself in desperate need of someone to talk to. Christopher Westwood she dismissed almost immediately. She did not believe she could rely on him. She thought of talking to Caroline Kilgaren, but decided against it. Finally and imperceptibly her mind turned to James Mullineaux. She wanted to confide in him. She wanted to be able to trust him. A few weeks ago she might have followed her instincts and sought him out, but now matters were different. Any closeness which there had appeared to be between them had proved illusory.

By the time the Stapleford masquerade came round, she had made no progress in her pursuit of further information of Josiah's death. Frederick's enquiries had drawn a blank, for Josiah's landlady had been silently unhelpful and the girl at the Guineas had sworn she knew nothing. The beadle who had arranged the burial had been found, but he had had nothing helpful to add; it seemed they had reached a dead end. Alicia was tempted to forget the whole matter, but something nagged at her to persist.

Alicia was already regretting her decision to accept Christopher Westwood's escort by the time that the party from Stansfield House reached the masquerade. Lady Stansfield had insisted on attending a tedious musical soirée before the ball and Alicia had sat wincing whilst an off-key tenor had warbled in Italian about the miseries of true love. Westwood had sat beside her, requesting translations of the songs, once more the possessive lover.

The masquerade was well advanced as they made their way into the ballroom. Ostensibly a celebration of Lord Stapleford's birthday, it was also yet another attempt to matchmake for the Staplefords' daughter Georgiana, who, at twenty-two, was now in every danger of being left on the shelf.

Because of the lateness of the hour, the ballroom was full and Alicia's hand was immediately solicited for a set of country dances which were forming. Etiquette was less strict behind the disguise of domino and mask, and Alicia observed that some fairly uninhibited behaviour was already taking place. No doubt that was why masquerades were so popular in the first place!

From her place in the dance Alicia was able to guess at the identities of some of her fellow guests—Caroline Kilgaren, in a white domino and matching mask studded with diamonds was in the next set, dancing with a gentleman in blue whom Alicia suspected to be Peter Weston. Marcus was over by the door to the refreshment room, chatting with another gentleman. In a group by the French windows stood Lady Corinna Dawe, voluptuous in a deep purple domino and playfully fending off the advances of a gentleman in grey in the sort of way that was intended to encourage rather than dissuade him. Alicia's heart missed a beat, but it was not James Mullineaux with Lady Corinna, for the gentleman was too short and stocky. Her ladyship was no doubt skilled in juggling her admirers, Alicia thought dispassionately.

Alicia herself was the recipient of plenty of stares, for even the relative anonymity of a domino and mask could not dull the instant impact of her beauty. The domino of jade-green complemented her colouring and she wore with it a mask of plain black silk. Indeed, the mask was a positive benefit since it hid her expression from view on a night when she did not suppose she looked very cheerful at all.

The dances became more lively and the crowds more animated, and still Alicia could not distinguish the Marquis of Mullineaux amongst the throng. She felt tired and depressed amongst such vibrant company. She had a constant stream of partners, but felt as though she was an outsider watching an event in which she had no part. Christopher Westwood watched her progress through the dances with jealous eyes, for his plans of spending the evening with Alicia had been overset from the first by Lady Stapleford. As one of the few acceptable young men who had shown Georgiana any serious attention, he was identified as a possible son-in-law by Lord and Lady Stapleford and they constantly threw him in her way. Georgiana herself, in celestial blue, was ably aiding and abetting this, gravitating to his side whenever she was free, attempting to flirt shamelessly with him.

The evening wound on. Lady Stansfield was holding court as usual in one corner of the room, surrounded by her elderly admirers. Alicia exchanged a few words with Caroline, who was obviously in high spirits and made her friend feel even more depressed as a result. Alicia danced every dance, smiled until her face ached and parried the more outrageous sallies of her partners. She realised that it had been a mistake on her part to try to distract herself at such a ball. The pleasure everyone else was having only served to underline her own worries all the more. The mystery surrounding Josiah's death dogged her heels and she could not shake it off.

Finally, to add to her woes, Westwood escaped Georgiana and came across to claim a dance, rudely cutting out Richard Pilton who had just approached Alicia on the same errand. Westwood's face was set in lines of deep displeasure and Alicia's heart sank even further.

'I have been trying to dance with you all evening,' he began peevishly as the orchestra struck up for a cotillion. 'Lady Stapleford has been pushing me in the direction of that spiteful cat Georgiana and I've barely been able to escape from her sight!'

'How flattering for you,' Alicia murmured, secretly thinking that Christopher and Georgiana rather deserved each other. 'No doubt she has her eye on you as a prospective son-in-law!'

Westwood grunted. 'Well, she'll catch cold at that! The whole of Georgiana's fortune is not enough to sweeten that pill!'

Alicia looked at him with a dislike fortunately hidden by her mask as Westwood continued in the same tone, 'I really wish you would reconsider my offer, Alicia! It would put an end to precisely that sort of speculation!'

'Thank you!' Alicia no longer tried to conceal her dislike. 'No doubt *my* fortune is sufficient to help you overlook those aspects of my character you dislike!'

Westwood looked affronted. 'Dash it all, Alicia, there's no need to be so sharp! You know I am at your feet—and have been for years!'

There was nothing remotely loverlike in his voice and Alicia wondered whether he had actually managed to convince himself that he loved her, or was merely repeating the fiction in the hope of convincing her. Either way, it only confirmed her belief that they would be badly suited and she was glad she had not seriously considered his proposal. A little while ago she might have been persuaded that he cared for her and that she was treating him badly. Now she felt that he no longer did care, if he had ever done so.

A moment later she was assailed with a jealousy far greater than anything Westwood could ever have felt. The Marquis of Mullineaux had come into the ballroom and had instantly been intercepted by Lady Corinna who was whispering intimately in his ear. Saturnine in a black domino, there was no mistaking his height and breadth of shoulder. He straightened up with negligent ease and the two of them disappeared together into the card-room. Alicia missed her footing, her anguish was so great, and Westwood caught her arm to steady her.

'Do take care, Alicia!' He guided her through the dancers to the edge of the ballroom without so much as a by-your-leave. 'I think you should sit this one out until you feel better!'

Resentment at his high-handed attitude now added to the mixture of miseries tormenting Alicia. She could not be bothered to speak, sitting in silence through the remainder of the dance and the polonaise that followed. Westwood attempted to engage her in conversation with determined cheerfulness.

Meanwhile, the Marquis and Lady Corinna had re-entered the room and joined the dance, which gave James the opportunity to study Alicia in a very similar way to that which she had been watching him earlier. His observation was subtle, but not covert enough to fool Lady Corinna, who was very shrewd in matters pertaining to her own sex. She gave an exaggerated sigh.

'Can it be that you still carry a torch for Lady Carberry, my lord? I fear that any hopes you may cherish in that direction are destined to be dashed!'

James raised an eyebrow lazily, not troubling to deny her allegation. 'Why might that be, Lady Corinna?'

Lady Corinna was too accomplished to disparage a rival directly. She pressed her body provocatively against his and gave him a melting smile. 'Oh, it is simply that Lady Carberry is renowned for her...coldness...to her admirers.' This was accompanied by a look which was the very antithesis of coldness. 'One might have expected that she would have wished for some fun after so tediously old a husband, but it seems not. One can only assume that such...pursuits do not interest her.' There was no mistaking the look she sent him with these words.

However, her statement did not appear to have the desired effect. As the dance ended, James renewed his scrutiny of Alicia with even greater interest. She was sitting quite still, head bent, with the unconscious grace which always seemed a part of her. For some reason he could not divine he was convinced that she was not at all happy. A man he took to be Christopher Westwood was talking to her animatedly and receiving little or no response.

'Of course,' Lady Corinna was saying to draw attention back to herself, 'she *is* very beautiful if one admires that style.'

The Marquis, who could recognise malice even when it was couched in such honeyed terms, agreed with deliberate obtuseness that Lady Carberry was indeed very beautiful. It earned him a sharp look and drove Lady Corinna further into indiscretion through sheer pique.

'Indeed,' she said spitefully, 'she has done very well out of those looks in the past. George Carberry may have been a nobody socially, but he was a very rich nobody and one who died very conveniently.'

Looking up into James's eyes, Lady Corinna thought she saw a flash of anger, but it was banished so swiftly by indifference that she thought she must have been mistaken. The movement of the dance took them onward and a moment later she knew she had miscalculated.

'Lady Carberry's marriage was very much a match forced by her father,' James said quite levelly, but in tones which could not be misconstrued.

Lady Corinna stared. Provoked into uncharacteristic jealousy, she gave a titter of artificial laughter.

'Lud, my lord, surely you cannot have fallen for that old excuse? Why, can it be that you are in love with her? How piquant! Or perhaps your relationship with Lady Carberry is not as innocent as the two of you like to make it seem?'

She knew it for a disastrous mistake as soon as the words had left her mouth. Before that moment the situation might have been retrieved with a tactful acknowledgement or a change of subject. But jealousy had driven her on and now it was too late. Lady Corinna had needed a reason to explain why James had not availed himself of her invitations to take their relationship further—much further. She did not think him obtuse, nor did his reputation suggest that he had lived as a monk. Yet all her most blatant invitations had been smoothly turned down in a way that could give no offence but which Lady Corinna had found both baffling and deeply frustrating.

But now she realised that her unguarded remark had hit quite literally on the truth, and that her next malicious comment had ended any chance she might have had of saving the day—or saving him for herself.

James caught her arm very tightly, swinging her round to face him. Until then their relationship had been characterised on his side by an indolence which had never revealed any deep feelings at all. Lady Corinna had, for her pride's sake, tried to make him fall in love with her, but he had shown no signs of doing so, no sign of any real feeling. Now, however, she could see genuine emotion in plenty and it chilled her to the bone.

James kept his voice discreetly low, but there was an edge of white-hot anger to it.

'I think it best, madam, that we forget your ill-judged observations.

However, should I hear them repeated I shall know exactly where they originated.'

He did not wait for a reply, but dropped her arm with a contemptuous gesture and, turning on his heel, strode away without a backward glance.

Alicia was finding Christopher Westwood's presence beginning to grate on her. He lurked at her shoulder like a gaoler, glowering at anyone who looked as though they might ask her to dance. He had even managed to frighten away Caroline and Marcus, who had gone off with a certain relief to dance together. Caroline was puzzled that Alicia, normally so spirited in her refusal to accept Westwood dictating to her, appeared to have become completely passive. She did not have the opportunity to ask her friend what was going on, but as the dance ended she steered Marcus towards where James Mullineaux was moodily watching the game of piquet progressing in the next room.

'James—' Caroline never wasted time '—I need you to go and save Alicia from Christopher Westwood!'

Marcus almost choked but James did not seem impressed. He did not laugh, but shook his head slightly.

'I'm sorry, Caro, I don't think I can help you.'

Caroline frowned in vexation. 'What is the matter with everyone tonight? You're sulking in here like a schoolboy and Alicia is letting Christopher bully her! James, for my sake, please do as I ask!'

James turned to Marcus. 'What do you think, Marcus?'

His friend gave him a level look. 'I think it would be very dangerous, James.'

James smiled reluctantly. 'So you've read me like a book again, Marcus? Damn it, the only time I'm behaving with circumspection, and your own wife tries to persuade me otherwise!'

Caroline stamped her foot. 'I have no idea what you are both talking about,' she said stormly, 'but if you don't like my idea I'll have to think again—'

James put his hand on her arm. 'Keep calm, Caro! I am persuaded! But don't blame me if you regret it later!' He put his drink down and disappeared into the ballroom. Caroline turned to Marcus, still frowning.

'Marcus, if you don't tell me what is going on, I shall scream with aggravation!'

Marcus laughed. 'I rather think, my love, that James has been trying to avoid Alicia. Or at least,' he corrected himself scrupulously, 'trying to behave towards her with impeccable respectability. He wishes to put his estates in order before he takes matters any further, but I believe

True Colours

his intentions to be completely honourable!' He met her eyes, wide behind the jewelled mask. 'You may imagine how difficult it is for him to behave in such a way! And now you have thrown temptation in his path!'

Gradually the group around Alicia and Westwood had dissipated, seeking more congenial company, and as the music struck up for a waltz Westwood turned back to Alicia again clearly intending to ask her to dance.

The figure of a black domino interposed itself somehow between the two of them.

'You must not seek to monopolise this beautiful lady, sir!' The black domino's tone was mocking. 'This dance is surely mine!'

Alicia found herself swept onto the floor before a scowling Westwood could even draw breath to object. The black domino smiled down at her from behind his mask.

'I apologise if you feel that I have forced your hand, my lady, but I had the strong impression that your companion would not yield to more gentle persuasion! And how else would I then achieve a dance with the most beautiful lady in the room?'

Alicia's lips twitched but she was determined not to fall immediate prey to this outrageous flattery. 'A pretty compliment, sir,' she observed coolly. 'You must be a practised flatterer! In a gathering like this how is it possible to make such a judgement between ladies?'

The dark eyes behind the mask were intent on her face. 'Easily. Beauty such as yours cannot be eclipsed by a mere domino and mask, madam.'

Alicia laughed. The lilt of the music carried them onwards. He always chooses the waltz, she thought, feeling the hard strength of the arm that encircled her. She felt light-headed, as though she had drunk too much, dizzy with a mixture of excitement and anticipation. She forgot his previous coolness, forgot Lady Corinna, and gave herself up to the exhilaration of being in his arms again.

As they turned, Alicia caught sight of Christopher Westwood glowering in their direction and smiled at her partner with deliberation.

'You are too generous, sir. I shall begin to suspect you of insincerity soon!'

'Oh, you should not!' The lazy drawl held a note of teasing she recognised. 'I am in deadly earnest. But then, I have the advantage over your multitude of other admirers because I would recognise you anywhere, and in any disguise, madam. Just as you would know me.'

Alicia felt a shiver go through her. There was no point in denying his words and he had invested them with a significance deeper than their surface value. She looked up into the dark face above her and forgot all her worries in the pure enjoyment of being held so close to him. She could read the heat of desire in his eyes, see that he wanted her, feel it in the touch of his hand. It was intoxicating, pleasure distilled. She wanted to drink deep. It was so overwhelming that Alicia felt her doubts and fears melt away as the exhilaration took her.

The end of the dance found them by the doors which led to the conservatory. James let Alicia go slowly, with a speculative look which did nothing to calm her inner turmoil. 'Will you consent to walk a little with me?' he asked.

Alicia hesitated. He was very direct. There was no prevarication about the heat of the ballroom or the need for fresh air. Seeing her doubt, James smiled suddenly.

'Come, Alicia, you used not to be so careful of public opinion! Will you trust me if I promise to behave with the utmost propriety?'

He proffered his arm and they sauntered through the double doors which led into the green darkness of the conservatory. The air was scented and humid here the light dim. Spiky shadows of fern and palm mingled on the floor, and couples wandered slowly amongst the plants, conversing in low voices. They walked for a little while in silence, but it was a silence sharp with awareness on Alicia's part. She was very conscious of the hard muscles of his arm beneath her fingers and the brush of his body against hers as they walked. It was almost enough to still her mind to the exclusion of her other concerns, but not quite. Unconsciously her head drooped as she felt the weight of her worries come back to haunt her.

James looked at her downbent head thoughtfully. 'I've been watching you this evening, Alicia,' he said gently. 'There's something troubling you, isn't there?'

Taken aback by his perception, Alicia prevaricated. 'Something wrong? Whatever can you mean, my lord?'

She saw a shadow of a smile touch his mouth. 'Why, simply what I say. I hope you will not think me arrogant if I say that I know you well enough to tell when something is worrying you. But I have no wish to pry.'

Alicia immediately felt ashamed. She made a slight gesture. 'I'm sorry,' she said contritely. 'I know I sounded ungracious. You are right, of course, but I did not realise that it showed.'

'Only to me, perhaps. I will stand your friend, if you wish to confide in someone.'

Alicia looked at him. In the shadowy darkness her eyes seemed huge and troubled, almost luminously green in her heart-shaped face. Once again she was completely trapped by her feelings for him. The impulse to trust him and tell him the truth was terribly powerful.

She had wanted to confide in him, and here he was offering her that chance.

They walked on slowly in silence. There were other couples loitering beneath the palm trees and flirting in the alcoves. Water splashed into an ornate lily pond where lazy goldfish flashed a fin. It was no place for confidences, being too well-populated.

'I would like to tell you,' Alicia said at last, a little hesitantly, 'but we must step outside, I think, to avoid being overheard.'

James gave her a questioning look. 'That would not be very prudent, perhaps, given your previous wish that we both observe the conventions!'

He had a point and Alicia was forced to admit it. To stroll in the hothouse was unexceptionable, since other couples were doing precisely that, but to step outside would be pushing the bounds of acceptability. She could hardly insist on certain rules one day, then persist in breaking them herself the next. But then, he did not yet realise the gravity of her problem and therefore could not appreciate that the Staplefords' conservatory was hardly the place to discuss murder.

'I can vouch for my own good behaviour,' Alicia said, without a smile. 'Can you do the same, my lord?'

It was a provocative question and James gave her a searching look. The heat had gone from his eyes, but there was still a tension in his manner as though he held himself on a very tight rein. 'No, not really! If there is something you wish to discuss it would be safer for you to do it here!'

Alicia sighed. She seemed to have no choice. She waited until they were close to the terrace doors, then said, in a clear, quiet voice quite devoid of feeling, 'Very well, I shall tell you here, then. I believe my cousin Josiah to have been murdered.'

Whatever James had been expecting, it was not that. Alicia, still holding his arm, felt the shock go through him like lightning. Without another word he steered them both through the doors and out onto the terrace, letting go of her when they reached the balustrade. The air was fresh and chill after the warmth of the house and the sky was very clear. Alicia took off her mask and swung it from her hands by the ribbons.

James was leaning on the balustrade, looking out across a line of cypresses which disappeared into the dark gardens. Eventually he said, in the same quiet tones she herself had used, 'Whatever can have led you to make such a deduction?'

Reaction was now getting to Alicia. She wrapped her arms around herself for warmth. 'Fordyce tells me that Josiah called to see me whilst I was away in Somerset. He wanted to warn me about something but he was too drunk to be coherent. Fordyce put him out of the house, but I think he regretted it later, for he said Josiah was in terror of his life.' She shivered in the cold air. 'And then Josiah died. Am I at fault in thinking it more than a coincidence?'

James straightened up and turned to look at her, still preserving an irreproachable distance between them. In the moonlight his expression was remote, impenetrable. He put back the hood of his domino with an impatient gesture and took off his mask.

'Perhaps not,' he said noncommittally. 'And what have you done to discover the truth, Alicia? Knowing you, it would be impossible to believe that you have let matters lie!'

Alicia prickled with resentment.

'I could not just ignore it!' she answered hotly. 'Leaving aside the matter of Josiah's death, there was a letter he wrote me, and a mysterious cousin who does not exist!'

She saw James raise his eyebrows in faint exasperation. 'All the ingredients of a gothic romance!' he commented dryly. 'You had better tell me the whole, I think!'

Alicia leant on the balustrade, relating the whole story from the moment Fordyce had told her of Josiah's visit to the current state of Frederick's investigations. It was a huge relief to share her suspicions with someone, even if she did suspect James was likely to tell her that her imagination was running away with her.

'We seem to have reached a full stop,' she said regretfully, at the end of her recital, 'and to have made no progress. I am at a loss as to what to do next.'

'Not to meddle any further would seem a sensible course of action,' James said sharply.

'But I cannot just let it go,' Alicia burst out.

James took a step nearer to her without appearing to notice. 'I was not suggesting it. As you are determined to pursue this, I am offering to put investigations in motion at Bow Street for you.'

Alicia hesitated. James asked, with the smile back in his voice, 'What is it? Do you not trust me? Or have you perhaps changed your mind?'

Alicia shook her head. 'No, I have not changed my mind. And it is a relief to me that you do not dismiss my concerns out of hand! But— are you sure, sir? You are under no obligation to help me.'

'The offer still stands.'

'Very well, then. I accept with gratitude, my lord.'

There was a silence between them. Alicia turned to go back inside, oddly at a loss as to what she should say now. As she took a step towards the doorway, James caught her hand.

'Just a moment, my lady. We have been out here some considerable time. You know what people will think?'

Alicia paused. She could no longer see his expression, for the moon had dipped behind the cypresses, leaving them in darkness. She felt almost empty with the relief of sharing her problem, and too tired to care about anything else.

'Let them think what they will. It's better than the truth!'

'That's so, of course.' She could hear the smile in his voice, though she could not see him clearly. 'But you look, if you will forgive me, like someone who has just been discussing murder, rather than someone who has just been thoroughly kissed in the starlight. It would be preferable for the Staplefords' guests to be certain of the latter, not the former!'

He pulled her towards him and Alicia's free hand came up hard against his chest. The hood of her domino slipped back so that her hair spilled out, its colour muted by the dark. She caught her breath.

'My lord, I thought we had agreed... You should not—'

James just laughed. 'No, I should not. But I did warn you, and you should know by now that in this at least you cannot trust me!'

'Yes, but I scarce supposed—'

Alicia's words were cut off as his mouth captured hers. Afterwards, all she could remember was the strength of his arms holding her hard against him, and the brilliant, dizzying darkness of the kiss as their desire spiralled up to engulf them.

It could have been five minutes or several hours later that James lifted his mouth from hers, holding her at arm's length, scanning her face. He was breathing as hard as she as he gave a shaken laugh.

'Well, no one is going to have any doubts now! Go inside, Alicia, before I forget all my good resolutions and kiss you again!'

Alicia paused. She felt cold now that he had let her go, and almost dizzy with longing. 'I think I shall go home now,' she said, a little uncertainly. 'I have no taste for the masquerade.'

James's face was still and shadowed. He did not answer her. His hands fell to his sides and he stepped back punctiliously to let her pass. Suddenly, inexplicably, there was a tension between them. Still Alicia hesitated on the threshold of committing herself.

'Will you accompany me, Lord Mullineaux?' she asked softly. 'I find I do not wish to be alone.'

James shifted slightly. His voice was once more his own—cool, remote and a little hard. 'Are you sure that that is what you really want, Lady Carberry? You might prefer to reconsider. Seeking out my sole company is hardly wise.'

Alicia put her hand on his arm and felt the tautness in him. 'Please,' she urged, very quietly. 'Don't leave me now!'

There was a very long silence. James's expression was unreadable.

'Then,' he said, very deliberately, 'you must go back into the ballroom and take your leave. It would not do for us to return together, so I shall join you in your carriage shortly.'

Alicia gave him a hesitant backward glance as she went in through the French doors. He was watching her with the same cool, remote expression in his eyes and somehow it chilled her. But it was too late now. She had made her decision and the die was cast.

Chapter Ten

James did not touch her at all in the carriage on the way back to Upper Grosvenor Street, nor did he speak. Alicia would have been happier if he had. She sat opposite him in the dark, watching in the faint lamplight the stern set of his face, his expression distant, almost severe. It daunted her. This was not as she had imagined it would be.

Alicia was half-appalled, half-exhilarated at what she was doing. It might have been the intoxication of the wine or the moonlight which had actually brought her to this point, but she knew deep down that it was what she wanted. She had been faced with the growing conviction that she would rather be with James on any terms than face the prospect of losing him. Whilst it was not in her nature to give herself easily, she loved him too much to want to live without him. She would settle for whatever he was prepared to give.

She stole another look at James, very aware of him in the enclosed space of the carriage. He had removed the black domino and the immaculate but severe cut of his evening clothes only served to enhance his physique, doing nothing to detract from his devastating good looks. His black hair was artfully dishevelled in the windswept style and there was an expression in his eyes which made him look, Alicia thought, the complete answer to any maiden's prayer and the epitome of a chaperon's warning.

For a moment her heart skipped a beat out of sheer nervousness. It's not too late to change your mind, a voice whispered inside her head. She drew on all the courage she could muster. She had thought about this, carefully considered her options. The thought of losing him to some dewy-eyed debutante or experienced flirt was not to be borne.

Besides, she might as well be honest. She wanted James, longed for his touch in a way quite alien to her previous experience. She could not draw back now, *would* not!

It was late and Fordyce had dismissed the servants in the expectation that Alicia would have stayed at Stansfield House for the night after the masquerade. Dawson, the night porter, was dozing at his post and woke with a start as the carriage drew up and its occupants descended. His eyebrows shot up into his hairline as he recognised the Marquis of Mullineaux with Alicia. He struggled upright, and desperately tried to regain a suitably bland expression.

'Madam! We did not expect—Do you wish me to wake the servants?'

'No, thank you, Dawson.' Alicia sounded far more composed than she felt. 'We do not require anything further tonight.'

Once again, Dawson, who had far less aplomb than Fordyce, fought to keep his amazement from showing on his face. 'Yes, my lady,' he said respectfully, and watched them cross the hall to the drawing-room. The door closed behind them with a firm click and Dawson stared at its panels in complete disbelief. He even pinched himself to check that he was awake. He was.

Alicia was finding this far more difficult than she had anticipated. She had not really thought beyond the point of making her wishes clear to James. Now she was not sure what she had expected to happen next, but whatever impassioned and ardent scene should have followed it was very different from reality.

James had taken the drink she had offered and was now standing moodily before the fire, his arm resting along the mantelpiece.

'Before we take matters any further,' he said quietly, 'may I be permitted to know why you have chosen this course of action? It seems somewhat out of character. Are you sure you know what you are doing?'

That was the last straw for Alicia. This clinical analysis of her behaviour was so far from her romantic dreams as to be a travesty.

'I thought that you were supposed to know how to manage these things,' she replied childishly. 'That's why I chose you!'

It wasn't true, but the words, born of disappointment and frustration, were out before she could bite her lip. James put his glass down on the mantelpiece with what seemed like exaggerated care and crossed to her with an intentness which belied his previous air of indolence. He leant on the arms of Alicia's chair so that she was pinned back and forced to crane her neck to look up at him.

'So now we come to the truth of it,' he said, very softly but with an edge to his words which frightened her. 'I did not believe you would go through with this, but it seems I misjudged you! A few weeks ago you were accusing *me* of a want of propriety, yet now I am to help you over the temporary inconvenience of your virginity, if I understand you correctly!'

Alicia winced at his words and the hot colour flooded her face. In all her calculations it had not occurred to her that he would react like this. She had assumed that were she to make her feelings clear he would take control of the situation. He had declined to play her game—worse, he had spoken with a cool calculation which only proved that he had no desire for her. Humiliated, she realised that she had misread the circumstances completely. True, James had indulged in a certain amount of flirtation with her, but it had not meant anything to him. And why should it, with the opulent charms of Lady Dawe all too obviously at his disposal? So she had made a complete fool of herself.

'You mistake me; I did not mean that—' she began desperately, concerned now only to retreat and cope with her embarrassment in private.

But James was not prepared to let it go so easily. She looked so young and vulnerable in the shadowed candlelight that it made her behaviour seem all the more outrageous. James tried to concentrate on her relative youth, her naïveté, her inexperience, but all his wayward mind seemed capable of presenting him with was a series of images which had nothing to do with innocence and everything to do with the deep, turbulent emotions which ran between the two of them. With his anger fanned to white heat by his own imagination, he cut her off ruthlessly.

'You did not mean what, precisely? To propose me as your first conquest in a career as a demi-rep?' He straightened up, still looming over her threateningly. 'Perhaps I misunderstood! Perhaps you intended only to become *my* mistress rather than to throw yourself open to the public? Thank you, but I prefer to do the asking myself!'

Since this had been precisely what Alicia had intended, her mortification now knew no bounds. She did not understand that James's anger sprang more from the temptation of her offer rather than its lack of appeal. And her pride was now seriously injured. How dared he humiliate her like this? She jumped to her feet.

'How very hypocritical you can be, Lord Mullineaux!' she said furiously. 'So the rules are different for you, are they, and for the likes of Lady Dawe? What blatant double standards!'

James clenched his fists with frustration. His mouth was a hard, angry line, but still he strove for self-control. 'My dear child, can you not see that respectable ladies simply do not behave in such a manner? Lady Corinna Dawe is the sort of woman whose behaviour should be as far removed from your own as...as the Prince Regent, and even you are not so naïve as to require an explanation of that!'

Alicia looked like an angry kitten, he thought dispassionately, all wide-eyed fury and sharp little claws. He almost expected her to stamp her foot.

'How dare you be so patronising, sir?' she stormed. 'I am a widow of twenty-six, not some immature child of eighteen! It is not for you to legislate for my behaviour! I have the right to act as I choose!'

James lost his temper finally and comprehensively. 'You have just proved your lack of understanding by your very words,' he said scathingly. 'You don't know what you're talking about! God damn it, this isn't some parlour game you can play and expect not to get hurt! What if half Society does behave as you describe? That is not for you!'

Alicia recoiled, her face stony, though her eyes were bright with unshed tears.

'Enough! You have said quite enough, sir! I understand you perfectly! But do not think that you have the right to dictate my conduct!' The sting was all too apparent beneath the sweetness of her next words. 'Though I may not appeal to you, I am sure that there will be others more...amenable...to my suggestions! I bid you goodnight!'

For a moment, James did not move. Alicia was standing between him and the door, so she was now perfectly able to see the almost murderous look of fury on his face as he started towards her. Her heart gave a sudden jolt as she realised that her bitter comment, meant only to salve her pride, had overstepped the mark by a long way.

James had given up the unequal struggle for self-control. Alicia's words had conjured up a vivid picture of her locked in Christopher Westwood's arms, or, worse still, Patrick Wickford's—he would not be so scrupulous in his treatment of her, at pains to protect the innocence which James had recognised and tried to preserve from both his own and Alicia's reckless actions. He took another step towards her.

Alicia quailed before his rage, instinctively taking a step back as he came closer to her. She recognised that her words had unleashed something elemental in him, something she could not control. Expecting him

at first to walk straight past her and out of the house, Alicia was gripped
by an unreasoning panic as he drew nearer. She backed away until she
felt the door panels digging into her back and half turned in a desperate
attempt to wrench the door open. But it was too late. James was already
beside her, reaching past her to turn the key in the lock with a finality
which both terrified and, at the same time, excited her.

'I've changed my mind,' he said roughly.

He was not gentle with her, but then, Alicia acknowledged numbly,
she had pushed him beyond restraint through her foolish provocation.
Suddenly it was a little too late to admit that she understood exactly
what he meant about not playing games which were too deep for her.

His mouth took hers without tenderness, showing only an urgent
desire which demanded satisfaction. It was shocking to Alicia to feel
the immediate and perfidious response within her as her body recognised and welcomed his touch, even as her mind struggled to assimilate
what was happening. She put her hands up to his chest, intending to
push him away, but the thought was already lost in the clamour of her
senses and instead she simply pulled him closer, sliding her arms about
his neck.

The ribbon restraining Alicia's curls was coming loose and James
put out an impatient hand to tug it free, spilling her hair around them
in a rich auburn cloud. His mouth returned to hers with a ruthless
intensity which incited feelings Alicia had never dreamed of. She would
have fallen had he not held her, so completely was she at the mercy of
her emotions. She felt his fingers trace a path of fire across her skin,
easing the dress from her shoulders with a touch that was very sure.
The low-cut bodice slid down to her waist, but before Alicia's shocked
mind could even register the thought properly James's lips followed the
path of his hands, brushing tantalisingly over the curve of her exposed
breast until it closed over the sensitised tip, making her gasp aloud with
pleasure. Alicia arched against him, conscious only for the need to be
closer still, to appease the deep ache within her with his body on hers.

She had no recollection of how she came to be lying on the chaise
longue, only that she was leaning back on the cushions, watching with
languorous pleasure as James hurriedly divested himself of his jacket
and pulled off his neckcloth. He crossed swiftly back to her side, and
she offered her mouth to his with a total lack of shamelessness. Their
kisses became wilder, as though they wished to devour each other, his
tongue plundering the sweetness of her mouth. Alicia's head fell back

as his lips traced the delicate line of her throat and took possession of her breasts again, teasing first one nipple and then the other with his circling tongue.

Her fingers dealt impatiently with the buttons of his shirt so that she could slip her hands inside, against his chest, pulling his nakedness against hers. She heard him groan and then his hand was pushing up her skirts so that they foamed about her hips and he could slide his hand up her silken stocking to the soft skin at the top of her thigh. Alicia gasped his name, digging her fingernails into his back in an agony of sensuous delight. She could feel his fingers parting her thighs and was within an inch of giving herself up completely to the searing pleasure which she knew was waiting for her, when suddenly James let her go, so violently that she almost tumbled to the floor.

Alicia caught her breath painfully, blinded by the swirl of her hair, bewildered, disorientated and deeply disappointed. Gradually, reality intruded. She was in her own drawing-room with the servants within call, and James, who had until a moment ago been making love to her to the exclusion of all other thought, was now shrugging himself back into his jacket, swearing most fluently under his breath. She had no idea what had gone wrong, but she instinctively straightened her bodice and smoothed down her crumpled skirts with hands that shook. Why had he stopped? He must have known that she had wanted him to take her there and then...

A moment's bewildered thought, and she rather imagined that she understood what James had done. No doubt he had set out to teach her a lesson and he had succeeded all too well, for she would remember this humiliation for as long as she lived! First, she had had the unutterable folly to try to seduce him, then she had responded to his calculated lovemaking with a total abandonment which made her burn with mortification at the recollection. And it must all have meant nothing to him, nothing at all. Her breath caught on a sob and she almost fled the room, remembering at the last minute that James had pocketed the key. Instead, she took refuge behind the huge desk she used for her business transactions, desperately hoping that her trembling legs would not disgrace her by giving way completely.

James himself was, in fact, no less shaken than she. He castigated himself silently and viciously for permitting his desires to overcome his self-control. True, Alicia had goaded him to it, but even so he could not blame her. He had wanted it as much as she. In fact, he was damn near being driven mad with desire for her! It had been bad enough to have to keep his distance after she had made it plain she thought his attentions meaningless. He had determined to show her the truth, but he had not wanted to propose until he could prove his estates were in good order and he did not need her money. In the meantime, Lady Corinna had proved a good distraction for the *ton*, who had been convinced they had been having an affair. Unfortunately, Alicia had thought so too.

Then, tonight, her unexpected proposition had completely floored him. He had known at the Bingleys' ball that her strictures to him to behave circumspectly had been almost in spite of herself. Alicia had wanted him, and only the fear that he might not care for her had held her back. Knowing that he would soon be able to declare himself, James had tried to possess his soul in patience. Then she had set out to seduce him.

At first disbelieving that she really meant to go through with it, James had been infuriated by her apparent attempt to use him. Deep down he did not really believe it to be true, but once he had let his self-control slip he had been as helpless as Alicia to avoid the torrent of passion that had followed. It was, after all, what he wanted. Now he could see no point in delaying further and intended to put his fate to the touch.

'You have nothing to fear from me, Lady Carberry,' James said dryly as he assimilated how she had chosen to distance herself from him, 'for I am determined to proceed with the utmost propriety from now onwards. It was not my intention to speak now, but it seems foolish for us both to carry on this most unsatisfactory of situations. I should therefore deem it an honour should you agree to become my wife.'

It was a considerably more handsome proposal than his previous one, but Alicia was no less surprised than she had been then. She had been waiting for his scornful denunciation and thinking that she preferred to have quite a large space between them, plus several pieces of solid furniture, when his words broke on her like a bombshell.

'No!' The word was wrenched from her. Seeing his frown deepen, she tried to move even further away from him and would have succeeded had he not caught her arm and held her still. 'This cannot be so, my lord! I thought…' She stopped and caught her breath while she tried to work out what she did think.

So he was not going to reproach her for her folly and wilful provocation. Alicia remembered Ottery, and James's determination to do the right thing despite his dislike of her. She must have misjudged him just now, she thought a little shakily. He had not manufactured the situation to punish her; instead, she had trapped him into a predicament where he felt the only solution could be to propose marriage and save her reputation. What had he said? That he had not intended to speak now... That, at least, she could believe to be true and it made clear to her her only course of action. She could not hold him to a proposal made under duress.

She freed her arm gently from James's grasp and looked up to meet the gaze that was fixed intently on her.

'I am sensible of the honour you do me, Lord Mullineaux,' Alicia said unsteadily, 'but I must decline. I cannot permit you to make me an offer out of pity, or propriety, or whatever else one might choose to call it!'

There was a taut silence. James was looking both astonished and annoyed. He ran his hand through his hair, only adding to its general look of dishevelment.

'My dear Alicia, what are you talking about? Is the prospect of marriage to me so disagreeable that you have to make excuses by crediting me with such false motives?'

'Yes! No! Of course not!' Alicia tried to get a grip on herself. 'I appreciate your reasons for asking me to marry you, sir, but it would not serve! It was foolish of me to meet with you alone tonight, and even more foolish of me to provoke you as I did—I see that now. But no real harm is done and, out of your generosity, I ask you to forget all that has happened. There is no necessity for anything more!'

A slightly grim expression came over James's face as he made a rapid reassessment of the situation. 'Alicia,' he said dangerously, 'do I understand you correctly? Are you suggesting that I have proposed to you only to protect your reputation, or even to make amends for what has just happened between us?'

'Certainly,' Alicia said, with a cool composure that was far from her real feelings. 'It is quite clear to me that both your recent proposals to me have been made out of chivalry! There could be no other explanation for your behaviour at Ottery, and, whilst I appreciate your kindness more than I can say, I cannot permit you to tie yourself to a loveless marriage just in order to do what you perceive to be right!'

At that moment, James was looking anything but kind. In fact, he seemed about to commit an act of violence. He could not believe that Alicia could have so thoroughly, so determinedly misunderstood him. Not long ago, he reflected with incredulity, he had relished the battle of wills between them. Now he was merely infuriated. Severe sexual frustration did not improve his temper.

'Well, here is a Cheltenham tragedy! I see that you are determined to martyr yourself, madam, so I shall leave you to do so in peace! It was too simple, I suppose, to have imagined I might have been prompted to propose because I love you—that *that* was the reason why I could see no point in us continuing to be apart! Allow me to say that you would try the patience of a saint! Goodnight to you, madam! I will see myself out!'

The door slammed behind him, leaving Alicia staring after him open-mouthed and, for once, silenced.

Deverson, James's very proper gentleman's gentleman, was startled by his master's reappearance so early in the evening, and in such a state of disarray. James's neckcloth was completely ruined and the jacket which had earlier fitted without a wrinkle now looked distinctly rakish.

Deverson's consternation grew as James's filthy temper became evident. Usually the most amiable of employers, he said barely a word from the time he entered the house to when he left it again thirty minutes later, with the air of a man setting out to get comprehensively drunk.

James did indeed turn in the direction of White's, but at his club fate decreed that he should meet up with Marcus Kilgaren, Charles Oxley and Peter Weston, who were in the card-room. They hailed him enthusiastically with the offer of a game of faro, but James declined and after a thoughtful look at him Marcus declared his pockets to let and got up from the table.

'You're looking pretty rough, old chap,' he commented critically as by common consent he and James moved off in search of a drink. He took two glasses from a passing waiter. 'Care to share the problem?'

He handed James the glass and watched with interest as his friend downed the contents in one mouthful.

'Steady on, James, this is quite a tolerable claret!'

James scowled. 'I have just proposed marriage to Alicia Carberry for a second time, and been rejected,' he said abruptly.

Marcus glanced round, but they were in no danger of being overheard. A couple of elderly noblemen were dozing over their newspapers before the fire, but it was too early for the young bloods, who were all still out on the Town or gambling for high stakes.

Marcus raised a quizzical eyebrow. Alicia's refusal must rankle indeed for James to speak so openly of it. 'Now you have surprised me,' he observed quietly. 'From what I know of the lady, I would have said that your suit would be welcome—this time around!'

James's scowl deepened. 'Yes, well, I was coxcomb enough to believe the same myself! I could have sworn—' He broke off. 'My mistake was a simple tactical error: I did not prepare my ground well enough before I advanced!'

Marcus looked at him with concern and a hint of amusement. 'This really doesn't sound like you at all, James! Have you lost your touch?'

'Since when have I had it in my dealings with Alicia?' James put his glass down and reached for another. 'Marcus, you would not believe the way in which Alicia was prepared to ascribe my reasons for proposing to her to all but the most obvious motives! Pity, propriety, chivalry...she had thought of them all!'

Marcus hid his grin by taking a sip of wine. 'Whereas I can discern immediately that you are suffering all the symptoms of a thwarted passion, old chap! However did all this misunderstanding come about?'

James gave him a baleful look. 'Like I said, Marcus, I rushed my fences! I'll spare you the details, for I don't wish to shock you! Suffice it to say that I have been finding self-denial a little difficult where Alicia is concerned, and tonight I nearly lost what little self-control I had!'

'Ah!' Marcus required no further clarification. 'Don't tell me—you, realising that to postpone your proposal further would only lead to more pointless self-sacrifice, offered Alicia your hand but perhaps did not mention your heart, only to be told that she understood your chivalric reasons for proposing and could not possibly let you sacrifice yourself!'

James stared. 'How on earth did you know that?'

'Common sense, old chap! If you didn't mention first that you cared for Alicia, your cause was already lost, I'm afraid!'

James began to see the funny side of the situation. 'Thank you for the philosophy—how about some practical advice on how I put the matter to rights?'

'Hmm,' Marcus looked meditative. 'That's the difficult bit!' He started to laugh. 'I have to say, James, that this is the most amusing turnabout! Who would have thought that you would have such difficulty in persuading a lady to marry you?'

'Thank you!' James tried to sound sarcastic but could not help laughing. 'It is not a problem which I had anticipated, certainly! So what can I do?'

Marcus raised a hand to beckon the waiter across. 'Lay siege to her feelings—prove that you love her!' He made an expansive gesture. 'I don't know—you are supposed to be the expert in these matters!' He gave his friend a mocking look. 'Brought low by a slip of a girl, James?'

But James had regained his good humour. He smiled. 'It was only a matter of time,' he said.

Alicia did not discuss James's proposal with anyone. Her feelings on the subject were still too raw. On the day following their encounter she developed a sick headache and sore throat, and when Miss Frensham found her in tears in the drawing-room it was easier for her to admit to influenza than try to explain to her companion that her misery also sprang from another cause.

It was ten days before she felt any better. The fever was followed by lassitude and depression, and she was prone to burst into tears for no reason at all. She spent much time lying in her bed, gazing unseeingly out of the window while her miserable thoughts centred on James and the hopeless mess she had made of their relationship. On the fifth day of her illness, a huge bouquet of lilies and snapdragons arrived from him, which prompted her to burst into tears yet again. She knew that he had called but she had refused all visitors except Caroline Kilgaren, whose brisk common sense had been tempered with so much kindness that Alicia had almost cried again.

James, meanwhile, had been true to his word and had gone to Bow Street to put in train an investigation into the death of Josiah Broseley. His requests for information had met with little enthusiasm. Josiah's name was not known to the Runners, a gloomily helpful man named Dundry had informed him, although that did not prove that he had not been mixed up in all sorts of nefarious goings on. Dundry had agreed that they would do their best to find out what his lordship wanted to know, and James had left him with the instruction that he should let him know at once if he had any useful information.

James was, in fact, finding it deeply frustrating not to be able to speak with Alicia. At first he had been confident of his ability to persuade her of his true feelings, but the passage of two weeks without seeing her had gnawed away at both his patience and the assurance that he could put matters to rights. He had called several times in Upper Grosvenor Street only to be told by an urbane Fordyce that Lady Carberry was much better, but still not receiving guests. It had not improved his temper.

Matters became progressively worse. At the end of the week, James's grandfather, the Duke of Cardace, was holding a magnificently opulent ball and James had rashly promised to help his maiden aunt Eugenie with the last minute preparations. This allowed him little time for social calls, so he tried to make do with despatching another huge bouquet of flowers to Alicia, with a note saying that he hoped she was better and looked forward to seeing her. On the day of the ball he was suddenly assailed by doubts and wondered if she would attend. Given that he had not been allowed a chance to put matters to rights with her, it seemed all too possible that she would not. Too late, he wished he had made time to call on her that day and found himself to be in an even worse temper. Adding yet another ruined neckcloth to the discarded pile, James reflected that the course of true love was proving tiresomely riddled with difficulties.

In the event, however, Alicia was not so poor-spirited as to fail to attend the ball. James, involved in the tediously long and boring process of greeting the guests, as well as also taking on a fair proportion of the host's role as a result of his grandfather's infirmity, was nevertheless able to pinpoint the exact moment when Alicia came through the door.

She was formidably ranked by the Dowager Countess of Stansfield on one side and the ubiquitous Christopher Westwood on the other, whom James was beginning to detest. In lilac silk Alicia looked at once impossibly exquisite and fragile, and her expression as she greeted him was serene and remote. James tried to place her mood but was unable to read anything beneath the surface. Already in an advanced state of irritation and frustration, he had to subdue a violent urge to take her in his arms there and then and kiss her out of her Society calm. Could this ice maiden be the same Alicia who had responded to him with such searing intensity only two weeks before? It seemed impossible. Wishing that he could regain his own lost equilibrium, James took her hand.

'You had my note, I hope,' he said, with a polite formality he hoped would mask his true feelings.

'Yes, thank you, my lord. And the flowers were beautiful.' There was no animation in Alicia's voice at all. She could match his own courtesy effortlessly. A faint, distant smile touched her mouth, but left her eyes blank.

James gritted his teeth. He considered—and reluctantly rejected—a very real desire to pick her up and carry her out of the ballroom to somewhere more private where he could dispense with the tiresome business of trying to tell her how he felt by simply proving it in other ways. Something of how he was feeling must have shown in his eyes, for he had the satisfaction of seeing Alicia recognise his expression and withdraw her hand from his rather hastily.

The queue was buckling behind them. 'I look forward to a dance later, Lady Carberry,' James said with the same smooth courtesy, and turned to greet Lady Stansfield, who had been flirting with his grandfather. She gave him a very quizzical look indeed, but fortunately made no comment. Alicia and Westwood moved away, he holding her arm in a proprietorial grip which made James want to hit him.

The reception of the guests was almost over when Lady Corinna Dawe arrived. Exotic in clinging yellow gauze, she had certainly dampened her dress to make it even more transparent, and appeared to be wearing absolutely nothing underneath it. She greeted James with confident aplomb as though their quarrel had never occurred, and looked him over with a distinctly seductive glint in her melting dark eyes. She clung to his arm, then reached up to kiss him lingeringly, smiling with satisfaction as she caught Alicia's eye across the ballroom.

'I see Lady Carberry has chosen your ball as her first social engagement since becoming betrothed,' Lady Corinna observed, with an artificial tinkle of laughter. 'How absolutely charming of her, and such a good way to refute any rumours linking the two of you together!'

Not a muscle moved in James's face. 'Just so,' he said calmly. 'Westwood is fortunate indeed. But is it yet an official engagement, or do you expect an announcement tonight?'

Lady Corinna shot him a sharp glance, but James's face was impassive. For a moment she had the frightening feeling that he had seen through her words for the fabrication they were, for he was not really reacting in the way she had hoped, either by showing any chagrin or turning his attentions to her instead. She gave a light, petulant shrug, provoked by James's very lack of reaction into taking matters further.

'As to that, I only know that the happy couple are to be congratulated,' she continued mendaciously. 'I hear that Lady Stansfield is *aux anges* at having achieved a family alliance!' And so saying she tripped away, pleased to have had the chance at least to plant her barbs.

James turned to watch Alicia, conscious of his exasperation growing with every moment. Alicia's usual coterie of admirers had gathered effortlessly about her and she was shimmering among them like a pale flame. It was an accomplished performance and James found it grated on him. Westwood clung to her like a burr and she did not appear to mind at all. Could it be true? he wondered suddenly. He was not such a fool as to fall for Lady Corinna's spiteful needling, but Caroline had mentioned a little while ago that Westwood had made Alicia an offer. He looked at her again, as though he would be able to divine the truth simply from watching her. Surely Alicia could not simply disregard the affinity between them and tie herself to a man of Westwood's stamp? James could not believe it; but equally he could not quite ignore that nagging doubt. A feeling akin to rage rose in him as he considered Christopher Westwood's smugly satisfied expression.

Leaving some very late arrivals stranded, James abandoned the receiving line and cut a path through the throng to Alicia's side. He knew it was not the time or place for a serious discussion, but at least he could try to establish some sort of contact. It was like a repeat of the scene in Mrs Bingley's ballroom—all conversation in the vicinity ceased as he reached her side.

'May I beg the honour of a dance with you, Lady Carberry?' James asked, smiling down at her.

Alicia's green eyes opened very wide. She plied her fan in a quick, nervous gesture. 'I am so sorry, Lord Mullineaux—' she even sounded nervous '—but all my dances are already spoken for.'

She saw the flash of real anger in his eyes before he bowed abruptly and turned on his heel to walk away. Her heart, which had been hovering in the vicinity of her feet, sank even further.

If James was suffering agonies of frustration, Alicia was feeling even more miserable. Her fortnight's illness had given her too much time to think. At first convinced that James had made love to her to teach her a humiliating lesson, then that he had proposed out of chivalry, she had been completely dumbfounded by his parting shot that night. She considered herself to be an independent lady, but she was aware that she could not simply ask him to confirm if he was in love with her. For two weeks she had agonised over whether it was really possible and she shuddered to imagine her embarrassment if she had misunderstood him. Besides, he had had plenty of time to change his mind. Earlier that evening, after all, she had seen him with Lady Corinna hanging on his arm again in apparent possession.

She turned her head to meet with the unappetising sight of Lady Corinna and James dancing the boulanger together with every appearance of enjoyment. Pain sliced through her and she damned herself for a complete fool. Even if James had been sincere, he hardly had a reputation for fidelity. In utter confusion, she wondered what she could have been thinking of, to consider committing herself to such a man.

If she felt miserable now, it was nothing to the grief she would feel were she to lose him to another woman after they had married.

Christopher Westwood was pressing her to dance again. Alicia turned listlessly to him and allowed him to lead her out onto the floor. She could smile and chat and dance, but she felt as though all life and light had finally gone out of her, and it was a pale ghost of herself that was left in the Cardace ballroom.

It seemed as though the gods were finally smiling on James, for just after supper he went back into the ballroom and found Alicia waiting for her partner for the cotillion by the French windows, temporarily alone. He took his chance quickly, catching her arm and pulling her out onto the terrace before she even had time to realise what was happening.

'Disgraceful conduct!' observed Mrs Eddington-Buck, watching their departure with avid eyes. She turned to her companion, her turban wagging. 'A scandalous example to set, do you not agree? But then, I fear they are lost to all sense of propriety, those two!'

Once outside, James did not speak, but ushered Alicia back inside the garden door to his grandfather's study, which he had thoughtfully left open for just such an eventuality. That he succeeded at all was mainly down to Alicia's stupefaction at the manoeuvre which had rendered her temporarily speechless, but by the time they were in the study shock had been replaced by outrage and James kept hold of her arm, correctly surmising from her look of fury that she would run away if he let go. Now that he finally had her to himself he fully intended to have his say.

Alicia was furiously angry, both annoyed and nervous to find herself outmanoeuvred by his high-handed behaviour. One touch of his hand had been enough to awaken all the feelings that had tormented her since that fevered night in her drawing-room, and it just made her more distressed. She drew breath for a blistering attack. It was the only way she could think of to protect herself.

'Lord Mullineaux, what is the meaning of this? Let me go at once!'

James ignored the request. 'I want to talk to you.'

'Well, I do not want to talk to you! We have nothing further to say to each other!'

James realised that Alicia was afraid, but his own emotions were by now in such a state of pent-up turmoil that he was incapable of defusing the situation. He had intended only to tell her that he needed the opportunity to speak to her properly. What he actually said came out quite differently.

'I think that there is plenty to say! For example, what is the nature of the relationship between yourself and Christopher Westwood?'

Alicia wrenched her arm from his grip. Far from the protestations of love and devotion she might secretly have hoped for, he was actually daring to interrogate her! She remembered the way in which Lady Corinna had draped herself all over him and felt a wave of defiance overtake her. He took too much for granted, behaving as he chose and yet expecting her to act like some poor creature whose happiness depended on his notice!

'If you must know, sir—not that I consider it to be *any* of your business—Christopher and I are betrothed.'

James went cold with shock. Regardless of what Lady Corinna had said, he had not really believed that she would do such a thing, either to spite him or to escape from him. He felt all his good intentions for reconciliation slip away as the situation slid irretrievably into all-out war.

'Indeed, madam? And is Mr Westwood aware that I consider you to have made a prior commitment to myself?' he asked, with cold menace.

Alicia's shocked gaze searched his face. 'You are mistaken, sir. There never was such an engagement.'

James gave her a look which brought the blood rushing into her face. 'I am sure,' he said with slow deliberation, 'that your...betrothed...would be glad to know of the circumstances under which I proposed to you!'

The colour left Alicia's face as quickly as it had come. 'You would not dare!'

'Would I not?' Even James could hear the insulting drawl in his own tones. It was as though one part of him, icy cold, was watching the other half make quite the most unforgivable mess of his whole life and was incapable of intervening. 'I assure you, my dear, that if that was what it took to get you to marry me I should not even hesitate!'

'And you may be assured, sir,' Alicia said with a cold magnificence that brought to mind her Stansfield forebears, 'that hell will freeze over before I ever accept your hand in marriage! You have clearly misplaced the manners of a gentleman during your sojourn abroad—that is if you ever had them.'

She turned on her heel with a whisper of lilac silk and James did not even try to stop her. The study door closed behind her with a soft click which sounded to James very loud and very final. A moment later he heard Alicia's voice in the corridor outside, speaking in low, impassioned tones, and Lady Stansfield's quiet response, then there was silence.

James reached automatically for the brandy decanter and noticed with the same detached interest that his hand was shaking. He could not even begin to analyse how he had managed to mishandle the situation so disastrously, for his senses seemed mercifully numbed except for a wholly understandable inclination towards violence. It would have given him great satisfaction to smash the brandy glass in the fireplace, but as it was one of his grandfather's finest pieces of crystal he managed to restrain himself. The dispassionate observer in his mind chose that moment to point out with sickening clarity that it was very unlikely that Alicia would ever speak to him again. Clarity was not something that he wished for at all, so he settled down with the brandy decanter and prepared to get seriously drunk for the first time since his salad days.

Several glasses of brandy later, matters had not improved at all. Marcus Kilgaren, coming in search of him, found James with an empty glass dangling from his long fingers and an expression of almost murderous intent on his face as he contemplated the things he would like to do to Christopher Westwood. Marcus, quick to define the cause, was not sympathetic.

'Devil take it, James, you really have made a deuced mess of this whole situation!' Marcus moved the brandy decanter beyond James's reach, and fixed him with a severe frown. 'You may come out now, for Lady Stansfield has retired from the ball with a sick headache, taking Alicia with her. It didn't exactly require Dr Johnson to tell which of them really was feeling sick—I've seldom seen Alicia looking so bad! Anyway, I am sent by your grandfather to recall you to a sense of duty!'

He took his friend's unresisting arm. 'Come along, you might as well go to the card-room. You know you play your best piquet when you are half cut!'

Deverson knew better than to disturb his master so early in the morning, particularly when he had had a heavy night. Or, he corrected himself morosely, a series of heavy nights. First there had been the Cardace ball, which had apparently had some kind of transforming effect on the Marquis. Gone was the fair and considerate master he was used to, to be replaced by an ill-tempered, impatient gentleman frequently the worse for drink. To be fair, James had not vented his bad moods on Deverson, but merely being in the same house with him was uncomfortable. Two nights of heavy drinking and heavier losses had followed the ball, and Deverson knew that his master would not appreciate being disturbed from his much needed rest.

However, the gentleman of the law who was currently standing on the doorstep had been most insistent that he should see the Marquis, and while they had been arguing the Earl of Kilgaren had also arrived, demanding entry. Deverson could not withstand the combined onslaught, but it was with a great deal of trepidation that he pulled back the bed curtains now and cleared his throat apologetically.

He addressed the heaped pile of sheets and blankets somewhat nervously.

'There is a gentleman to see you, my lord, by the name of Dundry.' He paused, then said in the tone of someone relating information in questionable taste,' I understand that he is a Bow Street Runner.'

James groaned as he turned over and the light struck his eyes. 'For God's sake, Deverson, what time is it?'

'Ten o'clock, my lord.' Deverson was quite expressionless. 'The Earl of Kilgaren is also here to see you, sir. I have shown him into the drawing-room.'

James struggled to sit up and winced as his head swam. 'Quite a host of early morning callers,' he observed crossly. 'What the devil can they want at this hour of the day? Tell them I will join them shortly, Deverson, and bring me some hot water. And an ice bag might help matters, too!'

'Very good, my lord.' Deverson backed hastily from the room as James, still clutching his head, attempted to swing his legs over the side of the bed and stand up.

When James entered the drawing-room a little while later, he found Marcus Kilgaren at his ease reading the *Gazette*, and Mr Dundry of Bow Street still on his feet, looking very uncomfortable. He was twisting his round hat by the brim and his equally round face was a florid red colour. On seeing James he immediately burst into speech.

'Begging your pardon for disturbing your lordship at such an hour, but you did say that if it was urgent—'

James winced as his head gave him a fresh spasm of pain. 'You did quite right, Dundry,' he interrupted abruptly, unable to cope with too many profuse apologies. He looked at Marcus, who was calmly folding up the paper. 'What can I do for you, Marcus? I hardly expected to see you so early.'

'Caro has sent me,' Marcus said, unruffled. 'She had a message from Alicia this morning which I thought to convey to you, to the effect that she has left Town for Somerset. But perhaps you should hear what Dundry has to say first? I collect that his is the more urgent business?'

'Caro must have the constitution of an ox to be up so early in the morning,' James grumbled, eyeing the entry of Deverson and the ice with disfavour. 'Well, you'd better start, then, Dundry.'

Mr Dundry cleared his throat awkwardly. 'It's like this, your honours,' he began. Then he frowned. 'Perhaps I should say at this point— as background, like—that we have been pursuant on our enquiries concerning the death of a certain Josiah Broseley ever since your lordship came to us with a request for information.' He nodded respectfully in James's direction.

Marcus, who had not previously had the pleasure of meeting Mr Dundry, began to perceive that the explanation might be a long one. James, however, had other ideas. His head was not up to taking any circumlocution.

'Any luck?' he asked directly, slumping in an armchair and applying the ice bag to his head.

Dundry looked scandalised at being hurried along in this manner. 'Yes, my lord,' he admitted, 'which is as why I'm calling.' He paused for thought.

'Mr Josiah died of drowning,' he said sententiously. 'That wouldn't be so rare in a man supposed to be a drunkard, but word is that before he died there were those out looking for him.'

Both Marcus and James were now listening intently. 'And do you think they found him?' James asked quietly.

Dundry permitted himself a small, grim smile. 'Aye, sir. A man— tall, fair, well-spoken and well-dressed—was seen talking to Josiah Broseley the night he died. The same man went to identify the body and claimed Broseley's effects.'

'It's not much of a description.' Marcus observed. 'Why, it could have been me!'

'You're pleased to jest, sir!' Dundry gave another small smile. 'I'll not deny it was difficult to put a name to the cove, but in the end we got him!' His tone conveyed his satisfaction. 'Name of Westwood, as is great-nephew to the old Countess of Stansfield.'

The effect on his audience was electric. James sat up a little straighter, his eyes narrowing. Dundry, gratified by this rapt attention, continued. 'Seems Mr Westwood, like Josiah Broseley, also owes a lot of money,' he commented thoughtfully. 'To money-lenders, to his tailor, and most of all to a certain Mr Bertram Broseley, who bought up his debts going back a long way. In fact, Westwood's done some work for Bertram Broseley, by way of payment, like.'

There was complete silence in the room. Marcus Kilgaren, who had guessed nothing of this, was looking incredulous.

'Westwood and Bertram Broseley? Why, I was not even aware they knew each other!'

'Why should we have known?' James said intently. He had abandoned the ice bag, Dundry's news having cleared his head more effectively than any other treatment could have done. 'I dislike the sound of this, Dundry. What sort of work does Westwood do for Broseley?'

'We're still making our enquiries, sir,' the Runner said, 'but I understand that it covers a little extortion here, a bit of blackmail there... Bertram Broseley is as nasty a piece of work as you'll find, sir, but word is that his business is failing and he needs money fast. Which brings me to the other aspect of Mr Westwood's plans which I think is germane to your interest.'

A brief spasm of pain crossed Marcus's face at the effort of following Dundry's parentheses. James, however, had completely shaken off his headache and was watching Dundry with a look that was grimly alert.

'I think that I can hazard a guess—Westwood has resolved to marry money,' he said levelly, the quiet tone belied by the keenness of his gaze.

'Just so, sir.' Dundry looked gratified at such quick deduction. 'Some time ago he apparently devised a plan to marry Broseley's widowed daughter—with Mr Broseley's connivance.'

'He needed no subterfuge,' James said, with bleak bitterness. 'She told me herself that they were betrothed. My God, if only she knew—' He broke off, for Dundry was frowning heavily.

'Oh, no, sir, pardon the liberty, but that can't be right! My sources told me that the lady had turned him down two months ago! Which is why,' he said with a triumphant flourish, 'Mr Westwood decided to abduct her—the lady being not willing!'

Both men looked at him incredulously. 'Are you mad, man?' James demanded. 'Lady Carberry told me quite clearly that she had accepted Westwood's suit! He had no need to carry her off!'

Dundry looked offended, but it was Marcus who interposed quietly;

'Just a moment, James. That may have been what Alicia told you, but was it true? Caro told me at least a month ago that Westwood had proposed and Alicia had rejected him! And even if Alicia told you at the ball that she would marry Westwood I would venture to suggest that it was mere bravado!'

'That's what I've been trying to tell you,' Dundry said eagerly. 'Her ladyship rejected Mr Westwood's offer, so he has abducted her!'

James clutched his head before the conundrum could revive the pain. 'This makes no sense,' he complained. 'Wait, let me think. Broseley and Westwood have been in business together for some time. Both are desperately short of cash. Westwood proposes to Lady Carberry but is rejected.' His gaze sharpened on Dundry. 'Are you saying that both Broseley and Westwood together are after her money? And that Westwood has carried her off to force her into marriage?'

Mr Dundry drew himself up with full, offended dignity. 'I've been trying to explain to your lordships! Lady Carberry decided two days ago to go back to Somerset and Mr Westwood offered his escort when he heard of her plans. All was falling out very conveniently for him! Now do you see, my lord? Mr Westwood has taken his chance to abduct her!'

Chapter Eleven

Two hours later the tension was beginning to tell on James. He had ordered some strong coffee and sat drinking it moodily, having been restrained from setting off immediately to the West Country. Marcus had pointed out quite reasonably that they needed to check first that Westwood had not re-routed the carriage from the start—even now he could be heading up the Great North Road. James had chafed at the delay, but had had to acknowledge the logic of this.

Other than having his curricle put to, there was little he could do at this stage. Dundry had gone off to check with the coaching inns on all the major routes out of London, and Marcus had sent a message to Kilgaren House to alert Caroline. He had insisted that they would follow James once they knew which direction Westwood had taken, and, bearing in mind that Alicia might need Caroline's comfort, James had not demurred.

It was a bare few minutes later that Dundry returned, remarkably succinct now that immediate action was required.

'They're on the Bath Road, my lord!'

'How many?' James questioned swiftly.

'Two ladies and a gentleman, sir. They passed that way yesterday, and I make no doubt that we should be able to trace them along the road quite easily. I have a good description of the carriage. The inn-keeper said that all three seemed quite amicable, but I imagine that is because Lady Carberry thought that she was going home, rather than—' He broke off at the expression on James's face. 'It's definitely our party, for the landlord described Lady Carberry.' He smiled reminiscently. 'No one is likely to forget that lady, sir!'

'I'm going after them now,' James said decisively. 'We won't be able to catch up with them, but we might be able to track them down in the end. I just pray we will not be too late, but if so—' He stopped, his face set.

'If only we knew where Westwood was intending to go,' Marcus said thoughtfully as James opened the door and shouted for his groom. 'It won't be Chartley Chase, for sure.'

'There's Broseley's place at Taunton,' Dundry suggested, a little diffidently. 'If the two of them have planned this together...'

'Good man.' James clapped him on the shoulder. 'It's worth a try at any rate! You'd better come with me, Dundry. Marcus, I take it you and Caroline won't be far behind?'

'Try and stop us!' Marcus replied cheerfully. 'Don't break your neck,' he added as James shrugged himself into his caped driving coat. 'That would be no use to Alicia at all—or Miss Frensham. I wonder what Westwood intends to do with Miss Frensham?' he added as an afterthought.

James swore. He had very little concern for Miss Frensham's welfare at that moment, but the vision of Alicia trying to defend herself against Westwood's advances was with him constantly.

'Leave us messages at the posting houses,' Marcus was saying urgently to Dundry. 'We might even catch up with you, given the speed at which Caroline likes to travel! And don't let him do anything too rash.' He looked at James thoughtfully. 'Damn it, he's been wanting an excuse to call Westwood out for months!'

For Alicia, the journey down to Somerset was assuming nightmarish proportions. When she had left Cardace House on the night of the ball, her only thought had been to escape from London and all future contact with James Mullineaux. She did not understand how everything had gone so irretrievably wrong between them; every true feeling was twisted and spoiled beyond recognition. All she could do was instinctively head for the place where she had been happiest, and that was Chartley Chase.

A long-suffering Miss Frensham had set about packing up in preparation for their departure the following day and they had left Fordyce impassively arranging to close the house in Upper Grosvenor Street indefinitely. Lady Stansfield had not spared her granddaughter's feelings, accusing her of rash, impulsive action, and Alicia had been vaguely surprised that Christopher Westwood had actually supported her to the extent of offering his escort for the journey.

She had not questioned his actions particularly, for her mind was obsessed with thoughts of James and she seemed incapable of making much sense of anything else. She had completely forgotten about Josiah's death and the fact that she had asked James for his help in finding out what had happened to him.

Now, as they neared Bath and the end of their journey, Alicia was beginning to regret her hurried departure. They had stayed overnight in a busy coaching inn where she had lain awake listening to the carriages coming and going, trying not to dwell on every encounter she had ever had with James. She had not been very successful. It was rather like a replaying of the dreadful time when she had first lost him, when every waking and sleeping moment had seemed to be haunted by his presence.

Her head ached from lack of sleep and her heart ached even more. The enforced inactivity of the journey gave her too much time to think, to try to retrace the progress of their relationship up to this miserable point. The rumble of the carriage wheels was making her head ache even more. She leant back against the cushions and allowed her eyes to close. Suddenly she felt very tired. Well, if there was nothing else she could do, she could at least sleep. The noise of the journey blurred and faded away, and Alicia was dead to the world.

When she woke up she knew instinctively that it was a very long time later. She was very cold and she felt horribly sick. Other sensations returned to her slowly. She lay still, listening half-consciously to the faint, plaintive call of birds outside. There was also an almost imperceptible smell...sandalwood...spices...which jogged a very faint memory deep in her unconscious, reminding her of her childhood... With an effort Alicia pulled herself awake, opened her eyes and flinched as the dim light caused her head to ache abominably.

She closed her eyes again immediately. The nausea ebbed a little and she tried to think. What had happened to her? She seemed to be lying on a lumpy sort of mattress and could feel the coarse material of a blanket rough beneath her fingers. Surely this could not be another inn? She moved her hand slightly and discovered to her relief that she was not physically restrained in any way. Not that she could move much in her present state. She felt as though any attempt at movement would result in violent sickness. What on earth was going on? Try as she might, she could not remember anything beyond falling asleep in the carriage.

The second time that she opened her eyes it was marginally easier to keep them open. She moved her head cautiously. She seemed to be lying on her back looking up at a high, shadowed ceiling. Meagre light was coming from a dirty window in the wall to her left, and she could make out rough plaster walls and bare boards on the floor, deep in dust. The iron bedstead on which she was lying was one of the few pieces of furniture in the large, empty room. The scent of spice was still there, faint but discernible, and the sound of the birds drifted into the room with no other noise but the lowing of cattle as a backdrop. It was all rather pleasant, and Alicia was tempted to allow herself to float back into unconsciousness and worry no more about anything.

However, it was too late. As she turned her head slightly to look about her there was a movement about the bed and someone spoke.

'So you are round again, my dear. How very fortuitous. I was afraid that I had completely overdone the dose and you would die. Even the Reverend Mr Skittle might draw the line at joining me in holy matrimony with a corpse!'

It was unquestionably Christopher Westwood's voice, and Westwood's face which hung over her. His words made no sense to Alicia at that moment, for she had more pressing preoccupations.

'I am going to be sick,' Alicia said, as distinctly as possible, and was gratified when a bucket appeared underneath her nose within a moment. Although unpleasant, the interlude made her feel much better. The nausea receded and her headache dimmed a little.

Westwood had removed the bucket with an expression of distaste on his face. Now he relocked the door and came back towards her. The first thing Alicia noticed about him was that he was very drunk. There was a hectic flush to his cheeks and a feverish glitter in his eyes, and, if further testimony were needed, a three quarters empty brandy bottle stood on the nearby table.

'Not quite your elegant style, is it, my dear, being sick in a bucket?' he jeered. 'But then, I suspect you will need to become accustomed to a few changes!'

There was a sneering tone in his voice which Alicia had never heard before. It was the voice of a bully, one who was very confident of himself. She tried to sit up but pain shot through her head and she sank back on the dirty pillow with a groan.

'I don't understand.' There was a quiver in her voice which was all too real. 'What's going on? Where am I? And where is Miss Frensham?'

Westwood stood looking down at her with odious complacency. 'Calm yourself, my dear. Miss Frensham is quite well, though no doubt a little distraught by now!' He giggled unpleasantly. 'I abandoned her at an inn near Bath, having encouraged her to step down to partake of some refreshment. You were asleep and nothing could have been easier than to trick her. I helped her down and said I would go back to wake you, but, of course, I simply gave the order to drive on and left her in the inn yard!' He giggled again with evident enjoyment. 'I can still see the look on her face as the carriage sped away!'

Alicia remained silent. It seemed the most sensible course of action until her head improved and she could think straight. At least the debilitating sickness had retreated, but she felt very weak and all the dust of the journey appeared to be clinging to her skin. Once again she attempted to sit up and this time she was successful. Propping herself against the iron bedpost, she cleared her throat painfully.

'Could I have a glass of water, please, Christopher? I feel very unwell.'

'Hardly surprising, I feel, with the dose of laudanum I gave you.' Westwood sounded pleased with himself rather than anything else. 'I think I must have overestimated the amount, but I did not want to run the risk of you waking too soon. As it is, you have slept the clock round, and very inconvenient it has been, too!' He sounded as though he expected her to apologise for her lack of consideration.

He passed her a rough beaker of water, which was brackish and warm, but tasted wonderful to Alicia. So this had been the reason why he had supported her when she had announced she was leaving London—and why he had offered the use of his own carriage. Alicia thought she already guessed why, but would make no assumptions.

'Why have you brought me here?' she asked, hitting just the right plaintive note. Westwood had seemed to appreciate her meek approach, so she decided she would try to maintain it, although it went rather against the grain. It would be foolish to provoke him when she appeared to be so thoroughly at his mercy—there was a lot she needed to learn.

Westwood drew his chair up beside the bed and gave Alicia a rather unpleasant grin. It was obvious that he was enjoying himself hugely.

'Why, to marry you, my dear!' He stretched out his legs before him and admired the high gloss of his boots. 'I asked you once before—do you remember?—but you refused me. This time I was taking no risks.'

So she had been right, Alicia thought. He was determined to marry her, and not because he was suffering from unrequited love either! His attitude towards her could scarcely have been more contemptuous.

'But you don't really care for me, do you, Christopher?' she asked, trying to sound piqued by his indifference.

Westwood gave a crack of laughter and swung backwards on the chair. 'Does it hurt your feelings that I don't bother to pretend any more? But then you ain't my type, Alicia! You're as cold as ice and I prefer my bedmates to have a little more spirit!' He tilted the brandy bottle to his lips. 'No, you hold no attraction for me, but your money...well, that's another matter!'

'Money? You mean Carberry's money?'

Westwood wiped his sleeve across his mouth and looked at her thoughtfully. 'Well, certainly that's part of it, of course.' How heartless he sounded. 'But I know Carberry's money is tied up in your do-good trusts, and it will take me a little time to break those. No, what I really need is ready cash and the promise of more. Your expectations as your grandmother's heiress are enough for now!' His tone changed from smug self-congratulation to bitterness.

'The old witch always meant to leave her fortune to me—I'd been living on the expectation of it for years, borrowing money to maintain the style of living I was entitled to! Then you had to come along and spoil sport! I thought she could at least be relied upon to disinherit you after you married Carberry, but the two of you always were so close she wouldn't even abandon you then!' He glared at her. 'So I had to spend the next seven years kowtowing to the old besom for the pittance of an allowance she granted me!'

Alicia marvelled at the casual cruelty of his words. Apart from his insensitivity over Josiah's death, none of this corrosive spite had ever spilled over onto the surface before. Westwood had always charmed Lady Stansfield with his attentiveness and anxiety to please, a consummate actor bent on gaining a fortune at any price. Alicia shivered.

'And if I refuse you again?' She tried not to sound aggressive, simply curious. Westwood laughed again, without mirth.

'You ain't in any position to refuse, my dear! In the first place you're hopelessly compromised and I doubt if even your grandmother would stand by you now! Besides, the shock might kill her if you claim to have been forced into marriage for a second time! She is not as strong as she was. It would create yet another monstrous scandal and you would be obliged to live retired.

'Anyway, there's no one here to listen to your cries for help and the Reverend Mr Skittle has been well paid to ignore your objections.' He paused and looked at her thoughtfully. 'And if you cut up really rough I expect I could manage to overcome my aversion to you sufficiently to ruin you. You would not really be in any fit state to refuse me after that!'

Alicia winced. The thought of marriage to Westwood under duress was horrible, but she knew he spoke the truth. She was hardly in a position to escape him and even if she did he would create another hideous scandal. She could never inflict that on Lady Stansfield.

Westwood had moved over to the door, presumably listening for the arrival of Mr Skittle. There was no sound, and once again Alicia became aware of the noises outside the room—the country sounds of the birds and cattle, the wind in the trees. So where was she? Not at Chartley Chase, although they were certainly somewhere in the countryside. If they had not altered direction after Bath, could they have carried on to Taunton, perhaps...?

Her mind was still working very slowly, for it was at least half a minute before she put together the elusive threads that were now all in her mind...the dusty, high-ceilinged room, the sounds of the country and the smell of spices...her father's plans for an arranged marriage for her, and an associate of his waiting in the wings... She had all the pieces of the jigsaw now, and they gently slid into place, to form the most incredible and horrifying whole.

'Christopher, what is your connection with my father?'

He had no warning and was too drunk to dissemble. She watched his mouth hang slackly with shock, an expression of stupefaction in his eyes. Finally he licked his lips and looked at her with a curiously wary expression.

'How the devil did you guess? Damn it, I've never said a word and I'm damned sure he hasn't! How did you know?'

Alicia shrugged. Despite her predicament she suddenly felt stronger, as though the balance of power had shifted away from him to her. He was on the defensive and she was determined to keep him there.

'It was you, wasn't it?' she said flatly. 'It was you who killed Josiah and pretended to be his cousin when you went to collect his possessions. You knew he had tried to warn me of the plot you'd hatched with my father and you wanted to make sure he never had the chance!'

An extraordinary expression came into Westwood's eyes, part malice, part triumph. 'That fool Josiah—he was a weak reed! He did some work for your father, but he could never bear to sully his hands! I tolerated him for as long as your father chose to protect him, but then he found out that we planned to use you and your fortune and he became nauseatingly sentimental!'

There was no expression in the glittering grey gaze as he turned to look out of the window. 'He said you'd always been good to him and you didn't deserve to be tricked again—the mawkish fool! He threatened to tell you all our plans. I went after him—he had to be silenced. And just when I thought all was safe I came to call on you and saw a letter from him sitting on your desk!'

Alicia closed her eyes against the memory of Christopher Westwood sitting in her library, immaculately self-possessed, with Josiah's blood on his hands. But Westwood was continuing.

'I took a big risk then,' he said cheerfully. 'I thought Josiah was too much of a fool to tell a straight tale, and I gambled on the fact that he would not have named me. And I was right, wasn't I?' He turned to smile triumphantly at Alicia and she could feel herself shrinking back against the hard iron of the bedstead, chilled to the bone by the madness she could see in his eyes. 'We knew you were already wary of your father, but you acted just the same to me. Same Alicia, cold as the driven snow! But I knew I had to move quickly. And you gave me the opportunity, didn't you, my dear?'

Alicia did not really feel that he required an answer. He must be quite mad to speak of murder and marriage in the same breath, but she was not going to test him further. She sat huddled on the bed, frozen at the thought of what she had uncovered. What could she do now, circumstanced as she was? To be forced into some conspiracy of silence was as bad in its way as being forced into marriage with him. When Westwood came back across the room and sat down beside her she tried not to cringe away. It was difficult, but he appeared not to notice her anyway, engrossed as he was by his own thoughts.

'I think I'll tell you it all,' he began conversationally. 'It'll pass the time until that tiresome priest gets here.' He drained the brandy bottle and some of the liquid ran down his chin, splashing on his shirt. Alicia felt a spasm of disgust go through her, but Westwood merely wiped it away impatiently with the back of his hand. He was flushed with high colour now, a triumphant glitter in his eyes which gave the lie to any claims of charm or good looks. Putting down the empty bottle, he thrust his hands into his jacket pockets.

'Where to start...?' he mused. 'I suppose that you are the start of the story, my dear, for you came to London and, as I've already said, supplanted me as your grandmother's heir. I'd always had a penchant for deep play and I was fathoms-deep in debt. In one of the dens I frequented I met your cousin Josiah.' He paused, picked up the brandy bottle and looked surprised that it was empty. 'Well, Josiah was very helpful. I confided all my troubles and he suggested that I should go to see your father. I knew nothing of Broseley's reputation then, but Josiah said he might help me.'

'And he did?' Alicia kept her voice neutral, allowing none of her horror to show. Fatal to make a slip now and draw his anger onto herself.

'It became apparent that we could do business together.' The self-satisfied tone had returned. 'Broseley bought up all my debts and in return I did some jobs for him.' Westwood looked at Alicia consideringly. 'No need to offend your sensibilities with the details, I suppose, though it's as good a joke as any that he is your father. Chalk and cheese!' He laughed. 'I expect you get your airs from your mother. He was always complaining of her vapours and die-away airs. Said he should never have married her, for she brought him nothing, and her death had been a great release for him... What was that?'

'What? I heard nothing.' Alicia's mouth was suddenly dry. Like him she had heard a faint noise on the stairs, but she did not dare to hope that any help was at hand. No doubt it was the corrupt priest whom Westwood had hired to perform his dubious nuptials. She waited, but there was no knock at the door and after a suspicious look Westwood appeared to lose interest.

'No doubt Castle is keeping an eye on things downstairs,' he murmured. 'You've guessed we're at Greyrigg, haven't you? But we've sent the servants away, so don't get any ideas about calling for help, my dear! Now, where was I?'

'You had done some work for my father,' Alicia reminded him quietly.

'Ah, yes.' Westwood settled himself more comfortably. 'Well, after a while your father called me in to discuss a proposition. He planned to marry you off to his business partner, George Carberry. They had plenty of plans for joint ventures. He thought the proposal would do me some good, too. He was sure that the marriage would be anathema to your grandmother and that she would disinherit you! I think he saw it as a fitting punishment for her,' Westwood said thoughtfully. 'She had always refused to receive him, and he knew your marriage to Carberry would humiliate her before the *ton*, when she had supported Mullineaux's suit!'

Alicia felt her eyes fill with tears. So, in the end, the whole tawdry affair had centred around Broseley's need for money and revenge. There was some kind of irony, she thought numbly, in the fact that Broseley's plans for vengeance had turned out to be the ruin of Westwood's own hopes of the Stansfield fortune.

'So my father removed me from your path by marrying me to Carberry,' Alicia observed. 'And what did you do in return?'

She saw Westwood smile. 'I owed him a favour—and eventually he called it in! Josiah was becoming more of a liability than an asset to Broseley's organisation those last few months. He would get drunk and spill dangerous information, in addition to his threat to destroy our plans by going to you. So he had to go. Your father had no compunction about losing a member of the family!'

There was no trace of remorse in his voice. Alicia, struggling with a feeling of unreality, felt as though she was trapped in some outrageous nightmare. How could he simply relate all of this without expression, without feeling? He had no concept of morality, for all that mattered to him was centred around the needs and wishes of Christopher West-wood. Broseley had indeed found a man after his own heart when the fates had sent him Westwood.

'I suppose,' Westwood said lightly, 'that the real villain of the whole piece was George Carberry, for dying so inconveniently. If he had lived you would have been shunned by Society and no doubt disinherited by your grandmother. Trust the old fool to make a mess of even that. He was only ever good for his money—but you inherited all of that, didn't you, my dear? Yes, Broseley was too clever for his own good there, and it has rankled with him ever since. Nor did you endear yourself to him last time you met, with your wilful rejection of his plans!' He turned to look at her, and there was something in his eyes which was thoroughly unpleasant.

'I suppose you were always my intended suitor,' Alicia said tiredly.

'I told your father that you would never agree to another marriage of convenience!' Westwood laughed again, clearly relishing the situation. 'He always thought he knew best! But I knew you, and I knew it was madness to suggest either a business arrangement or a match! All I could do was insist that he did not disclose my identity so that he did not queer my pitch with you. I knew it would hardly be to my advantage if you realised I was in league with him!' He sighed. 'You are always so headstrong, my dear! But that is all in the past now. With me as your husband I am sure you will conform!'

Alicia was sure that he knew any number of ways to enforce his will and she shuddered at the thought. She drew the rough blanket closer around her for comfort. Thank God he had not yet exhausted his story—she did not like to think what he might do if once his attentions became focused solely on her again. Without flinching she faced the fact that he was quite capable of fulfilling his threat of forcing himself on her to compromise her beyond saving. She was not sure how she could cope with that.

'Anyway, I decided to try my luck with you under my own colours,' Westwood was saying. 'I thought I had a good chance of persuading you to marry me—you seemed to enjoy my company and I knew you were lonely. I invested a lot of time and energy in being pleasant to you, Alicia.' He kicked moodily at a loose floorboard. 'Unfortunately, I'd left it too late, hadn't I? You had already met Mullineaux again and were no doubt cherishing some sweet romantic dream that the two of you might be reunited!' There was an ugly expression on his face. 'Damn it, if only I had proposed sooner I'm sure you would have accepted me!'

Alicia shuddered to think that this could be true. The Christopher

Westwood she had known until recently had been charming and good company, solace in her loneliness, kind and pleasant. She might well have accepted him simply to enliven her solitary existence, little knowing that she had a tiger by the tail. But James Mullineaux had changed all that. Meeting him again had shown her just what a sham it would be to accept any other man, and no one else could ever be a substitute for him. Suddenly Alicia understood the change in Westwood's behaviour of late, as he had realised that he had left his proposal for too long. He had become sharp with frustration as he had seen his chance with her slip away. The mask of his good nature had faltered, but not sufficiently for her ever to suspect the truth.

Once again, her attention was attracted by a slight noise outside the door—the scrape of something on the wooden floorboards. It stopped almost immediately, but Alicia frowned a little in puzzlement. Surely Mr Skittle had no reason to be surreptitious in his approach?

Alicia's head was beginning to ache again with the effort of holding back the tears. To think that she had told James in a fit of pique that she had accepted Westwood's offer. Now she was well-served for all that foolish pride which had prevented her from telling him that she loved him. She imagined him receiving the news of her marriage to Westwood and the contempt it would engender. Little would he know of the truth of the matter, and she could never tell—not while Lady Stansfield lived. And when Lady Stansfield had died could she really come out with the truth of Westwood's criminality—and her own enforced connivance in it? She struggled against the fog of tiredness and misery that was clouding her mind.

At last there was the sound of steps on the stair. Westwood jumped up with barely concealed impatience.

'Can that be that damned priest at last? God alone knows what is taking him so long to get here!' He hurried across to the door, and unlocked it again.

Alicia was hoping that God would indeed be very tardy in sending his dubious representative along to conduct the marriage service. It was not, in fact, Mr Skittle who came into the room, but her own father. She was not surprised to see him. Westwood had confirmed that her prison was one of the attics at Greyrigg, albeit one in which she had never been before. The top floor of the house was riddled with interconnecting rooms and passageways which could conceal any number of dubiously imported goods or an entire army of men. She steeled herself as Broseley strode across the bare floor towards her, an oleaginous smile pinned to his face.

'Well, my dear, history repeats itself, does it not? I hope that Christopher has been persuading you of the good sense in accepting your fate this time!'

'I find him no more acceptable as a bridegroom than I did George Carberry,' Alicia said coldly. 'Furthermore, you cannot possibly think that a marriage conducted here by some questionable priest will ever be recognised as valid. I certainly will not honour it!'

Broseley turned his slimy gaze on Westwood. 'My dear Christopher, have you been wasting your time here? You assured me that she would be eating out of your hand by the time I arrived to act as witness to your marriage!' He turned back to Alicia. 'You must allow that he's a finer figure of a man than poor Carberry, my dear, and unlikely to die from the exertions of your wedding night! Indeed, I had quite expected to find him anticipating those delights already!'

Alicia's expression showed her contempt, but she would not lower herself to answer him. It was Westwood, apparently piqued at the aspersions thus cast on him, who burst into speech. 'Your daughter, sir, holds no charms for me besides her money!'

Broseley just laughed. 'But you'll marry her just the same, my boy! All we need now is the Reverend Mr Skittle to set the seal on matters!'

As if on cue, there was a knock at the door. Westwood caught Alicia's arm and practically dragged her off the bed as the door opened. Alicia had intended to struggle as much as she could, but to her horror she found that her legs were as weak as cotton-wool and she could barely stand, let alone put up a fight.

'Mr Skittle—' Westwood began, then broke off.

'Skittle is temporarily indisposed, I fear, my dear Westwood,' said the Marquis of Mullineaux in very smooth but infinitely dangerous tones. 'Your butler, sir,' the Marquis added, turning to Broseley with utter courtesy, 'has also succumbed to a mysterious ailment which has rendered him completely unable to move.'

He made a slight gesture with the wicked-looking duelling pistol he held negligently in one hand. 'I must beg you to unhand that lady, Westwood.'

Broseley had not moved, but Westwood took this instruction very badly. 'Be damned to you,' he snarled. 'You'll have to kill me first.' He shot a furious glance in the direction of the doorway, saw Marcus Kilgaren lurking there, and turned back to James like an animal at bay.

Mullineaux's mouth twisted in a travesty of a smile. 'If I must, I will,' he murmured, 'but much as I would wish to rid the world of you, Westwood, I am reluctantly compelled to leave you alive to stand trial.'

Westwood burst out laughing. 'Trial! You jest, Mullineaux!'

'I fear not.' James was so expressionless he might have been discussing the weather. 'You have just confessed to Lady Carberry that you murdered her cousin. Both myself and the excellent Mr Dundry of Bow Street heard every word through this door. We were here long before your proposed father-in-law—' he nodded grimly towards Broseley '—came stumbling along to act as a witness at the wedding. And, of course, as well as murder there is the matter of the abduction of a lady. Plenty of work, I feel, to keep Mr Dundry busy over the next few weeks!'

Westwood had lost colour as James spoke and the extent to which he had condemned himself out of his own mouth became apparent. His mouth hung slackly in a face of pasty white. He turned to stare at Broseley. 'You old fool, how the hell did they get in? Castle's supposed to be a professional! Damnation take it that I ever trusted you to organise any of this!'

'Shocking lack of servants in this part of the country,' James drawled. 'Certainly not enough of them to keep an eye on all the comings and goings in a big house like this! But we waste time, Westwood. Let the lady go.'

Neither Westwood nor Broseley paid him much attention, for they were too wrapped up in their mutual hatred. Westwood was still muttering, 'Of all the stupid, incompetent fools—' when his employer turned on him with a fury beyond anything Alicia had ever seen in her father before.

'Hold your tongue, you dolt! Haven't you done enough damage? I can't believe what I'm hearing here!' His West Country accent was very strong. 'So you thought you'd pass the time in telling tales of your exploits, did you? Something to impress your future wife? God damn it that I should ever have soiled my hands with you, you worthless bastard!'

For a split second Westwood's grip on Alicia's arm slackened out of sheer shock, and it was all the chance she needed. With more strength than she realised she possessed, she drove the elbow of her free arm into his stomach with a satisfying impact and twisted herself out of his grip. Westwood let out a gasp of both surprise and pain, and doubled up, coughing.

James, with great presence of mind, caught hold of Alicia and dragged her free of the maelstrom as Broseley hurled himself upon Westwood. Whilst he was twice the age of his opponent, he was not drunk and fury gave him an added strength to counteract Westwood's relative youth and agility. It was not much of a fight, however. As the two of them locked bodies with a grunt, Westwood got an arm free and Alicia suddenly saw the glint of a knife in his hand.

She drew breath on a scream as Broseley also saw the knife, but too late. As it slid between his ribs he had a look of ludicrous surprise fixed on his face. His weight fell against Westwood, setting him off balance, and the drink did the rest. Westwood lost his footing, stumbled sideways and fell onto the bare floorboards, Broseley's body half across him and a choking cloud of dust rising from the floor. The knife slipped from his fingers and went skittering away, aided by a well-aimed kick from James Mullineaux. Then it was all over as Dundry rushed into the room and began the words which spelled doom for Westwood.

'Christopher Westwood, I am arresting you for the wilful murders of Josiah Broseley and—' he cast a significant look down at the prone body on the floor—'Bertram Broseley...'

Some time passed, but Alicia was not really aware of it. James carried her downstairs, wrapped in the noxious blanket from the bed, which Alicia had half-heartedly tried to push away. In the drawing-room was Caroline Kilgaren, pale and distraught, who jumped up eagerly as they came in, her worried gaze going to Alicia's face.

'You have her safe! Thank God! And James—you are not hurt yourself? I was beside myself with worry... Put her down here...I will fetch some water...'

James put Alicia down gently on one of the lumpy sofas and drew Caroline aside, speaking to her in a low voice. Their voices washed over Alicia, who lay with her eyes closed, in a state between waking and sleeping. Presently Caroline came across to her and tried to encourage her to drink, but she merely turned her head away on the cushion and did not open her eyes.

An unquantifiable time later she was recalled from this dreamlike state by the unpleasant smell of burnt feathers being wafted beneath her nose. She opened her eyes crossly and met the amused gaze of the Marquis of Mullineaux.

'I thought that would do the trick,' James said cheerfully. 'Pity the poor fowl we had to pluck them from! Don't frown at me like that, Alicia—you may sleep presently, but for now I need to talk to you!'

To her complete horror, Alicia immediately burst into tears. She felt the puffy sofa give as James sat down next to her and gathered her into his arms without a word. She just clung to him, her face turned against his chest. None of the questions such as why he was there or how they had found her mattered at all for the time being.

For a while James said nothing, simply holding Alicia close so that the warmth and reassurance from his body transmitted itself to her and she began to relax. It was so amazingly comforting to be held like that

that after a time Alicia found herself yawning involuntarily, and felt rather than saw James laugh. A little shyly, she raised her head and looked at him.

'I haven't thanked you yet for rescuing me...' she said diffidently. 'How did you find me? And so quickly!'

James loosened his grip a little, much to her disappointment. He smiled down at her. 'Quickly! It didn't seem quick to me, I can assure you! You do know that you were unconscious for a whole day, don't you? It was two days ago that you left London!'

Alicia blinked a little, but she was too tired to make much sense of this. 'I didn't realise...so I had been asleep all that time!'

'Fortunately for you,' James said, his tone grim. 'Otherwise you would probably be married by now—or worse! He didn't hurt you, did he?' he added, his tone suddenly so sharp that Alicia jumped.

She shook her head tiredly. 'No... He didn't beat me, if that is what you mean!' Her mouth curved in a slight, sleepy smile. 'Nor did he molest me—he told me that I was not at all appealing to him, and too cold for his taste!'

She felt James's arm tighten about her for a moment as he smiled.

'Well, we must be grateful for your shortcomings in that respect, my love! Though I doubt I will have much complaint to make in the future!'

Alicia just snuggled closer to him. She was bored with talking, feeling so happy and warm that she simply wanted to sleep. There had been some disagreement between them, she remembered vaguely, but none of that mattered now. Nothing mattered, except—

'Miss Frensham!' she exclaimed, sitting bolt upright. 'Whatever has happened to her? Christopher said something about leaving her behind at a coaching inn...'

James laughed. 'Yes, indeed, we found Miss Frensham at Bathampton, ensconced in the landlord's best bedchamber with three doctors in attendance! She had such a strong fit of the vapours after she was abandoned that they feared for her life! She is a little recovered now, and Marcus has arranged for her to be taken to Chartley Chase, so you need not worry about her any more!'

He glanced down at Alicia and realised that the finer points of any explanation would have to wait. She was almost asleep where she sat, her head resting against his shoulder, her eyes closing irresistibly. He gave her a little shake.

'Listen, Alicia, it's going to take a bit of time for you to sleep off this stuff Westwood gave you, particularly with the shock you've had as well. Caroline and Marcus are going to take you back to Chartley and look after you. I must return to London with Dundry and sort things out once and for all. I'll come back as soon as I can, I promise.'

None of this made sense to Alicia except the unwelcome news that he was going to leave her. Her mind slid over the bits she did not understand—who was Dundry, and what were the Kilgarens doing there?—and fastened on what really mattered to her. Her face puckered like that of a petulant child.

'Why must you go? I want you to stay here with me!'

James pressed his mouth against her hair. More than anything he wanted to stay there too, not least to prevent anything else going wrong. But he knew that someone had to break the unwelcome news to the Countess of Stansfield. It was the least she deserved.

'It won't be for long, Alicia. By the time you are feeling better, I shall be back, I promise. I don't want to go.' His serious gaze sought hers. 'You must understand that. But I have to.'

He gave her a quick, hard kiss. Caroline was hovering in the doorway and it was time to go. James stood up and wrapped the blanket closer around Alicia, as though she were a child. By the time he had reached the doorway she was already asleep.

The day was warm with the promise of summer as James Mullineaux rode into Chartley village almost two weeks later, and he felt his spirits lift with the hope of one who felt that he had at last reached the end of a long journey. He had stayed with friends near Bath on the previous night and had left his luggage to follow as he took advantage of the fine weather to ride the rest of the way.

It had not been a pleasant couple of weeks. Christopher Westwood had sung from the rooftops in an attempt to incriminate others and free himself from blame. To James had fallen the uncomfortable task of telling Lady Stansfield the truth of Westwood's corruption and she had aged almost visibly as she had absorbed the news. Her main concern, however, had been for Alicia's welfare. Only James's reassurance that Alicia was safe and would visit her as soon as possible had prevented her from posting down to Somerset immediately. Finally, James had been to see his grandfather to gain his blessing for his forthcoming marriage and had at last set off for the country with a heart lighter than it had been in weeks.

The village was very quiet. A few ducks splashed lazily on the pond and the sound of children's voices floated on the air. Over the heather-clad hill lay Monks Dacorum and James suddenly felt a rush of uncomplicated pleasure to be back. They would settle in the country, he decided, then laughed aloud at the change in his own outlook. He turned into the approach to the Chase and the pebbles of the driveway scattered beneath his horse's hooves. A groom, alerted by the noise of his arrival, emerged from the stableblock to take the horse and James dismounted to hurry up to the front door with sudden impatience.

His anticipation was now almost at fever pitch. Chartley Chase, always peaceful, seemed almost sepulchrally silent. James knocked vigorously on the door and a moment later Fordyce's firm tread could be heard crossing the hall to the main door.

'Good day, Fordyce. I hope that you are well?' With barely concealed impatience, James hurried into the hall, divesting himself of his coat. The sunlight dappled the polished floor, and the scent of lilies filled the air. It was beautifully serene and tranquil, just as he remembered it. But James could not help wishing that the calm might have been broken. He felt that he really did deserve a hero's welcome.

'I am very well, my lord, I thank you.' Fordyce was closing the door with what seemed to James to be agonising slowness.

'And Lady Carberry? How is she?'

Fordyce paused. James could barely curb his frustration. What was the matter? Where was everyone? Fordyce spoke with lugubrious deliberation.

'Her ladyship is much better, my lord. However, she is from home. The Earl and Countess of Kilgaren are in the drawing-room, should you care to—'

But James was gone.

Caroline had never seen James enter a room so precipitately. She had been sitting on the window-seat in the sunshine, dozing contentedly over a book, listening to the soft rustling of the pages turning as Marcus read a two-day-old copy of the *Gazette*. Then the door slammed and James had erupted into the room like a tornado.

'I understand Alicia is from home!' he began, without preamble. 'What the devil is going on here?'

Marcus put down his newspaper and got to his feet in a leisurely manner.

'Good day, James,' he said mildly. 'How nice it is to see you again!'

James had the grace to look a little ashamed of himself. He shook Marcus's hand and came across to the window-seat to kiss Caroline.

'I beg your pardon. I hope that you are both well. I have but this minute arrived, and been told by Fordyce that Alicia is not at home! I apologise for the fact that it put all other thoughts out of my head!'

Caroline put down her book and rose to her feet, smiling. 'It's too fine a day to be cooped up indoors. Come outside and we will tell you what has been going on here! But first tell us what happened in London. Is Westwood safely locked away?'

She slipped her hand through James's arm and steered him out of the French windows. Beyond the formal terrace stretched the woodland garden, and the three of them strolled through this as James gave them the details of what had been happening in London. The grassy glades were thick with bluebells and they sat down on a couple of rustic benches in a patch of sun as James turned expectantly to them.

'Well? You must know that I am positively expiring with impatience! How can it be that Alicia, who should by rights be considering herself an invalid, should go off visiting or whatever at such a time?'

'You mean,' Marcus corrected dryly, 'how can it be that Alicia, who should be here waiting for you in a fever of gratitude and impatience, should have the bad taste to be from home when you choose to call!'

James scowled at him. 'Well, I'll allow that I did expect some show of appreciation, even if it was too much to expect the wretched girl to fall into my arms!'

Caroline sighed, propping her chin on her hand. 'I don't know what's going through Alicia's mind at present, James, for she does not speak to me. At first when we brought her home she simply slept all the time. We called Dr Pym from Bath, but he said that no real harm had been done, though, of course, she was deeply shocked and distressed. After a few days she seemed a little better, but she was quieter than I have ever seen her and she barely spoke a word. She wasn't difficult about anything,' Caroline added thoughtfully. 'In fact she was quite docile and passive, but it was most odd—and most out of character!'

James raised his eyebrows, struggling to come to terms with this completely alien description of his beloved. One might describe Alicia in many ways, but mild and submissive she was not. God forbid that her experiences had turned her into a mouse!

Marcus smiled slightly. 'Yes, I must admit I've never seen Alicia like that before! Caro finally got her to talk about Westwood and the ordeal she'd been through, but Alicia showed no emotion whatsoever and when Caro tried to turn the conversation to you James, Alicia simply wouldn't speak at all!'

Caroline's mouth drooped despondently. 'It's true, James,' she said unhappily. 'Then two days ago we got your letter telling us to expect you soon, and Alicia said nothing, but—'

'Yesterday she rose very early and left without a word!' Marcus finished for her. 'She left a note apologising for abandoning us like that, but said she could not face you at the moment and needed time to think. Nobody knows where she has gone!'

'Well, Fordyce knows,' Caroline amended, 'but he told us that Alicia had sworn him to secrecy. Oh, it really is too bad of her! When I see her again—' She broke off with a rueful smile as Marcus took her hand in his in a soothing gesture.

James was tight-lipped with annoyance. 'So Fordyce knows, does he?' he asked, getting purposefully to his feet.

'James,' Caroline called after him, hopelessly, 'don't make him tell you... Don't!' But it was too late. James's tall figure could be seen cutting across the terrace and into the house without a backward glance. Marcus gave a resigned sigh and pulled his wife to her feet.

'What a delightful place this is—when our friends are not here to cause us problems! Come along, my love! We may be needed to keep the peace!'

'Fordyce,' James said directly when the butler had made his usual stately entrance in response to the bell, 'I understand that you know of Lady Carberry's present whereabouts. Is that so?'

Fordyce permitted himself a small, discreet nod of the head. 'It is so, my lord.'

'Where is she?'

'Her ladyship gave instructions that her whereabouts be divulged to no one, I fear, my lord.'

James gave him a hard stare. He had his impatience well in hand now, but he was still taut with annoyance.

Fordyce maintained a prudent silence. Every last one of the servants was behind the Marquis of Mullineaux in his courtship of Lady Carberry, but it was evident to them all that she was making things extremely difficult for him. Fordyce considered Lord Mullineaux thoughtfully. He suspected that he was the sort of man who could be relied upon to bring matters to a successful conclusion and would very likely brook no opposition. The delicate question from Fordyce's own point of view was how much help he should offer. He decided to test the water.

'Her ladyship is expected back in a few days, my lord,' he offered. 'If your lordship would be good enough to wait—'

'No, thank you.' James was polite but firm. 'I have an alternative plan. I wish to go and meet Lady Carberry.'

Fordyce swallowed hard. Both Caroline and Marcus, who had not said a word, were looking at him with identical quizzical expressions. Fordyce capitulated.

'I hope, sir,' he said severely, looking at James very straight, 'that you will understand my motives for divulging the following piece of information. Her ladyship is visiting her sister, Mrs St Auby, in Taunton. She has sent a message to the effect that she expects to set out for home the day after tomorrow.'

James's face broke into a grin. 'Thank you, Fordyce. You're a good man! I know you have your mistress's best interests at heart, and I assure you that in that we are at one!'

Fordyce could not be said to have smiled, but he almost did. 'Very good, sir. Shall I give orders for the carriage to be prepared?'

James laughed. 'Certainly, Fordyce.' He turned to look at Caroline and Marcus as Fordyce made his stately exit from the room. 'We are all three going on a journey to Ottery!'

Marcus groaned. 'You push the bounds of friendship a long way, James! In the last few weeks you've dragged us halfway across the country!'

James came across the room to them. His face was alight with amusement and a new determination now that he could at last plan a course of action. 'Patience, Marcus! I know you would both wish to be present at my wedding! Here is what we shall do...'

It was a sunny afternoon on the road to Ottery. The sky was a bright, clear azure without a cloud in sight and a light breeze blew across the levels, carrying the scents of summer.

The brilliant splendour of the day suited Alicia's mood ill. She had spent a miserable few days visiting Annabella, who had been loud in her discussions of their father's death and tiresomely superior about her own married state. It was easy to see, however, that matters were not very happy in the St Auby household. Although Annabella had proved to be Bertram Broseley's sole heir, his fortune had not been as great as expected and tempers were short.

Annabella's ill-concealed enquiries about Alicia's future plans all too obviously stemmed from her own self-interest, so in the end Alicia had told her that she was thinking of retiring from Society and living as a recluse. Annabella had appeared delighted, pressing her to stay as long and as often as she wished, exchanging a glance of obvious complicity with her young husband. Alicia had felt vaguely sickened and was glad her visit was but a short one.

Now, of course, she had ample time to consider her own situation. Once the shock of her abduction had faded, she had chafed at the idea of sitting waiting for James to come back to Chartley. She really did not feel that she could bear to face another proposal from him. Would he forever be rescuing her from the consequences of her own folly? It was intolerable to consider. Despite her own deep feelings for him,

Alicia was even more determined that he should feel under no obligation to offer for her. If the only way to avoid him was to live retired, she would quite happily do so. She even considered living abroad in order to ensure that she kept out of his way. It was a miserable thought, but it had to be considered. Once James realised that she was determined not to accept his suit, surely pride would ensure that he left her in peace?

Alicia was so lost in her thoughts that it was a moment before she realised that the carriage had stopped. They were a couple of hundred yards away from the village of Ottery, for she could see the spire of the church against the sky and the stone walls of the first cottages. Alicia would have chosen just about anywhere else to be delayed, the village bringing as it did memories of her first encounter with James a bare few months before. She sighed with vexation and pushed the carriage window down.

'Jack! What is going on? Why have we stopped?'

There was a pause before the voice of the coachman, noticeably expressionless, floated down to her.

'There's a gentleman here wishing to have speech with your ladyship. He requests that you step down from the carriage.'

A strong premonition seized Alicia. She could not see around the front of the coach, but then she did not really need to in order to know who was there.

'Ridiculous!' she snapped. 'I will do no such thing! Drive on at once, Jack!'

There was another pause before Jack spoke again.

'Begging your pardon, my lady, I cannot.'

'Cannot?' Alicia stuck her head out of the window in exasperation. 'From whom do you take your orders, Jack?'

'Why, from you, ma'am, of course.' Jack sounded infuriatingly placid. 'The trouble is, my lady, that the gentleman has a pistol.'

Inside the carriage Miss Frensham heard this and began to twitter. She had been extremely highly strung ever since the episode at the inn outside Bath, where she had spent a very uncomfortable time until being rescued by Marcus Kilgaren.

'Oh, Lady Carberry, I cannot bear it! Do as he says, I implore you!'

Alicia ignored her. 'You surely cannot believe that he would use it, Jack! Drive on, I say!'

'I have a responsibility to my passengers and for the horses, ma'am,' the coachman returned. 'I cannot risk injury or damage. Please dismount, ma'am.'

Alicia slammed the window shut in fury and wrenched the door open.

There was no doubt about it—she would have to face James, for she was sure it was he. As she let down the steps he came alongside the carriage, smiling wickedly at her furiously flushed countenance.

'Alicia, did your grandmother never tell you that it is very bad *ton* to cause a scene on a public highway?'

Alicia's voice was squeaky with annoyance. 'You are the one causing the scene, Mullineaux, with this outrageous behaviour!'

'Then step aside to speak to me, my love,' James said whimsically, 'before I add to the scandal further by dragging you bodily from your carriage!'

Miss Frensham, an interested bystander, gave a little scream. Having been robbed of her chance to defend Alicia on the previous occasion, she threw herself into the part now.

'Oh, that I should ever live to see such goings on on the King's highway! You, sir—' she pointed her umbrella at James '—are a black-guard and a bounder masquerading as an honest gentleman! To think that Lady Carberry should be subject to such an outrage...'

James was smiling broadly. 'Doing it too brown, ma'am! Never fear, I mean Lady Carberry no harm! My apologies for interrupting your journey—Jack will convey you to Ottery Manor, where you will find the Earl and Countess staying with the Squire and Mrs Henley. If you would be so good as to ask them to join us at the church, we may proceed with the nuptials!'

Miss Frensham subsided on the seat, her face the picture of affronted dignity. 'A runaway match! And with the connivance of the Earl and Countess of Kilgaren! Well I never—'

'Just so, ma'am!' James turned back to Alicia and held out his hand with a grave courtesy to help her descend.

Alicia, who had stood by all this time in astonished silence, looked at him thoughtfully. He was looking particularly handsome, but also definitely unyielding. In an undignified tussle of wills or, worse, a phys-ical struggle, she was certain that she would lose. She put her hand tentatively in his and felt his fingers close round hers strongly. There was a glimmer of a smile in the look which he gave her, then he closed the carriage door on Miss Frensham, gestured to Jack, and the carriage set off at a brisk pace, leaving James and Alicia alone in the road.

'Don't say a word!' James ordered as he heard Alicia draw breath to speak. 'Hear me out and then you may say whatever you wish, but do not, I beg you, refuse my offer of marriage before it is even made!'

Unusually persuadable, Alicia remained silent, and after a moment James's stern demeanour relaxed slightly, although he did not let go of her hand.

'On the first occasion that I proposed to you, Alicia, you accepted me without question. Things were very easy then—you knew that I loved you and you trusted me. A lot has happened since then to dispel that love and trust, but I can only hope that it's not too late and that you do still care for me.' He took a deep breath. 'Because, whatever has happened, I know that I have always loved you. I might have pretended otherwise—I tried very hard to convince myself I disliked you—but in the end I knew it was not true. Now *that* is what I should have said when I proposed to you last time and I beg you to believe me, because you have put me to an unconscionable amount of trouble just to find you and say it!'

That sounded more like the real James, Alicia thought as, suddenly shy, she concentrated on one of the large mother-of-pearl buttons on his driving coat. Looking up after a moment, she saw that he was watching her with unwonted seriousness.

'If you are really sure...' she said hesitantly, and was swept into his arms in a way which left no room for doubts.

A breathless, shaken time later, James let Alicia go sufficiently to turn her in the direction of the village and start walking.

'I almost forgot...' The wicked smile was back in his eyes. 'Our wedding guests will be wondering if you are cutting up rough at my high-handed tactics! No doubt Theo March will be trying to decide how long to wait for us! Come along, before I kiss you again in the middle of the road and scandalise this entire village!'

'James!' Alicia stopped dead in the road. 'You really meant what you said to Miss Frensham, then...you had arranged the wedding before you even asked me?'

'How many times am I expected to ask?' James enquired with perfect reasonableness. 'Twice you have rejected my suit with no consideration for my feelings and I did not intend to give you the chance to do so a third time!'

'And now,' Alicia said, looking down at her crumpled green travelling dress with disfavour, 'I am expected to get married in this, and I don't doubt that I look a shocking fright!'

James removed a leaf from her hair. 'Indeed, my love, you look delightful! You had all the traditional trappings of a wedding at your marriage to George Carberry—this time I hope you will accept that the advantages of the groom far outweigh any superficial considerations of dress or decoration!'

'How obviously complacent you are,' Alicia marvelled, trying to sound cross. 'And to think I have not even said that I love you!'

James gave her a look which made her retreat a step. 'Not in so many words,' he said thoughtfully as he followed her, 'but I am reasonably certain! Perhaps, however, I should put it to the test—'

Alicia warded him off with both hands. 'I am content to admit it!' she said, with a wary look for an old crone who had emerged from the nearest cottage and was eyeing them suspiciously. 'Save your demonstrations for later, when we do not have an audience!'

As they approached the lichened church, the carriage from Ottery Manor could be seen drawing up at the lych-gate. Alicia stopped again.

'James...'

'Yes, Alicia?' There was a sudden tension in his voice as though he expected that she was about to change her mind.

'When we are married, may we go and see my grandmother straight away? I feel that I have neglected her of late, leaving her alone to hear of Christopher's arrest and now this...I don't want her to hear from anyone else that we are married!'

'Of course.' Tension had given way to amusement in his voice. 'We will go up to London at once—but I hope you do not intend to stay long, for I have other plans for our honeymoon!' He stopped to kiss her again. 'Well, maybe we won't go immediately,' he said thoughtfully, when they had stopped for breath, 'for I also have other plans for tonight!'

He let her go at last very reluctantly. 'We must see if we can get as far as the church,' he finished, a little huskily. 'I have had a special licence burning a hole in my pocket for four days now and if we do not manage to get married soon I cannot answer for the consequences!'

He took her hand and they completed the final thirty yards to the church gate. Theo March was waiting in the church doorway, and his anxious face broke into a smile as he saw the two of them.

'James, my boy! Alicia! I was so glad when James told me... And thrilled to be able to be of service...' He looked at their radiant expressions. 'No need to ask you if you are sure,' he said comfortably, 'for it is written all over your faces!' A slight frown of puzzlement touched his features. 'It's strange,' he reflected thoughtfully, 'for when you met at the vicarage I was sure you did not even like each other. Yet now...'

Alicia, glancing at James a little shyly, saw that he was smiling. He took her hand again. 'We were just extremely good at hiding our feelings, sir!'

Theo beamed. 'So even then...'

'Yes, sir,' James said, giving Alicia a look which made her feel both warm and dizzy at the same time. 'Even then!'

* * *

The Dowager Countess of Stansfield was feeling disconsolate. The news of Christopher Westwood's criminal activities had quite overset her and, to make matters worse, Alicia had chosen to bury herself in the depths of Somerset without a word. Only that morning, Mrs Eddington-Buck, in the most gently malicious of terms, had hinted that Alicia's reputation was now so tarnished that she doubted Alicia would ever dare return to Town. Lady Stansfield had given her the rightabout, but when the outraged matron had left she had slumped back in her chair, feeling sick at heart.

She stabbed viciously at her embroidery to give relief to her feelings. To think that she had been driven to take up needlework to pass the time, she who was used to so many more exciting occupations! But there was no Christopher Westwood now to flatter and cajole, no Alicia to bring light and youth into her life.

The door of the drawing-room opened softly, but her sharp old ears still caught the butler's tread.

'I do not wish to be disturbed, Masters!' she snapped irascibly. 'I am at home to no one!'

'Of course, your ladyship.' Masters was even more smoothly deferential than Fordyce. 'However, I am persuaded that you would wish to see the lady and gentleman who are waiting below. Indeed, I have already told them that you will receive them.'

Lady Stansfield stared at him in outraged amazement. Had he taken leave of his senses?

She swelled with wrath. 'Ho, have you indeed? Well, Masters, you can now go and tell them that I am not at home!'

'No, madam.' The butler appeared impervious to her wrath. 'I am certain that you will make an exception.' He executed a slight bow, then turned to throw open the drawing-room door with more than his usual aplomb.

The embroidery fell unheeded from Lady Stansfield's lap as she got to her feet. Alicia ran into her grandmother's arms. She was followed across the room by James Mullineaux with the broadest smile on his face that Masters thought he had ever seen. Not to be outdone, he cleared his throat with great deliberation.

'The Marquis and Marchioness of Mullineaux!' he announced grandly.

* * * * *

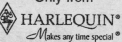

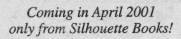

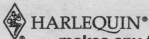

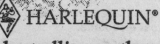

HARLEQUIN®

bestselling authors

Merline Lovelace
Deborah Simmons
Julia Justiss

*cordially invite you to enjoy three
brand-new stories of unexpected love*

The Officer's Bride

Available April 2001

HARLEQUIN®

Makes any time special ®

Visit us at www.eHarlequin.com

PHOFFICER